Utterly Monkey

Also by Nick Laird

Poetry
To a Fault

Utterly Monkey

NICK LAIRD

FOURTH ESTATE • *London* and *New York*

First published in Great Britain in 2005 by
Fourth Estate
A Division of HarperCollins*Publishers*
77–85 Fulham Palace Road
London W6 8JB
www.4thestate.com

A catalogue record for this book is
available from the British Library

ISBN 0-00-719748-9

Typeset in ITC Garamond by
Palimpsest Book Production Limited,
Polmont, Stirlingshire

Printed in Great Britain by
Clays Ltd, St Ives plc

For the Lairds

'For God's sake bring me a large Scotch.
What a bloody awful country.'

Reginald Maudling,
Secretary of State for Northern Ireland,
on the plane back to London after his
first visit to Belfast, 1 July 1970

WEDNESDAY, 7 JULY 2004

Moving is easy. Everyone does it. But actually leaving somewhere is difficult. Early last Wednesday morning a ferry was slowly detaching itself from a dock at the edge of Belfast. On it, a man called Geordie was losing. He'd slotted eleven pound coins into the Texas Hold'Em without success – not counting a pair of Kings which briefly rallied his credits – and had now moved two feet to the left, onto the gambler. The three reels spun out into *click* – a bell, *click* – a BAR, *click* – a melon. Fuck all. Geordie's small hands gripped each side of the machine as if it was a pulpit. He kept on staring at the symbols, which again and again represented nothing but loss. Then he sniffed loudly, peeled his twenty Regals off the machine's gummy top and sloped away. Eighteen quid down and they hadn't yet left the harbour.

The boat, the *Ulster Enterprise*, was busy, full of families heading over for the long July weekend. Geordie bought a pint of Harp from the gloomy barman and slumped onto a grey horseshoe-shaped sofa in the *Poets Bar*, then sat forward suddenly and took a pack of playing cards from the black rucksack by his feet. He started dealing out a hand of patience. A short man in a Rangers track-suit top stopped by his table, swaying a little with the boat, or maybe with drink. His shoulders were broad and bunched with muscle. He held a pint of lager and a pack of Mayfair fags in one hand. The other was in his track-suit top, distending it like a pregnancy. He had a sky-blue baseball cap with *McCrea's Animal Feed* written across it. He looked as if he'd sooner spit on you than speak to you and yet, nodding towards the other pincher of the sofa, he said: 'All right. This free?'

Belfast, east, hardnut.

'No, no, go on ahead.'

The man sat down carefully, like he was very fond of himself, and held Geordie's eye.

'You think we'll still have McLeish next season?' Geordie continued, looking at his tracksuit top.

'Oh aye, I think so, though he's a bit too interested in players and not enough in tactics.'

'You on holiday?'

'Spot of business.'

'Oh right. I'm seeing some friends. You heading to Scotland?'

'Naw, on down to London.'

'Oh aye? Me too. You not fly?'

'Taking a van.'

Geordie paused, to see if the offer of a lift was forth-coming. It wasn't.

'Hot enough today, eh?'

'It'll do all right. Better that than pissing down.'

They talked the usual talk. About pubs and places and discovered that the stranger was the nephew of one of Geordie's dinner ladies. Which was how they swapped names. Ian. Geordie. They played whist and matched pints for the next two hours as the ferry ploughed through the water to Scotland. Just before they got in Geordie went out on deck to clear his head. Outside he shivered and watched the wake turn lacy and fold back into the sea. He felt off. His mouth was dry and the ache in his head suggested that afternoon drinking hadn't been such a great idea. He turned slightly, to take the wind out of his eyes, and Ian was standing beside him, smiling secretly out to sea. Geordie nodded briskly at him and went in to the toilet.

When he came back to the table Ian had dealt the pack out and was in the middle of a round of pelmanism. Seeing Ian concentrating on the cards, crouched forward, intent, just as he had been doing earlier, made Geordie feel suddenly well-disposed towards him.

'You not play patience? It's a better game.'

Ian turned over the Jack of Hearts.

'No skill in that. This', he tapped the back of a card, 'exercises the memory.'

Staring hard at the grid of cards, he turned over a matching Jack, clubs, then placed them both into a dis-card pile at the side. Geordie said it first.

'Listen mate, I'll be in London for a while later on this week as well, and I don't know so many folks down there. If you give me your number maybe we could meet up for a jar or two?'

'Tell you what, you give me yours and I'll ring you if I'm free.'

'Aye, do. That'd be a laugh. We'll go out and get slaughtered.'

*   *   *

The solicitor Danny Williams was looking in his baby-blue refrigerator. His pinstripe grey suit jacket sagged over the narrow shoulders of a kitchen chair. He had discarded his tie and shoes. The room was dim and the only light came from this massive fridge. It was like a UFO opening its door in his kitchen. 'Take me to my dinner,' Danny said out loud in the empty flat, without humour, as he stood snared in the pale luminous strip. An empty jar of mayonnaise sat by itself in the middle of the top shelf, like a judge on his bench. Danny found it difficult to look in his fridge when he was alone. It witnessed his failures. He would often wander round his airy flat, peckish, open it, see nothing he fancied (or could eat without risk of illness) and walk away again. Danny was skinny. The fridge clicked off its light and Danny resolved to make toast, a Saturday visit to Safeway. The doorbell went. He walked down the hall, unslid the chain, and opened his life.

Geordie Wilson was standing on the step. His small frame was silhouetted against the London evening sky. He looked charred, a little cinder of a man. His navy tracksuit hood cowled round a narrow and freckled face and his bagged eyes looked very blue and watery in the light from the hall. He had several days' beard growth. He could have been Death's apprentice. *Geordie Fucking Wilson.* In the slowed-down moment, Danny registered a furious argument being conducted further down the street between a man and woman out of sight. It was in Russian or maybe Polish.

'Someone's for it, eh?' the figure on the doorstep said, snapping his elbow into the air. Danny felt his head lift suddenly. He shuddered, and realized just as quickly again that Geordie, this burnt-looking thing, was not going to draw a gun and shoot him.

'Easy up big man,' said Geordie, reaching a hand out for his shoulder and smirking. 'It's me. Geordie. How are you? What about you? Surprised?'

'Hello,' Danny said slowly, blinking in exaggerated shock, 'Geordie Wilson. I knew it was you. What the hell brings you here?'

They would go to the King's Head, but first Geordie came in and dumped his bag on the sheeny wooden floor of the hall, and they edged round each other, like novice ice-skaters, as Danny moved towards the kitchen to get the jacket of his suit. He slipped it on, felt its impropriety, like armour at dinner, and slipped it off again. He was wearing his grey suit trousers and a white shirt, which, though open-necked, still displayed cuff links as tokens of a serious man. He pulled a navy zip-up fleece off a hook, and then decided to wear his scuffed Levi's jacket over it. He looked like a social merman: pinstriped lower, denimed upper. Geordie stooped and removed his fags and lighter from the rucksack. It was only when they'd left the house that Geordie asked where the pub was. It was an incontrovertible fact that this was where they were heading. Some friends you take to cafés and cinemas, some to concerts, others to matches or shopping, but some, the ones you grew up alongside, meaning the ones you learnt to drink with, you always always always take to the pub.

As they walked, Geordie was forced to half-skip to keep up with Danny, whose eyes, still varnished with surprise, were trained on the pavement. Gum studded the cement like the beginnings of rain. It was too warm for a jacket and he could feel sweat beginning to prickle along his spine. His face was tight with goodwill, his stomach with nerves and he wasn't certain that what was happening was happening. *Geordie Fucking Wilson*. He needed a drink.

The King's Head was a nasty little place but close, with a chubby cream cat that had the run of it to such an unreasonable extent that customers would be standing, possibly shivering, possibly pregnant, whilst it stretched and yawned and dreamt on a seat in front of the fireplace. It had the look of a theatre bar. All busy carpet, threadbare velvet and smeary mirrors, and signed sepia photographs of stars, faded with smoke and sunlight to the same dulled obscurity as their subjects. Its landlord was the obese and charmless Gerard, who sported a lame goatee in a lame attempt to define a lame jaw. Years back, when Danny had been looking for an evening job during law school, he tried all the local pubs for bar work. Gerard had immediately said *Sorry mate, hardly enough for meself here really.* Danny had persuaded his then-girlfriend to call in and ask. Tamara, a delicate woman whose distinctive nose exacerbated her accent and deportment into something approaching minor nobility, had put her head round the door and Gerard had offered her work immediately. They then couldn't decide if Gerard was sexist or anti-Irish or just anti-Danny.

Still, it was the closest pub and proximity – to lazy men in the city – is worth an acre of stripped floorboards, battered leather sofas, and four elastic student barmaids, which was what the second nearest, Pravda or Molotov or something, offered.

Geordie wandered to the far end to get a table and Danny stood at the bar. *Geordie Wilson. How weird is that?* He looked very well, really, considering, Danny thought, watching Geordie tap his lighter on the table at the far end of the bar. Chirpy. They hadn't seen each other for a long time, not since 15 August 1995, the summer Danny came back from his first year of uni, though neither remembered the incident. Danny was driving his father's grey Volvo estate up the widest main street in Ireland, Ballyglass's High Street. Ballyglass is really only this street. Other thoroughfares run off it at right angles before petering out into lanes and housing estates and fields. Geordie was crossing the lights by Union Street and Danny was waiting at them, holding the car on the clutch. Geordie saluted him and Danny, reclining, lifted a finger off the wheel and nodded a greeting. Both passed on feeling a little gladdened, a little embarrassed. Old friends know too much.

While Gerard stood and sullenly stared at the two jars of Guinness, waiting for them to settle, Danny watched Geordie fidgeting. He never could sit still. When they were at school, Mr O'Neill the maths teacher had told Geordie that he had no brakes. Danny, remembering that, pictured it literally: Geordie driving through Ballyglass in a car on which the cables have gone. Up Fairhill and Oldtown he could keep pace with the traffic. His car would look like the others, accelerate like the others, and he would sing along tunelessly to the songs on Townland Radio just like the other drivers. But downhill, to James Street, to the Ballymore Road, the car wouldn't slow. He might try to warn you, flash his lights, beep his horn but he'd still collide and send things flying: other drivers, rickety cyclists, grocery shoppers, idiot dogs. *Geordie Wilson, a bad bastard who lacks the ability to stop, and he's come to see me.* Danny delved for his loose change and counted it out while he waited for Gerard to steer his bright blue paunch, like the front of a bumper car, around the open drawer of the till. Gerard performed the manoeuvre quite neatly, pausing in front of the cash register to slam it shut with his side, and then pressed at the optics with two highballs, growling. Danny placed his scuffed Adidas on the brass footrail and shifted his weight onto it, keeping his balance by holding onto the side of bar. What *were* these rails for? To tie your pet to? He turned again to watch Geordie, sitting at the table, idly aiming and flicking a match, unlit, at the fat white cat which sat a few feet from him, defiantly licking her paws.

Gerard set the two pints down in front of Danny on an already sodden Carlsberg towel, and noiselessly accepted the exact amount (*I think that's right*) proffered by Danny. He splashed the coins in the open drawer of the till, and went back to watching some sportive tangle of colour and shouting, wrestling perhaps, on the telly in the corner.

Their table was round, too low, and pocked with circular marks, a Venn diagram of sessions of previous drinking. Their lack of back support forced them to lean forward, conspiratorially. They looked like grandmasters. Geordie moved first.

'All right fella. Sorry to drop in on you like this. You look a bit shocked.'

'No don't be stupid mate. It's good to see you. What's been going on?'

'No no, you go first boss. Last I heard you were doing the law.'

'Yeah. I'm a fully paid-up lawyer. Qualified almost three years ago. Working in the city. Good money, bad hours. But here, what about you? Let's hear your news.'

'Aw, you know me. Bit of this. Bit of that. None of the other. Some of the above.'

Danny had forgotten this, how Geordie spoke. It struck Danny now that maybe it was because he felt awkward. He sounded like a client squirming, mixing bonhomie with avoiding your eye. Danny waited.

'Well, I'm officially an unemployed labourer.'

'That what your business card says?'

'It's what my dole form says. I wish to labour. But no suitable labour's available. Suitable's the key. You wouldn't believe what they've made me go on. I've been apprentice, trainee, new-starter, jobseeker.'

'So you just living off the bru?'

'Off the bru and on the . . . ' Geordie lifted his pint and nodded towards it, 'brew.' He then laughed too loudly, a little hysterical.

Danny eyed him quizzically. 'You're still a funnyman. Funny peculiar.'

'Sorry mate, I'm a wee bit caned. I had a smoke in that park at the end of the road before I came to see you. What have I been doing? Well . . . ' Geordie puffed his cheeks and blew breath out for a second. Danny felt the heat of it and moved slightly back. 'I was doing a bit of cab work with Tommy Vaughan's Taxis. Driving the old biddies to and from the Bingo. Leaving them over to their friends' houses for tea and chat or up to the church on a Sunday.'

Danny was reminded of what he'd wanted to ask him when he'd been at the bar.

'How did you know where I lived anyway?'

'Just phoned your mum and mentioned I was coming over and she told me. Got your phone number as well but thought I'd just call round, surprise you.'

Damn sure you did. Otherwise I'd have produced a bulletproof excuse. Danny also suddenly realized why his mum had called him at work that morning when he'd been on a conference call: an e-mail from Jill, his secretary, had popped up on his screen asking him to ring her back. He'd forgotten, as usual, but this seemed a disproportionate and cruel punishment.

'Yeah . . . You look well. It's good to see you. How long are you here for? What are you doing here? You know, in London?'

Geordie moved nothing in his face now except his lips.

'Not sure yet. See how things pan out.'

They drank fast, and let drink do the unpeeling for them. After setting down each new round on the table there was a moment when they waited for the pints to finish settling. It is difficult to get going on a Guinness. There is nothing aesthetic about other refreshments. Lager and cider just slop in their glasses, fizzing at you to get at it, to raise it and down it. Guinness is complete in itself. The first sip is like cutting a wedding cake. After the measured pouring, then the storm in a pint glass, the spindrift apartheid of grains and galaxies settling. And the Guinness was working. Danny began to feel a kind of warmth for this hard-bitten short-arse in front of him. It *was* good to see him. There was the other thing, of course, that Geordie brought back: guilt. But for the moment that could be disguised with drink, with smoke and mirrors which, indeed, the pub had in abundance. Danny had some knowledge he'd been chewing on for the last hour. It was time to spit it out. He cleared his throat and started, 'I heard you had some bother a while back.'

The bother was a bullet in the back of each of Geordie's calves.

'Ach, you know the way it goes. I wasn't really up to anything. I was seeing . . . '

He looks up, expecting an interjection. None comes.

'Budgie Johnson's sister. Just for a wee bit of action, nothing serious, and he took it hard. You ever see her? Something else altogether.'

'Which one is she?'

'Janice. With a wonky eye and great fat tits.'

They were grinning. Geordie knew that Danny probably didn't usually have this sort of chat. Danny knew that Geordie knew.

'Works in Martin's Chemists?'

'That's the one.'

'What happened?'

'Greer walked in on me and her. Getting to the pitch. On his sofa.'

'You're joking?'

'No joke. I didn't know whether to come or shit myself.'

Budgie, also known as Greer, was the eldest of the Johnson brothers. There were two others, Chicken and Brewster, and two younger sisters, Janice and Malandra. Chicken was called Chicken because Budgie was called Budgie, though why Budgie was called Budgie was nobody's business and anyone's guess. He probably bit the head off one. Budgie was an animal. He'd knocked over every premises in Ballyglass at least three times. A big lean man like a knife. He looked the part. Shaven headed, serious. You didn't fuck with Budgie. He ran several things – drugs, local racketeering, a rash of pot-sheen stills up between The Loup and Cooperstown – but there was some confusion as to how far his fingers went, and into which pies exactly.

'You weren't done just for that?'

'That was the real reason.'

'Well, what did they say you were done for?'

'Nicking cars . . . '

Danny eyed him with a level twenty-twenty.

'Tha' wee bit of dealing maybe.'

'What sort?'

'Puff mostly. A few pills. Coke at Christmas.'

'You twat.'

'They all do it.'

'So they're not going to want you cutting in.'

They supped. Geordie removed his fags from the front pouch of his hooded top, and leaned back to squirm the lighter out of his jeans.

'When did it happen?'

'I've told this thing a million times.'

'So tell it again. You're still one whiny bastard. You should be glad of the attention.'

12

Geordie lit his fag and blew smoke out. Once, twice. He took a sip and wiped the froth away with the back of his hand. Everyone prepares their body before they tell a story.

'It was around one in the morning, on a Tuesday night. Five months ago or thereabouts. I'd been playing pool in the new pool hall. You won't know it, it's down behind the carpet warehouse. Then I'd gone to the Gleneally for a few pints with Den Spratt. You remember him?'

'Rat-face Spratt.'

'The very same. More like a chipmunk now. More meat to his cheeks.'

'Come on.'

'I was lying in bed, bit pissed, dozing. Mum's staying at her sister's in Bangor. Dad's flat out snoring. There's a bang of some sort and it wakes me. I figure it's a car door banging just outside. So I look out the window. My bed's still beneath the sill. There's two cunts in the fucking garden in balaclavas. The streetlights are giving off good light and I know them. Not just to see, I know their fucking *names*. And they're standing back. Not even keeping a lookout but watching the porch, so I know that there's others and they're at the fucking door. And I figure that bang was my fucking door going in.'

He stops and fingers a Regal out from its box. Danny realizes that the story, for Geordie, has slipped from urgency into theatrics. Danny lifts the pack and raises his brows. Geordie nods as he lights his own. Danny draws one out for himself and is struck by how clean and neat it is. Perfect. He looks over at Geordie's fag, smouldering, spoiled. Geordie's nails were bitten down so badly that the tops of the fingers puffed out baldly over the remains

13

of the nail. Numerous hangnails hung from their pink tiny divots. Danny bends his head to the flame Geordie's offering.

'So I do what you'd do, what anyone'd do. I grabbed my jeans and jumper from the floor and legged it to the bathroom. I threw the clothes through the window onto the roof of the scullery and stood on the cistern. I don't know why I didn't lock the bathroom door. If I'd locked that fucking door . . . I'm wriggling out through the window, the wee one. We only have a wee window in there, and it's awkward because I'm going head first and I'm about to fall onto the scullery roof on my face and break my fucking neck. It's about ten feet or so. But it doesn't fucking matter anyway because I hear footsteps pounding up the stairs. And I hear my dad shouting my name. He's screaming it. Geordie, Geordie. Over and over. And I'm halfway out the window. Caught in the window really, like in a mousetrap' – Geordie slides the first two fingers of his right hand between the thumb and index finger of his left, and wriggles them to show the swimming of a man caught in a window – 'and I feel this whack on my left leg. They don't pull me in. They just stand there beating the tripe out of my fucking legs. I'm screaming at the top of my voice, I'm waking the whole fucking estate.'

They break stares, both a little embarrassed. Odd how intimate it is to look into someone's eyes. Like staring at the sun. You can only do it for a second. Danny is feeling relaxed now, forthright, made in Ulster. Geordie's story's reminding him of differences and how he doesn't have to wake in the night to find four thugs coming for him like the apocalyptic Horsemen. He waits for Geordie to go on and glances round the pub. No one's near enough to hear. Or young enough. There's only two old guys sitting up at the bar, huddled, with stares that stall in mid-air. It's like a care home in here, he thinks. With Gerard pickling the residents in order to preserve them.

'So there's four of them. And I know them. In fact you know one of them too. Jacksy Hewitt, from out past Fairhill.'

Danny nods but can't think of the face. 'From McMullen's class?'

'That's the cunt. Well, Jacksy sticks a blue pillow case over my head and I'm standing in my own bathroom and I piss myself. I actually piss myself. On my legs and the floor. And one of them is saying to me. *Not so tough now sweetheart, not so tough now.* And they push me down the stairs, I'm stumbling, and one of them is pinning my da against the wall with a baseball bat. And he says to him *We'll be back for you granddad.* And they tape my hands behind my back with that silvery gaffer tape and lead me out through my own garden and trip me on the pavement. I'm lying on my face in my fucking keks in the middle of the estate with a pillow case on my head. Two of them lift me and dump me in the boot of some crappy wee Astra or something and I can hear them hooting and laughing as they start her and tear off. We take a right out the estate so I know we're going towards Ardress or round the back of the town.'

Eyeballing Danny now, Geordie's showmanship is giving way to something hard like fear. He slows right down as if he's suddenly exhausted.

'It was the industrial estate ... That's where it was. Behind Harrison's Meats ... I know. You used to fucking

15

work there. Could have done with you there then, Danny boy. You and a big meat cleaver. You and big Mungo and me with a cleaver each. We could have done some damage.'

'What had they got? I mean, what else apart from the baseball bats?'

Geordie shakes his head, and sets his mouth as if he's disappointed.

'Pack of stupid bastards. Idiots. Eeeeeejitttts.'

He shakes his head and elongates the word like an Englishman doing an impression of an Ulster yokel. A seahorse of smoke rides out from the cigarette tip.

'Bats, yes, and a shotgun, it was an old farm gun, double barrelled, and the pistol. And they had a children's torch. A fucking *children's* torch. Green, with a wee purple dinosaur on it. Couldn't even get proper torches. *And* the batteries were shit in it or whatever so they had to reverse the car and put the headlights on me . . . You've heard this bit before haven't you?'

Danny had. Everyone in the county had, he figured, seeing as his mother'd rang him to tell him.

'Aye but go on.'

'So that fucker Jacksy? You know who I'm talking about?'

Danny nodded.

'He takes out the wee peashooter pistol. And two of them are kneeling on me back and I'm squealing, absolutely squealing like a pig. And it's against my calf, I can feel the barrel of it, cold, pressing into my calf, and he tries to fire it and it fucking *sticks*. Unbelievable. So they work at it, blaming each other, bickering, and one kneels down by my face. And my face's all cut, mouth full of gravel from the car park.'

He pauses. He can tell a story, Danny thinks.

'I'm fit to be tied. I don't know whether I'm coming or going so one of them slaps me. Hard. And he says *Wake up sunshine*.'

He does this clipped, chirpy little voice.

'*Now, we'll let you choose. Either we wait for another shooter or we use the bats to break your legs. Your choice. What'll it be?* Well you know the score, I'd probably never run again and maybe never walk if they use those bats. Smithereens. You're completely fucked. So I waited. And I knew they weren't going for my knees. I knew they were going to do the calves. I knew them and they knew I knew them. It was a warning really.'

He pauses, does a little stoic sigh. 'The pain's gone nearly completely. Only a stiffness now. And a wee limp. A wee limp for Hopalong Wilson.'

Danny's annoyed he's skipped the main bit.

'So what *did* you say, when they gave you the choice?'

'I think I said *Fuck off*. Maybe more than once. Maybe more than twice.'

Geordie emits a little mocking, breathy laugh through his long nose. Then stretches his upper lip down over his teeth. It looks for a second like he's wearing a gum shield. Then he opens his mouth with an audible *puck*.

'And then, when they started messing around, swinging the bats, I said I'd wait. So Jacksy got in the car and left, spinning the tubes and swerving round me. I was begging them, then, to let me go. I was like a kid. Screaming that I'd learnt my lesson. That I'd leave the fucking country. That I'd marry Janice. That I'd never deal a thing. That I'd deal everything they wanted. That I'd skin myself and make them coats. Anything, anything at all I thought would work. It seemed like hours. Me lying there crying and whingeing, stinking of piss, and the three of them left are kicking me and telling me to fuck up. And then that cunt comes back. And then two get down across my back again and I feel another barrel against my calf again, the left, and I black out.'

'Fucking hell mate.'

'Yeah . . . One of them telephoned my da from a phone box somewhere and told him where I was. Da was sitting there in the living room, crying apparently, with the police round making him cups of tea. I woke up in the Royal . . . '

Geordie looks up and grins. Danny can see a practised line coming.

' . . . with the world's worst hangover and the best kneecapping surgeon in the Northern Hemisphere sitting on my bed. He was just sitting grinning at me like he was my fucking uncle.'

Geordie leant back on the stool and gripped it with his hands, keeping his arms straight, like a man on a rodeo. Danny turned his empty glass in his hand, as if tuning in for the correct response. He looked Geordie straight in the eyes for maybe three, four seconds, and then said, with a slight shake of his head, 'Your round.'

Later, Danny and Geordie were sitting staring at two tidemarked pint glasses and Danny asked him again, serious now, 'So, how come you're *here*?'

'Well, I stopped the *anti-social behaviour*, the joyriding. But I was still seeing Janice, and still dealing a little and then, yesterday evening it was, I got the word to get out.'

LATE EVENING

The word had come in through a friend of his dad's that Geordie's name had come up, again, and that he should scarper. And sharply. He'd never been on a plane and wasn't going to start now, so he needed to get the ferry over to Scotland. That very evening he'd wangled a lift from Fergie, who drove one of Turkington's laundry vans, to Dungannon, from where he'd caught the bus to Belfast. He'd stayed at his Auntie Val's overnight in her spick Sandy Row redbrick and she'd driven him up to the docks in her purple Corsa the next morning. In the terminus, after a cardboard cup of coffee and a Danish pastry that resembled a trilobite (in consistency as much as shape), he spent thirty-seven pounds fifty on a single passenger ticket for the next Stranraer boat. Easy. Another country.

He'd left only once before, if you don't count a day trip to Rathlin. His Uncle Pat had taken him to a Rangers game for his sixteenth birthday. The fabled Ibrox. So many people in the one place. His eyes had scanned the rows and rows of men all standing watching the same thing. What did they all do for a living? How did they all afford this? Where did they all live? It was like five Ballyglasses all shaken out, lined up, and filed in. And he knew this other feeling was not just wonder but pride. When they'd stood and sung his chest was so tense, so strung with emotion that he thought he might cry. It was an Old Firm game, of course, and Celtic had lost 2–1. Ideal. He'd chugged eight cans of McEwans on the ferry home and spent the bus journey back to Ballyglass puking into his rucksack, with Uncle Pat sitting on the aisle seat telling him to hush down and quit his sobbing.

And then, on what might even be the same boat, Geordie had lost some money in the machines, drank a few pints, and met Ian McAleece. When Geordie'd stood out on the deck and felt the ferry engines shudder, he'd thought suddenly of fucking Janice, of coming inside her, of her tiny gasps, and of climbing out through her bedroom window. The shudder, the leaving. The boat seemed to enlarge when the engines started, and take on another, a somehow fuller dimension which lasted all the way to Scotland. Geordie, a naturally small man, delicate even, benefited from this effect too. He was constantly in motion. Sitting in Danny's living room, after they'd wandered back from the King's Head, fidgeting, smoking, shifting around, he seemed bigger than he actually was.

They were slumped on Danny's battered blue Habitat sofa. Danny had brought some cold cans of Heineken out from the fridge and a stupefied silence weathered round them. Their talking had gone the way of most male conversations. They'd lolloped through anecdotes in the pub, the *mind-that* and *mind-this* of teachers and football matches, and the *there-was* and *you-never* of some night in Cosgroves, paused a little at politics on the walk home while glancing at family, before spinning down gently through jokes into women.

Geordie now picked up a photograph from the top of a little stack of books, face down in a bamboo frame.

'Who's this then?'

A pretty straight-backed blonde seated, opposite the photographer, in a restaurant.

'Well, I said I was seeing someone. That's her. Olivia.'

Geordie whistled softly. '*Olivia*. Very nice, *very* nice. Very tidy.'

'Yeah, she's beautiful. But a little mental. In fact she's coming round tomorrow evening to collect her stuff. That's one of her piles.'

Geordie had already started grinning, preparing a wind-up involving haemorrhoids – but Danny was up and into the bathroom.

The television was on but on low and they sat dully watching *Eurotrash*: a blonde woman with swollen silicon breasts restrained by a silver tassled bra sat on a comic Frenchman's lap and mouthed something in Italian. Danny jabbed the remote control and Jools Holland appeared, playing the piano, his droll agile face looking down, slightly surprised, at the blur of his hands, as if they weren't part of him.

'Ach,' said Geordie. 'Put it back.'

'So what are you going to do mate? What's the plan?'

Danny had developed the habit of setting the pace

and subject of conversations. After interviewing scores of witnesses in order to draft statements, he'd realized that almost everyone has the capacity to bang contentedly on about, say, tungsten-tipped screws and talk shows and grades of wallpaper, for ever, if you let them. Danny didn't. He considered himself to have mastered the art of asking questions, but Geordie had managed to talk about everything so far except his future, and Danny wanted to know about it – specifically how much of it, if any, included him and his boxroom.

'I'm just going to stay in London for a while, a few months, and then go home. If not to Ballyglass, then Belfast or somewhere.'

At the words *a few months* Danny's knee twitched. 'You can't,' he said, referring to the first half of his statement.

'Course I can. The whole thing'll be forgotten,' Geordie countered, referring to the second half. 'They've bigger fish to fry. It's getting to be time for the wild men again.' Geordie's eyes opened wider when he said *wild*. Something excited his face.

'What do you mean?'

'Everything's starting up again. Everyone's fed up with waiting for something to happen.'

'Like what?'

'You know, people in the know with the right sympathies. And semtex, and guns, all that. Apparently. That's what people are *saying*. Around the town anyway.'

Danny read the *Belfast Telegraph* and the *Mid-Ulster Mail* online but was more concerned with stories about five-legged lambs being born in Magherafelt or poetry competitions won by arthritic eighty-six-year-olds than

politics. He watched the news and watched the breakdown of the Executive but just thought it more posturing
and gamesmanship. Danny had a sense that there was
no way back into the Troubles. How could people go
back to that? He thought every political postponement
and disagreement was just another stepping stone, slightly
submerged or slime-slippy perhaps, but the only way
across the river. Danny'd kind of assumed it was all over
bar the shouting, and the occasional shooting.

'I meant to tell you. I met a guy on the boat on the
way over. Mrs McAleece's nephew.'

'Who's that?'

'One of the dinner ladies at the primary school. You
know. The one with the big wide face like a satellite
dish and hands like shovels.'

'What's he called?'

'Ian McAleece.'

'I think I remember her. She looked like Nanny from
Count Duckula. Was he all right?'

'Yeah, all right.'

Geordie had produced another picture frame, this one
silver, from under the pile of books by the side of the
sofa. The same blonde girl, this time with her hair up,
wearing heavy framed black glasses, was sitting on a
wooden bench holding a glass of wine. She looked beautiful, and sad.

'Put that back mate. I've sorted all her stuff out and
you're messing it up.'

There were several discreet piles of her stuff collected
round the flat: monuments to the death of something. A
pile of clothes sat neatly folded on the chair in Danny's
bedroom. Eight CD boxes sat separated from the main

pile on the shelves by the living room window. Two columns of novels leant against each side of the sofa like bookends, and three videos and a couple of DVDs sat on top of the TV. Separation, Danny was learning, involves a great deal of separating. He felt the dead weight of failure settle on his chest.

'Listen, Geordie, you want me to ring you a cab? Where are you staying?'

'Well, actually Dan, I was *hoping* I could stay here.' Danny managed to keep his smile from slipping down into his shoes. 'Just for a night or two, 'til I get myself sorted. I was hoping to just kip on the sofa.'

Danny's smile increased its wattage. 'Yeah, yeah, of course. No problem. Stay here. I have to get up though and head to work tomorrow, and I'm not sure I've spare keys for the house.' Danny knew that two sets of keys, one of which had recently been attached by a silver chain to Olivia's pink leather purse, were in the drawer under the coffee table about a foot in front of them.

'Sure if you leave me yours, I can get a set cut.'

'I could do I suppose. I'm not sure if you can though. One of them's a security key or something. You need a letter from the managing agent.'

'Well, if I can't I'll just make sure I'm here when you come back.'

'Yeah, okay then. Sure.'

Geordie leant down and produced a lump of hash about the size of a bar of hotel soap from his rucksack. Danny watched him surreptitiously as he deftly skinned up, and passed the spliff to Dan to spark. Soon they both turned motionless, glassy-eyed as fish.

When the third spliff came round, Danny had lit a cigarette which he passed to Geordie to smoke when he smoked the joint. It was intimate and odd, all this. But not unworkable, Danny thought, this might be all right, this might even be fun.

The evening was ending. Danny, feeling too trashed to be anything but at ease with Geordie staying over, and too trashed to clear a space on the floor of the box-room, locked the front door and tossed Geordie a sleeping bag, bulbous in its carry-sac, and a lank pillow without a cover. In his bedroom he locked his laptop and his diary into a drawer in his desk and climbed messily, many-limbed, into bed.

My office worker's collar turned unselfconsciously
up . . . I return home . . . feeling a slight,
confused concern that I may have lost for ever
both my umbrella and the dignity of my soul.

Fernando Pessoa

THURSDAY, 8 JULY 2004

A minute after waking, Danny padded into his shower.
His mornings were efficient. He dressed in beige cords,
a blue shirt that he rubbed at for a bit with an iron that
leaked and was only ever tepid, and strapped his black
cycle helmet on his wet hair. His leather satchel slung
over his shoulder, he lifted his bike off the hook on the
garden wall and set off through the smouldering traffic
to work.

Geordie shifted from facing the back of the sofa to
facing the room. He farted a slow crescendo and went
back to sleep.

Danny locked his bike in the underground car park
and walked through the office courtyard to a side door
into his building. Danny worked at Monks & Turner, a
Magic Circle law firm. Which meant that his firm was,
supposedly, one of the five best in the country. It was

certainly one of the biggest. It felt to Danny like just another institution in a long line of places where you got told what to do, and did it. He had attended Ballyglass Nursery, Primary and High School and had done pretty much everything right. He was a gaunt truthful child and his teachers had been surprised, and a little perturbed, when they realized that he wanted to know as much as he could. His mother still rang to tell him that one of his old teachers had been in the office telling her how they kept his essays to read out to their classes. He never got less than an A and as he got older it began to seem more and more important not to. It seemed that every A raised the tightrope he was walking on a little higher, so that his fall would be even greater when it came. And then, suddenly, he was at the other end and in university.

His school had filled out his application for Cambridge and he'd signed it. He'd decided to choose history for a degree. There was so much of it. He'd gone along and been interviewed by a large Australian woman, covered in cream drapes like a dustsheeted wardrobe, and a neat little ginger Englishman. Danny was accepted, worked, thrived, and as he'd promised his father, applied to law firms for a job after graduation. Monks & Turner was the first interview and when they accepted him, he'd cancelled the others. Two years of law school in Tottenham Court Road, living above a Perfect Fried Chicken take-away in Turnpike Lane, saw city life settle down on him like smog. He became a first-class Londoner.

When he arrived at Monks, a grimy Monday in September, he had sat in Corporate, specifically insurance work. His trainer had just moved into the new office they were going to share. Their new name plaques, *James*

Motion and, underneath of course, and slightly smaller, *Daniel Williams*, had been put up to replace Townsend Hopkins. Townsend was an infamous old boy partner who'd been given the heave-ho for not bringing the work in. The firm constantly restored itself like that. It put Danny in mind of some vast ruminant. The main entrance, painted, polished, was its mouth, the corridors and meeting rooms served as intestines and organs, and the lawyers were like teeth, yellowy-pale, varying in sharpness, and renewable. Like teeth, they varied not only in sharpness but also in purpose, and some would get clients, others retain them. All, though, were grinders. Danny, when he qualified, had joined Litigation, the only seat he'd done which felt like law, and he was now a two-and-a-half-year qualified solicitor-advocate in the Commercial Litigation department specializing in International Arbitration. Danny sometimes thought that the only job worth doing was one which was covered by one word. Plumber. Joiner. Farmer.

A year ago Danny'd been given his own office, about the size of a garden shed. When his three bookcases and two filing cabinets had initially arrived he'd felt slightly claustrophobic. Now he felt snug. He could reach almost everything in his room from his desk. His computer screen faced the window. He faced the door. His desk had a panelled front on it and Danny had developed the habit of nipping below it, where he kept a duck-down sleeping bag and a cushion embroidered with sunflowers that his sister had made, for a kip either before, during, or after lunch. He would make sure the route to his desk was barricaded by briefcase and recycling box, then slink off his seat, suddenly boneless.

Danny's central friend at Monks was Albert Rollson, a Brummie who'd ditched his accent in favour of a mid-Atlantic twang. Rollson was neurotic. His terrors included other people's illnesses and he would get out of a lift at the next floor if someone in it coughed or sneezed. He'd flinch if someone accidentally came too close or brushed against him in passing, and grimaced if hugged. Which is not to say that he was cold, he simply, proudly, possessed an over-developed sense of propriety. It informed his distrust of Antipodeans. And Americans. And Europeans. And was the reason he worked in law. He was born to its hierarchy, its wheels within wheels, its concurrent bitchings and slobberings, its dog-eat-dog, backstab, leapfrog. And it allowed him to dress like Cary Grant.

Danny had shared an office with Rollson when they had qualified, two years after arriving at Monks. They had argued relentlessly over plants. Danny's view was that offices are the ugliest, most sterile places in the world. Everything is synthetic. You see nothing that is actually growing, bar the perceptible fattening of some of the most sedentary lawyers and secretaries. Danny wanted a real plant in the room. He told Rollson that the lack of flora in the workplace was the reason lawyers started office affairs. There was nothing else to look at but people. The obscene clashing decor, the generic tacky prints, the background corporate hum from air conditioning, VDU and photocopier: people looked at each other more closely. Rollson however, perpetually single, quite liked the idea of people looking at him more closely. Plants were there simply to steal more of his oxygen in a city where there was scarcely enough anyway.

30

He was allergic to anything natural. On a school outing to a stables near Dudley, a large grey mare had once licked his face and he'd never recovered. That rough slobbery smothering tongue. The smell of it. He quite liked seeing the countryside from the motorway, the space, its potential, and he'd once bought a David Attenborough series on video, although he hadn't watched it.

Danny walked into his corridor. He noted that the doors of Andrew Jackson, departmental senior partner, and Adam Vyse, departmental managing partner, were open. He removed his bag from his shoulder, placed the helmet in it and carried it close to his body. In this way, and by performing two complicated body-spins at just the right moments, he could walk past the partners' doors without it being immediately apparent that he was just arriving. It was 9.43 a.m.

Geordie stretched out an arm to the coffee table, encountered the remote control and switched on *Trisha*. He noticed that he'd drooled on his pillow.

Danny's phone was flashing. This always scared him a little. Either it was a message from last night (which meant that somebody had expected him to be there after he'd left) or from this morning (which meant that somebody had expected him to be there before he'd arrived). In the worst case scenario (the WCS, as Rollson would have called it) there would be two messages from the same partner, one from last night and one from this morning, and in the very WCS, that partner would be Adam Vyse. Danny listened to his messages. Two. First message, yesterday: 7.05 p.m. Carrie, Adam's calm and pretty secretary, was cooing that Adam wanted to see him as soon as possible. He loved the fact that Carrie refused to say *a.s.a.p.* We're not Americans, Danny always thought when he heard it used, we have time to say the whole sentence. Second message, today: 8.11 a.m. Adam. 'Danny, give me a ring soon as you're in. Something big's come up.' *Ach fuck*, Danny said, a little too loudly.

Vyse was notorious for handing out difficult work and not supervising it. He would demand a briefing just prior to seeing a client and then, in the meeting, repeat to the client what you had just told him, word for word, before turning to you, smiling encouragingly, and asking whether you agreed with his *preliminary views*. Danny stood at Vyse's open door. He was leaning back in his leather easy chair, with his tailored arms crossed behind his slicked head and the phone cradled between his neck and chin.

'Yes, of course. No you're quite right. We don't need any more of them. Oh yes? . . . Fourteen. No, no about two hundred acres. Uh-uh . . . A Jet Ski. Well, you know what I say? He who dies with the most toys wins . . . No, this is *it*. They need to consolidate and we aren't going to give them time to. We need to hit them hard now . . . I know . . . *Yes* . . . '

Danny looked in at the office. A wooden golf putter was propped a little forlornly in the far corner, as if it dreamt of real grass. Aside from Adam's own enormous bureau, reminiscent of the White House presidential desk, another sheeny table, an eight-seater for team meetings, dominated the middle of the room. The oak-veneer cabinets fronted with glass held silver and crystal ornaments given to Adam for successful corporate claims or defences. Danny could read the largest one, a glass rhomboid, from here: *Jackman Thorndike Litigation*

1998 – The Best Team Won. An open wardrobe displayed navy and grey pinstripe suits, a shelf of shirts and a row of pegs from which numerous ties hung down, entwined. A sky-blue baseball cap hung on one of the pegs. Its motif was illegible but Danny knew that it said *I Wouldn't Say Boo To A Gooson*, Gooson being a corporate client involved in a billion dollar insurance dispute which had taken a team of twelve associates and three partners two years to resolve. Danny also knew that Adam had a matching sky-blue polo shirt with a matching logo. After the case had been settled the whole team, in their team outfits, had flown to the firm's headquarters in Atlanta for a week-long junket. The pictures were still on the noticeboard in the corridor outside. Team Gooson at the check-in. Team Gooson in the departure lounge. Team Gooson at the baggage terminal. They reminded Danny of the Gateway outings for mentally handicapped kids he used to help with at school. It was to do with the grinning. On the meeting table sat an array of executive toys: an Archimedes' cradle, little metal monkeys on a magnet that could be built up into shapes, a Rubik's cube sponsored by a pharmaceutical company with different drug logos on each side. On a far shelf, Chopin was seeping softly from the big black speakers that stood, close as bodyguards, on either side of the little silver stereo. A copper plaque above the desk stated, in gothic lettering, *Teamwork divides the task and doubles the success.* On the far wall photographs were aligned in a row, five of them, like the house's face-up poker hand. Each contained posed shots of Adam and his family. His wife (Amelia? Amanda?) was pretty much what you'd expect

33

if you watched television on Sunday evenings. Something of the period drama about her. Slighty sad, as if she'd expected something slightly different, skinny (tennis, Danny supposed), naturally blonde. The kids were all versions of either of their parents, and all the shots appeared proprietorial somehow: two of the blondies on a yacht looking more bored than they should; one astride a grey pony which, bearing its teeth, seemed to be grinning for the photograph; the perfect husband and wife posed at their fireplace, holding the lintel (*Team Marriage,* thought Danny); one of the wife in a manicured garden (of at least two acres) with a lifted glass of wine; the whole family on a ski slope clutching each other and not for balance. They looked happy.

'I know ... Quite ... Well, I looked at him for a moment and said *If that's the way you want it we'll have no option but to seek an injunction.* It was either put up or shut up. We have them by the balls ... Yeah, fuck'em ... Okay, we'll talk soon ... Okay ... take care ... Bye ... Bye bye.'

Adam swivelled slightly, and with one fluent gesture succeeded in both replacing the phone and waving Danny into the room. 'Danny. Yes, great. Come in, come in. Shut the door.'

Danny was tempted to nod at the telephone and solemnly ask 'How *is* your Mum?', but thought better of it and stepped inside. He sank slightly into the deep-pile carpet.

'Sit down. Now, how are things?'

This means, in law firms, *Can you do this piece of work for me, this piece that I am keeping up my sleeve? If you are seriously considering saying no, you need a reason better than I have no time or desire or consciousness or limbs.*

Danny could have quite enjoyed these non-conversations, where both sides spoke in this unwritten code, like pig Latin, if they didn't result in pain for him, which they invariably did. There were several responses to Adam's question, and none of them could save him. Danny's favoured one was to hedge as much as possible until the work had been described and then try to sidestep it or, if it looked okay, enthusiastically accept it. First off, Danny liked to describe how busy he was, at great and enthusiastic length, in order to strengthen his hand when he would try to brush off the incoming work. He replied, 'Fairly stuffed at the moment. I'm working on this *massive* arbitration between a Brazilian company, our client, and a German electronics manufacturer. That's with Carol and Alastair. And I'm running the disclosure on a new claim for Cartwrights against a ballbearing manufacturer. That's with Jonathan. We're fighting over the size of it at the minute.' Adam's eyes were scanning a point about six inches to the right of his head. Danny couldn't remember whether there was a mirror behind him. I haven't finished yet, he thought, so at least look me in the face. 'And a couple of pro bono issues have just gone live. The homeless charity I work with are disputing marketing fees, and my death row case in Jamaica is up for review by the Inter-American Court of Human Rights. Then there's also the coroner's inquest that I've been doing with Amanda.'

Adam, rather shamelessly, looked bored. 'Right, right, great. Now I've a piece of work I'd like you to look at for me. It's fairly intensive but really interesting.' Danny's simultaneous translation ran on: *Stop fucking around. I know you have work. We all have work. And you are about to get some more. And it's going to be horrific. C'est la fucking vie.* Still, even this was unusual. There was normally the pretence of an option. He'd have to force it. 'Well Adam, I'd really like to *help* you on it.' *I'm not doing all of it mate.* 'But I really will have to check with the other partners on my matters, Carol and Jonathan, as to whether or not it's feasible.' *I have friends in power-ful places and they will come through for me. Back off tiger.*

'I've already spoken to them and they're fine about it, as long as you get everything done of course.' *Checkmate. Stop your snivelling. You're fucked for the foreseeable. Forget about your holiday, your friends, your sleep.*

'Okay, great.' *Dead man walking, dead man walking.* Danny heard a bright, happy voice come out of his own mouth. 'And will there be someone on this to help me?' *If I really really have to do this, I need to share the shit around.*

'I'm sure you'll be able to find a willing trainee.' *Screw you wiseguy.* 'Here's the file.' *I've cleared my desk! I've cleared my desk!* 'Hard work is character-building, Danny.' *Go fuck yourself.*

'Of course, of course.' *I'm eating it up.* 'Though my character's already built, thanks.' *Fuck you too.*

'Look, Danny, the thing is, it was one of Scott's pro-jects and he's had to clear out to Australia for a while unexpectedly.' *We all know what happened so settle down.* 'We're in a bit of a bind.'

Scott Atkins had come home from work on Monday, at 1 a.m., to discover that his wife had moved back to

Australia. She had left a factual note on his pillow telling him that they had spent a total of two hours together in the last five weeks, aside from sleeping in the same bed, and that she was going home to Melbourne.

Danny nodded. Adam continued, 'It's the Ulster Water takeover. You know what I'm talking about? It's not really your line but things being as they are the Corporate boys need all the help they can get.' *Don't misunderstand me, I think you're a piss-poor lawyer.*

'Ulster Water?'

'Yes.'

'My part of the world.'

'Really? I always thought you were Scottish.'

'No.'

'Oh. Well, Syder Plc are launching a takeover offer for them. Yakuma are making a rival bid. We're acting for Syder. You'll have a quick conference call after lunch with the Syder MD, a Mr Tom Howard, where you can introduce yourself.' *You're on your own. I know nothing about this.* 'I understand he can be a pretty difficult customer. In the meantime you need to go speak to the Corporate department. You'll be overseeing the litigation due diligence and maybe heading off to the head office this weekend. In Belfast. John Freeman's the partner on it. Okay? Thank *you*.' He turned abruptly but neatly in his chair and started reading his e-mails.

Danny started back up the corridor. He hadn't heard of John Freeman. He started listing all the consequences that had flowed from previous hospital-passes, those spinning cases that you catch in mid-air and which end with a sudden high tackle or headbutt from nowhere. One, involving a counterclaim between crisp bag manu-

facturers, or more specifically between a crisp bag manufacturer and the company that manufactured the machines
that manufactured crisp bags, had caused Danny to begin
taking anti-depressants. Another, involving suing the
Bulgarian Government for reneging on promised subsi-
dies for a hydro-electric power station, forced him to
miss his grandmother's funeral. Danny spent approximately ten per cent of every working day looking at job
sites on the Internet.

Albert was waiting in his office. He was sitting in
Danny's seat, clicking out a length of lead from a plastic
pencil, one of several that peered out of the handker-
chief pocket of his jacket. He'd walked past Adam's office
and witnessed Danny nodding sagely as Adam stitched
him up. Rollson had been returning from the stationery
stores in the basement with a new haul. He visited them
every few days to check out any new pens, pencils or
interesting objects that might have arrived and hadn't
been listed on the intranet stationery ordering facility.

'Well?'

'I'm in serious trouble.'

'What on?'

'Takeover of Ulster Water. One of Scott's old cases.'

'The due diligence on that's *huge*. You are *fucked* mate,
truly.'

'I need a trainee on it.'

'You might get the lovely Ellen.'

'Fat frigging chance. Come on, get out of my seat.'

The lovely Ellen. Danny and Albert had been having lunch
about two months ago when they agreed on a girl. This
was noteworthy because it was rare, rare enough to have

never happened before. Though neither liked a specific type (aside from Albert's self-hating weakness for sloans, pearls, turned-up collars) each would say about the target of the other's amorous (read lewd) remarks, that she was too tall, too small, too fat, too thin, too loud, too quiet and so on. Albert had pointed her out to Danny in the canteen. She had been expertly gathering tomatoes at the salad bar with two primitive wooden utensils, the sort that look like souvenirs from a holiday in Tonga. She was wonderful. They agreed on Ellen. Everyone agreed on Ellen. Albert knew who she was, of course, and which office she was sitting in. Danny had since looked her up at least five times on the intranet to see her picture: those almond eyes levelly staring the camera down.

Ellen was a trainee on the ninth floor in the Banking Litigation department. Danny worked on the tenth floor in the Corporate group. That morning, after his meeting with Adam, and a leisurely dander to Starbucks, he sent out a sequence of increasingly desperate e-mails to the entire Litigation department. There were two positive responses. One from a meat-headed trainee called Bradley who wore a variety of different shades of pastel shirts, all Ralph Lauren, with the sleeves rolled up to display massive pale forearms, like shanks of lamb in a butcher's window. Bradley's offer of help, evidently compelled by his trainer, was so loaded with qualifications, and his work of such low quality anyway, that Danny was about to send out a seventh request, addressed only to the senior associates, begging them to allow their trainee to assist him, when Albert's uncommon optimism came uncommonly good.

Ellen Powell was about to qualify into the Employment

department and had been doodling the last seat of her training contract away downstairs on the ninth floor, avoiding work as much as she could and sneaking out the building by way of the catering lift at 6 p.m. Her trainer had gone on secondment and when Ellen returned from reading the newspapers in the library on the fourteenth floor, she had thirty e-mails in her inbox. After reading through Danny's six requests, and checking Danny's picture out on the intranet, Ellen e-mailed him offering to help. It had just pinged into Danny's inbox when she appeared in his doorway. She was standing very straight: a tall, black girl wearing a black trouser suit and a double-cuffed blue and white pinstriped shirt. Her hair was braided and tied back. Her long legs and narrow hips made her seem taller than she was and it was only her breasts that prevented her body from appearing purely athletic. Her face had something reserved and angry about it. She was closed to the general public. Danny grinned.

'Something amusing?' A posh bone-dry voice.

'No. I'm smiling in a friendly manner. It's the Monks & Turner spirit. You're Ellen?'

'And you're the man with too much work.'

'I'm one of them. Please. Come in, come in. Sit down. Now, how are things?' And thus we do the evil we have done to us.

EARLY MORNING AGAIN

Two miles and forty-seven yards away, Geordie was skinning up a morning spliff to lessen the stress of *Trisha*. Two men were arguing over an enormously fat girl who was dressed from head to foot in Adidas. The two men were both at least three times her age, which appeared to be around thirteen. Man One and Man Two would periodically stand up and shout at each other and then sit down. Like little figures wheeled out on the chime of a fancy wooden clock, they'd wave their arms, clang around for a while and retreat. The fat girl's brown hair was scraped up away from her face and sat in a tuft on the top of her scalp, like the green parts of a pineapple. It was becoming apparent that Man Two was the girl's father and that Man One drove her school bus. It was also becoming apparent that Man One had fathered Pineapple's baby. This, the offspring of Pineapple and

41

bus driver, was now being brought on stage for some kind of curtain call. It was a pink-faced wailing package and nobody wanted to hold it.

Geordie took the last hot drag on his spliff, and stubbed it out, crooking it like a baby finger. This was interesting. He was alone in Danny's flat. He stood up. He was wearing only pale blue creased boxers. He lifted his rucksack from the foot of the sofa and emptied the contents out onto the sleeping bag. He replaced everything bar one white plastic bag. He set about counting the cash it contained. Geordie had not left home empty-handed.

The morning of his going he'd been fit to burst with worries about what to take and where to go and how to get. The usual going concerns. He'd rang Janice at work and asked her to meet him in the old children's playground over in Kildrum. It was out of town and across the road from a housing estate that was being emptied out, house by house, to swankier estates. The windows on some houses were boarded up and some were flung open on the warm summer sky. The place had the look of an advent calendar. Janice had taken her lunch hour early from the chemists and driven out in her wee red Fiesta. Geordie watched her carefully and clumsily reverse the car into one of the outlined spaces in the car park, even though it was completely empty. She sauntered up to him. Tight scant denim skirt, white trainers, a navy V-neck top and a long open maroon cardigan. Her hair was tied back and Geordie fancied she'd been crying or maybe it was hay fever. She looked good, great even, if you forgave the wonky eye, and Geordie did, as he held her waist and kissed the soft swell of the top of her breasts.

'Jan, I have to disappear. You know your fucking brother has put the word out on me.'

'I heard Brewster talking about it in the kitchen. Geordie, I don't know what to say. It's my fault. I tried to talk to Greer but he wasn't having any of it. And Da said to shut up or he'll turf me out. Should I come? Should I come with you? Where are you going?'

Good old Janice, Geordie thought. Good old stupid sexy Janice, with her little waist and little feet and big lips.

'Better not, at least not yet. I'll try and send you a message at Martin's when I get something sorted. I don't know where I'm going, to be honest Jan. And I've no cash. I was thinking of Australia but there's visas and stuff to be sorted out and I'll have to do that in England. You could try and come over and meet me in London maybe, or in Australia even, in a few months. You could do your hairdressing again and I could work in a bar or drive a cab.'

'Geordie, if you need money, I can get you money.'

He had turned her round and she was leaning into his lap as he drifted slightly on the swing, pleased with the airy movement. He was considering whether or not she'd let him slip her skirt up and fuck her gently from behind, here and now, as a little leaving gift.

'How can you get money? You can't nick it from work Jan. They have security cameras in there.'

'Geordie!' she snapped a little, 'I love that job. I wouldn't steal from Mr and Mrs Martin. They've been really good to me.'

'Aye, Charlie Martin's been very keen to be really good to you. Mad keen. Mad keen to get you in the back of the shop all alone and be *really* good to you.'

43

'Shut *up*. Listen to me. Greer has money in a box behind the panel in the bath. He doesn't know I know it's there. You have to work the panel off with a knife or screwdriver but the other day I was in there and Da was shouting to let him in the bathroom but I was shaving my legs and I turned round to let him in for a piss and kicked the side panel of the bath and it made a clangy sound, like metal. *Geordie*, I can *feel* you.'

Geordie had slipped his hands inside her cardigan, which she'd zipped up, and he was cupping the under-side of her breasts. His cock was running lengthways to the left, over the side of his thigh. 'Hold on,' he said, and slipped one hand under the pinch of his jeans and pulled his cock up straight, to fit in the shallow inden-tation that her tight skirt allowed her ass to make. 'Go on then. What about the bath?' He pulled her tight to him now, holding her hard little waist. She was rubbing a little against him and her voice was softer, sinking.

'What? Oh. Well, I let Da in and then when I went back in to finish my legs I took Brewster's penknife from the cabinet, which Malandra had in there cos it's got tweezers on it, and I took the panel off and there's a metal box, with a lock on it but the key was in it, and it's full of money. I mean *full* of money. It must be Budgie's. No one else in the house has cash like that lying around.' Her voice trailed off as Geordie moved one hand down and under her and touched the warm, wet patch of her cotton knickers.

'You're full of money.' He slipped a finger in under the strict elastic and felt that smallest part of her hardening. With his palm on her thigh, holding her legs apart, his finger moved down to feel the lips loosening, moistening.

'Geordie, not *here*. Come into the car and we'll park down by Macklin's river.'

'Ach, come on, there's no one round. It's the last time we'll see each other for a while. Are you saying, Janice,' and here he moved the other hand up over her breast and freed it from her bra. Loose and soft and billowy. He held the dense little nipple between his finger and thumb, gently, then firmly, 'that you'll steal Budgie's money to give to me? What *are* you saying?'

'You've nothing to lose. I'll deny everything. No one knows the money's there. He never checks it. That first night I put a hair between the panel of the bath and the wall so that if someone took the panel off the hair would fall and Geordie, the hair was still there this morning. I'll take some of it. Just enough to see you right. Come on.'

Clever girl, Geordie thought. Janice stood up, shivery, adjusted her bra under her top and tugged her skirt round to straighten the seam. She dragged him by the hand to the car, and as she walked she felt the friction tingle between her legs, as if his fingers were still down there. Geordie pulled his checked blue shirt out of his jeans to cover his cock: it had thrust its angry head over the parapet of his belt.

Driving back into town, after a frenetic half-hour at Macklin's river, feeling sated and lazy and sexy, Janice told Geordie to meet her back at the playground at two, and to bring a bag. She went back to work and told old soft Mr Martin that she wasn't well. *Woman's problems.* He was getting ready to complain when she pushed her chest up against him and made as if to cry. He told her to go straight home and get to bed. They could manage without her. She drove to the semi-detached house at the edge of the Dungiven estate she shared with her parents, Malandra and a varying number of brothers (Budgie's marriage had faltered, as predicted, almost immediately, and Jackie and little snub-nosed Greer Junior lived with her mother over in Coagh, and Chicken had just moved across town into his girlfriend Jenny's flat which was, too conveniently, above the offy). She told her mother, who was sitting at the dining-room table doing a jigsaw of two poodles in a pram, that she'd period pains, and needed to take a bath and some aspirin. Her mother, holding two edge pieces between her pursed lips, looked up, nodded and then looked down again. Some old sitcom was on the telly. Janice thudded up the stairs into her room and emptied her toilet bag onto her bed. She carried it into the bathroom and set it on the edge of the bath. She leant against the sink and looked at herself. The mirror was overcast with dust and constellated with stray white flecks of toothpaste. Janice thought how old she looked. She stretched the skin at the side of her eyes to flatten the little crow's feet that were appearing. She must remember to wear her glasses more when she drove, not squint so much. And she should stop smoking, they say that's not good for the skin. She turned and looked at herself from the side. Her breasts were still high and still firm, for breasts that size. She cupped them as if weighing them, and thought how last week some asshole down at the building site on the Benaghy Road had shouted after her, as she passed on the way to the solarium at lunchtime, *You don't get many of them to the pound.* She felt like kneeing him in the balls as she had Budgie, when he'd tried to get into her room three years ago, drunk. No way José. She hadn't let him in since she was sixteen and he never tried any more. She lifted her top. Her stomach was still flat and still hard. Good. She could do with losing some weight off her bum she decided, and suddenly, a little viciously, tugged off her top and wriggled out of her skirt and knickers. She stepped cleanly out of the puddled clothes, and looked at the pale mass of herself again. Skin and then inside that flesh and inside that bone and then inside that what? Didn't people say the marrow of the bone? People had bone marrow transplants didn't they? As she stood and stared in the mirror she saw her face waver and emerge as if it was fifty years old. Fleshy cheeks, a corrugated brow, eyelids thickened and heavy. She blinked and came back to herself. You're getting old Janice, she thought, you're beginning to die.

She opened the bathroom cabinet. A dimpled strip of Boots paracetamol clattered into the sink, triggering a loose scree of assorted plasters. An ancient bottle of Calpol, still in its stained cardboard sheath, stood at the back of the top shelf. A stippled pink ankle support covered some squat and sturdy pill bottles. It dated from the time Budgie, up playing on 'the pitch' (really a partly gravelled field behind the Costcutters which had been earmarked for a car park that never appeared) had his ankle sprained by a dangerous tackle from Jackie McMenemy. That was the first time Budgie had been in trouble, apparently, according to Brewster, as Janice had only been one or two then. As payback Budgie had lifted a broken brick from the pile they were using for one of the goalposts, hobbled over to Jackie, who was sitting cross-legged nursing his own ankle, and smashed it in

his face. Her dad had given the McMenemys money so
that Budgie wouldn't go to borstal. You still saw Jackie
round the town on a Saturday, holding the hand of one
of his wee boys who'd look up, wailing or smiling, into
the gap-toothed grin of a village idiot. You can fix that
sort of stuff now, Janice thought, wiping her tongue like
a polishing rag over the neat ornaments of her own front
teeth.

There were pumice stones and scalpels and bunion
and corn plasters for her mother's gnarled feet (the legacy
of twenty years standing behind the counter in Marshall's
bakery). And there was Brewster's penknife with the
tweezers that saw heavy usage. The hair on Malandra's
body could best be described as adventurous. Her eyebrows, left alone as they had been for approximately
fifteen years, had sent out expeditions to explore the rest
of her face. The small of her back had fleeced itself. She
was pretty, Janice knew, and unlike her was dark, which
was really why the flecks of downy, shadowy hair on
her face used to be noticeable. From when she was
twelve, if she ever pissed any of them off, they'd called
her Elvis, what with her sideburns and all. Which was
why there were four half-empty tubes of Immac in the
cabinet, and the tweezers were kept busy applauding in
the natural light by the bathroom window.

Janice banged the cabinet door and pulled out the
blade of the knife with her thumbnail. She wedged it in
between the panel and the side of the bath. The panel
shifted slightly ajar. She turned on both bath taps: they
squealed as she twisted their heads, and dripped in some
gloopy orange bubble foam. The panel was a sheet of
plywood, painted white, and the green deposit box was

still behind it. She pulled it out from its hiding place. It was lighter than she remembered. She put the lid of the toilet down and sat on it, the box and the lid burning her bare thighs with cold. The cash was in rolls packed in little plastic bank bags. They reminded her of messages in bottles somehow. She hadn't time to count it or estimate how much it was. She quickly took the bags out and pushed some into her trainers, and then pushed her socks in after them. The rest she stuffed into her toilet bag. She stood up then, and touched, gently, as if in remembrance, the cool damp hair between her legs. She would miss him, she thought, and his lovely big cock. Maybe she would try and meet him somewhere. Fuck Budgie. It had been a long time since she'd felt anything but hate for him. Fuck Greer and Chicken and their vicious mouths and fists and friends. Fuck the lot of them. Except Brewster. He was all right, just a bit pathetic. He floated around like a ghost, shocked to be noticed at all. She went to the toilet, wiped, stood and yanked the chain. It was an old-fashioned toilet with the cistern up high on the wall. It glugged and then whimpered, filling up. She stepped into the bath and hunkered. It was too hot to lie down in. She could hear the bubbles in the foam popping softly, audible as an opened can of Coke. She lowered her ass into the water and raised herself again. She cupped some water and let it drizzle down over her knees, onto her thighs, into the nest of hair between her legs. She sat down properly and then, with the dragged, reverberant sound of skin on wet plastic, slipped down into the bath to submerge herself completely. Pinching her nose closed, she felt the water funnel into her ears. She could hear the sounds of the house much clearer here: the television spilling canned laughter in the living room, and the steam whistle of the kettle on the gas ring, and then her mother's chair scrape back on the lino tiles as she got up in her sheepskin slippers and shuffled into the kitchen to warm the teapot. I live underwater, she thought suddenly, and pushed her feet against the bottom of the bath to surface for air and shampoo.

Geordie then had a bagful of cash. Janice had put the money in a white plastic bag and he'd placed it in the front pocket of the rucksack he'd nicked from his little sister Grace. As soon as he'd got on the ferry (until then he was still expecting Budgie to appear suddenly, behind some window, tapping softly as rain) he'd nipped into one of the disabled toilets, and sat on the floor and totalled the cash. £49,250. Not bad at all.

Sitting on Danny's sofa, Geordie counted it again, dealing the notes into piles like playing cards. £49,300. He recounted it. £49,450. *Fuck it*, he thought, *I've a rough idea*. He lifted two of the Bank of England fifty pound notes, pushed them into his left trainer and placed the rest back into the plastic bags. He started to look around Danny's place with replenished interest. Where the hell could he hide it? He wandered through the flat like a prospective buyer, looking up at the plaster cornices and down at the skirting boards. He tapped walls. He opened cupboards and drawers. He peeled back the carpet, like sunburnt skin, from a corner of the living room. The pale epidermis of unpolished floorboards. He didn't know what he was looking for. He sat down again, heavily, on the sofa. And then it was obvious. He'd hide it where Budgie had hidden it. Geordie lifted a small fork from the cutlery drawer, which was still lolling out like a tongue, and carried the bag into the bathroom.

The bath must once have been new and white. And that must have been some time ago. It now had a discoloured ring around it, close to the top, like a high tide-mark and the base of it was grained by smaller rings and various stains, all of them bad. The panel was plastic and when Geordie inserted the handle of the fork, it scraped open almost immediately. Behind the panel was a paper bag filled with nails, a magazine from July 1995 called *Smash Hits* (featuring Take That and their magnificent teeth) and an empty bottle of Johnson's Baby Shampoo. He pushed the plastic bag right to the back, past the roughened underside of the bath.

Geordie, to the tune of 'The Farmer Wants a Wife', was softly singing *Fifty thousand pounds, fifty thousand pounds, hey-ho ma-dearie-oh, fifty thousand pounds.* Janice was an idiot. She reckoned that kind of money was Budgie's, that it was the proceeds of one scam or another: bleaching red diesel to white, flogging counterfeit DVDs or videos to the stallholders up at Nutts Corner, offering 'protection' to the chippies and offies that lined the main street. That kind of folding didn't come in from that. Not, leastways, all at once. Fitting the panel back into its gap, Geordie started to get a little unnerved. Maybe *he* was the idiot. Everyone'd heard the rumours. Something was starting up or going down. Something was being unleashed. Maybe he had Something's money.

Geordie showered, dressed himself in yesterday's garb, and set off towards Dalston. Danny's flat was in Stoke Newington, according to Albert, Olivia and his postcode, but Danny himself admitted Dalston was spiritually, if not technically, its home. He had given Geordie brief instructions last night: *turn right out the house, then right again, then buy some food for dinner.*

Stoke Newington High Street runs from the white liberal enclave of Church Street (homeopathic healers, designer clothes shops, independent bookstores) through the Turkish community (men's clubs with no discernible purpose, kebab shops) to the African and Afro-Caribbean end (hair shops, furniture stores selling coffee tables fashioned from ceramic tigers). Geordie began to walk down it. He passed a mobile phone shop and remembered he'd not brought his phone out. Stupid of him. He'd not seen so many different shades of skin before. Geordie, Danny had learned last night in the pub, had never tried garlic or pasta, unless tinned spaghetti is pasta. Neither had he drank wine outside a church or eaten an aubergine, a courgette, or a sweet potato. Geordie felt himself in a new position: the outsider. He felt white. He couldn't stop looking at the black people he saw. Their skin looked polished. They were beautiful. In Ridley Road market he thought he was about to get his head kicked in for staring. He was looking at a broad-shouldered young black man wearing a brown leather jacket and a gold-buttoned white shirt with a Nehru collar.

'Wadchu looking at liddle man?' Geordie realized he was talking to him. The man was repeatedly tilting his head back, as if brandishing his chin like a weapon.

'Nothing,' Geordie mumbled, shaking his head, scurrying, suddenly animal.

He came to a butchers, entitled Halal Meat, on the corner of the market. It was one long glass counter open to the street. Bald dead chickens clustered upside down along the back wall. Three men, slick and confident as bartenders, swayed between each other and served the docile queue. They wore white coats smeared with blood. They made Geordie think of a war movie he'd seen once in which sleepless doctors tended to the wounded. He inched to the front.

'Yes? Help you?' said Omar Sharif's plumper little brother.

'Can I have a pound of bacon and four chicken breasts please?'

The moustache behind the counter leant right across and tapped his cleaver on the glass: 'Are you taking the piss my friend?' He rolled the 'r' of 'friend' and toned the phrase as Goldfinger did to James Bond. Geordie, angry, shook his head and then softened his face and shook his head again.

'No bacon. How many chicken breasts you want?' Sharif Jr straightened up behind the counter.

'Four, please,' said Geordie, a little stunned.

He crossed the road to the Kilkenny Arms, received his Guinness from the bleached Australian barman, who actually said 'G'day', and sat at an empty table. His ears were burning. He felt somehow embarrassed. This was the capital of his country and he felt a million miles from home. This was London, home of Big Ben, unfailingly chiming on the news every night, home of the Houses of Parliament and Churchill and the Union Jack and all the unchangeable symbols the orange banners displayed. Geordie realized he hadn't seen a flag all day.

Mooning over his Guinness, Geordie thought about Ulster, that little patch of scorched earth. It had stayed loyal to England and now England didn't want it. England was completely indifferent to it now. Geordie remembered Jenny McClure, this girl he'd known at primary school, who was tall and blonde and posh, which meant that her family lived outside the town and owned two cars and her dad played golf. She was clean and prim and perfect. And all through P6 and P7 he'd asked her to the cinema and made her little Valentine cards and warned the other boys off and waited after school just to walk ten paces behind her to the gates where her pert and pretty mother waited. And all that time she either ignored Geordie, or got her friends to tell him to leave her alone. Geordie remembered the lunchtime when, in an empty classroom, he'd poured the jar of dirty paintbrush water into her school bag. One day you wake up and hate.

At the Orange parades the police would stand on the fringes, attentive and static, like curious strangers who've stopped to watch a wedding party leave the church. Geordie remembered sitting on tarmac in fierce bare sunlight watching old Andy MacLean, a friend of his da's, unwrap the Lambeg from the oilskins with a deft patience. He remembered the clipped neatness of his white rolled shirtsleeves. The snap and flutter of the tendons in his forearms. And how his thin wrists arched as the drumsticks twirled like spokes in front of him, and under his jutted chin how the ordinal drum had pounded and pounded and swung. He remembered how the lodge's banners had advertised their faithfulness, as if faithfulness was all that mattered. But how could one stay devoted to someone who wants to leave you? Well, they wanted us once, Geordie thought. He stayed on in the pub for an idle hour, opposite a toothless old timer, folded into himself, dressed like Geordie's dead grand-father, grey suit, flat cap, reading the *Irish News*. When he stood up to slope past him, the old guy raised his tumbler of whiskey to eyelevel, as if he was toasting the two of them.

Outside the pub a tattered newspaper was lying against the curb and the wind was freeing it sheet by sheet. Some pages blew about restlessly further up the pave-ment. One had managed to wrap itself around a lamp-post and was flapping gently like a drunkard trying to hail a taxi. Geordie stopped to watch an African man, in a brown lounge suit and a piano keyboard tie, across the road. He was preaching about Jesus and reminded Geordie of the McNulty brothers, who, on a Friday night when he was shuttling from pub to pub on Ballyglass main street, would be standing out in suits they were too young to need for work, beseeching the sinners to repent. Geordie wandered back up the High Street and turned left past the school into Sofia Road. The playground was filled with kids shouting and running and taking every-thing very seriously. Kids don't really have senses of humour, Geordie thought. Everything seems so impor-tant. One little boy, Arabic looking, was standing in uni-form by the wire fence looking particularly grave. Geordie looked back, just as level and serious. The kid sneered, casually flipped him the middle finger, and walked off.

In the house Geordie slumped down on the sofa and turned his phone on. He'd two texts, both from Janice. BUDGIE KNOWS UVE CASH said one. RING ME said the other. Geordie needed to piss. He jumped up and went into the bathroom. He was jittery. It was always going to happen, he reasoned, but he didn't realize it would happen so quickly. He'd need to think. There was no way Budgie would know where he was. It wasn't like he was still in danger. He zipped up, flushed the toilet, and then checked his voicemails. One from Janice. She'd been crying. He'd probably slapped her about. The second voicemail was from Ian McAleece. Something about a drink. He wasn't in the mood for that. As he was setting the phone down on the table it rang. He answered it, knowing he shouldn't, but angry suddenly. 'Geordie? It's Ian here. From the boat.'

*　　*　　*

At eight o'clock that morning, just as Danny was rising soberly from bed, and the sleeping Geordie was making the repetitive gurgling sound of a broken cistern, Ian McAleece was sitting on the side of his sagging single bed in Kilburn Park's sad little Lord Gregory Hotel. He was intently jabbing his mobile phone buttons with his stubby index finger. In Ballyglass Budgie Johnson woke suddenly and hoarsely answered his little silver Motorola: 'Hello?'

Yes, it is a small small world. And Ulster but a button on its coat.

'Budge, listen mate. Get a pen. I need you to get the cash to Mervyn. He's bringing it across tonight. He needs to get it left in to this hotel. You got a pen?'

'Okay, okay. What's the address?'

Seven minutes later, Budgie Johnson went to the makeshift cupboard and found that the cupboard was bare. Wearing his boxer shorts patterned with the prison arrows of Christmas trees, he had locked the bathroom door, knelt on the damp bathmat and slipped his house key in the crack between the wall and bath to lever the panel off. He'd pulled out the green metal box, flipped its lid and gaped. After very slowly mouthing *fuck* several times, he put the panel back in place, set the box on his bed and banged on Malandra's door.

"Landra, open the door. Ah need ta ask you something.' Budgie was not yet angry. He was so terrified he felt like he was floating.

A scrape and a click and a tousled, dark, pretty Malandra, in a Bart Simpson nightshirt bearing 1986's legendary injunction *Don't Have a Cow Man*, appeared, holding a mug of tea.

'What?' Voices from the portable in her room came into the hall and were chanting *Four, Three, Two* . . . in some competition on breakfast television.

'I had a box under the bath. There was stuff in it. And now there's not. You know anything about it?'

'What sort of stuff? Drugs?'

Either she was very sly or knew nothing. Budgie spun round and knocked sharply on Janice's door.

'Jan, open the door.' Malandra waited, interested and leaning against the door jamb, with one leg arched neatly so the heel of her foot rested against her other ankle. She looked poised to execute some daring entrechat or pirouette.

'What? What is it?' came a voice from the bedroom, unmistakably issuing out from a head on its side with one cheek pressed into a pillow.

'Open the *fuck*ing door Janice.' Budgie was no longer floating. His thoughts were beginning to settle: he was up to his neck here. His stomach contracted. His fists were itching. He punched the door once, and again. Hard.

'Okay, okay. Hold on.'

A ratchety noise and the door inched open.

'What is it? Greer, this is *my* day off.' Her tone suggested that her brother didn't have *any* days on. Budgie smacked the door fully open with the palm of his left hand and Janice was shoved backwards. He strode into the room and grabbed a fistful of her hair.

'Where the fuck is it you wee bitch?'

Janice was only aware of Budgie's breath, his stinking morning breath, on her face, and the sharp pain in her scalp. Her hair was lifting her up onto her tiptoes. Then she registered Malandra screaming as her terrified face appeared over Budgie's naked shoulder, her arms pulling at Budgie's neck. She noticed how hairy Budgie's shoulders had got. And then she started to scream as well. Budgie spun round and in doing so pushed her onto the bed. He launched Malandra into the hall and shut the door and pushed the bolt across.

'I think you've something to tell me.'

'Greer, I don't know what you're talking about. *Who* the fuck . . . I was *asleep* and you *just* force yourself in here and . . . you've no fucking right . . . '

Budgie moved across the room and neatly slapped her across the face with the back of his hand. 'Janice stop fucking about. I *know* you took it. Now where is it? You've no idea what you've done.'

'What fucking money? I don't know what you're talking about.'

'I never mentioned any money Jan.'

Janice looked scattered, stunned. Budgie sat down beside her and took her hand in his. He started to bend her index finger back. Very calmly he said, 'I'll break your fucking finger Jan I swear it. I won't even blink. Now tell me where the fucking money went.'

'I didn't know it was yours. I just found it. I've spent it.'

'Don't talk shit. You better fucking hope that's shit. Did you give that money to your little boyfriend? Cause if you did, he's a dead man. He's fucking dead Jan. You've killed him.'

'He didn't know it was yours. I told him it was mine.'

'Yeah, cause *you're* going to have fifty grand in your pocket. You stupid stupid bitch.'

When he said 'fifty grand' Janice's eyes flickered. Budgie read it correctly.

'You didn't even *know*. You didn't even know how much you'd given him. God, but you are an idiot Jan. You're nothing but an idiot slut.'

Casually, Budgie punched her hard on her left temple. Jan crumpled onto the duvet and began crying. He stood up.

'I need that money. You better tell that little thief I'm going to come after him and rip his fucking head off. You better tell him to get that money back to me. Or he's dead, and you're dead, and his family's dead, and everyone his family's ever fucking *met* is dead. You hear me Jan? This is big boy rules. You stupid fucking *stupid* bitch.'

Budgie was breathing hoarsely. He opened her door. His mother and Malandra were standing in the hall. Malandra was crying and sniffing while his mother just stood there watching, bovine and floral in her nightie, open-mouthed. Budgie considered shutting it for her but instead feinted a lunge at them. They flinched and Malandra screamed. Budgie snorted. Back in his room he rang Ian who answered weirdly.

'Hawwwo.'

'Ian, everything all right?'

'Yeah, brushing my teeth. You speak to Merv?'

'No, not yet, listen there's a minor problem.'

'What sort of problem?'

'The money isn't quite ready.'

'What do you mean not ready? It's *been* ready for months. Mervyn's flying tonight. I swear to God Budgie if you've taken any of that money you'll be dead by dusk.'

The same tone he'd just used, the same threat he'd just made to Janice. He suddenly wished he could step out of the way completely, instead of being smack in the middle, making death threats and receiving them, like a domino stood on its end in a row of them, waiting for someone to touch the first one and topple the lot.

'I swear I never touched it. I kept it safe but there's been a fuck-up. Not my fault. My . . . my little bitch of a sister . . . I think she's taken some of the money.'

'How the *fuck* did she get at the money? What sort of fucking treasurer are you?

'No listen Ian. It's fine. Calm down. I know who has the money. I'll get it back.'

'Don't tell me to calm down. I'm your fucking CO. Now who has the money? Where is the fucking money?'

'Ian, I'm sorry. It's a guy we told to get out of town. Geordie Wilson. It seems she gave him some money. But he's just left, he's . . . '

'Geordie Wilson?' Ian started to laugh.

'What? What's funny?'

Budgie heard a tap run, and then one, two, three spitting sounds. Then the jangle of a plastic toothbrush being set in a glass.

'Mr Wilson and I became acquainted on the boat over. I have his mobile number. You're a lucky man Budgie, stupid but lucky. How much money do I need to retrieve from him?'

Budgie grimaced. 'About fifty thousand.'

'Fucking hell Budge. This is the last time you look after the cash for the boys. I'll see to that. You and me'll be having a chat when I'm back. If I have *any* fucking problems getting this . . . Well, I'll be coming to see you anyway. That's a promise. I'm going to give Mr Wilson a call and arrange to meet for a drink. Now, meantime, here's what you can do . . . '

'Listen mate,' Ian said, 'you fancy a pint this afternoon? I'm at a loose end. Waiting for something to arrive.'

Geordie was leaning back on the sofa but frantically jiggling his right leg. It hadn't stopped jiggling since Jan's texts.

'Well, I'm a bit busy at the minute. Something's come up.'

'Mate, I won't take no for answer. Seriously. Non-negotiable. Meet me in the centre. What about O'Neill's off Chinatown? Go to Leicester Square and walk through Chinatown. You can't miss it. Four o'clock say?'

'Maybe. Look it's just this thing's happened and I need to think about . . . '

'Yeah great. Tell me about it later,' Ian interjected, 'I've got to go now.' He hung up. Geordie set the phone on the wooden coffee table and leaned back again on the sofa. He looked up at the ceiling. White paint flaking off the pale pink plaster meant the near corner looked like a sky ragged with clouds. He breathed out heavily, utterly deflated. He picked the phone up and texted I'LL BRING THE CASH BACK to Janice, and immediately turned it off. He looked at the ceiling's mackerel sky again, and thought how when he was a kid at scout camp in Gosford, his patrol leader, the ruthlessly cheerful Terry Green, had told him that a sky like that meant good weather was on its way. Yeah, right. Where's Terry Green now? Six feet deep and filled with worms. No good weather came for him, Geordie thought, and it isn't sunshine that's heading for me. All those homespun proverbs, country wisdom, local knowledge, old wives' tales: what a load of shit.

AFTERNOON

Danny told Ellen as much as he knew about the Ulster Water case, which was nothing, and neglected to mention that they might be going to Belfast on Saturday. She dutifully took notes, which quickly amounted to at least three times the number of words that he'd used, and sat opposite, listening attentively and asking the appropriate questions. Danny referred to part of the due diligence as 'real monkey work' and her efficient face broke into a smile. She had one slightly askew front tooth. It just made her look even sweeter. The bump in the Navaho rug put there to placate the gods. Danny could already feel he might be getting himself into trouble. He listed her faults to counterweight the effect she was having; she appeared to be business-like, brusque and hard-nosed; she might be a little humourless; she had a tiny stain, possibly toothpaste, on the left lapel of her jacket. He told her he'd ring her in a hour or so and she should come down for the conference call. It was noon.

He'd let Freeman, the Corporate partner, bring up the trip to Belfast, if it was still on the cards. If the two of them had to go Danny knew they'd sit in a dark hallway somewhere, being brought boxes of documents by surly admin staff, admin staff who would make it clear they knew Danny and Ellen worked for the company trying to buy them and sack them. They'd spend hours looking through contracts for onerous undertakings or impending litigation that could influence Syder's decision to buy. However, unless Danny found some clause stating that in the event of a takeover Ulster Water would collapse like a broken deckchair, and leave Syder sprawled on the sand cursing and rubbing its coccyx, the bid would go ahead. Danny knew he would draft a detailed and lengthy due diligence report that would weigh, in unusually elegant language, any abnormal and arduous clauses in all of Ulster Water's contracts pertaining to employment, intellectual property, information technology, outsourcing, even the sodding vending machines, and that it would not be read by anyone. It was, he supposed, possible that the conclusion might be perused but it would be so heavily qualified ('In light of the short time available ... given the limited resources and lack of information ... due to the hostility shown by the target company and the corresponding impossibility of obtaining proper financial documentation etc. etc.') that any deductions he'd draw would be completely worthless. At least legally. *You ain't getting us.* This is every law firm's secret motto. Every lawyer is a virtuoso of the 'On the one hand' line. *We can only give you the facts as they appear to us. The decision, of course, is yours.* Of course. And the decision was never Danny's. So he needed to find out whether he would in fact be spending his weekend in his homeland. And whether he was still having this party tomorrow night.

Danny had no idea why he'd agreed to have a party. Admittedly it was his birthday next Wednesday but that had never before given him sufficient cause. The idea of planned fun bothered him on a fundamental level. The original idea and impetus for the party had been Olivia's, several weeks ago, and dates had been bandied about. But since Olivia and he had finally split he'd re-resolved, at Albert's instigation, to ask everyone else he knew round to his house to get drunk, and possibly, though improbably, get laid. That plan had shrunk somewhat. Danny had then e-mailed about ten friends a week ago telling them that he might be having some people round next Friday and maybe they'd call by. If they were free. Now he had to reconfirm. He opened a new e-mail on the screen, clicked on the appropriate recipients: *Dinger, Tippy, Thunderclap Jenkins, The Elephant King of Sodom, Fishboy, Tuzza, Rollson, Renault Minivan, Little Turk,* and *Simon.* Most of these were colleagues, exercising the small freedoms of setting e-mail nicknames. Those were the same recipients who'd received the initial e-mail. Danny then went through the rest of his address book and clicked on random names: five university friends he hadn't seen for months, three law school mates he saw solely to take drugs with, his friend James who'd dropped out of law school and now lived in Guildford, selling rubbish compactors (or compactors of rubbish, as James would correct him), and Clyde, his oddest cousin, who

65

worked as an environmental health inspector in Hounslow.

He wrote:

> Party. No exclamation marks. It's my birthday on Wednesday. I'll be receiving guests from 9ish tomorrow night. If you have nothing better to do, please call in. Bring your own whatever.

After opening another Internet window and typing in the address roadmap.co.uk, he brought up Sofia Road, copied the link and pasted it into the e-mail.

> Click here for the map: www.roadmap.co.uk/mxccsofia/n16.
> It's No.23. The blue door. Get off at Dalston Kingsland Overland on the Silverlink and turn left. Or get the no.73, 112, 43 buses.
> Many thanks, kind regards,
> Admiral Sojourner Watkins

He always signed off with an assumed name. It wasn't meant to be funny, at least not any more. It was a way of articulating the other lives he could have tried and which were slowly closing up elsewhere. He clicked on *Send*. Danny thought how if someone transcribed the twenty-five years or so of his speech they would be hard pressed to justify ever using an exclamation mark. When he answered the phone, even at work, people invariably asked him whether they'd woken him up. He never understood why everyone else was so excited by life. He was either bemused or enraged at their effortless joy. Three *Out of Office* messages pipped into his inbox.

He called Rollson to tell him how lovely Ellen was in person. Rollson groaned and pretended to choke on his pain au chocolat in a jealous fury. Albert was working on a settlement agreement, something to do with four-wheel drive jeeps which hadn't yet been made, and which he'd worked on 'til three the night before. He was on course for another late one, waiting for New York to wake up and send him comments on his last draft. He'd been on a conference call all morning and now wanted to chat. Danny agreed to nip round for five minutes.

Rollson's room was like a show office for the ethical employer, or, more precisely, the employer who is worried about being sued for RSI. He had the desk raised on four wooden blocks for some odd reason, odd given that he was five foot five, and therefore also had a specially high chair, one which Danny called the Wimbledon Judge Seat. The chair raised and lowered itself by levers and Rollson would, as a distraction, frequently drop himself a foot or so in the middle of an argument if he felt like he was losing. The chair also had a special lumbar support fitted, and his keyboard was the new-fangled angled kind allowing maximal access for the wrists to rest on their own special pad. His VDU had a transparent screen fitted on it to reduce glare and even Rollson's mouse was ergonomically designed and different to every other lawyer's. It had three buttons and was about twice the normal size: more canine than rodent. His mouse pad contained a further wrist rest, one which Rollson, in his over-enthusiasm at receiving another toy from the company's full-time physiotherapist, had upsettingly described as feeling like a thirteen-year-old girl's breast. It should be clarified that overall Albert Rollson wasn't a particularly sick or delicate or querulous man. He was just very very bored, and had found that the best way to counter the ennui was to exercise all of the pointless opportunities offered by an enormous company. He had them change the pictures on his walls every six weeks. He attended training seminars on using a Dictaphone. He attended a two-day course in Northampton on speed-reading at which the tutor had said 'the main trick to it is just to read faster' and they had all lowered their heads and obediently tried. He visited the in-house doctor at least once a month and though the doctor had prescribed him a variety of beta-blockers and anti-depressants, he hadn't yet suggested that maybe Albert should change his job.

Danny stood in the doorway but didn't go in. Something was different.

'Mate, why is your room reminding me of the Blue Grotto?'

'I know, the fluorescent light was making a buzzing noise so I rang down to Business Services and got them to send a man up to change it, but they've installed a blue one. It's like sitting in a brothel.'

'Is it?'

'Yes. It is. Aside from the lack of hookers.' Albert did a newsreader shuffle of the papers he was looking at and set them aside. He did look wrecked, and unusually for Rollson, his clothes were a little rumpled. His Windsor knotted red silk tie was still on but the top button of his white shirt was open. A stray hair curled out from the gap and his dark brown eyes were underlined for emphasis by thick black lines of sleeplessness.

'You have to ask her to your party tomorrow night.'

'Ellen?'

'Yes, Ellen. You just rambled on about how amazing she is. You have to ask her.'

'She's *working* for me. It'd be weird.'

'No, it wouldn't. And she's working *with* you, not for you. It would be weirder not to mention it. Just casually throw it into the conversation. Who else've you invited?'

'You saw the e-mail. That lot plus Geordie.'

'Who is this guy?'

'I'll tell you about it at lunch. He's an old mate from school.'

'You haven't mentioned him before. Where'd he spring from?'

After Danny and Ellen had spoken on the conference call to John Freeman, the Corporate partner overseeing the Ulster Water bid, it became apparent that there would be no lunch. Freeman was a short and angry man. The anger was obvious. The shortness Danny inferred from his photo on the firm's intranet. He was shiny-pated, overweight, and had tiny black perforations for eyes which were looking upwards to the camera. He looked like a malevolent medieval abbot. After Freeman's secretary had patched the two of them into the call, Freeman launched into the conference without giving Danny time to introduce Ellen. There appeared to be several accountants and clients on the line, aside from the whole Corporate team, presumably down on the second floor, hunched in anticipation round Freeman's speaker phone. As always, Danny found it difficult to focus at times like these. His ability to concentrate decreased in proportion to how important it was that he did. He could, for example, intimately describe someone he had sat opposite on the tube several days before but couldn't tell, when asked directly, whether or not he'd sent a holding letter to the lawyers on the other side or indexed a file of documents. As the voices coming from the speaker phone on his desk discussed logistics Danny, sitting opposite Ellen, felt himself unwind, as if the speaker phone was a radio and he was lolling in the bath. She was really quite something, this girl. Absolutely remarkable. Danny found himself staring at her breasts and quickly shifted his eyes onto the pad she was scrawling on.

'Will that be possible, Danny?' Freeman's tensed vocal cords were flinging something at him.

'I'm sorry, we seemed to get cut off there. Could you repeat it?'

A derisory snort issued from the phone. Ellen, her face inspired with concern, was holding up her pad opposite him. CAN YOU GO TO BELFAST ON SAT MORN. She grinned. He grinned back.

'I mean, it sounded like you were about to ask me whether or not I could take a team to Northern Ireland this weekend, but then there was silence.' Danny winked outrageously at Ellen. 'If you hadn't progressed further than that then the answer's yes. I've a trainee briefed and we're aware of what the exercise will involve. Obviously, I've a few specific questions to ask about the set-up, but we don't all need to be on the call for that.'

The Corporates were mumbling assent. Freeman took hold of the conversation again, a little too quickly, as if another child had tried to take it off him.

'Quite, quite. Well, I'd anticipated that and sent you an e-mail with a contact list for Syder earlier.' Danny heard the tap-dancing of far-off typing and an e-mail, headed SYDER CONTACTS, from Freeman, appeared on his screen. Danny stopped listening again.

*   *   *

Ian was leaning back, unfolded, with his hands locked together behind his head. His posture was one of a man who has taken the board on and won, but his stare was fully engaged, and directed now at three men in suits sitting two tables over. They were laughing loudly and Ian was willing them to stop. Geordie hadn't turned up yet, though it was ten past and he was starting to think he'd underestimated the little shit. One of the suits was working himself up to say something, but had looked to be doing that since Ian sat down twenty minutes ago. The main mouth, an overweight owl who smiled reflexively and broadly after everything he said, was telling another anecdote.

'So I leaned across to him and said *You'll just have to trust me.*'

The three of them laughed loudly again. One of his attendants, grinning, asked, 'Why didn't you tell him to just, you know, foxtrot oscar?'

The fat one rubbed his thumb and first two fingers together while pursing his lips and lowering his eyebrows so his phizog was puckered in close, as if he were trying to squeeze his facial features through a bangle.

'Money. All about the lettuce. Even Dave knows that.'

He nodded towards the other man, who tilted his head, guffawed obligingly.

Ian brought his open palms down on the table so they made enough of a noise to attract the attention of all three men, then stood, pressing hard against the table to flex

71

his triceps in their tight blue polo-shirt sleeves, and walked purposefully to the swing door. It wasn't that he minded people enjoying themselves. He minded them talking rubbish. And he minded people being impressed by slick and noisy idiots. Ian had the kind of dislike for blokes in suits that men can have who only don a two-piece when they're in serious trouble (before the bench, at the altar, in the coffin). As he was standing in front of the pub door, looking out, Geordie's face appeared like a mismatched reflection. For a second they were shocked to see each other so close, even through glass, and Ian shuffled back, embarrassed, as Geordie pushed the door open.

'Big man,' Geordie said. Ian took the outstretched hand, and felt Geordie's pipe cleaner fingers bend in his clasp. Malleable. Ian had ironed out some options, and shelved them in order of desirability. His mind was as neat as the pebbledashed terraced he shared with no one. Ideally, Geordie would spill everything and tell him where the money was. Then, if that didn't happen, he wanted Geordie to get drunk and ask him back, today, to the house of this friend he was staying with, or, if for some reason he couldn't swing that, he wanted an invite to go round there, and soon. All of this might go out the window, of course, if Geordie appeared to be a risk. He might just beat the shit out of him. Ian, however, prided himself on judgement. He could read a man the way the others in the wing had read the *Sunday Sport*. And while they read the *Sunday Sport*, he had been reading his Machiavelli and Sun Tzu. He was politic and ruthless. And he would get what he wanted, which was things in order.

Geordie, conversely, wanted distraction, and one of its major subsets, drink.

'And what about your business down here? How's all that going?'

They were both settled at the table, one hand chilled round a Guinness, the other, propping a lit fag, beginning to smoulder.

'Not bad. I've got it all lined up. Just waiting for one thing to arrive and then I'll probably be heading back over.'

'What is it then, that you do, I mean?'

'Import-export really. Just starting up. Having a look round. Seeing what opportunities are out there.' Ian was gently bouncing his head forwards and backwards as he spoke.

'I'm looking for work myself you know. Over here. If you know anyone.'

'Yeah? I'll ask around. I might have something for you actually. A mate of mine is starting a business in London.'

'Oh aye? What kind of thing?'

'Opening a bar. Really plush. Needs cash though. Not the sort of money either of us would have.'

'No, you're right there.'

Ian watched Geordie's face. Nothing coming through it. Like the grimy windows of O'Neill's. Strike one, Ian thought. The conversation turned to how expensive London was, then how you could have a better standard of living in Northern Ireland, and lastly to politics. When two Ulstermen sit down together, there's probably an even fifty-fifty chance they'll try to kill each other, but Ian and Geordie were getting on. Geordie sat and sneaked looks at Ian's bulbous biceps, his cylindrical neck, the thickness of his wrists and their cord-like veins. Geordie was slight, and fascinated by men like this. They seemed a different species to him. Bull-men, stone-men. Aside from his bulk though, there was something else that held the eye. There was a sense of potential about him, something trapped and coiled and waiting. He was like a box of fireworks.

For his own part, Ian enjoyed being watched. When the listener admires, the speaker performs better, and Ian was no exception. He flexed his right bicep behind his head as he scratched his back. He nodded kindly at Geordie when he spoke. He bought them pint after pint, and began to think Geordie was all right. He was a good kid at heart. And in fact the kind of kid who'd do better for them than some fucknut like Budgie. Smart, a listener. Surprisingly, he found he was telling Geordie about himself.

Ian McAleece had got into the business of fear quite late, at least late for Northern Ireland. He had been sixteen for three days when his dad was shot in front of him. Twenty-six times in the chest and neck and shoulders, as it turned out. Alfred Robert McAleece had got home from his bread-round and reverse-parked the van, white and emblazoned in red with *Hutton's Bakers*, along the kerb outside the house. He opened the van's back door and lifted out a wooden pallet containing two vedas, one wheaten, and eight apple pancakes. The family always got what was leftover, although Ian was pretty sure it wasn't exactly leftover so much as nicked. His dad, still holding the pallet of bread, had shut the back door of the van with his hip. Ian was about to leave for school. Swinging his sports bag over his shoulder, he opened the front door. Seeing him, his dad continued to waggle his hips as he crossed the pavement, doing a waltzy little dance with his tray of bread. All of these things took for ever to happen. It was like sitting in a boat drifting down a slow river. It was that passive. Ian remembered tiny details of it, the round brass knob of the porch door. It had been misted with the February cold as he turned it.

A red transit (stolen in Lurgan three days before) was parked just up from the bread-van. Everything happened together then. It was like the boat suddenly tipping over a weir in the river, plunging, slippage, the multiple angles of falling. The transit doors banging open, two men out on the road, all in black, in balaclavas, with semi-automatics, shouting, and then that monstrous sound as they opened fire. Ian's mum had run out in her socks into the road. The transit was gone in a screech of tyres, leaving behind it a chemically sharp smell of rubber and gunfire. Ian stood in the small green patch of lawn in front of his house. His mother was kneeling by his father. Parts of his father were splattered over the paving stones and against the back of the bread-van. His mother had run out carrying a two-litre bottle of Coke for some reason. She must have been looking for something in the big cupboard by the fridge. Ian watched her crouch forward and try to wipe blood away from her husband's face. Then she opened the bottle of Coke – it fizzed and hissed like someone stage-whispering *shush* – and she poured Coke over his dad's face, and tried again to wipe the blood off. Then she leant over him and tried to mop at it with her baggy white T-shirt. Alfie's face had looked all shiny and sticky.

They'd got the wrong man, some said. They'd just gone for a Prod, said others. The IRA said they'd got the treasurer of the local UVF. As Alfie McAleece, apolitical and apathetic in everything but football, had seen three businesses fail and twice been declared bankrupt, this seemed the least likely of the explanations. But if you throw enough shit, some of it sticks. A man at the funeral called Gerry approached Ian. He thought that the bastards who'd done this should pay. He was from the Organisation. And that was that. As it turned out, well, Ian was here and now none of that stuff mattered any more. He recounted the story of the shooting to Geordie in three short sentences, all of them broken with curses and pauses.

Geordie nodded, a little embarrassed by the new knowledge. Ian seemed a nice enough bloke. Bit lonely maybe. Geordie responded with a few stories of his own: a friend of his dad's beaten to death in a pub; his uncle, a policeman, shot dead through the jaw at a checkpoint; how his cousin was killed with a red-hot poker pushed into his throat. He didn't tell him about his own shooting, the kneecapping. Ian probably knew enough to have noticed the stiffness in his gait, and Geordie felt, obscurely, that he couldn't tell him because he didn't want Ian to see him as one of the victims, the losers, the ones sobbing face down in the car park, covered in gravel and piss. Geordie bought two more pints of the black. The pub was starting to fill up with people skiving off early from work. He remembered Danny and his agreement to make dinner. He'd slip off after this next one.

'Well why don't I come back with you to Danny's? We can get a few tinnies on the way home.'

'No mate, I can't do today. But Dan's having this party tomorrow evening so come round for that, yeah? We'll make a proper night of it.'

'Yeah, all right. Gis the address then.' Ian couldn't be bothered to argue. He felt exhausted. He was sure Geordie wasn't going anywhere. And tomorrow night was fine. He could stay late and find the money in Geordie's things or, failing that, beat it out of him. He wouldn't be any problem. Geordie might still just tell him about it anyway. You never knew. And he might be a useful wee fella to have round.

*   *   *

Cycling home, Danny felt relieved that Geordie would be there when Olivia came round to pick up her things. She would cause a scene. She would start to cry. And he would feel that he'd made the wrong decision. They had met through a friend of hers who worked on a cricket magazine with Danny's mate from uni. He pulled his brakes and slowed to a stop at the Old Street roundabout lights. A bus pulled up beside him. She had managed, in only a few months, to push him right over to the side of his life. Albert had pointed out to him one day that before he arranged to do anything he had to ask her permission.

The lights changed and Danny pushed off, fairly sure that a kid on the bus was giving him the fingers but not wanting to give him the joy of turning around and seeing it confirmed. Tonight then, he would make sure that when she turned up her stuff would be sitting out for her in his sky-blue hallway – sky-blue because she'd decorated it. Not actually decorated it, but she'd told Danny what colours to paint it and had been instrumental in finally getting it done. She recycled the colour cards as bookmarks, and had left them in the various novels she'd begun and abandoned. Over the last two months, rereading Graham Greene, Danny had learned the colours of the walls in his bedroom and boxroom: apricot and cinnabar. The card wedged between the twelfth and thirteenth pages of *The Great Gatsby*, his favourite novel and the one he'd pulled out from the shelf, sleepless, to reread three nights back, had revealed the kitchen to be either cowslip or mustard, depending on the light. Someday, possibly, Danny might learn that his hallway was, in fact, teal, if he happened to make it past the fifth chapter of Colleen McCullough's *The Thorn Birds*, left behind by the flat's previous owner.

Danny was turning into Sofia Road when he noticed Geordie at his storm porch, trying to turn the Chubb lock. He looked like the wiring for a man, with none of the casing, and he was shuffling and mumbling. He's been drinking, thought Danny, amused more than dismayed. He pulled up onto the pavement and freewheeled towards him.

'All right wee man,' Danny shouted when he was right up at the gate. Geordie electric-fenced it into the air.

'Aw you cunt, you scared the life out of me. Fuck off out of that.'

'Where you been causing trouble then?'

'I went into the centre there, to meet that fella from the boat, Ian. I've told him to pop along tomorrow night.'

'Okay, why not.' Geordie still hadn't opened the front door.

'Here, you hold this.'

Danny leaned the bike into Geordie, who held it gingerly for a second and then nimbly hopped on and started pedalling along the pavement and out onto the road. He turned some very small circles in the centre of

the street and then expertly bunny-hopped back onto
the footpath.

'Here, Danny, mind we used to do the slow-pedalling
game. I always beat you. Watch. I was the king of this.'

Danny turned round in the doorway, having opened
the door and dropped his cycle helmet and satchel inside,
to see Geordie cycle in slo-mo for about a metre along
the pavement, before wavering slightly, and then leisurely
tipping away from Danny over onto the concrete. He lay
there laughing and snorting. Danny started to smile, and
was suddenly in fits and gusts of laughter. Geordie hadn't
even tried to put his foot or arm out to break his fall.

'You just cowped over.'

Danny was cooking and Geordie was skinning up on
the kitchen table. Danny's repertoire of meals was pretty
limited. Aside from toast, he was a fan of eggs and fond
of chicken. He had always wanted to make a chicken
omelette but the actual concept of mixing the dead bird's
flesh with the dead bird's – what? offspring? No, their
periods, he supposed – was too repugnant. Danny stood
at the kitchen counter, chopping and dicing tomatoes for
a salad on a wooden slab. He was going to make two
ham and cheese omelettes. Geordie's chicken breasts,
fresh from Halal Meat, were lying in the fridge but Danny
wanted to eat quickly and Geordie just wanted to get
caned.

Olivia was due to arrive any minute. In preparation
Danny had uncorked a cheap Hungarian bottle of
Cabernet Sauvignon and was now on his second glass.
Her belongings were laid out in the hallway: a stack of
books and some folded clothes in a plastic bag, another

plastic bag of more books and some CDs, and a large
bunch of dried flowers that she'd bought for his kitchen,
which he'd untied from above the window and leant in
the corner of the hall, beside the door. They'd reminded
him of the bouquets left on the grass verge of roads back
home, propped against a fence or hedge, to commemo-
rate the murdered or the accidental dead.

Danny was melting a scrape of butter in the frying
pan when the doorbell rang. He turned the gas off,
widened his eyes at Geordie as if to say *Here goes*, and
set off down the hallway. Olivia was standing on the
front step, looking small and shivery and heartbroken.
The yellow light spilling out the door from the hall gave
him the sense of having come upon some animal in the
road, trapping it with brightness.

'Hello fucker,' she said.

'Hello.'

Danny moved towards her, to kiss her on the cheek,
but she pulled back, glaring.

'Sorry, God, sorry. Look do you want to come in? I
have your stuff here for you,' Danny pointed at his right
shoulder with his right thumb, 'but I mean come in if
you want.'

'Just give me the bags. This is hard enough . . . I can't
believe you're doing this.'

She gave a tiny stamp of one foot in its neat black
court shoe. Her grey trouser suit and palpable sadness
were like something out of Charlie Chaplin. She had her
fists clasped, her knuckles boned.

'Let's not go through this again.'

'No, that's easier for you isn't it? Whatever makes it
easier for *you*. You're such a coward Daniel. No one can

believe you're doing this.' The *no one* was of course a reference to Olivia's friends, the eternal committee, always in session on the subject of Danny's interpersonal skills.

'Please. Livvy, I just can't do it any more. It wasn't right. You know all that.'

'All I know is you lied. I *miss* you, Danny, really. Don't you miss me?'

'Of *course* I miss you. Of course I do. But it . . . it just wasn't working. It wouldn't work.'

'Give me the bags Danny. I can't believe you. I can't believe you're doing this.'

She stepped forward into the hall, her hands up as if to push Danny out of the way but really only to prevent any contact. Danny moved back obediently. She looked so small, a tiny scolded but defiant child. Danny bent to pick the bags off the floor for her but she snatched them up before he could. She looked at the dried flowers.

'I don't want those but I don't think I want you to have them either. I'll take them and bin them.'

She picked them up, and wedged them in one of the plastic bags, then turned around to face him. She looked up at him, timid again, scared.

'This is it then . . . I can still e-mail you can't I? Maybe go out for a drink every once in a while . . . At least 'til one of us starts seeing someone else. That's how it works isn't it?'

'E-mail me whenever you want. You can call me too. Everything's going to be all right Olivia.'

'I know that Danny. No one's died. I just feel sad.'

'I know. I'm sorry. I do too.'

'I know this is normal but it doesn't feel normal. This much sadness can't be normal.'

Her face was breaking up into tears. Danny couldn't bear this. Just when it seemed that he would have to pick her up and hold her, ask her to forgive him, she turned and was away, clattering down the path. Danny listened to her footsteps diminish on the pavement. He closed the door and stood there, his hand resting against the door jamb.

This is what it was to be single then. Not a pleasurable emotion. A kind of hollowness that began in the chest and spread to the head. He felt brittle, like he was all shell. He went into the kitchen to get drunk and get stoned but Geordie had moved into the living room. He must have passed them in the hall when Olivia was there. Danny hadn't noticed. He was lying across the sofa, his feet dangling over the edge, watching *The Simpsons* and smoking.

'You all right mate? She was a looker. Very nice.'

'Yeah. I don't know mate. I don't know. Maybe I've done the wrong thing. How *do* you know?'

'Shut up. There'll be others. Plenty of women everywhere. Here, have some of this.'

How easy it is to make a ghost.

Keith Douglas

THE HAPPENING

Danny hadn't spoken to Albert about Geordie. Partly because they were both busy – Albert was waiting in for a new adjustable footrest from the physiotherapist – and partly because it was unexplainable. They *were* old friends, but more than that. The tie that bound Danny to Geordie was not simply the sky-blue and red stripe of Ballyglass High, or even the burgundy and grey of Ballyglass Primary. Wilson and Williams. Of course they were put at the same desk. And of course they caused trouble. And of course they were parted and moved back together.

It was the summer of 1990. In June of that year Miss Woolmington the chemistry teacher, a jittery Bristolian, proud possessor of the only English accent most of her pupils had ever heard in person, set fire to the wing of her batwinged jumper by leaning across her own Bunsen burner. Their class learnt several things that day. The

English pronounced *Fuck* quite differently from them. Man-made fibres (in this case a wool-acrylic mix) can be dangerously flammable. And life is remarkably unfair. Total self-immolation had been prevented only by Geordie joyfully throwing Miss Woolmington's coffee over her, then mopping at the sodden black mess under her armpit with her own anorak, while she stood there shrieking that he was touching her breasts. Geordie's actions had been interpreted as over-enthusiastic and he'd been suspended from the last week of term. Two days later a bald statement appeared on the grass slope overlooking the school car park describing the headmaster's pedigree (parents unmarried). It had been written in weedkiller: the font was bleached white and five foot high.

Danny had watched the whole batwing incident and joined with the rest of the class in outrage. They wrote a joint letter stating that Geordie, no matter what considerable joy he had taken in his actions, had been the first to act and had acted well. In fact he'd been up and halfway across the Portakabin classroom before Danny had even registered the smell of smoke or Miss Woolmington's shrieks. After the suspension Geordie had told Danny about nicking the two gallons of weedkiller from McConnell's Filling Station and Danny'd kept shtum. It was one of the first secrets he'd kept. Danny knew the school would not have treated him or any other kid in the way they'd dealt with Geordie. In response Geordie'd started running with a bad crowd who'd already been expelled, Budgie and his lot.

It happened on 12 July, the Province's Glorious Twelfth, and two days before Danny's fourteenth birthday. The main street was thronged. The bands hadn't started, but here and there among the crowd there were hints of the coming pomp and ornature. A gold epaulette sparked on a red jacket as its portly owner climbed out of an old-style grey Granada. A silver emblem weighed a beret on the head of a little girl who pouted her way up a queue for ice cream. Another young girl stood at the open boot of an estate car, carefully unpacking her tuba. It looked like the enormous ear of some bronze colossus. There were pensioners in dark suits and ties – at the top end of the age and clothing range – and then younger ones in white shirts with their sleeves rolled up: serious men about to get down to business. Listless adolescents in trainers and the football shirts of certain teams, and a baby in a stained bib, hot-faced and bonneted, twisting away from her mother.

One of these adolescents was Danny, whose dad had an estate agency at the top of Black's Hill. Outside it, one of the town's two arches was raised, straddling the road. It declared, carefully, *Welcome Here Brethren*. When Danny saw the arch again, after coming back for the summer from his first year at university, he'd suddenly realized it was designed to be read for what it didn't say as much as what it did: *Brethren are welcome but the rest of you aren't. The rest of you can put it into reverse and fuck right off.*

This was Danny's first parade. The Williamses had always been away before, Eurocamping in France, or once, captured for ever on video camera, an argumentative too-hot fly-drive through California. But this year Danny's nana, his father's mum, had been ill and his parents had gone to stay with her over in Antrim. Danny and his two sisters were being looked after by their babysitter Karen. Danny had spent a sizeable portion of the last week imagining how Karen might declare her love for him and then ask him if he'd touch her breasts. Today though she had walked her charges down to the Oakdale Park, and now smooched and smoked on a bench with her boyfriend Brian. The girls, Annie and Jane, seven and eight respectively, and to all intents twins, were see-sawing and singing 'Wheels on the Bus'. Danny was across the park throwing a tennis ball against the gable of the first terrace on Palace Row. He was bored and felt awkward near the sulky Karen and Brian, brawny in a plaid shirt. Danny mooched over to their bench. He was heading off for a while. He'd see them back at the house. Asserting her right to give permission, Karen, trying to light a cigarette and simultaneously remove her gum, declared that Danny was old enough to do what he wanted. What Danny wanted was to go to the marching.

He met Wee Jim and Del from his scout troup at the Oldtown Corner. They were waiting for Jacksy, the same boy who would later shoot a bullet through each of Geordie's calves. Del opened his rucksack and showed Danny seven or eight cans of Top Deck shandy and three Hamlet cigars. He hushed his voice, as if the contraband was asleep: *We're going to get wrecked.* Just then Jacksy came slouching around the corner, hunched with his hands tucked tight in his jeans. *Awright lads.* His voice was lower than everyone else's. He was a skinny cock-sure kid who suffered from eczema. His hands reminded Danny of sunburn. He rarely took them out of his pockets.

They took a can each. Danny wasn't sure if the Top Deck was alcoholic. It didn't seem to say on the cans although it tasted like beer, but less sour. They decided to head over to the wide kerb outside Martin's Chemists.

UTTERLY MONKEY

There was a bench there and, after five minutes of standing around her, the old biddy on it got up and tottered off, clutching her shopping with both arms in front of her, as if the boys had been very taken with her cat food and her toilet roll.

The way things worked was this. After school, the boys would walk home together, anything from four or five to ten of them. Some days they'd 'shoot some pool' down Eastwood's Pool Hall, other days buy brown paper bags of vinegary chips from the Brewery Grill and eat them in the back attic room of McGurk's Undertakers, whose youngest son, Wee Jim, was part of the gang. James McGurk was not only an undertaker, but also, like Danny's dad, an estate agent. Danny had often wondered if business for the latter was dependent on the former. He must benefit by being around when the relatives discussed the sale of the deceased's caravan or bungalow or castle. In the back attic, reached by walking through two offices and along a curtain-corridor that ran along the side of the funeral parlour, Big Jim McGurk had stored or dumped about fifteen mattresses and a threadbare snooker table short several balls, mostly reds. There were also, propped along the wall, three display coffins. It lent the place the look of a particularly louche Pharaoh's tomb. It was an odd place for an after-school club. One of them, Del maybe, had done a sign with a black marker – *The Coffin Boys* – and Blu-tacked it to the wall beside the big oak boxes. The top left-hand corner had come away and leaned outward like the gelled tufts most of them sported.

McGurk's back room had been one of their places for years but became central after the hostilities broke out: on one side was Slim and his gang, and on the other, the third years. Slim was the rangy fourth year who'd stand outside McLaughlin's with his sidekicks as they all waited for their buses out to the country. For months it had just been a bit of shoving and tripping but then there'd been some kicking and the third year boys, the Coffin Boys, had begun to cross the street in order to walk home. Then the older boys had crossed it too, and started to chase them up it. Then last week Wee Jim got a split lip from Micks, Slim's lieutenant, at the bowling alley.

Sitting squashed on the bench (all four were jammed in), Danny saw Micks, in a Man U baseball cap, across the street. He was stood with his mum, a small plump woman with a tight black perm that looked like a helmet her glasses were securing to her head. Micks seemed to be looking towards something she was pointing at. She lowered her bare arm then and said something to him. Then the peak of his baseball cap turned towards them. Danny told them, but breezily so as they wouldn't think him scared.

'Here, boys, Micks McManus is over there.'

'Fuck him. There's four of us. Let him come and try it.'

Del was the worst possible combination for a friend: mouthy and very fast on his feet. The marches were starting. In front of them the Drumgavy Loyal Sons of William Flute Band were assembling. They were all in peaked military-style caps, purple with yellow piping, and purple jackets buttoned to the neck with yellow epaulettes, although the women and girls flapped in grey A-line skirts whereas the males sported trousers. All the banter had stopped now. The parents of the youngest flautists had waved to them and now stood waiting, a little anxious. The players ceremoniously lifted their silver flutes to their mouths and stood there in silence. Their

heads were all inclined a little, as if each one were trying
to see round the marcher in front. The crowd hushed
suddenly when the bandleader, facing sternly forward,
shouted something incomprehensible and very loud, then
stamped his foot once, twice, and a hundred exhalations
made the flutes all squeal together. 'And they're off,' Del
shouted, like a horseracing commentator.

The last of the Drumgavy majorettes were going past,
twirling their batons and flashing the kind of smiles that
would turn a dentist suicidal. Danny thought how this
could almost be the stadium of the Denver Broncos, say,
or the Washington Redskins, or some other fabled team,
and that this could be the half-time of the Superbowl,
rather than a Thursday lunchtime turning grey on Ballyglass
High Street. Through the gap that the band were leaving
behind them the boys could see, across the street, that
Micks had been joined by Slim and Philly Stewart, a spindly
ginger kid who, the rumour went, had been caught getting intimate with his neighbour's labrador. The boys discussed it endlessly. Philly was pointing across at their
bench. Next thing they were sauntering over through the
gap behind the band. All of the boys saw it. Wee Jim
exhaled an *Oh fuck*. Danny felt his legs go tingly, as if
he'd just finished a long run. He also felt curiously secure
by being in the middle of the bench, with Jacksy to his
left and Del and Wee Jim to right. It was like sleeping in
the middle of the tent when they'd go camping out at
Drum or Davagh: even though you might hear noises outside or things brushing against the canvas, you knew you
weren't going to be the first to suffer.

'Well girls, how are we today?' Slim was standing in
front of them, his crotch pushed out as if someone was

behind him, trying to shove something into his bum. Micks had picked the rucksack up off Del's lap. Del had made a sad little grab for it and Micks had pushed him, hand on forehead, back into the bench. He opened the rucksack carefully, as if something might jump out, and peered into it.

'Top Deck, heh boys? Fucking shandy. You *wankers*. Here, I've been needing a new school bag. Slim, what do you think?'

Micks chucked the bag to him and he caught it one-handed. Del half stood up and tried to grab it again. This time Slim smacked him on the forehead, open-palmed, and Del flopped back onto the bench. Danny looked round to see if anyone was watching or he could see someone he knew. The bands were in full flow now and everybody was facing them. The bench was a few feet away from the edge of the pavement, so that when he looked to either side all he could see were people's backs. Slim was swinging the bag round and round and bringing the trajectory nearer and nearer to the boys' faces, before pulling it back. Jacksy reached up to shield his head. Philly Stewart, who was standing behind the bench laughing, slapped Jacksy on the ear.

'Keep still or I'll break your fucking necks.'

'I've heard his bark's worse than his bite,' Del whispered.

Danny heard and felt a constriction of laughter move up from his chest to his throat. He managed to hold it there. Wee Jim was sitting very quietly and looking solemnly ahead. His eyes were shiny, as if he was about to cry, and his lip was still swollen, in profile, from Micks splitting it at the bowling alley a week ago. Philly flicked Del's ear with his index finger, causing Del to flinch forward, within an inch or so of the rucksack that Slim was still swinging towards their heads.

'What'd you say you poof?'

'Oi, no need to be so rrrrough.' Del growled the last word – rrrrufff – and Danny knew he was about to laugh out loud. Fuck. Just in time, at least for Danny, Wee Jim squeaked a laugh out of the side of his mouth. Philly punched the back of his head, hard, and brought Wee Jim's forehead into the orbit of the rucksack. There was a heavy clunk and Wee Jim clutched his face. Slim started to laugh. He dropped the bag on Danny's feet. Danny looked down. He noticed that Slim was wearing shiny silver trainers with Velcro fastening instead of laces.

'Let's go. These pricks are boring me already.'

Danny thought *You're the fucking prick, the fucking prick who can't even tie shoelaces*. Danny said, 'You're the fucking prick, the fucking prick who can't even tie shoelaces.' Everyone paused, as if someone had suddenly spoken in Hebrew or Swahili. Micks looked rooted to the pavement and Slim was waxwork in front of the bench, agog, his mouth wide like that of an especially vacant fish. He still stood with his crotch thrust out, the main man, the big swinging dick. Danny was at the level of his groin and it suddenly occurred to him how, if he wanted to, he could just lean forward and sock him in the balls. Danny leaned forward and socked him in the balls. A good, hard shoulder-to-fist punch. A dim thud, a keeling. Slim was doubled up on the pavement. Danny still had his arm out, locked in place like he was holding something up. 'Oh fucccck,' Del shouted and there was a scrabbling and rasping of rubber soles on pavement. The boys were up, weaving, scattered.

Danny too was on his feet. He heard Jacksy scream 'Nice one Williams,' and then he found himself pelting up the main street towards his dad's office, even though it was closed and his dad miles away. He glanced back and saw Micks pounding after him. The other boys had gone, probably down Molesworth or up the Burn Road, legging it, laughing. Danny was pinballing through the crowd, shouting 'Sorry' as he went, as much to Slim as to the tutting people he was knocking into. He was electric, shocked. What the fuck had he done? He'd cut his own throat.

Danny took the entrance into the gravel car park behind his dad's office and ran to the wire fence at the back of it. There was a gap in it that his dad had been going on about getting fixed for years. Danny, giving thanks for his father's laziness, had one leg through it when he heard Micks' brays from the other side of the car park. He didn't appear to be using words. Danny ducked his head down through the gap and felt a tug at his neck – his yellow Nike T-shirt was caught on one of the cut wire prongs. Micks was running across the car park, sending up little flurries of stones as he ran. Danny yanked the rest of himself through the fence and heard the T-shirt rip. He legged it over the field. It sloped down over the course of a few hundred metres onto Monkey Lane, which ran alongside the Glencrest estate. Clambering over the gate at the bottom of the field, he paused and glanced back up the hill. Micks was standing behind the fence watching him. When he saw Danny look back, he waved, perfectly normally, as if he was waving him off from his doorstep. It was terrifying.

Danny made as if to walk down Monkey Lane and out onto Taylor Road, but instead crouched down after a few metres and doubled back behind the hedge that ran along the field. He could cross the Glencrest estate to his own road. He squeezed through the straggly privet, popped out the other side (the branches folding their arms again behind him) and hunkered down on the pavement. His T-shirt was now an off-the-shoulder number. And his breathing was raspy, like his dad's when he was angry. Staring at the pavement he noticed minute red bugs, a score of pinpricks, meandering over the paving slab. They didn't seem to have any sense of direction or purpose, veering off this way or that. Danny smeared one into the grey with his thumb. It left a tiny scarlet blur. He stood, pulling his T-shirt up to cover his thin shoulder, and started to dander across the estate. It was Protestant, this place, and therefore pretty empty. Everyone was either at the marches or on holiday. The houses were private, not council, and built only a couple of years ago though already the pebbledash white was discolouring – like snowfall thawing out to slushy grey. A kid's bike had been abandoned on its side on one of the neat front lawns and the wheel was still spinning. Danny had an urge to cross the lawn and press his hand against the rubber, to stop its ticking, but he walked quickly on to the estate's entrance. He was about to exit onto Milburn Road, his own, when Philly Stewart walked past on the far side of the road, heading towards Danny's own house. Did he know where Danny lived? Danny didn't know. Philly was doing his simian shoulder roll and staring blankly forward. Danny felt his legs go, and he leant into one of the redbrick entrance pillars to steady himself. Philly's peculiar gait made it seem he was pushing an imaginary wheelbarrow: his arms hung out by his sides and his shoulders were arched and lowered. He pushed it on up Milburn as Danny spun slowly around on a crack in the pavement and headed back into the estate.

Danny was walking swiftly again but unsure where to. He'd have to hang about in the estate, find a hole in the ground and sit in it for a year or so. When he passed the house again with the bike outside, its wheel spinning slower now, he heard a car from somewhere nearby, pulling away sharply. He glanced over towards the screech of tyres and saw, instead, Geordie running along the top of the T-junction. Danny shouted 'Geordie' and set off after him. Geordie slowed down and he caught up. Geordie looked edgy as always.

'All right Williams, how's things?'

'Fucking wick. Me, Del and Jacksy and Wee Jim were watching the march down the street and fucking Slim and Micks and Philly came along and started hassling us. I don't know what happened but I ended up smacking Slim in the balls. He's going to go through me for a fucking shortcut.'

Geordie's face broke into that overwhelming grin. Danny started to laugh, from relief.

'Fucking hell, Williams. Slim's hard as nails. They'll be looking for you.'

'Aye I know. And Micks chased me down through the back field onto Monkey Lane and I just saw Philly walking up Milburn towards my house. What you doing round here?'

'Nothing really. Here, c'mere. Follow me for a sec.'

Geordie turned around and walked back in the direction he'd just come from. He walked up towards the back

gate of an orderly corner house with two hanging bas-
kets, ablaze with pansies and fuchsia and geraniums. The
estate was still deserted, although a television could be
heard blasting from the open windows of the house next
door: the parades' hullaballoo occasionally narrated by
the respectful, deep-voiced and slightly bored observa-
tions of an anchorman.

'Here. We can nip in round the back. It's me uncle's
but they're all down at the parade. I just been to see
whether they're around.'

Geordie pushed at the back gate with one hand and
it swung open, banging against the pebbledashed side
of the house. A pebble skitted off and landed on the
paving stones, joining the others that were scattered across
the path.

'Will he mind? I mean just for an hour or so. I could
just sit in the garden or maybe use his phone and get
Karen to nip down and get me or something.'

'Well he's not here so he won't know, will he? I just
told you that, didn't I?'

Geordie looked quickly at Danny who nodded assent.
Round the back of the house there was an ornamental
pond, much too big for the garden. Its water pump gar-
gled, unseen amongst the overgrown foliage. Danny went
to the edge of it. Two carp, luminous bars, hung in the
dirty water. As Danny's shadow moved over the surface
they flicked away. Danny called out, not looking up:
'Your uncle's got two carp in here you know Geordie.
My dad says they're worth a lot of money depending on
how big . . . '

Danny glanced up to see Geordie standing on top of
one of the bins. He had his arm in through the small

95

window of what must have been the downstairs toilet. The windows of it were all frosted over.

'What're you doing? We can just wait here 'til your uncle gets back or head off in a bit anyway. They're not going to miss all the marches in order to get me.'

'Naw, I always do this. It's fine. C'mere. Give me a booster.'

Danny moved across and stood beneath Geordie. He interlocked his fingers and Geordie placed one track shoe, flecked with grit, into the makeshift stirrup. Danny lifted and Geordie went halfway through the window. A scrabble, rubber-screech on glass, and he was all the way in.

'I'll come round and open up. Hold on.'

Danny sat on the grass beside the pond. The pump had changed its sound and was now respiring hoarsely, unhealthily. He heard the back door open. There was no key being turned, just the scrape of a Chubb lock. The back door opened directly into the kitchen. Danny started to wipe his feet but Geordie said, 'Forget about that. Get inside.'

'But I've mud on my gutties. I don't want to get it on your uncle's floor.'

The kitchen was spotless. Either no one here cooked or they were incredibly tidy. Danny said, 'Do you think I could get a glass of water?'

Geordie was leaning against one of the work surfaces. His forehead was varnished with sweat and he looked obscurely worried.

'I'm sure you could.'

'It's all right to be in here, isn't it?' Danny said, opening a cupboard to look for a glass. There was only a single cornflakes packet inside it. Danny accidentally slammed the cupboard door shut.

'Is your uncle married?' Danny went on, but Geordie didn't respond. Danny turned on the tap and there was a loud rattling of pipes. He twisted the tap further to stop the sound but the banging increased. Sticking his head under the flow, he pursed his lips to catch the water. Running from Micks had left him incredibly thirsty. When he eventually lifted his head up, he said, 'I must have drunk three pints of ... ' but Geordie was gone. Maybe he's finding the phone, Danny thought. He turned the tap off and walked out into the hallway. Then everything stopped.

The hallway was an elevator, jerked to a stop, mid-floors. It was a carriage in a stationary train shunted from behind. It was a rollercoaster car tipping over the brink of the slope. It was entirely silent.

Geordie was standing at the far side, by the glass-panelled front door. Between him and Danny there was a body. A man was lying splayed on the paisley carpet. He was in his forties maybe, wearing a dressing gown that was hitched up round his middle. He wore old blue Y-fronts and the lower part of one of his spindly legs was bent up under the thigh. The knee was all pink and bulgy. The man's neck was twisted round too far to the left. Danny could only see a little of his face but it was waxy and completely white. He had a few days' beard growth. He looked terrified. One eye stared straight ahead. Danny followed its gaze to the skirting board. He was dead. The man was dead.

Geordie said, 'We need to get the fuck out of here. Come on.'

Danny still stood there. He felt a shaking rise within him. The bones of his body were banging inside him like the water pipes. Geordie pushed past, back into the kitchen. Danny looked at the body, and then turned and followed him. For some reason Geordie had pulled off his T-shirt and was rubbing the kitchen cupboards with it and the taps. Danny stood watching him stupidly. Then he went into the bathroom and Danny trailed automatically after him. Geordie rubbed the door handles. He was professional somehow, agitated and upset but professional. He strode outside and rubbed at the outside window and frame of the bathroom while Danny leant against the sharp pebbledash of the back of the house. He could feel his legs going and tears coming. Lastly Geordie rubbed the bin lids and then yanked the T-shirt back over his xylophone frame. 'NOW,' he suddenly shouted and Danny jumped, then followed him, running, back round the side of the house and down through the estate. They hit the Milburn Road and legged it through Danny's open front door and past the living room where the girls were building a lego metropolis and up the stairs into Danny's bedroom. Geordie closed the door behind them and stood against it, leaning into Danny's too-small blue velour dressing gown. Danny perched on the edge of the bed. They were breathless.

'What the f-fuck are you doing? Don't you want to see if your uncle's all right?'

Geordie looked at Danny like he was about to punch him.

'Something happened, something awful happened. That wasn't my uncle's house. It was Barry Hughes's. From the school.'

Of course. The man was Barry Hughes. He had looked familiar, even like that. Barry Hughes was a vice-principal and maths teacher at Ballyglass High. Danny had never been taught by him though he was known to be strict, despite wearing daft patterned jumpers and singing snatches of operas in the corridors.

'*What?* Why the fuck did you do that? Why did you think it was your uncle's? How'd you get the wrong house?'

'Danny, it wasn't my fault. I just found him there. He was lying at the bottom of the stairs. It wasn't my fault. I just saw him. I went up to him and looked at him but he was a funny colour and he wasn't making no breathing sounds and that leg was twisted back behind him.'

'But why'd we go in there? Why Hughes's house?'

Geordie's eyes were filmy. Danny thought he was going to cry as well. His stomach was all jittery. 'Why'd you go in the house at all? Did you know it was Hughes's house?'

'Look.' Geordie pushed at his own forehead. Danny had seen men do that on television when they were upset. It looked fake when Geordie did it, like he'd seen the same TV shows. 'I knew it was Hughes's house but I thought he'd be at the parade all right? An' I thought we could just go in and use his phone. *You* were the one who wanted a place to hide out.'

'YOU FUCKING TOLD ME IT WAS YOUR UNCLE'S HOUSE.' Danny stood up.

'Aye I know. But you helped me break in.'

'Fuck you Geordie.' Danny was shaking his head and biting his lower lip. 'We have to call the police and go back to the house. He might still be alive.'

'He wasn't alive, Danny.'

'He must have heard us come in and then slipped or something, fallen over the banister. He must have thought we were burglars. But we would have heard him fall. He would have shouted.' But Danny was thinking of how loud the pipes had been banging. And how noisy the tap was. His T-shirt was still wet from the water. They wouldn't have heard anything. And Danny had slammed the cupboard door. He must have frightened him. He had killed him. 'But we would have heard him,' Danny said again, slowly this time. 'We have to go back. He might be alive still.'

'He's not alive Danny. He was *white*. Chances are he never heard us. He could have been dead hours for all we know. Dead for days. We're not calling the fucking police. They'll say we killed him. We'll be sent away. For breaking and entering. For murder. There's nothing we can do but keep quiet. It's not our fault Danny. It's just one of those things.'

Geordie slid down the door. Danny's dressing gown slithered off the little plastic holder shaped like an elephant, its trunk the hook, and fell onto his head. He pushed it off and it draped over his shoulders like a cape. He was a boy playing at being a superhero. Danny felt a tear break from his eye and run down his cheek.

'We can't do nothing. We have to tell someone.'

'Shut up. Just *shut* up. *I'm* the one who'll get it. *I'm* the one who'll be in trouble. *I'm* the one they'll blame.'

'Well it's your fucking *fault*.'

'Danny, I didn't do nothing wrong. I was just going to go in and get the phone. *You* wanted the phone. I was only trying to help you.'

It is pretty to see what money will do.

Samuel Pepys

FRIDAY, 9 JULY 2004

They'd smoked, talked, and eyed the box, then Danny'd
stood up abruptly, mumbled about the length of time
until work (seven hours), sloped off to bed, and they'd
slept. They hadn't talked about Hughes. They'd never
talked about Hughes. As his house had been locked and
there were no signs of forced entry, the death had been
regarded as an accident: a fall over his banister, accounted
for by a loose rug on his landing and the alcohol in his
system. He'd broken his neck.

Danny had thought about him occasionally over the
years but ever since Geordie'd arrived he'd been noticing
the names Barry or Hughes turning up everywhere, and
references at work or on TV or in conversations to teachers
or maths or opera or death. This is how obsession works.
You acquire a sense that the world is trying to talk to
you. It's as if a theme's being pushed like a skewer

through your life. At night the private cinema of his retina showed one main feature: Hughes's fish-eye staring accusingly at the skirting board.

Danny was woken at 7.30 a.m. on Friday morning by his radio alarm. He jabbed it off and rolled over, then opened his eyes slowly. It was somehow 9.06 a.m. Time is something else that can't be trusted. Danny left for work unwashed and left Geordie lying sound asleep again, facing into the sofa's back, his breathing like someone steadily sweeping a floor. Danny didn't get to the office until past ten. After he'd locked his bike in the underground car park, he walked across the courtyard where the senior partners parked their jags and mercs. It looked like an upmarket second-hand car lot and, strolling across it towards him, between a Range Rover and a Beamer, was its chief salesman, slicked and erect and smiling: Adam Vyse.

'Good morning *Mr* Williams. Gosh, almost good *afternoon* in fact.' He pretended to check his watch. Ha ha. Ha ha ha.

'Morning Adam. Yeah, I'm running a bit late today. I had a doctor's appointment this morning.' *You like that? You like that bald-faced lie?* Danny smiled at him pleasantly.

'Oh yes? Nothing serious I hope?' *Cancer perhaps?*

'No no. Just warts, as it happens. But all over my genitals.' *I am insane.*

Adam looked like he'd just eaten a chilli: his tongue hung out, frozen at the beginning of whatever word he was about to say. Danny walked past him, trying his best to imitate Vyse's earlier grin, the one employing the mouth but rejecting the eyes. *Be more mental*, he repeated to himself, *be more mental. They might make you redun-dant.*

Danny had twenty-three e-mails waiting for him. A woman who worked in the Property Library called Nessa Pamplemousse was selling *Gladiator* on DVD. Four people, none of whom he knew, were holding leaving drinks. Lesley Hornbridge from Private Client was giving away a free candy-striped two-seater sofabed, although you had to collect it from Eastbourne. Danielle Winton was trying to sell a showjumping pony. Apparently it was carefully produced, very bold cross-country, never had a day off work and was 100% traffic, clip, box, shoe. Gibberish. It was serious money, though: £8,000. Maybe he should buy it and ride to work everyday. Kathy De'Ath was cel-ebrating her thirtieth birthday in the Coachman's Arms this evening. Danny said the name out loud, to test it – *De'Ath* – as he deleted, unopened, the rest of the e-mails from strangers. Those left were from some of the invitees to his party: it looked like people were coming and, as people hunted fun in packs, even bringing others. He clicked open his Sent folder, found the original inviting e-mail and forwarded it again to everyone on the address list who hadn't replied, with the heading: *Tonight. My birthday party. It might be a laugh. Someone might trip on the stairs. Do come.* Before he sent it he stared at the e-mail for a full minute, thinking, then typed *Ellen Powell* in at the end of the list of addresses and hit *Send.*

Danny stood up and went out of his office, intending to go and see Rollson. Standing in the corridor he could easily touch both of its opposing walls with his hands. He pushed at them for a moment, like a preppy Samson between the pillars. He was feeling curiously light; the endorphins from his ride into work had gelled with his amusement at telling his boss that he was carrying a minor venereal disease. On the way in he'd cycled past a blonde waiting at a bus stop in Old Street and her posture, as if a string was pulling her head straight up, reminded him of Olivia standing on his doorstep, dignified and abandoned. But it is very difficult to sustain sadness during the day, there is too much to see, and he now felt oddly charged, happy even. And Ellen of the almond eyes might come tonight. He walked up the corridor, dragging his finger along the front of the filing cabinets. They had ridged doors that allowed them to roll back into the sides of the cabinet and he consequently made a thrumming sound, like a truant dragging a stick against railings. When he passed Andrew Jackson's room, and the partner looked up at him, grimacing, Danny gave him the First-Class Vyse-Certified Shit-Eating Grin.

Rollson was being attended to by the in-house physio, a ginger woman who dressed like a district nurse. Rollson was her best client. He was getting fitted for a new lumbar support.

'But Albert, if you actually sat up straight then you wouldn't have a gap in here,' – she inserted her hand into the space, wearily patient – 'between your back and the seat.'

'I know but how do you sit up straight for fourteen hours at a stretch? It's not possible. I'm only human.'

'Everyone else seems to manage it.'

'They get curvature of the spine. Richard III, Quasimodo, they all worked here.'

He made an impassive expression and blinked very

slowly at Danny, to suggest the suffering he was going through. The physio sighed. Her badge read Eleanor Broom.

'Well, this support pad is the best we can get. It took four weeks to arrive and I had to get special partner authority to order it.'

'Okay, I understand that, but I want you to record in your notes that I'm *not* comfortable in this seat.'

This was meant to scare the physio, intimating that he was preparing a claim against the firm for health problems. She sighed again and looked hurt.

'I'll see what I can do. Let me talk to the firm that makes these. Maybe we could order a new foam one to be specially moulded to your back or something.'

Albert, out of sight of Eleanor, who was still fussing with his current lumbar pad, grinned at Danny.

'Well I suppose if that's all you can do, it's all you can do.'

Danny slid into the seat opposite him just as his phone started ringing.

'Okay, I'll pop off back downstairs now. E-mail me if there's anything else.'

The physio swished out, leaving a vapour trail of perfume. Albert had, instead of a telephone receiver, a handsfree headset, à la Madonna circa 1990, and he flicked it over his head.

'Thanks Eleanor, thanks *so* much . . . Albert Rollson, hello?'

Danny looked at the desk between them. It had an angled book rest on which there were two large sheets of blotting paper, patterned with the squiggles of dozens of dried signatures. There was also a free-standing magnifying glass, several small jars of vitamins, a tube of Berocca, and a box of man-sized tissues, whitely erupting. The Kleenex had been purchased on Monday, which Danny knew because Albert had spent a large proportion of Monday afternoon standing in the doorway of his office arguing that man-sized tissues should, in fact, be the size of a man, even if it was only a little man who didn't care much for food.

'Uh-huh. Uh-huh. Yes. Okay. Mr Haroldson, would you mind awfully if I set you on speaker phone while I get the file? Please do go on.'

Rollson gestured to Danny to shut the door and he did so, quietly. Rollson set the handle of the Dictaphone, the part you speak into, by the telephone. From a drawer under his desk, he lifted a transparent cassette, on which ROLLS was daubed up the side in Tipp-Ex, slotted it into the Dictaphone, and flicked the machine on. It hummed into life.

'Hullo, Albert? Albert? Can yuh hear uz? Can yuh hear uz now?' Northern, a sixty-a-day timbre to it. The kind of voice you'd like to talk to your grandchildren in.

'Perfectly Mr Haroldson. If you and the team want to give me a summary of events from 1992 onwards, right up to the present day, I'll take notes. Just tell me everything you can think of and I'll keep my questions until the end. Maybe each of you could speak in turn?'

'Right-o, Albert. June. June? Get June in here. June should go first.'

Albert mouthed to Danny, DID YOU INVITE HER?

Danny mouthed back, ELLEN?

They nodded at each other simultaneously. Albert mouthed, COFFEE?

They left the wobbly voice of June describing her filing system to the Dictaphone and walked down the corridor to the facilities room. In here the buzz of the office was intensified. There was an enormous bovine photocopier, ingesting, digesting, egesting. From under its lid Danny could see the strip of light zip up and down the glass panel, the dawn horizon strapped into a box. The fax machine, water fountain, sink, taps, shredder, scanner and vending machine all glugged or beeped or munched or whirred or clicked in here. It was the modern farmyard. Danny pressed 71 on the vending machine's sticky pad and a brown plastic cup slotted into the gap. A thin ribbon of water started to fill it, running colourless at first and then very dark. Albert repeated the process. He looked faded, exhausted. Danny felt impelled to give him a hug but instead patted him, awkwardly, on the shoulder. Even this physical contact occasioned Rollson to take a step back and lean against the snorting copier.

'You okay mate? How's the settlement coming? What time d'you get away at last night?'

''Bout three. I feel pretty dreadful. But I'm coming to your do this evening, although it might be later rather than sooner. What did Ellen say?'

Albert pulled some paper out from the large circular dispenser and ripped it off. He wiped carefully round the lip of his plastic cup before he drank from it.

'I didn't speak to her – just added her name to that reminder I sent round. I'll go check for a reply in a minute. I think I'm losing it though. I told Adam Vyse I'd genital warts this morning.'

'Why?' Rollson rearranged his face into a smile but

Danny could see his disapproval. It was too direct a
revolt, too unsubtle. A little bit naff.

'I was late. It seemed like an amusing thing to do.'

'How'd he take it?'

'Not sure yet. I'll let you know.'

'I'd better get back to Mr Haroldson and June.'

'Just say you went to get their file.'

Albert nodded and sipped at the coffee. Danny was
staring across the white room at the shredder as if he'd
only just noticed it. Just to the above and left of it,
attached to the wall, was the paper roll dispenser Albert'd
just used.

'I wonder,' Danny began idly, 'if we fed a bit of that
paper into the shredder and turned it on, whether it
would keep going by itself, until the roll ran out or the
shredder was full?'

'I think it just might,' Albert said, pouring the rest of
his coffee into the sink.

'Interesting thought.'

'I'll see you later Dan. I've got to go and ask some
pointless questions.' Albert hurried out.

Back at his desk Danny had no reply from Ellen. He'd
need to e-mail her about Northern Ireland in a minute.
It could be embarrassing if she didn't mention the party
e-mail at all. Maybe she thought it was too friendly and
weird. Jill had already booked their Belfast flights and
the Europa, the most bombed hotel in Europe. He'd save
that fact for the plane. It was only for one night, they
just needed to have a quick look through the main contracts. If it appeared that there was going to be too much
work to do in a day and a half Danny had decided that

he'd get the documents copied and sent over to London, should Ulster Water be amenable to the idea, which seemed unlikely. Danny opened the matter's correspondence file on his desk. Scott had left it in a mess. Post-it notes hung from it with numbers and names scribbled on them. There was a perfect coffee ring on the file's cover: a No Entry sign. It didn't even seem to be in chronological order. Danny pulled out a summary sheet from the file's inside flap. Their client, Syder, were going to asset strip and sell off Ulster Water's businesses. There was a rival bid from the Japanese company Yakuma who were going to invest in the company and expand it. If Syder's bid was successful the first step of their business plan was to sack 4,000 people. It was the largest private employer in Ulster.

Danny turned around in his chair and put his feet up on the air conditioning unit that sat below the window. He looked out at the dozens of windows of the office block opposite. They were like stacks of televisions all tuned to the same channel. A programme about a mythical monster: half-human, half-desk. The only way for Danny to see the sky from here was by its reflection in the very upper opposite windows. Today it was an invariable cinereous grey. He assumed his own window reflected the sky for the lawyers or accountants or bankers across the road. Who knew what they did? They all dressed alike. Their chinos and blue shirts and brown brogues, their sensible haircuts and smart-casual misery.

Danny had worked on cases he'd disliked before. He realized that lawyers always allow themselves the casuistry of arguing that everyone is entitled to take part in the legal process, everyone is entitled to justice. And this is true. However lawyers don't work for everyone. They work for who pays them. And usually the sinned against don't carry the readies. And usually the best lawyers work only for the richest. The trick for your conscience is to put on lawyer's gloves before you dirty your hands. Danny wouldn't consider working for some of the companies or organizations he had as clients and yet, in fact, he was. He'd worked for a cigarette company acting against smuggling allegations. He'd worked for the pro-hunting lobby. He'd worked for one of the largest arms manu-facturers in Britain, defending it on charges of illegally selling weapons to various Middle Eastern countries. He'd worked for crooks and liars. He'd won cases he wished he hadn't. And now he was trying to get 4,000 people sacked in Ulster. Another sophism Danny's colleagues utilized was that if they didn't do it, someone else would. So let them, Danny was thinking, as he stared out at the reflected grey of the sky, let someone else do it.

They were to fly on Saturday morning at 10.30 a.m., collect a hire car at the airport, and drive straight to the Ulster Water headquarters, just outside Belfast. It was the twelfth of July weekend so there would be marches and possibly trouble. They'd just go about their client's busi-ness and then head over to the Europa. A drink and some dinner, and they'd fly back on Sunday, in either the morning or evening, depending on how far they'd got in the diligence. Danny started to read the file.

At noon he e-mailed Albert to see about lunch. Albert mailed back that he couldn't today as he had 'to go off to box now'. This actually meant that Albert was off to attend his boxercise class along with a score of female secretaries and lawyers. There was only one other man who attended: Tel, from the print room by the South Street entrance. Albert was always paired with Tel for the partnered exercises and Tel was terrifying. He was an East Londoner, and appeared to suffer from the East London disorder of considering accidental eye contact an act of overt aggression. He was squat, broad, wide-mouthed: an angry toad with powerful limbs. When he wasn't staring in generalized hostility around him, Tel was incredibly friendly, at least in that fearsome and dominant manner in which the drunk in the pub's toilets is incredibly friendly. Last week, when Danny and Albert were eating lunch, Tel had shouted *Wotcha Rollsy* across the canteen, and Albert had frantically lifted his arm to return the greeting, though, by neglecting to set his fork down first, he had newly patterned his pink Gieves & Hawkes tie with arugula and pine nuts washed in balsamic vinegar. There was a perverse pleasure for Danny in seeing Rollson dishevelled and unkempt: embarrassment is most devastating for the normally shevelled and kempt. Rolls had thought Tel okay, really, though he always made his shoulders ache when he had to hold the punch pads for him, but two weeks ago he'd noticed SKINS tattooed on Tel's arm, when they were in the changing room after the class. He now worried at length about whether Tel knew he was Jewish.

Danny e-mailed Rolls back: Don't forget your legwarmers. And your Combat 18 headband. He supposed he might as well look at Scott's preliminary due diligence on Ulster Water. He'd ask Ellen to come down and help him. She'd already looked over some stuff on it. He could just brazen it out, mention the party and see what she said. He sent her an e-mail, formal and brusque, and she duly appeared, formal and brusque, holding a stack of the files she'd been reviewing.

'Mr Williams, I have a document for your attention. It's very important.' She looked serious.

'You're the second person to call me Mr Williams today. Please don't. It would upset my father. What's the document? Anything that will get us out of going tomorrow?'

Ellen set the files on the pull-out shelf in the filing cabinet and slipped a white card off the top of them. *Danny* was written on the back on it. She had a schoolgirl's careful script.

'Afraid not. Happy Birthday.' She smiled, unguarded suddenly, showing the slightly crooked tooth again.

'A-ha. My first and undoubtedly only birthday card. That's very kind of you. How did you know it was my birthday? Though my birthday's not 'til Wednesday actually.'

'It was in the e-mail. About the party? You said it was your birthday party.'

'Of course. Thanks.' Danny was waggling the card in his hand and watching her. Ellen looked away, at the files. Stop looking at her, Danny thought, you're acting like a weirdo.

'So are you going to come? To the party?'

'I'll try to. I'm meeting some friends from law school later. I might come after.'

'Bring them along. Bring your boyfriend. The more the merrier.'

Your boyfriend? The more the merrier? What the hell was he saying? Why was he talking like he was in a sitcom?

'Well, if I find one before tonight I'll make sure to bring him.'

She turned to the files stacked on the shelf and started sorting them out. Danny looked down, a rush of pleasure at her admission, and opened the card. It said *Happy 40th Birthday* and showed a bottle of champagne, with its cork popping.

'I wasn't sure what age you were going to be so I guessed.'

Danny glanced up to see her grinning cheekily.

'I'm going to be twenty-eight thanks very much. Only a year or two older than you.'

'I'm twenty-three actually.' Fuck, Danny thought, I'm going to be too old for her.

'You're just a baby.'

'Yes.' She sat down, smoothing her skirt over her thighs.

'Let's have a look at what we've got on Ulster Water then.'

Danny stood up and lifted the box of the first load of documents that Scott had been sent. It was surprisingly heavy and he stifled a grunt as he set it on the seat next to Ellen. As she read out the types of contracts, flicking through the pages, Danny tried to note down something useful. The sunray expanding on his desk had now reached his glass of water and was complicating it with light. Danny kept looking at the blackness of her delicate fingers against the white pages. He decided he needed to go outside. He still felt a little unstable, and didn't trust himself not to reach over and touch this beautiful girl's hand or face or neck. The air conditioning, and the spliff last night, seemed to be making his mouth completely dry despite his constant attempts to rehydrate it. He needed some food.

'My head's splitting. I'm going to nip out for a sand-wich. Can I get you something?'

'Well if it's all right, I might come for the walk.'

'Yeah of course, although I'm going to buy an iron first.'

Danny didn't know why he'd said that. He *did* need an iron and had wanted to buy one today but he could have done it later, on his own. He realised that he wanted her to come with him and lend her calm firm air to the proceedings. They stood now, side by side, a little awk-wardly, waiting for the lift. Its doors drew open and they joined a pale woman who was breathing hoarsely and smelt of cigarettes and coffee. The three of them stood in silence. Outside, the street was abuzz with dark suits and the white triangular bibs of shirts, brushing past each other, swerving, reversing. They walked through St Paul's churchyard. A rabble of Japanese schoolkids, with their harmoniously glossy black hair and discordant Day-Glo rucksacks, blocked their path and stared at Ellen. Danny realized he wanted to stare at her too. When they were waiting to cross Ludgate Hill a van driver tooted his horn at her and shouted something, thankfully incomprehen-sible. Danny was suddenly embarrassed to be near a woman so publicly beautiful. Everyone seemed to accept it. Danny said that they should walk on down to the water and, once there, they continued, buffeted slightly by wind, onto the Millennium Bridge and stood, leaning over the open side, watching the Thames mosey beneath. More schoolkids waved at them from a red pleasure cruiser headed for Greenwich. He felt he'd stumbled by accident on the centre of the world. Back in the city, with the two of them swinging their mini-carrier bags of lunch – a Pret à Manger sandwich, a vanilla yoghurt with Brownies, juice – they'd gone into the Robert Dyas hardware store just round the corner from Monks & Turner. It was full of office workers, hurriedly trying to patch the rips in their clockwork harried lives: slug pellets, Polyfilla, teasmaids. Danny felt that it was somehow Future Time, when everything has worked out, and it was a Saturday and he and his wife, whom he loved, had gone shopping for domestic appliances for their neat and lovely terraced house. Danny applied the universal rule for choosing wine in restaurants, and picked out the second cheapest iron as Ellen explained the significance of the descaling plug.

At the till she said to the chubby blonde girl who was prodding despondently at the cash register, as if trying to keep it awake, 'Bet you can't wait 'til half-five.' The girl's face broke from sullenness into a grin. 'It's been like this all day. Really busy for some reason.' Danny felt something slip a little inside him and settle, like a combination lock coming right. Everything's sparks and particles, shivers and jottings, approximations, but maybe sometimes you know why you turn one way and not the other. Ellen smiled at the Robert Dyas girl and asked her was she going out tonight. The girl chatted on like she'd known her for ever, and when Danny leant over the checkout desk to endorse the Switch receipt, he felt himself signing up to something else entirely.

EVENING

'It's like this, you see, I wouldn't do it if it wasn't providing a service. We keep the restaurants clean and the streets quiet. If people sleep safe and in peace in their beds at night it's basically because of us.'

Danny's cousin Clyde was talking. This was not unusual. Clyde was an environmental health inspector in Hounslow. He was very pale and possessed an abnormally large head which, as his hairline was receding, still appeared to be growing, and which he jerked around a lot when he was animated. Which he frequently was. Everything amazed Clyde. Particularly himself. He was one of life's excitables. Leaning against the sink, he was talking to a chubby pigtailed blonde perched on the kitchen counter, and peering down her substantial cleavage. She said something inaudible and raised her pencilled eyebrows. Clyde bobbed his balloon-head wisely.

'Well I suppose so, but the police are less important than you'd think. To be honest with you, they're more back-up for us. I mean, they'll come round if we're having trouble getting a party to turn it down or something but normally we prefer to work alone.'

The flat was almost full. Ben, Danny's friend from law school, had arrived at eight with the boot of his Fiesta packed with speakers, an amp and decks. He had immediately set about organizing the furniture in his quietly capable manner. He'd moved the table to the corner of the living room and the sofa against the wall to create floor space, then set the sound system up on the table. He was now standing behind it, an ear cupped to one of the headphones (his 'cans' he called them), playing Stevie Wonder's cover of 'Light My Fire'. Several people were swaying and jiggling on the floor in varying levels of comfort and confidence, index-linked to sobriety.

Danny had arrived home at 7 p.m. to find Geordie lying flat out on the sofa, almost exactly as he'd left him, but awake, smoking the ubiquitous spliff, and watching a programme called *Dogs with Jobs* on one of the cable channels. Danny sat on the arm of the sofa, beside Geordie's feet. Still holding his bicycle helmet, he asked him if any of the dogs were lawyers. Geordie grunted. Maybe some of them were cleaners, Danny said pointedly, looking around him.

The coffee table was stacked with beer cans and ashtrays, and Geordie had artfully managed to drape the few clothes he possessed around the flat. Every room was claimed by at least a rolled-up sock. Even the fact of him, his sentience, his being, and particularly his being on Danny's sofa, made the flat seem cluttered and too small.

'Come on wee man, get up. I need this place sorted out for the party.'

'Two minutes Dan. I've just lay down.'

'Bollocks you have. Get the fuck up. You can go and get a takeaway for us while I tidy.'

Danny suddenly just wanted him out of the house, so he could open the windows, Hoover the floors, and dump all his stuff in the tiny boxroom. He wanted the place to smell fresh, homely, of a bunch of flowers or something cooking on the stove, a shank of lamb braising, not of this Ulsterman, his feet, his breath, his ashy sour scent. He wanted to open a bottle of wine, white, French, not a six pack of Heineken. He wanted his flat back.

'All right all right. Keep your hair on Captain.'

Geordie had spent the day floating around the locals, smoking and worrying about what to do with the cash. Ian had rung him three times to check about tonight. He seemed madly keen to come. Must be lonely. Geordie knew how he felt. All day he had watched the other piss artists and timewasters sit round and do crosswords, argue, eye the boxy comforter in the corner showing other people doing things, and thought how none of them had his problems. He was the man apart. He was half-considering telling Danny about the cash or even asking him to take it to Belfast tomorrow. He could just tell him it was a present or something for Janice. Or he could run with it. Become the man who disappears. He'd rung Janice and she'd cried on the phone. She was in Martin's so couldn't speak for long but her voice had sounded funny, muffled like she'd been at the dentists,

119

and Geordie'd asked her why she was speaking weird and she told him Budgie had busted her lip. Fucking Budgie. All of this, everything, was Budgie's fault. He was going to repay him some day, with a ton of interest. Cripple him with the fucking interest. Janice had asked him to bring the money back, to bring it back and apologize. Yeah, right. Like Budgie was going to take that. Like he was going to pat little Geordie on the head and buy him a pint in the Gleneally. She was stupid, Jan. Poor bitch. Sweet though. You could do worse than settle for her. She'd keep you warm, would Janice. That cracking body, a real peach. But not the brightest. Poor wee Jan. Forever fucking up and getting thumped. He sometimes thought he loved her.

'Any birds coming tonight that aren't totally monkey?'

Danny laughed. Totally monkey. He hadn't heard the phrase for years. There are always a hundred local words that mean 'ugly' or 'rough' and another hundred that mean 'drunk'. It's what makes a dialect. The most popular synonyms for 'totally monkey' had been gypping (as in 'she's a gypping trout'), minging, manky, boiling, munting, rancid, and raw. 'Chewed' and 'melted' were also popular.

'A few, aye. All out of your league though mate.'

'Fuck off. They might fancy a bit of rough.'

'Not that rough.'

'They be more into pretty rich boys like you then?' There was a hard centre to Geordie's voice, a wire running through the words.

'All right calm down mate. I was just joking.'

'Aye, well . . . you and me, mate, we're not so fucking different.'

'I know, I know. Let's clear this place up.'

Geordie left and brought back cod and chips and Danny tidied, filling three bin bags with rubbish. They wolfed the takeaway, both adding loads of ketchup, and sank matching pint glasses of milk. They watched MTV. The incredible black girls in the videos reminded Danny of Ellen.

'There is one girl who might turn up tonight that's really fit. A girl I work with. She's coming to Northern Ireland with me tomorrow.'

'Oh yeah? Nice. Point her out to me.'

*   *   *

'It's a responsibility to the general public.' Clyde was still talking. 'I have their lives in my hands and on my con-science. I've seen some things in restaurants. Rats the size of dogs.'

'You sure they weren't actually dogs? Were they on leads?'

The pigtailed blonde had disappeared and been replaced by Ben the DJ, who had been caught in a conversation while filling a mug from the cold tap. There were no glasses left. The bathroom door was closed and there were two people outside it waiting. One of them was Ellen, who'd just arrived, and been let in by Fishboy who was sporting a pink Christmas cracker party hat which he appeared to have brought with him. The other was her friend Rowena, a tiny pretty Indian, who was gripping Ellen's arm and gravely predicting that she was about to wet herself.

The kitchen contained Clyde and Ben (who was repeating that he had to get back to his decks) and sev-eral friends of Danny's from Monks. They were leaning

121

against the work surfaces and swapping wisecracks. During one of those unfathomable and sudden silences that strike at parties, Tuzza, who was in the corner by the fridge talking to Simon, was heard to say 'because he's an oily little prick', and immediately everyone else in the room swivelled their faces towards him like so many tracking satellite dishes. Through the open kitchen door you could see ten or twelve people standing in the garden. It was a warm and sticky July evening. The sky was mostly grey but in the west, over Islington, it was blushing pinkly. The windows of the houses backing onto Danny's were lit and quartered by their frames. They almost looked like faded yellow flags hung out for the party.

On the patio Jennifer Bauer, a depressive leveraged finance lawyer, was sitting on an upturned red bucket, in floods of tears after drinking eight gin and tonics and trying to kiss Adela, the sylphic friend now crouched beside her stroking her knees. Another group, consisting solely of men and led decisively by James the compactors salesman, were trying to throw pieces of gravel into a plant pot by the back door and yelping angrily or joy-fully as they missed or made it. At the far end of the garden, by the metal bin where Danny kept the seca-teurs and watering can, four men were standing in an approximate square, facing each other: Ian, who'd arrived with four cans of Carlsberg and his usual serious air; Albert, who'd brought a bottle of Veuve Clicquot and an ex-girlfriend called Claire; Geordie, who was already drunk; and Danny, who was wondering if Ellen was coming and swiftly knocking back a bottle of Sauvignon Blanc.

Ian had stood in silence for the first half-hour, after introductions and after he'd politely knocked away any direct questions put to him. If he spoke, he spoke fast, as if he didn't have much time to waste. Albert was describing in detail his latest vision. It had come to him while he was walking past one of the gyms on the Finchley Road and had noticed the Lycra-ed gerbils on their treadmills and stairmasters and elliptical machines.

'Now I figure that running six miles in fifty minutes would burn about four hundred calories.'

'How do you know that?' said Geordie, suspicious as a thief.

'I have experience of exercise, as you can see.' He pinched a roll of fat, tremulous, above his belt. Albert was continually making succinct forays into fitness, such as the boxercise class ('to sandpaper me down even smoother'), but hated the locker-room friendliness or unfriendliness (hated even that pressure of whether to speak). He disliked how the disinfected smell reminded him of school, and became too aware of the proximity of foreign bodies, and those sideways methods people had of glancing at each other.

'And then I thought, calories, of course, are units of energy. We could harness all of this power.'

'But those machines need electric,' Geordie again.

'An ordinary exercise bike doesn't. It must be easy to rig them so they run off their own power. And it could work for all the machines. It's brilliant.'

'I like it,' said Danny, definitively, as a way of closing the conversation down.

'It's textbook genius. This makes use of something people want to discard. Their fat. Imagine the incentive of knowing you can't watch *Coronation Street* unless you row for a thousand metres first. Fat would drip off them.'

Ian watched all this like a father at his son's birthday party: bemused, uninvolved, a little bored. Albert turned to him and said, 'Well, what do you think? Has it got legs?'

'I think there's better uses for your energy than the gym.'

Geordie snorted a little. 'Yeah, like you don't go to the fucking gym.'

Ian clenched both his arms in front of him. His shirt reshaped itself, tight, over the muscles which sprang into tension. Ludicrous contours and bulges. Smiling widely, he said, 'But my energy's directed towards generation.'

'And what are you going to generate?' Danny asked, unimpressed.

'Justice,' Ian stated decisively.

'Right,' Danny sighed. 'Anyone got any fags left?'

Danny was watching Ian. All that crap about generating justice was designed to wrong-foot Albert and him. Ian wasn't to know Albert couldn't be wrong-footed by an avalanche. Where the hell had Geordie pulled this tosser from? He watched Ian rub at his massive right bicep with a stubby little trowel-hand. He seemed to have Geordie marked out as a wingman and him as the enemy. When Ian shouldered his way to the toilet, Danny turned to Geordie and asked, impatiently, 'Where the hell'd you find him? He's wound like a spring. And what the fuck's he talking about?'

'Lay off him, he's all right. He's Northern Irish. You mightn't remember what they're like.'

'Hello stranger.' Ellen, at his back, trailing Rowena,

newly returned from the toilet and much relieved. Ellen was wearing a white fitted Burberry shirt and dark blue bootcut jeans. Understated and beautiful. Even the languid way she looked around her made Danny lose confidence. She seemed to have the ability to slow time right down, so that it clung to her, reluctant to let go.

'Hey. I didn't know whether you'd make it. How long have you been here?'

'We just arrived. Some guy in a cracker hat let us in. This is Rowena, Danny, and,' she looked at the others, 'I'm Ellen.'

'This is Geordie, a friend over from Ireland, and Albert, you might know him from work.' Danny gestured at each in turn, and flicked his eyebrows at Geordie to let him know this was *the* girl. And here was Ian back, looking at Ellen as if he was slightly puzzled.

'And this is Ian, a friend of Geordie's.' Ian nodded stiffly.

'Sorry I'm not being a good host. Let me get you two a drink. What would you like?'

When Danny returned with two plastic cups brimming with wine, Ian and Albert were standing, patiently, listening to Rowena loudly recount her journey here. The story appeared to involve her losing a shoe en route, although she was wearing two now. Both Albert's and Ian's eyes were widening as her voice grew louder and louder. She was practically screaming, in case, it seemed, someone should try to interrupt her.

Geordie had turned away from the group to corner Ellen, and was sitting on the metal bin. Ellen had asked whether he and Danny had been friends since school, and he was now regaling her with some story,

125

gesticulating, charming. Danny gave Rowena one cup ('OH GREAT, THANKS DAVY') and handed Ellen hers. Geordie was leaning slightly back and his head was level with Ellen's chest: 'So we were in the local nightclub, the Pink Pussycat it's called, though we always called it Clubland, dint we?'

He looks up at Danny, who nods.

'And Danny had pulled this bird from Dungannon called Stacey, about twenty she was, and I'd copped with this fenian called Orla from Pomeroy. We were only wee fellas. Wee boys, fifteen maybe.'

Danny suddenly knows what's coming.

'Shut up Geordie.'

Ellen looks up at Danny, her plastic cup about to touch her lips.

'Just a bit of fun. Just giving Ellen all the facts about you. What friends from home are for, mate.' The last word was a barb, a tiny hook like his grin.

Ellen sensed the acrimony. Embarrassed, she looked over the back fence towards the dark houses. Their windows, yellow as the eyes of cats, seemed to be watching them now. Danny was raging, but said nothing, and downed the whole half-pint of wine in his tumbler.

'And then Danny scoots off down Monkey Lane with this bird for a bit of scobing, and ... do you want to tell the rest Dan?'

'Geordie, please, leave it out mate.'

Ellen is interested now, more interested because Danny's reaction to the story is actually physical. Even in this muted summer light, it's apparent that he's flushed not just with wine but embarrassment.

'No, go on, what happened?'

'If the lovely lady wants to hear it, I'll just have to tell it I suppose.'

The other three beside them had turned to listen now. Parties: where everyone is always waiting for something to happen.

'So Dan disappears down Monkey Lane with this bird and reappears about twenty minutes later when me and Orla, or Carla or whatever she was called, are sitting on the bench outside Martin's eating gravy chips and peas. And Dan goes off to buy Stacey a gravy chip and I know he's fucked her, I can tell by the look of him, but he's still not looking happy so I leave the two birds together and follow him up the street.'

Geordie looked up at Danny now, triumphant. Danny has edged back until he's almost against the fence. He looks trapped by the story.

'So then I goes into the Brewery Greaser and goes to Dan, *So what happened?* And the story is that they're getting down to it, they're snogging in the side doorway of the St Vincent de Paul and then she says,' Geordie puts on a really high coarse voice, '*Listen darling I need to go – howld on there for a minute,* and she struts off up the alley but only a few yards and crouches down beneath this fire escape for the furniture shop. And Danny's telling me this, and he's looking really upset. And *Geordie*, he goes, *Geordie, she only fucking took a dump. Not even a piss. A fucking dump. She fucking takes a shit when I'm standing there watching her.'*

Ian shot a short hard laugh. Albert looked at his glass. Rowena giggled a little and then stopped, glancing at Ellen. Danny watched her too. She was trying hard not to look dismayed, and failing.

'And then the worst bit, the pits, I ask him, *But Danny, did you do her after? You didn't fucking do her afterwards did you?* And Dan goes, *Aye, damn right I did.*' Geordie laughed and took a swig from his can.

'And then on the Monday after school me and Del went down Monkey Lane and there was this great turd still there, under the fire escape, drying out. Fucking disgusting. And then after that we always used to say, if a bird was rough, is she Monkey Lane? Is she completely monkey?'

He looked directly at Danny, and said, slowly, smiling malignantly.

'Is she totally – utterly – fucking – monkey?'

Danny returned his stare. He looked at Geordie as though he wanted nothing more than to push him backwards off the dustbin so he'd smack his head against the fence, and in fact he was thinking of nothing else but how he'd love to push him backwards off the dustbin so he'd smack his head against the fence. And then kick the shit out of him. But he knew he wouldn't.

Inside, Ben was playing Marlena Shaw's 'California Soul' at full blast and the crowd on the dance floor had thickened. Jennifer Bauer had cheered up enough to thrust her limbs around and once more love her friend Adela from afar. James was in the kitchen, burping simultaneously as he repeated the names of the two girls who were standing across the room from him. The girls, Emma and Nicola, were standing at the counter, ignoring him and organizing a round of six tequila shots. The glasses stood in a neat row, aglow like tiny jars of honey brimming with sloppy gold. Semilunar lemon slices and a little pile of salt were arranged on a saucer beside them.

Outside the toilet door, Clyde, over-excited now for this was real news, and worth not a little attention, had found the pigtailed blonde again and was anticipating enjoying her complete concentration, if only for a second or two: '*Bloody* hell. Unbelievable.' He shook his head dramatically, bounced from foot to foot.

'What?'

'Outside. Did you see it?'

'*What?*' She still wasn't quite convinced.

'In the garden? Did you see it? Did you see Danny?'

'*No*, what happened?'

'He just pushed that Geordie bloke off the dustbin and smacked his head against the fence. They're kicking the shit out of each other.'

LATE EVENING

It was hardly balletic. Danny had pushed Geordie backwards, not meaning to start a full brawl but wanting to unsettle him suddenly, just as he had been. Geordie'd looked genuinely surprised as Danny's two hands had gripped his shoulders and pushed, though as he was falling his eyes had flicked left, to Ellen, in a faked glance of appeal and shock. Danny noticed. His response was to kick the metal bin lid so it gonged, as though announcing to the party the start of the main feature.

Geordie was momentarily wedged, legs in the air, between the toppled dustbin and the plank fence before he nimbly rolled onto his side, laughing now, and bounced to his feet. He brushed himself down, still chuckling, and then turned and flung himself at Danny in a chest-height tackle. Rowena shrieked. The little group who'd gathered at the other end of the garden, now including Clyde and

Pigtails, emitted the hushed *Ooooh* of a centre court crowd impressed by a dexterous drop shot.

They went over together, heavily. Danny was flat on his back when they landed and Geordie fell on his side. Danny tried to sit up but before he got straight Geordie sprang neatly onto his chest, pinning him down. His knees were almost on Danny's shoulders and Danny's tracksuit top was pulled right up so the dark flat line of the hair on his stomach was showing. 'Your trainers are getting mud on his top,' Albert pointed out in a pained voice. Geordie was slapping Danny on the cheeks, a little harder than playful, while Danny was forcing a smile. The scene could still, just about, be brushed off as horse-play. Ian was grinning at them like a proud father. Ellen had turned to look at Rowena, her eyebrows raised to perfect circumflexes. Only Albert was visibly distressed. He was manically stroking his neck as if there was an insect on it.

'Come on guys. Let it go. Geordie, get off him.'

He stepped forward, not to lift Geordie off Danny (he wasn't touching anyone), but simply to chide them from a closer vantage point. As he did Ian moved into his way and gently set one stubby hand on Albert's chest, politely refusing him entry. Albert stumbled backwards immediately, intimidated.

'Let them sort it out themselves.'

'They're not exactly sorting anything out.'

'Well,' Ian moved to stand beside Albert and face the two belligerents, 'this is how *we* do it.'

Danny managed to twist Geordie off him and stood up, one hand holding the top of the fence for balance. Geordie, chuckling again, got to his feet, and they stood a couple of feet apart, breathing hoarsely and out of sync.

'You cunt,' Geordie said, as if discussing the weather.

'*You're* the cunt,' replied Danny, almost equally implacably.

'I'm not the one who fucking started it.'

'Yeah you did. And you've been a real prick all day.'

Geordie moved closer to Danny, so that only Danny could hear what he was about to say, but there was no aggression in his movement and it looked to the others as if they were making up. The group at the end of the garden started to unbristle and turn inwards again.

Geordie quickly whispered: 'Williams, you're a real jumped-up wee tosser, with your wanker friends and your poncy flat and your suits and trying to impress some bitch, some fucking bla . . . '

Before he could finish the sentence Danny had him in a headlock. They were wheeling and stamping around, and resembled a disrobed pantomime horse except Danny was facing the wrong way. He was shouting 'Calm down. Just calm down,' as Geordie kept swinging upwards to try to connect with a punch. Eventually Geordie ran Danny against the garden fence which gave a condoling groan, as did Albert, who was now plucking at the skin round his adam's apple. Geordie, still headlocked, had his feet angled on the lawn's verge like starter blocks, and Danny was standing in the flowerbed, splaying the dog daisies, with his back to the fence. Geordie, facing the ground, noticed the red handles of the long-bladed secateurs that had fallen out of the bin and scooped them up. Simultaneously, Ellen and Rowena screamed 'Danny' and 'DAVY' respectively. Geordie swung the clippers and smacked the blades against Danny's left knee. Immediately Danny grunted and let go. Geordie popped up straight, opened the blades and pushed the sharpened V upwards at Danny's throat. The two men stood entirely still, Danny with his hands on the outside of the blades, Geordie gripping the handles. They looked at each other. Geordie spoke softly, with cartoon menace. 'Not so smart now eh batman?'

Ian laughed. Danny could feel the cold blades just touching his neck. They were roughened with spots of rust or dirt and he could feel flecks of Geordie's spit on his face. Danny looked at Geordie. His eyes were wide and alive for once and he was grinning at him and repeating 'Not so smart now eh?' Danny noticed a tendon standing out in his neck, taut with exertion, and he thought of a brake cable at full stretch, which suddenly snaps and lashes about like an eel. Then he thought of his own neck's tendons and pulled his head back from the blades, into the garden of the Somalian family next door. He looked over Geordie's head. Both Ellen and Rowena appeared upset but it was Albert's face that surprised him. It showed not just fear but a peculiar distance. He was looking at Danny like he didn't recognize him. This had to finish.

'Geordie, come on mate, we're both being pricks.'

Geordie sensed a comedown. He looked along the garden at the crowd watching him and realized what they were watching: a man in a flowerbed holding big scissors. He laughed again.

'*Mate* . . . sure we were only messing.' He lowered the blades, and then, as if to show that he had always been playing, sliced at a tendril of the creeper that was sneaking over the fence from the Aidids' side and said 'Snip, snip' in a squeaky voice.

'Sorry mate, I shouldn't have pushed you. I just fucking hate that story. *And* you know it . . . Anyway, let's leave it.' Danny just wanted the thing fixed now, put back together as quickly as possible. It didn't matter if it didn't work any more.

'Aye.' Geordie seemed disappointed somehow, smaller.

'We'll talk later yeah?' Danny couldn't really look at him.

'Aye.' Geordie dropped the clippers into the daisies. Danny felt a blast of utter sadness, the slipstream left by fear passing him. He put his arms out onto Geordie's shoulders, almost for support.

'Don't be at that, for chrissake.'

They nodded at each other and Danny clapped him half-heartedly on the shoulder.

Danny picked the hedge clippers up and put them back in the bin that Albert had righted. He then placed the lid on it. He looked around for something else to put in order, another action to imbue with dignity and delay him from having to look in their faces, but there was nothing left to do.

'Here's your drink.' Ellen, handing him a glass of wine.

'Ta.'

'You all right?' Her tone was deliberately flat, the kind you might use when you haven't seen someone since they went upstairs to have a bath. Danny was glad. Any emotion might cause him to collapse under the leylandii and start hyperventilating.

'Oh aye, fine. Geordie's an old mate but a bit of a header.'

135

She nodded very slowly. She was deciding how to put something.

'I'm going to head off, I think,' – she glanced at him – 'Get the overland to Highbury and then catch the tube.'

'Ellen, no. I'm sorry about this. Too much drink. Stay. Just for a bit anyway.'

Danny knew he was too drunk. He was going to say too much and be too much. He bent down and snapped off one of the few daisies still standing. A thin trail of sap dangled from it, white like saliva. He wiped the stem on his sleeve and handed it to her.

'Here. Peace. Have another glass of wine. We'll go inside.'

She looked reluctantly at the flower but took it anyway, and twirled it slowly between thumb and forefinger.

'You don't have many of these left.'

'No.' Danny gazed stupidly at her.

'Your garden's nice though.' She looked down it, appraisingly.

You can have it, Danny thought, *and the flat, whatever you fancy.*

'And your kitchen's a nice yellow. Same as the middle of this.' She waggled the flower, almost under his nose.

'I think it's cowslip, the kitchen,' Danny said. 'Or possibly mustard.'

Ellen laughed and started walking to the back door. Danny watched from behind for a second, the dip of her waist and the curve of her ass in her jeans, and then followed, obedient. He felt like skipping. Ellen didn't stop to talk to Rowena and this, Danny noted, was a good sign. It suggested that Rowena had been primed not to interfere if Danny and Ellen went off somewhere. Or maybe she just hadn't noticed: she *was* still talking. Albert was standing beside her and looking like he could, just about, imagine some other place he would less like to be, although he'd need a week or so to think of it. He lifted his eyebrows as Danny walked by to ask him if he was okay. Danny nodded. His eye was throbbing. Somewhere during the proceedings he'd been thumped in the head.

Ian was demonstrating to Geordie some sort of open handed punch to the neck that knocked people out for hours . . . *if your arm's sufficiently twisted . . . finish'em for good*. Geordie was nodding and trying to look calm but his breath was still coming in gulps. Danny thought he heard Ian say *You should have used them* and wondered if he meant the hedge clippers. As he walked through the enlarged group at the bottom of the garden (most of the party seemed to be out here now), he found himself tempted to limp. Someone patted his back but when he turned to speak to them it was a girl he didn't know, holding two bottles of Becks, who just wanted him to move out of her way.

Everyone was drunk inside too. And it was clear the party hadn't gone alfresco, it had just got bigger. Phone calls had been made. Friends of friends had been advised and turned up. Parties are another thing subject to natural selection: a good party thrives and multiplies, a bad one dies out. Ben had now moved on to Philadelphia funk and was playing a stomp with the wonderfully dysfunctional chorus *You can have my husband but please don't mess with my man*.

Ellen stopped in the hall and turned to face Danny just as Clyde appeared from the toilet behind her. He made a leery grin at Danny and then wobbled his enormous head in Ellen's general direction. It was like trying to point with a football. Danny ignored him by squinting slightly and making a confused face. Ellen had moved so close to him that her breasts brushed against his top. They were standing directly under the white paper lampshade and she was staring very intently at his face. Danny suddenly thought *We're about to kiss*. The phrase *Go on my son* arrived from nowhere and settled in his brain. Or maybe Clyde had just said it. Please let Clyde not just have said it. He looked up, but Clyde and his head had both gone. Ellen was still staring at him. She touched his cheek, tilting his head slightly. *This is it* Danny thought. Her lips were plump, budded, open.

'I *knew* it looked funny.'

She tilted his head again, the other way this time so his left cheek was directly under the light. 'You're going to get a black eye. It's already swollen.'

'Oh . . . Yeah, it *is* sore actually. I think Geordie kneed me in the face.'

'You'd better get something frozen on it.'

'I don't think there's any ice left.'

'D'you have any peas in your freezer?'

She strode purposefully off back into the kitchen, pleased to have an objective. Danny touched his left cheekbone exploratively. It felt raw and new and not a part of him. He thought of a terrorist he'd read about in the Sundays recently: this guy had turned state's evidence in Belfast and re-emerged after reconstructive surgery, months later, in the foreign living room of a Plymouth semi-detached. He'd described touching his face like this, amazed and terrified to be alive. Danny remembered the photo of him sitting looking out through the double-glazed windows onto a strange new estate. They'd blacked his eyes out in the picture so it looked, appropriately enough, like he was wearing the blindfold of a condemned man. Danny was still absently tracing his cheek-bone when Ellen arrived back with a saggy unopened bag of frozen petit pois. She held a tea towel in her left hand that Danny's mum had given him when he went off to university. The tea towel had a picture of a tractor on it, pulling a trailer full of pigs across a green hillside. Their quizzical snouts poked out between the trailer's side-bars and the tagline at the bottom read *The Sperrins: where there's time for good things to happen.* Though not to those pigs, Danny invariably thought when he saw it. The strange fact of Ellen being suddenly in his things, in his domestic life, made Danny stop for a second: all these objects that ramified for him now being touched by her. He had always considered the moment the person starts using *your* stuff a certain pivotal stage in the relationship process and now, though he wasn't even seeing Ellen, here she was, casually wringing his tea towels, at ease in his dust and his hallway. And he hadn't wanted her to set his things down somewhere safe and move off swiftly. This was a good sign. Even by the way she quickly folded the tea towel and peas into a bundle, she somehow demonstrated a competence so effortless that it seemed a *style*. She *moved* well, contained and easy. Danny wanted to kiss her, to slide his hand into the absolute fit of her cheek and ear and cup her face like a flame up to his, as if he was lighting his own face from hers, and to kiss her, to taste her, to touch her.

She handed the makeshift compress to him. There was

139

something of the perfect nurse about her, Danny realized. That was part of what it was. Her unfussy capability was soothing: around her he felt that sedative tingle he got in the back of a black cab or when he was having his hair cut. You have nothing to do but keep still and watch. It was like entering sleep's antechamber. He realized he was staring again.

'I might sit in the bedroom then and hold this on my face for a few minutes,' he said, trying to win back some authority. 'We could just sit in there for a while, get out of this madhouse.' Madhouse? *Madhouse?* Stop talking now, he thought.

'All right then. Is there more wine in the fridge?'

'I think so. There's some red in the cupboard beside it if not.'

She was off again, being capable. Ian shouldered past him into the toilet, not pausing or glancing his way. He heard the rasp of the lock slide across. Ellen returned brandishing an opened bottle of red Rioja and two squat brandy glasses he didn't recognize. Holding both glasses in one hand she shook them out – she must have rinsed them – and a drop of water spun off to splatter on the hallway wall. She didn't notice. Danny walked across to his bedroom door and knocked. A girl's voice said, 'Yes?' He turned to Ellen, gave a little shrug.

'Can I come in?' Danny said, feeling ludicrous.

'Yes.'

He opened the door and Claire, Albert's ex, was perched on the edge of his bed beside the chubby pig-tailed blonde. Claire had a gaunt beautiful face but the correspondingly gaunt figure of an eight-year-old boy. Her long brown hair was draped across her features and, as she brought her head up from her knees, Danny saw that she'd removed his framed photograph of George Best from the wall, balanced it on her lap and was employing it to snort coke off. George would be pleased, Danny thought. As Claire flicked her hair back she flashed them a winning and angular grin.

'Daniel, sweetheart, how *are* you? I hope you don't mind us in here.'

Pigtails was already greedily lifting the photograph off Claire's knees and on to her own.

'Claire, long time. Albert said you were here. How've you been? This is Ellen by the way, at M & T as well.'

'I *love* your top. I'm always looking for a fitted white shirt,' Claire said, looking Ellen up and down and then glancing back at Danny and widening her eyes. Ellen smiled at her, but awkwardly.

'I suppose you two want us to leave now?'

'No, no, whenever you're ready. I was . . . I got a black eye, I think, and I was going to hold this . . . ' He lifted up the small bundle of tea towel and peas. Claire looked at it like he had presented her with roadkill, which, in its lumpish wetness, it was beginning to resemble.

'You poor *darling*, Melissa told me all about the fight. Was it awful?'

Presumably Melissa was Pigtails because although her head was now in her lap, a ten pound note sticking out of her nose, she carefully raised her left hand in greeting. The manner in which Melissa then snuffled her head sideways reminded Dan of the pigs on the tea towel.

'Oh your poor eye. Is it *very* sore? But think how manly you'll look, having fought over a girl, and *what* a girl . . . ' Claire said stupidly, coked up to her eye-

141

balls. She stared at Ellen voraciously again. Ellen stepped in slightly behind Danny.

'It wasn't over . . . anyone, Claire. We were just drunk. The whole thing got out of hand. Anyway . . . if you've finished.' He took a step towards the wooden chair in the corner of his room. He'd rescued it from the pavement outside his old flat in Turnpike Lane.

'Danny, how rude of me. Have a line. And you,' – Danny realized she'd already forgotten Ellen's name – 'Both of you. Here.'

She delved into her elegant Indian silk camisole, and on into her redundant bra, and pulled out a small white wrap. She waved it at them. 'Here, here we are.'

Danny was thinking a little line wouldn't go astray, but when he turned to Ellen she was already shaking her head.

'No thanks, not for me,' she said.

'Yeah, no thanks Claire,' Danny repeated.

'*Okay*, well we can see we're superfluous here, can't we?' She looked at Pigtails and then fluttered her fingers around in front of her, playing an invisible piano. Perhaps to signify walking, Danny thought, or maybe she's waving goodbye to the room.

'We can indeed.' Pigtails set the photo frame on top of the chest of drawers, licked her finger and expertly wiped it over the glass, picking up any stray specks of cocaine.

'All right, we're out. Let's leave the lovebirds to it.' Claire grinned and blinked dramatically again, then pouted, kissed Danny on both cheeks and swirled out of the room.

'Was that the coke or was that her?' Ellen said, when the door was closed.

'A little bit of both. She's nice though. Recruitment consultant.'

Ellen nodded in such a serious and sympathetic way that Danny laughed.

The bathroom confirmed the existence of a party. The white floor tiles showed a muddy turbulence of footprints. A single clump of grass and soil had been trampled into the middle of the beige bathmat so that it resembled a scale model of an oasis in a desert. There was no toilet roll on the holder but several pieces were stuck to the tiles, and two full rolls, both sodden for some reason, sat on their ends in the bath. A cigarette butt turned slowly in the toilet bowl and a full glass of red wine stood abandoned by the sink, as though its drinker had caught a glimpse of themselves in the mirror and decided they'd really had enough. A clean silver ashtray was pristine on the windowsill. Ian took his fags out of his Rangers top and lit one. He was getting angry. He'd already sneaked into the boxroom where Geordie's clothes and bag were and rummaged through them. Nothing there but an assortment of stains and a bar of hash. Where had that little gypsy put the money? Ian knocked the toilet seat cover down with the toe of his trainer and sat on it. He'd either have to wait around tonight, which could take for ever, and the gangly lawyer would still be here, or he could come back tomorrow. Danny was off to Belfast in the morning with that black girl. Geordie'd be on his own. Maybe he could invite himself round for lunch and stay 'til he got the cash off him. Only way. Ian flicked his ash on the floor and stood up. He rolled his shoulders in front of the mirror, set his fag in his mouth, and ran his left hand over his number one crop.

143

In Danny's bedroom, Ellen had chosen to sit on the chair in the corner while Danny was attempting to recline in a semi-recumbent posture on the bed, in a manner which seemed both natural and inviting. It was not going well. Ellen was looking around herself and sipping at her wine. Danny was alternating between furiously knocking his Rioja back and dabbing at his face with the soggy parcel of melting peas. Ellen got up from the chair and set her glass on the chest of drawers, beside the photo of George Best. She moved to his bookcase and scanned the shelves. When she reached up to pull a book out – the *Times Atlas*, in fact – her white shirt hitched up and showed the small of her back and the top of her knickers above her dark blue jeans. Her back was taut, hollowed, and a deep brown, the warmest colour conceivable. The glimpse of her knickers showed they were gold. Gold!

'Your knickers are gold.' It was too late. Ellen turned round, her arms folded, the atlas a breastplate behind them.

'My mum gave them to me for Christmas. I didn't buy them. Anyway I like them.'

'I like them too. I was just surprised. You don't see enough gold clothes these days.'

'And why are you looking at them anyway? You're supposed to be covering your eye with that ice. I *was* going to ask you to show me where you're from – in this.' She tapped the atlas twice with her right thumb. Her arms were still folded across it.

'Okay then. C'mere.'

She took one step towards the bed and then looked at him seriously suddenly.

'You know I don't do this with just anyone.'

'Do what? We haven't done anything.'

'Sit on their bed and look after them. I just feel sorry for you.'

'Thanks.'

'Although I don't even *know* you.'

'Of course you know me. You've advised me on the purchase of domestic applicances.'

'Yeah, true. I know you a bit I s'pose,' she cocked her head to one side, pouted and looked at the ceiling. The pose looked practised. Danny smiled and said nothing. She sat down on the other end of his duvet and opened the atlas between them. Countries and colours. He looked at her lips, and then up to her eyes. He wanted to look at her breasts but knew that he shouldn't, or shouldn't get caught. He set the peas and tea towel on the bed-side table. His sleeve and forearm were cold and wet from the melted ice. He lifted the book onto his lap. One page had a map of the island of Ireland. He found it and turned the atlas round to face her. He pointed at his home town.

'Right in the centre. Just to the left of Lough Neagh, the biggest lake in the British Isles. A wee place called Ballyglass.'

Ellen was looking at the map. This isn't exactly flowing, he thought, and went on, 'It's beside where the High Kings of Ulster, the O'Neills, were crowned at Tullyhogue Fort. My house is near there. But there's nothing left now really – just a ring of trees where kids go to get drunk and have sex.' Ellen looked up.

'I thought you'd be near the sea.'

'Well, it's only an hour or so away. Everything in Northern Ireland is only an hour or so away . . . We're going *here* tomorrow.' He tapped Lisamore, a town just outside Belfast.

'This is where Ulster Water is. Have you been to Ulster before?'

'I've never been to Ireland.' Ellen said. She shut the book and rested it on her knees, then made a show of checking her watch, a sensible little wind-up thing with a black leather strap. Am I boring you? Danny thought, irritated that she hadn't asked him about Ballyglass.

'I'd better find Rowena. She'll be wondering about me.'

'Okay,' Danny said quickly, feeling flattened.

'But let's have a look at this eye first.' She leant over him and turned his bedside light on. He could smell the wax she used to straighten her hair. It smelt edible, like coconut.

She pushed the head of the mini-Anglepoise back so it shone on Danny's face. There was already a carmine-coloured spot just below his left eye and the cheek was jaundiced-looking and swollen. Some small dark thing seemed to be trying to break out of his face. She touched his left cheek gently.

'God, your face is *cold*. But you're going to have a black eye tomorrow. Should keep those peas on it.' Her fingers were still on his face. Danny was trying to work out whether it was a purely maternal instinct that kept them there when she swung forward and kissed him swiftly on the other cheek. Then she was up and across the room.

'Right, I'm off to find Rowena and then we're going home.' The door opened and closed and Danny sat on his bed alone. He grinned and touched the swelling on his left cheek, then moved his fingers across to the faint wetness on his right.

146

LATE NIGHT

There are those who know when to go and there are
those who don't. Some people, like Albert, never stay
longer than you want them to, possessing a sixth sense
for the host's wellbeing, for mixing and amusing, for not
becoming too drunk. Most importantly, they order their
own taxis at a suitable time. Others hang about, drifting
from emptying room to emptying room until you've strug-
gled into your pyjamas, picked up your teddy bear, and
manhandled them out the front door. Clyde could
unpeople Egypt, Danny thought, as he watched his cousin
the lummox sitting on the sofa, engrossed in picking his
nose. The living room was empty. Everyone had left.
Even Ben had packed up his decks and gone home. The
furniture was mostly back in its place. Clyde was now
contentedly watching television, an athletics tournament
in Copenhagen. He had made himself a cup of tea and

was eating some crisps he'd found at the back of a cupboard. He'd also, Danny'd noticed, set a Chinese Chicken Pot Noodle on the kitchen counter and Danny was now listening out for whether the kettle was being re-boiled. It might have been four in the afternoon but it wasn't. It was, as Danny had just exclaimed to Clyde in a deliberately surprised tone, four in the morning. The flat was a hell's angels' squat. Danny turned all the lights on in the living room and slowly orbited the planet of Clyde's head, gathering empty bottles and cans from the floor and dropping them into the bin bag he was trailing behind him.

'Do you want to sleep here mate?'

'Yeah.' Clyde was delving into the crisp packet for the last few crisps and slowly licking his fingers. He seemed subdued, as if he'd finally noticed he was alone.

'Do you want a duvet and stuff?'

'Hm-mmm.'

'Geordie?' Geordie was buttering toast in the kitchen, having sobered up into hunger.

'Yeah?'

'Can you kip in the boxroom on cushions from the chairs? If Clyde stays over on the sofa?'

'Yeah.'

Clyde was already asleep and the light in the boxroom was off when Danny came out of the bathroom. After he had set his three identical travel alarm clocks to go off at staggered five minute intervals – one on his bedside table, one on the chest of drawers, and one on top of his suitbag packed and ready by the door – he lay face down on his bed, still fully clothed. His pillows had the smell of old smoke on them. They smelt like Geordie. What on earth was he going to do about him? That fucking monkey story. The hedge clippers. In front of all his friends. He'd have to sleep on it, but to get to that point, there were first the issues of undressing, and of turning off the bedroom light, and even before that was the issue of becoming vertical. As he rolled over to slide off the bed there was a knock at his door, two shy taps, soft as an embarrassed cough.

'Dan?' Geordie, rueful.

'Come on in. I'm still up.'

The door opened and a shrivelled Geordie Wilson entered. He sloped to the bed and balanced neatly on its edge.

'Mate, I've got to be up in . . . ' Danny picked up the bedside alarm clock to look at it, 'three hours – Jesus Christ – to get my flight. If this is about earlier, I *am* sorry, really. It was my fault.'

Geordie was staring straight in front of him, at the far wall. He looked tiny and still and very far away. Danny moved up the bed so he was sitting on the pillows with his back against the wooden headboard. Geordie turned towards him. He had the deferent, hopeful face of a man who's about to try and sell you something.

'I know mate, I know. I went overboard. We were both stoked. And I'm sorry about your eye – that *was* an accident . . . The thing is, there's something else, something I need to talk to you about. And I need to talk to you about it now.'

He stopped, and went back to facing the wall, shrugging a little, as if the room were his cell. His voice dropped a pitch.

'So when I came over . . . when Janice knew I was coming over, she gave me some money.'

'Right.' Danny drew the word out into two syllables.

'It wasn't hers. She found it in the house.'

'Oh yeah?' Danny nods, interested, and then realizes, '*No.*'

Geordie nodded in reply. He was still sitting at right angles to Danny. He set his jaw in a curious way, pushing it over to the right so the teeth were all mismatched, and then sighed and nodded again.

'Yep. Budgie's, and he went ballistic when he found out. Smacking Jan round, smashing the house up, screaming.'

'I'm not surprised. How much are we talking about? You have to give it back. Tell me you've still got it.'

'Oh I have it all right, but I've been thinking. About Jan. She's got herself in such a fucking mess for me. She's not the sharpest tool in the box, but you know, she's been good to me. Not for any reason really. I wasn't so good to her.' Geordie was still staring at a certain patch of the wall like he was reading his speech off it. His voice was a singsong.

'True, true enough.'

'So I thought maybe she could come back with you, back to London.'

'*What?* Why does she have to come back with me? Why don't *you* go back and get her – or get her to come over by herself?' Danny sat forward and the headrest knocked against the wall.

'Sure how can *I* go home? I'd be dead the moment I set foot in the town. Dan I've never *flown* before. I couldn't get in one of those planes. I thought you could bring the money back and swap it for her. There's no way Budge would let her leave *before* he got the cash and to be honest I can't see him letting her leave *after*. It has to be a swap. You just have to pick her up and put her on the plane with you on Sunday.'

'Mate, she's not a fucking carrier bag . . . ' They both sat very still for a few seconds and stared at their hands. Danny started again. 'So hold on. You want me to just see Budgie Johnson and say *Oh by the way here's the stolen money – Geordie's awfully sorry about that – He went a bit mental – Can I have your sister now? Cheers* . . . Wise up.'

'You could do that. You could do that easy.'

'And where does she stay? *Here?*'

'Only for a wee while Dan, like only for a few days. We could kip in the boxroom. Do it up nice. She's a trooper Dan, honest to god. She'd be helpful, good to have around the place.'

'Jesus, Geordie. I'm going to Belfast to do due diligence on a takeover. I'm a lawyer, not the Scarlet fucking Pimpernel . . . I'm not even a good lawyer.' Danny lowered his voice for the last sentence, sat back against the headrest again.

'Danny, it's a *wee* thing, a wee favour,' he looked up at Danny and did the bloodhound gape – big eyes, dark rings, dolorous. 'We go back, you and me, big man, we have history.'

Danny looked intently at Geordie's profile and said nothing. There was something unsaid here. The word *history* held the shock of a gunshot. Did Geordie mean Hughes? Was that the history they shared? They'd never spoken of it. Danny watched Geordie pick a fleck of tobacco off his white T-shirt and drop it on the wooden floor. Then he started to chew on a ragnail on his left hand. He rearranged himself, crossing his right leg across his left knee. His unusual period of stillness was over. Back was Mister Fidget with his metaphysical itch.

'Look, maybe I *could* drive down on Sunday morning and pick Janice up. You could just get her to meet me, keep it a secret from Budgie, and then after she gets here, you could send the money over by courier or money transfer or something. On Monday morning say. I'm *not* carrying it. You can send him a fucking postal order.'

'Well if you're going to pick her up you might as well take the money. Just give it to Budgie or leave it at the house . . . '

'How much is it?'

'Near on fifty.'

'Fifty what?'

'Fifty grand.'

'*Fifty grand?* You took fifty grand of Budgie Johnson's money. No way mate. I'm not carrying fifty grand around and certainly not across to Belfast on the plane. And I'm not going to Budgie's house with it. You can arrange for me to pick Janice up somewhere, and get her to keep it completely quiet. Budgie isn't going to be watching her every minute. We can do it early on Sunday morning. But I'm not taking the money. *Seriously*. You can send it to him after.'

'All right . . . Good man. I'll ring her in the morning.'

'You need to get her on the three o'clock flight from Belfast City Airport to Heathrow. It's British Midland and it'll be expensive.'

'Three o'clock. Okay. Thanks mate.'

'Listen, there's a spare set of keys in the drawer under the coffee table. You can use those when I'm away. I need to go to sleep now.'

Danny pushed his curtain aside to look out and the room was turned a little paler by the dawn light. Cars were huddled along the street and a large tomcat was trotting up the pavement, its sleek back moving like a wavelength. Everything was a shade of grey, overwashed and exhausted.

'Yep. Sorry I kept you up. Have a good time at home.'

Geordie walked to the door, still springy and light on his feet. Danny had decided just to fall asleep as he was.

'Turn the light off please.'

'Aye . . . Here, Dan?'

'What?'

'What do you reckon he's going to spend it on?'

'I don't know.'

'D'you reckon it's drugs?'

Danny's voice came from the pillow.

'I reckon I don't care.'

The market has no morality.

Michael Heseltine

SATURDAY, 10 JULY 2004

The taxi was late. Danny was sitting on the arm of the sofa, dressed in his smartest pinstripe and sporting, jaunty as a carnation in his buttonhole, a big black eye. It was nearly perfectly round and ranged in colour from the ripe purple of a damson to an apricot's pearly yellow. His face was a well-stocked fruit bowl. In the shower earlier he realized he needed to think of a good excuse for his bruise. He'd considered two options: the kitchen cupboard or the heroic intervention. He still hadn't decided. He felt like shit. Clyde was in the bathroom, doing what he termed his *ablutions*. After Clyde had spent ten minutes explaining how Hounslow was actually on the way to Heathrow, Danny'd agreed to take him somewhere west in the taxi and drop him off near a tube station. Now the taxi was outside sounding his horn and Clyde was still abluting.

After they'd climbed into the cavernous black cab, which seemed appropriately sized for Clyde's head, as if the vehicle had been adapted specially for him, the cabbie drove off. A few houses down Danny saw a white transit van parked by the kerb. A guy in a sky-blue base-ball cap was sitting slumped in the far corner of the front seat. Clyde was discussing Pigtails' breasts and how near he had come to *unleashing* them. 'You're an animal,' Danny said placidly, looking out the window.

Ian had been parked outside Danny's for thirty min-utes. He'd been considering going in when the taxi had pulled up and tooted, so he'd waited. The grey sky was heaped up with clouds. All of the streetlights clicked off together suddenly and other lights came on in the houses, singly, like stars. A bedroom window was raised by a Rastafarian wearing an alice band, a Turkish woman dragged a pushchair over a doorstep and onto the street before going back into her house. She re-appeared a second later carrying a large package shaped like a child, so substantially bundled there was just a slit left for two eyes to peer darkly out. She fastened it into the chair, locked her door and strode off wheeling the buggy. Then Danny came out of his house swinging his suit bag, and that cousin of his who wouldn't shut up all night was tramping behind him, still talking. Danny's eye looked mashed up. The cab drove past and Ian slinked down in his seat. He got out and locked the van. To business.

The doorbell was ringing and ringing and in Geordie's dream it was a phone that he couldn't find, hidden some-where in his old bedroom in Ballyglass. He jumped from his single bed, tugged open his wardrobe, the door of which still stuck after these twenty-odd years, and ripped all the clothes out of it. The shelves held piles of shirts, folded, soft as flags, and of every colour imaginable, which he knew he had never owned or even seen but which, in dream-logic, he understood to be his. Flurries of them fell onto his feet, a rainbow of silks and soft cottons, and as he delved further into the cupboard he could see more and more of them stacked up behind, lemon and cobalt and ivory, then checked and striped and embroidered like blouses, and still others of lace and damask, calico, satin, stiff linen. And the ringing continued. If he could just find the phone he could get out of this room. He woke with a jolt. There was a second's delay before he knew where he was. Then the doorbell went again, two rings, pause, two rings. He stood up gingerly, one hand against the wall, and then jerked open the door of his room so hard that it banged. He shouted, 'Danny, your cab's here.'

The door banging had echoed in his head, and it hurt it still further to shout. The flat was heavy with silence. He stage-whispered 'Danny . . . Clyde?' then tugged on his jeans and walked down the hall to the door. He opened the snib and Ian kicked the door so hard that it smashed into Geordie's forehead. He clutched his temples with both hands, like a See No Evil monkey, and pulled the palms apart in time to watch Ian enter and neatly close the door behind him.

'*Fucking* hell.'

'Morning Geordie. You and me are going to have a little chat.' The word *chat* was staccato, a punctuation point. Ian shoved him into the living room and pointed to the sofa. Geordie sat down. Ian leaned against the table looking at him.

157

'Fucking stinks in here. Did you sleep in here? It fucking stinks.'

'No . . . Did I piss you off last night?'

Ian snorted and stared hard at him.

'Well, did you forget something?'

'Yeah, I forgot to get the *fifty grand* you owe me.'

Geordie experienced a kind of inner freefall. His throat landed in his stomach, his stomach dropped into his knees, and his bowels tried to escape to his ankles. He attempted to keep a steady face. Ian said, softer, 'I know about the cash Geordie. I know you took it from Budgie. Well you have to give it back to me. Right now and right here. So let's make this easier on both of us and you just pay up like a good wee fella and then I can go home and have my cup of tea.'

Geordie's stomach was still leaden with dread but he decided, almost as a reflex reaction, to try to bluff it.

'I don't know what you're on about Ian. I don't know anything about any money or who Budgie . . . '

The sound of bone meeting flesh is always lower in pitch than you remember. It sounds like a pack of flour dropped on a tiled kitchen floor. Ian had stepped across the room and punched Geordie in the chest. Although it was an ungainly movement – Geordie was sitting on the sofa and therefore too low for Ian to get a decent purchase – it was sufficient to cause Geordie to sob. It sounded like laughter. Ian stood over him.

'Give me the fucking money Geordie.'

Ian cuffed him on the ear, almost fatherly.

'I was going to give it back. I'm *going* to give it back when Janice comes over, as soon as she gets to London.'

Ian sniggered adolescently.

'Who the fuck's Janice? Geordie, I don't think you get it. I need the money *now,* in *London*. Budgie was looking after it for me. You were unlucky to meet me, that's all. Ulster's a wee place.'

Geordie looked up. He started to repeat, in a miniature voice, 'I *don't* have . . . ' but Ian was lifting his hand again.

'*All right.* All right. It's under the bath. I'll get it. I'll get it now.'

Geordie scrambled to his feet and Ian followed him, sighing, paternally patient. Geordie fished his keys out of his jeans and squatted down to work at the side of the bath. Ian felt relaxed. He leant against the sink. Geordie'd just made a mistake. But now, by working together, they'd been able to fix it.

'You see Geordie, this money's important.' Then he added, as an afterthought, 'Anything the 'RA can do we can do better.'

'Right,' said Geordie as the panel edged open. He lay down on the floor on his front, halfway in and halfway out of the bathroom, and reached in under the bath. His chest held the dull ache of Ian's punch and his forehead was already swelling.

'Here it is.' Geordie pulled out the white plastic bag filled with money. It was dusty and had ripped on something.

'Excellent. I'll take that.' Ian leaned down and snatched it. Geordie was on his knees, one elbow leaning on the bath. The cold tap had a droplet of water hanging from it. He watched it elongate then draw in its waist and wobble. It broke off and hit the enamel with a wet click. Ian jiggled the bag. 'Let's count this out shall we?'

159

Geordie levered himself up from the floor as Ian sat heavily down on the sofa and emptied the bag onto the coffee table. He started arranging the notes in piles. Geordie looked at himself in the bathroom mirror. His forehead was a red bump and you could see he'd been crying. He entered the living room and sat down on one of the dining chairs.

'Now, let's see what we got. Make us a cup of tea Geordie. Just milk, no sugar.'

When Geordie came back into the living room carefully carrying the brimmed mug of tea, Ian had the money in three neat piles, all with the Queen's head on top. There was her imperturbable smile, her mute watchfulness. No one has seen what money has seen. All those arguments she must have witnessed, those atrocities she must have caused. A Helen of Troy, 2-D, with pin curls and thin lips. Starter of wars. He docked the tea gently on a black slate coaster beside the banknotes.

'I make forty-nine thousand, three hundred. How much did you spend of it?'

'None, nothing at all.' This was not strictly true. Geordie had spent almost two hundred quid. He sat down again on the dining chair beside the TV.

'I'll be checking with Budgie.'

'Ask him, he'll tell you.'

Ian leant back on the sofa and looked at Geordie. Putting his hands behind his head, he crossed his ankles, so completing his favorite pose: The Man at Home in the World.

'You see, a man has to work out what he wants from his life. For example, what do *you* want from life?'

You leaving would be a start, Geordie thought, but mindful of his injuries, he nodded, looked pensive, and replied, 'What everyone does, I suppose. A nice house, nice car, a nice wife.'

'Not everyone wants that. There's bigger things. There are some of us who'll do whatever it takes to protect the rights of our friends and our families.' Ian was smiling grandiosely.

'Do you see what I'm saying Geordie?'

'Not really.' Geordie was touching his chest tenderly now, checking for all of his ribs.

'Look at this *cunt* who lives here. *Danny*.' Ian made such a face when he pronounced Danny's name that it seemed he was picking the word out of his teeth. 'He doesn't care about Northern Ireland, or give a fuck about anything but his own life, about making money for big business, about buying a bigger flat, buying more *crap* to fill it.' He looked around the room disdainfully. 'The crimes those big corporations commit . . . he's just a foot soldier for them.'

Geordie nods. He tries, gently, 'I suppose he just wants an easy life.'

'Yeah well, the life of a turncoat *is* pretty easy. Pandering to the English while they betray his country. He's been bought.' Ian brought his arms from behind his head and folded them across his chest.

'He's been in England for years. I don't see how the *English* betray . . . ?'

He was cut off by Ian sitting forward suddenly, and raising his voice, 'Of course they fucking do. They think they can walk all over us, that our rights as British citizens are some kind of fucking gift from them. You did

161

well to beat the shit out of him last night. Look at this place. Look at his friends. Who the fuck does he think he is?'

'Right.'

'He's just some fucking twat from Ballyglass. Did you hear his poncy accent? Sounds like he was fucking born and bred in Kent or somewhere.'

Ian was getting himself exercised into a fury now. Geordie sat quietly and watched. He took a couple of slow breaths through his flaring nostrils and the rage seemed to subside. Watching him it was apparent to Geordie that this was a technique Ian used for controlling his anger. He must have learned it at her Majesty's pleasure in Maghaberry or the Maze. Ian leaned back on the sofa, and smiled, reasonable again.

'The way it goes, Geordie, is that the squeaky wheel gets the grease. You know it, I know it, and the Irish Republican Army certainly fucking know it. And how they've squeaked. Squeak squeak squeak. Well we should squeak for a while. Our turn.'

'Okay.'

'You see I'm a contractarian, Geordie.' He waited, staring, until Geordie nodded.

'As *I* see it, the state has a relationship with its citizens, *whoever* those citizens are, Protestants, taigs, blacks like those ones last night,' – he waved a hand expansively – 'or whoever. The point is this . . . ' – suddenly noticing he hadn't touched his tea, he leaned forward and carefully picked it up. 'The point is this, a right is a *right* and not the *gift* of whatever government's in power. Our loyalty's to the *Union*, not to the English . . . and that Union's defined as people united *not* by religion, or race, or whatever, but by recognition of the *authority* of that union ... Are you with me here wee man?'

'I am. I am, Ian. You're on to something there.' For God's sake go, Geordie thought.

As if he'd heard his thoughts, Ian suddenly seemed embarrassed to still be there, and talking so volubly. The anger flicked back into him like voltage.

'I'm trying to *educate* you. Someone like you could have been something, instead of a snivelling feckless little thief. You could have made a difference.'

'Yes.' Geordie nodded, agreeing to everything to get him to leave.

'Anyway, you are what you are. Pity.'

Ian stood up and Geordie did too. Then Ian shrugged, a minuscule relaxation of his ox-shoulders, and Geordie mirrored the action. He was like Ian's wobbly skinny reflection in a playground mirror. Geordie had a momentary urge to offer his hand, feeling obscurely that their transaction had been a success.

'I'll see myself out.' Ian nodded at him, workmanlike.

'Okay.' Geordie sat back down on the chair. He folded his arms, feeling shattered and oddly embarrassed.

On the street a female black parking attendant was standing by Ian's van. She was wearing a too-big official jacket and a cap that came down low on her head. It made Ian think of a child dressed up in her father's livery, or those African women called up to fight who have to wear a male uniform. She was writing the registration details of Ian's van into an electronic clipboard. Ian slammed the front door behind him and walked over to her. He was smiling broadly.

'All right? Just had to nip in there for a second, bring some groceries round to my nan? Yeah? She's very sick. Can't walk.' He touched his right leg as if to confirm it.

'Sir,' the traffic warden sounded tired but spoke very precisely, 'your car has been parked here for over fifteen minutes. I first noticed the vehicle parked at 8.32 and it's now,' she tapped her pen against the LED display, '8.48 a.m.' Ian strode up to her, stared in her face, menacingly at first, before switching to an unpleasant grin. He said, 'Fair enough. The law's the law,' and gently took the ticket she was holding out before getting into the van.

Black cabs are to cars as cathedrals to houses. It is partly the vaulted roofs, the spare air and the silence, but most importantly it's the meditative aura they encourage. They provoke an impulse not to do but to be. When you get in a cab you'll find out what's bothering you. It will rise to the surface. And Danny was snared in contemplation. Staring vacantly out at a London so quiet it was as if the mute button was pressed. He'd dropped Clyde off at West Acton. His black eye, in the clean light of outside, had shifted to a predominance of primrose and violet shades. His face was an amateur flower arrangement. He picked at a dried fleck of food on his tie. He hated his job.

Each of the other check-in queues for British Midland was inching forward and when it became clear that he'd chosen the wrong one and should change lines, someone else would appear and bustlingly join the queue he was about to move into. One of the lines was disappearing so fast it seemed to be staffed by Mr B. Midland himself.

Danny's queue on the other hand, chosen for its apparent shortness (the first mistake!), was behind a desk manned by a very stoned twelve-year-old with numeracy issues. Three times the couple at the head of his queue had repeated *No, three bags* to his wide-eyed and pitted face. They were a beautiful couple, all glossy like something from an advert, and had now turned sideways to the desk, allowing Danny to watch them in profile. The husband was standing behind his wife, whispering into her ear. She giggled like a geisha, shyly, behind her hand.

Danny had arranged to meet Ellen in the check-in queue at terminal one but had seen when he arrived that there was more than one line, and that they weren't all within sight of each other. He had to keep leaving his bag and ducking out under a red velveteen rope to get to a clear view of the others. Standing out in the open he heard Ellen before he saw her, a repetitive clipping sound on the marble floor. She was pulling a neat black bag on wheels behind her and looking very seriously at him.

'Good morning.'

'Good morning. You look very smart.'

'I'm worn out. Oh your eye's awful. You look like a hooligan.'

'I don't feel too clever either.' Danny moved towards her to kiss her on the cheek but she'd bent her head to retract the extended handle on her bag. Danny found his nose an inch or so from the top of her skull. He could see the line on her scalp where her hair was parted. It wasn't quite straight. He pulled back.

'No, I don't expect you do.' She looked up again at him, puzzled at his nearness, and then glanced around her. That bored thing again. Danny followed the direction of her stare but saw nothing distracting.

'So, have you got the files? Shall we check in? My suit bag's already in the queue.'

'All in there.' She nodded at her own bag, now brought to heel.

*   *   *

On the plane they'd independently decided to sleep. This solved the problem of discussing last night, any of it, and they were both exhausted anyway. Danny had been careful to let her have the arm rest but in the event she'd simply leant against the window and dozed off immediately. He imagined she was the kind of person who never had any trouble sleeping. He could hear her breathing soften into a regular rise and fall. It struck Danny as oddly intimate to listen to it. He looked over at her, keeping his face angled forward as much as possible in case she should open her eyes. She was wearing a trouser suit, black with a faint chalkstripe, and under it a pink shirt, the wide double cuffs of which poked out from under her jacket sleeves, emphasizing the slimness of her wrists. A thin gold chain lay loosely round her throat and her hair looked polished, delicately straight, as if touching it would break it. Her lips had the plush sheen of gloss on them and were in a petulant pout. Her nose was wide and trimly flat and her lashes thick. Mascara, Danny thought and remembered Olivia had put some on his eyelashes once. They'd been getting ready to go out to a New Year's Eve party, laughing in his bathroom. He'd been quite taken with it. He glanced back over at Ellen's figure, feeling a tinge of guilt for doing so but knowing that just looking at her would block out the thought of Olivia. Her thighs were slim but solid beside his own, and almost as long as his. He picked up the British Midland magazine and looked at an article on basket-weaving. There was no way he could sleep.

At Belfast City Airport it was raining heavily. Behind the Avis desk sat a fat woman with short black hair and a skinny bald man. They were each about fifty and sitting, through necessity, very close together. They looked like an unhappily married couple waiting to get in some-where, a divorce court perhaps. As Danny and Ellen walked over to them Danny had already, in his head, christened them Jack Sprat and his wife. The lady, who could eat no lean, hauled herself up when they got to the desk, evidently excited to have customers.

'Hello. It's under Williams. We're to collect a car until tomorrow.'

'I'm Jackie and if you have any questions about . . . '

Danny had accidentally knocked her speech off course. She gave a tiny grimace and looked at her desk.

'All right. Can you fill this out please?' She pushed a pink form across the counter. Her fingernails were a darker pink against it and were too raised from the skin to be real.

The car was a silver Ford Focus and seemed in good nick. Danny had forgotten how the Northern Irish regis-tration system worked so he couldn't figure out how old it was. It bothered him that he couldn't remember. He used to sit up straight in the back seat and tell his can-didly uninterested parents the county and year of each car going past. Danny hated forgetting things, something he knew was due partly to his upbringing: memory being much more prized in Northern Ireland than intelligence.

Danny got behind the wheel without hesitation. He had been thinking about driving at home on the plane and was looking forward to it. Ellen put her bag in the back and got into the front. Maybe he should have asked her whether she wanted to drive. He looked over to offer but she was pulling her seat belt across and humming some tinny pop song that had been playing in the terminal. The first time they'd been in a car together. Again he felt that odd twinge of chance intimacy. The seat belt was pushing against her breasts. Danny briefly imagined that this was his wife and they were driving home from their honeymoon. He felt deflated suddenly and wound the window down to let a little air in.

When they had circled the car park twice and still couldn't find the exit Ellen started giggling. After their third orbit Danny asked her to stop. She nodded and bit her lip, but little bubbles of laughter kept escaping. She almost seemed to be nervous. He needed to get out onto the road and turn the radio on. Getting to Lisamore should be pretty easy – through Antrim and follow the signs. A man appeared in front of them suddenly, dressed entirely in yellow waterproofs and a yellow plastic fisherman's hat. His outfit inexplicably caused Danny to think of ducks. He waved them frantically towards a gap in a row of parked cars and pointed. Danny waved back, 'They don't want us to leave. That's Northern Ireland all over.'

In the car they listened to Cool FM, the province's premier popular music station. Danny had spent years in his bedroom listening to Cool Goes Quiet every evening with the lights out. It was an hour of saccharine love songs between eleven and twelve. Danny hadn't liked it for the music but instead for the maudlin stories that lay behind each of the song requests. A million different case histories. *Sean has been cheated on by Sharon but he is leaving her anyway for Jennifer. This is from Jen to her man Sean. 'I'm not in love . . . so don't forget . . . '* That kind of thing. Sometimes people rang up and recited their tragic histories down the phone, times and dates of heartbreaks at the ready. Fifteen years later and Cool FM was now a dance music station with a DJ who shouted and laughed continually. Mary J. Blige came on and Danny noticed that Ellen was doing a tiny shoulder shimmy to the music. She leaned forward and turned the volume up.

AFTERNOON

The rain had stopped by the time they arrived in Lisamore and found Ulster Water's headquarters. It was a squat grey building surrounded by pebbledashed houses, and had the evening shadow of a large tarmacked car park, empty now except for seven or eight cars clustered by the entrance. They were all Mondeos and Astra Estates, vehicles for mid-ranking executives, and each sat neatly by a low signpost planted in the grass verge. Danny pulled into the first spot lacking a sign, beside the Deputy Finance Director's empty space, and turned the engine off. He looked out through the windscreen at the sky. It seemed to hang precariously low over the drab office block. Danny opened the back door and removed a slim leather business folder he had brought in his suit bag. Across the seat from him Ellen had opened the other door and was sorting out files.

'I hope the Deputy Finance Director hasn't gone too

far. I might want to see him.' Realizing how arrogant this sounded, Danny added, looking up at her, 'Although I'm sure his secretary'll do.'

'Or hers,' Ellen said brightly.

'Of course, or hers.' Danny stood upright then and placed the documents folder between his knees in order to perform what Albert termed *the preliminary shooting of the cuffs*: he pulled one white cuff down below the sleeve of his pinstriped jacket, as far as it would comfortably go, and repeated the manoeuvre with the other cuff, this time pushing his chunky diving watch under it. He fastened the middle button of his single-breasted. Ellen was beside him, having put her coat back on. They looked well-mannered and ruthless, although Danny's shiner tinged their efficiency with a surreal *Clockwork Orange* atmosphere. As they walked across the tarmac to the door, Danny suddenly pulled Ellen to a stop by the elbow. 'What's the name of the MD again?'

'Shannon, Jack Shannon.'

'Of course. Good, good.'

Danny's nervousness could appear aggressive and he had to remind himself before he went into any meeting, never mind a hostile company's headquarters, that these people were just, as he was, doing a job. But he was going to be firm and professional. His first trainer's mantra, *Never apologize, never explain,* ran through his mind. Wetting his lips as a preliminary to speech, he pushed open the glass door. To business.

Mr Jack Shannon was in a wheelchair. This was the first surprise, although it shouldn't have been, as Ellen reminded Danny, or at least no more of a surprise than that registered by Mr Shannon when a black woman introduced

herself to him. He blinked twice and was late with his
smile. The second surprise was how fast Mr Shannon's
wheelchair could go. He whizzed along the corridor in
front of them, shouting incomprehensible orders. Danny
couldn't tell whether the instructions were for them or the
workers sporadically dotted in offices along the corridors.
It was all he could do to keep him in eyeshot.

'Mr Shannon, excuse me . . . '

Danny was praying they'd hit some stairs soon. That
would slow him down. At one point it seemed they'd
lost him but he suddenly glided alongside them, now
with a large bottle of Ballygowan water nestled in his
lap. He disappeared again after finessing a tricky chicane
made by two piles of boxes but when they rounded the
next corner there he was, halted outside two silver lifts.
He was twisting around in the wheelchair and staring
irritably over his shoulder at them.

'I have to go in one of these. You can take the staircase. Fifth floor.'

'We're happy to go up with you,' Danny said amiably.

'No room.' He had pushed his chair right up against
the lift and was staring straight ahead at the metal door.
They started on the stairs.

'So you two work for Syder, do you?' said Mr Shannon.
He was sitting on one side of a huge round desk, flanked
by three other men. All four were facing them. Ellen and
Danny, nodding hello, had just entered the room. Having
climbed the five floors Danny could feel each of the
cigarettes he'd smoked the night before unionizing against
his lungs. He felt overheated. Ellen had reset into her
default mode of inscrutable composure.

'Not for Syder, no. We work for Monks & Turner, Syder's solicitors.'

'In Belfast?' Shannon again.

'No, in London actually.'

'We had some Australian here for a couple of weeks looking through files. He was from Monks & Turner. But you're a local boy, aren't you?' The three other heads made tiny nods of agreement.

'I am. Ballyglass.'

'My wife's from Ballyglass.' The pleasant-looking forty-year-old to Shannon's right had spoken. He had an unfashionable moustache and reminded Danny of a footballer from the nineteen-eighties, though he couldn't think which one.

'Oh right.' I don't want to have this conversation, Danny thought.

'What's your name?' Shannon again.

'I'm Danny Williams and this is Ellen Powell.'

'Williams. Do you know it?' Ignoring Ellen, who had started to say hello, Shannon turned to the footballer.

'Well there's quite a few Williamses around Bally ... ' Danny started to say but the footballer cut him off, 'Anything to the estate agent, Mark Williams?'

Danny nodded, fourteen again, caught mucking around by an adult.

'I'm his son.'

'He sold my father-in-law's house. Nice man. Very helpful he was. But you're in London are you?'

'I am. I'll let my dad know you said hello, Mr ... ?'

'McManus, though he'll know my wife's family, the Connollys. Her father's Tom.'

'*Tom Connolly*,' Danny's voice had unexpectedly

pitched itself at castrato. He hastily dropped it to gruff-
ness. 'Sure I know him myself. He used to take us for
Scouts on a Tuesday night.'

'That's right. Still does as far as I know.'

'Small world.' Danny was smiling now despite himself. Northern Ireland. Forget about six degrees of
separation. Everyone in Ulster was just a person away,
sitting on their other side, waiting to lean forward and
say hello.

'It is that.' Shannon looked happier anyway. He
pointed at his own face with one hooked finger. 'You
get thumped on the plane or something?' Danny forced
a short laugh.

'No, no, I caught my head on a cupboard.' He had
spoken too quickly for it to sound truthful. *Caught my
head?* What a ludicrous phrase. He tried to salvage it.
The four men were staring at him, looking more interested about this than they had about anything else.

'I was bending down to get something, and I stood
up. Caught my head.' *Stop saying 'caught my head'.*

'I snagged my face,' *Snagged my face?* 'on the door of
the cupboard. Pretty painful.' Danny reached up and
touched his eye. It felt puffy.

'Looks like you were thumped.' Shannon said defiantly. The footballer nodded in considered agreement.

'Well, anyway, shall we get started? Have you a room
put aside that we can use?' Danny brought his hands
together as if to pray, but quickly, with the result that
they made an unexpectedly loud clap. Ellen flinched and
the MD looked at him with open bemusement.

*   *   *

175

On Kilburn High Road, where things get arranged and sold in pubs, there is a café on a corner that has started to rival the taverns as a place to do business. It has established itself as a favoured haunt of the East Europeans who've pitched up to replace the influx of Irish. It may be that the café's synthetic cream reminds them of the kind used in the monstrous confections sold in Warsaw and Prague. It also may be that the large glass façade, which comprises both the front and one whole side of Pastry Nice, allows nervous men a safe and open meeting place.

Ian had chosen a table for four in the glass corner of the café. An empty coffee cup sat in front of him. Although he was trying very hard to keep still, his leg was jiggling. The coffee, which he normally rejected as a domestic drug, had made him jumpy, but the café had no orange juice and he refused to pay for mineral water. The queue that had formed behind him by the time he reached the cash desk looked like an ID parade for a crime that had been committed by Lech Walesa. Is there a collective noun for moustaches? There was a gaggle of moustaches behind him in the queue. Ian paused to consider whether he could ask for just a glass of tap water but then quickly ordered a coffee, and so his leg was now jumping and the Poles would think he was nervous. He was waiting for two brothers, Bartosz and Tomek. Or Bartek and Tomasz. He couldn't remember, although he had written it down in the exercise book he'd left, stupidly, at the hotel. When he'd returned from seeing Geordie he'd rang Budgie, exercised in his room, showered, slept for ninety minutes, and then dressed. Ian emphasized function and serviceability in his wardrobe choices. Today he was wearing straight cut stonewashed jeans (too narrow and tight to be fashionable), a tucked-in white shirt (with button-down collars), a black leather belt, and brown leather shoes. He had a denim jacket, which almost matched, and which he'd placed on the seat beside him.

About four years ago he had done business with an antiques dealer in Yorkshire, a bald, bespectacled man, pious and stealthy as a verger. The Selby man's indulgences appeared to be bow ties and sherry but he had also a less obvious interest in weapons. He was a quartermaster to the underworld. He had sold Ian twelve deactivated handguns, fifteen deactivated rifles and a deactivated submachine gun, plus the tools and manuals to re-convert them back to weapons. Ian had found him through a small classified ad in an issue of *Guns & Ammo*. The advert detailed a weapons list and stressed the simplicity of the conversion kits. Ian didn't know if it was legal or not but it was an improbably easy way to buy guns. He had assumed bringing them back would cause him more trouble, at least until Cleaver the Yorkshireman had offered to arrange their delivery for ten per cent of the weapons' cost. It had all been remarkably smooth. Cleaver, when contacted last year about further objects of desire, had promised to supply Ian with a phone number, but he would have to call for it at the house. Ian had obediently done so on Thursday, taking a cup of tea with Cleaver's senile wife who had started to cry as he left. That evening, parked at a Welcome Break motorway service station near Watford, he had phoned the number and made the arrangements. This was the result. Pastry Nice at 1 p.m.

Budgie had been pathetic on the phone. He couldn't focus on the events in hand. An amateur mind, Ian thought, and when he had asked him who Janice was, his reaction was completely unprofessional. He'd got really wound up.

'My wee sister. The one who took the money.'

'Ach of course, I should have realized that.'

'Why? What'd he say about her?'

'I think she's coming over to meet him.'

'She fucking *isn't*.'

'I'm just saying what he said.'

'The *fucking* bitch.'

'We'll talk when I get back.'

'Fucking *bitch*.'

'Budgie, we'll talk when I get back.'

* * *

Geordie hadn't wanted to call him. He hated being made to look stupid. He was always the fall guy and the whipping boy and the scapegoat. And this had turned out no differently. He had to tell Danny that the money had gone back to them, to Budgie and Ian, and he had to ring Janice and tell her to get ready to leave, but he couldn't find his mobile. Surely someone hadn't nicked it? They'd all dressed nice and had that healthy shine that money gives. Geordie rang his own number with Danny's terrestrial phone. One of Danny's shoes in the boxroom started vibrating. It must have fallen off the shelf and landed in it.

Across the Irish Sea Danny was cheerful. It turned out Scott, the Australian, had been both methodical and industrious, and there were only eight boxes of contracts for them to index and review. They should easily be finished by five. Danny was sitting in a large meeting room at the back of the building. From it you could see the Lisamore River, a few hundred metres away in open countryside. When his phone rang he'd excused himself from the two Ulster Water admin staff that were searching for missing documents, and moved across to the window. The river looked solid and grey in the afternoon light, like a road winding through the fields. He didn't recognize the number displayed on his phone.

'Hello?'

'Dan, it's Geordie.'

'All right mate.'

'You know Ian?'

'The bloke from last night?'

'Yeah. It turns out he knows Budgie.'

'You're *joking*.'

'No joke, and he's just been round here and tore me to ribbons. Smacked me in the face with the front door . . . ' Geordie sniffed, reminded.

'Fuck. Did he get the money?' Danny was suddenly aware of the other occupants of the room. Ellen was next door but the two administrators, both fifty-something women, were looking at him horrified. One of them was clutching the cross that hung around her neck. Danny nodded at them, smiled reassuringly, and stepped into the corridor. He hadn't heard Geordie's reply.

'*Well*? Did he get the money?'

'I said yeah. I tried to bluff him, tell him I didn't have it but he's a *fucking* animal. My chest . . . I think he might have broke one of my ribs.'

'You'll be all right. Is my door okay?'

'Fuck off. Your door's fine.'

'What about the rest of the flat, did he break anything?'

Geordie grimaced.

Danny edged back solemnly into the meeting room.

'Sorry about that.' Danny waved the mobile phone at them.

'Everything all right love?' one of the admin assistants asked.

'Yeah . . . It was my brother . . . He just got mugged.' Danny figured, on the hop, that this would both explain his question and excuse his swearing.

'Margaret! Did you hear that?'

'Mugged! *Dear* god. Is he all right?' Margaret had heard and was clutching her cross again.

'Oh no he's fine, just a bit shaken up.'

Sometimes a lie echoes until it becomes deafening.

'Where did it happen? Has he reported it?' Margaret had now set her file down on the table and was just looking straight at Danny.

'I think he's sorting it out now.'

'Where was he dear?' the other one spoke again. Stouter, and perhaps slightly older, she had the centred, confident air of a matriarch.

'Um . . . in Belfast. He was in Belfast, in the centre.'

'In the city centre. On a *Saturday* afternoon. I suppose it's the twelfth weekend. Lots of rowdies,' Margaret said and nodded to her friend, who was already nodding sympathetically at Danny. Just to complete the round, Danny nodded at Margaret. She looked distraught and went on, 'Would you believe it?'

No, not sure I would, Danny thought, and felt the prickly heat of guilt.

'Whereabouts in the centre was he, love?' The matriarch, picking up the baton.

'Just . . . in the very centre . . . by the shops.' Danny

was trying to think of the name of the big glass-roofed shopping mall, but he couldn't remember it.

'Near Castlecourt, was it love?'

'Yes, just by there. I don't know too much about it in fact. Only a short phone call. He's very upset.'

'I'm sure he is.' Margaret again.

This was like talking to two of his aunts. There was a pause and Danny thought it was over. He tried to think of a way to draw them back to their work but . . .

'Does he live in Belfast dear, your brother?' The matriarch spoke. Her dyed-brown hair was thinning, Danny noticed. He looked down at the top of his pad where he'd written the names. Margaret and Lillian.

'Yes, Lillian, he does.' In fact he used to *have* a great-aunt called Lillian. She'd smelt of soap and hadn't looked unlike this one.

'Is he working there?'

'Studying. He's at Queens.'

After glancing at Margaret, Lillian said, 'My Stephen's at Queens. What does he study?'

Just then Ellen opened the door of the meeting room, a large box of documents balanced on her hip.

'Here, I'll take that.' Danny walked over and lifted the box from her.

'Thanks. There seems to be a whole set of Intellectual Property contracts missing. I can't find any which are post-1990.' Danny looked at the index she'd set on the table. Margaret stood stiffly up and adjusted her cardigan over her redoubtable chest, then marched over to Danny and put a hefty arm around his shoulders. Looking at Ellen with something like pity she said:

181

'His brother's just been mugged dear, don't worry him too much.'

'I didn't realize. Is he all right?' Ellen looked at him quizzically.

'Yeah, he'll be fine . . . maybe you and I should look at this stuff next door?' Danny hoisted the box and walked towards the doorway while Margaret sighed and looked pleadingly at Ellen.

'I thought you said you had two sisters.'

'I do. It was Geordie on the phone. He was telling me something weird and then I said *fuck* and they looked as if they were about to jump me, so I made something up. Sorry.'

'Don't apologize to me. If you want to lie to those two nice ladies you just go right ahead.'

'It's not that I want to lie . . . '

Ellen was grinning at him. She was finding him amusing. Amusing was good. He could handle amusing.

It was 1.15 p.m. and the Poles hadn't showed yet. Ian was watching two men loitering across the High Road. They were leaning against the metal railings that lined the street. Their backs were rigid, their faces sharp and hard. They'd walked past earlier – muscular gaits, as if their limbs were painfully welded together – and had then disappeared. Now they were back, standing opposite Pastry Nice, glancing over, and one was on his mobile, gesticulating energetically. They were both short, even shorter than Ian, but broad and dangerous looking. They had high cheekbones but wide flat faces, one of which had been flattened even further by a broken nose.

Their heads were cropped and their clothes cheap and nondescript: jeans, dark anoraks, white trainers.

They crossed the road and entered the café. Ian watched them nod towards the girl and make their way over to an old man in a long heavy coat sitting at a table at the back. He stood up when he saw them, lifted a blue plastic bag off the seat beside him, rolled up his paper and pointed at Ian with it. He then walked out of the café, pausing at the door to pull a large and ursine hat out of the bag and onto his head. It seemed a bit excessive in the summer heat.

They sat down heavily at his table without looking at him or speaking. Ian moved his right hand from the tabletop down onto his leg to stop it from jiggling but saw that his action immediately affected the one with the broken nose. He had gripped the sides of the table, as if ready to overturn it, and was watching his brother for direction. Ian swept his hand back up and placed it on the glass surface, awkwardly, with the palm upwards so they'd see it was empty. It resembled a dead man's hand. Ian turned it over and gave a tiny rap with his knuckles on the table. As if he had called the meeting to order, the one with the unbroken nose looked at him, and spoke.

'You are Ian, yes?'

'Yes.' Ian nodded at both of them in turn.

'I am Bartosz and this my brother, Tomek.' The broken nose nodded.

'Great. Ian.'

'Yes, I know.'

'You got the stuff we discussed on the phone?' Ian *was* nervous.

183

'We have everything which you requested. But first and more important, are you with money? You made us to understand half now and half Monday.'

'I am. I am with the money,' Ian replied. 'But not on me.' They looked at him emptily.

'I mean I don't have the money with me now.'

'So you are *not* with money.' Bartosz said, as if he'd tricked him into confessing. Tomek, the one with the divot where his nose should be, spoke for the first time. His voice was deeper and his accent even thicker than his brother's. He leant forward.

'You get money now and come to the barber's.' He jerked his head towards the street. 'Ask Jerzy to show you the yard. Tell him Bartosz sends you. And you will need a car yes?'

Ian looked across at the barber's over the road. A huge man, a little flabby but enormously strong-looking, wearing tight black leather trousers and a white T-shirt, was leaning in the doorway. As he turned to go back into the barber shop a stringy ponytail flicked out behind him.

'No, I'm all right. I've a van with me. Can I park it outside the barber's?'

'I think rather not. You should put it down there.' Tomek pointed to the next street off the High Road. 'Then, on Monday you can drive in under the bridge. We must show you.' He meant the railway arches, Ian realized. The yard behind the barber's must be in one of the railway arches.

'Okay. I'll be twenty minutes or so.'

'Good. Remember to ask Jerzy. He is very big and has hair tied like a woman's, yes?'

Bartosz smiled weakly at his brother's comment. Ian nodded and stood up. The two Poles rose simultaneously. Their eyes were the same shade of gunmetal grey. For a second it seemed as if something was about to happen, as if they were all going to lift the table or shake hands, but then Ian turned, picked up his jacket and left.

On the side street Ian parked the van outside a derelict house. He hated seeing something left to rot. It made him feel helpless. The door had been boarded up and was badged with yellow council notices. It must have had squatters. Three empty beer bottles sat in a row on the wall outside it as though set up for target practice. There were little tufts of weeds around the front, and the upstairs windows were broken. Shards of glass rose and hung from the frames making the windows look like animal mouths, fanged and dark. Ian locked the van and set off to the barber's. He carried a white plastic bag with twenty-five grand wrapped in several other bags inside it – the other half was back in his room in the hotel, sealed in an envelope in the base of his holdall. He wasn't nervous now. Carrying the money actually lent him *more* confidence. He didn't have to think what to do with his hands. The barber's was opposite Pastry Nice and, as if in reply to that syntactical oddness, it displayed in large letters above its own glass front, a hand-painted sign plainly stating BARBERS. There were several posters in the lower half of its window and the dates for the events (a Polski Hip Hop Night, an African Spiritual Revival, a Young Ireland boxing match) had all passed, suggesting that the posters were there for concealment rather than advertising. Someone on the street could see and be seen by the standing barbers but couldn't tell who was inside on one of the four chairs, or seated on the long wooden bench waiting. Ian entered and clocked a twenty-something bloke: skinny, a little goatee, reading Autotrader and sitting on the bench. One of the barber's chairs was occupied. An almost perfectly bald head sat at the peak of a cone formed by a brown cape. The seat was pumped up so high the occupant's brown brogues were dangling in mid-air, and, bending almost tenderly over him, waving a pair of scissors, was the enormous Jerzy. Although losing his hair, Jerzy had kept his pony-tail, a lank affair tied with a brown elastic band. After nodding at Ian as he entered, he had gone back to the shiny bonce in front of him, click-clicking the scissors around it but not making contact with the customer's few surviving hairs, which were mostly clumped above, and coming out of, his ears. Ian nodded back and walked straight up to this giant in leather trousers.

'Jersey?'

The man swivelled his shoulders round, slow as a building crane. He raised his eyebrows the tiniest fraction but kept his face vacant.

'*Bartosh* sent me. He said to ask *you* to show *me* the yard?' The big man nodded, said something in Polish to his customer, and jerked his head towards the rear of the shop. Ian followed him, watching the sail of his T-shirted back ripple as he moved. For his enormous size, he walked very lightly.

LATE AFTERNOON

Janice had been in the chemists since eight that morning. She came in early on Saturdays to help Mr Martin stock the deliveries: cheap perfumes, medicated shampoos, carbolic soap and novelty bubble bath. The merchandise hadn't changed much in the five years Janice had been there. They'd sell a few foot spas and hair driers at Christmas, but the year-round trade was no-nonsense toiletries and the prescriptions Mr Martin dispensed from the back of the shop. Janice worked on what she called the *cosmetics counter*, and it did indeed sell lipstick, in three different shades normally, though they only had two at the minute, and mascara, in both brown and black. The rest of the top shelf displayed face masks, two pedicure sets, and a curling device for eyelashes. The condoms and Canesten were kept in a glass cupboard behind her. The middle shelf catered for old people: pill boxes,

an electric feet-warmer, rubber sheets, and several different denture pastes. At the bottom of the counter was
an array of tablets for ringworm and fleas, a lotion for
liver fluke in cattle, and a gallon-jar of foot-rot spray for
sheep. She'd arranged them from left to right in order of
colour, darkest to lightest. Nothing had moved in the
counter for some time, not since last Saturday in fact,
when she'd sold one of the lipsticks to Joyce Hartley's
daughter who couldn't be more than twelve. A Boots
chemists had opened up just across the main street and
even Janice now bought her own make-up in there. She'd
go over at lunchtimes, telling the Martins she was just
popping out to buy a sandwich, and then smuggle the
make-up back in her handbag. She always thought Boots
big smiley security guard (Declan someone) was going
to stop her on the way out and look in her bag. She'd
have to show him the receipt and explain that she worked
in another chemists, a less well-stocked one. Sometimes
she thought she should have applied to Boots when
they'd first opened. Their cosmetics counter was amazing,
like some enormous paint box: row after row of shades
of concealers, lipsticks, mascaras and eye shadows. In
fact they had a whole separate range of waterproof mascaras, and that special thickening kind that plumped the
lashes. They even had all the metallic shades of eye
shadows, and Declan was cute in his own goofy way.
The shop girls in there all looked like doctors in those
spick white coats, hurrying down the aisles as if they
were rushing through Accident & Emergency. Compared
to that, Martin's was more like the Geriatrics ward. Both
Mr and Mrs Martin were about seventy, bordering dod-
dery, and Janice's shop coat had turned grey over five

years of washing. Five years in the same shop, standing in the same spot behind the same counter, but the Martins had been good to her, or good enough to persuade her to stay. Even when the place was turned over and everyone knew that Budgie had done it, they'd never said a word about it, or not to her anyway.

Janice didn't like Saturdays in the shop. The view of the street – of the far side of it from O'Hagan's Bakery on the left up to Robertson's Bikes on the right – was blocked by a lorry selling flowers and plants. There had been a market in Ballyglass since the 1600s, when James the First had granted a Royal Charter to John Stewart, a local landowner, and the townland of Ballyglass, most of which he owned, had become a livestock fair. Now the main street was lined on both sides with stalls. They sold everything a Ballyglassian could want: fake designer T-shirts (the trademarks smudged or slightly askew), rugs embroidered with Indian tigers, plastic shoes, jewellery (home-made from baked dough), carrots still covered in soil. There were at least three burger vans. One stall sold only mobile phone covers, branded with everything from Rangers or the Union Jack to Celtic or the Tricolour.

There was an intricate balance to Ballyglass. For every Protestant business, a chemists, say, like Martin's, there was the Roman Catholic equivalent, sometimes right next door. It was an instance of the parallel universe becoming visible, as if two separate towns existed and somehow inhabited the very same space. There were different local papers, schools, churches, pubs, clubs, bars, restaurants, shops, petrol stations, dentists, estate agents, insurance brokers, newsagents, car dealers. The odd thing was that now peace (of sorts) had come, the big businesses from

189

across the water had started arriving. The Boots which had been causing Mr Martin sleepless nights had also caused problems for several of the good people of Ballyglass: was the chemists classed as a Protestant or Roman Catholic operation? There was talk of contacting the shareholders. The same went for the barn-like Tesco's and Sainsbury's supermarkets which had opened on the edge of town. The Protestant greengrocer, who'd always favoured carrots in his window display, and his Roman Catholic equivalent, who'd been fonder of cabbages and broccoli, were now closing, along with various butchers and mini-marts. It was becoming apparent to the place that peace had its own difficulties, and it was only the troubles that had kept the community structure. Now, with the Army barracks dismantled, the two concrete sangars gone from the main street, and the invasion of the multinational chains, Ballyglass was starting to look like it could be in Yorkshire or Surrey. It had turned out the threat of losing your identity hadn't been from the foreign governments of Dublin or London after all, but instead from the money-makers, the profit margins, the businessmen.

Mrs Burnett spoke very softly. It was as though she was scared of being overheard. Mrs Burnett was not a well woman. She wanted a new toothbrush and looked very intently into Janice's face just as Jan's phone started ringing. It was set to the Mexican Jumping Bean tune – Malandra had done it – and Janice didn't know how to change it. She led Mrs Burnett – poor Mrs Burnett who'd lost husband and son, one to cancer and the other to prison – into the middle of the shop, to the toothbrush rack, and then went back to her counter to answer her phone. 'Geordie!' Janice squealed it and Mrs Burnett turned slowly round. She was looking for a toothbrush with soft bristles, not the harder kind which hurt her gums.

'Hello tiger. How you going?' Geordie felt something unscrew a little inside him, come looser. He could see her behind her counter, examining her nails, watching the street.

'Fine, I'm fine. But are *you* all right?' Mrs Burnett was now leaning against the toothbrush rack. It seemed to be the sole means of keeping her upright. Janice edged out round the counter and over towards her.

'I think something's wrong. Budgie's gone weird. He never mentioned the money at all yesterday.' She put one hand on Mrs Burnett's shoulder and gently eased her away from the wobbling carousel.

'It's all sorted out now. I met an associate of his over here and delivered it to him.'

Geordie was sitting on Danny's sofa. The horseracing was on the telly but a sunray had successfully censored the picture. He couldn't be bothered to get up and close the curtains.

'Thank God for that. Does Budgie know?'

'He should do now. Listen, Jan, can you talk? Is Martin around?'

'He's in the back . . . but I've a customer with me.'

Mrs Burnett, though, was not really with anyone. She had wandered over to the wooden chair by the rack of walking sticks and sat down. Some shopping spilled out of the two bags she'd dropped by her feet: a small tin of beans, a single banana. She was holding two different toothbrushes in their extravagant packets and looking at them, hard. Her perm was coming out and her hair looked greasy.

'I can call you back later.'

'No go ahead. It's fine.'

'Okay. I thought maybe . . . do you fancy coming here? To London?'

'For a weekend?' Janice's voice was shrill with surprise.

'For good, I mean, for as long you want. You could stay here, at Dan's. He doesn't mind.'

Some relationships are always going to be serious (when you decide to begin seeing, say, a devout Christian, or your best friend) and some just aren't. Sometimes, though, one thing slips into another, the sex becomes tender, and you realize you're enjoying your pillow talk more than you thought. Janice was silent for a few seconds. She liked Geordie more than any of the others she'd been with. He was funny, and he didn't care about acting hard or fighting. She thought he might be clever. And he *was* good at sex. He enjoyed it and wanted her to as well. With other boys it had seemed almost like fighting – being held down and tugged at – but with Geordie it was like they were playing together, like they were sharing an amazing secret. She hadn't expected him to like her though, not like this.

'I could come over for a while.' She pressed at the lid of her wonky eye, something she did when she was concentrating hard. Mrs Burnett was unconsciously, and with some difficulty, demonstrating the brace position, having dropped one of the toothbrushes under her chair.

'Good.' Geordie stood up in Danny's living room and yanked the curtain across. The TV screen coloured. 'I miss you Jan. More than I thought I was going to, you know.'

'I bet you don't. I bet the women over there are just

too snobby for you.' She was swaying a little behind the counter.

'Do you not miss *me*?' Geordie asked, his little boy voice.

'Course I do, you know I do. Listen, I'll have to ask, you know, about getting some time off.' She looked over at her lone customer, who, still in her seat, had pressed her forehead against the Quit Smoking poster. 'We're pretty busy at the minute here.' Geordie felt irritated. God, she really could be slow. Here he was telling her to come live with him for good and she was talking about asking old man Martin for a holiday.

'Jan, I'm *serious* about this. I want you to come over and *stay* here. *Chuck* your job. I've arranged for Danny to pick you up tomorrow morning.'

'*Have* you now? And when were you going to let me know?'

'Well, I'm telling you this minute, aren't I?' He knew from her voice she was smiling.

'You're very full of yourself Geordie Wilson, you know that. What if I'd decided not to come?'

'Well then he wouldn't be picking you up. Don't muck around Jan. I still have to sort your ticket out. You can fly back with him and Ellen tomorrow.'

'Who's Ellen?'

'Girl he works with, and I think he's seeing her now. They're over in Belfast on business. He said he'd get you at 10 a.m. by the Esso garage on Moneyronan Corner. Do you know who he is?'

'Of course I know who he is. He's gorgeous. Big tall thing.'

'Easy up.'

'I'll have to call you back.' She switched the phone off. Mr Martin had come out from the back of the shop and was stooping over Mrs Burnett, his hand on her arm.

'Janice, I think you should make Mrs Burnett a wee cup of tea. Would you like that Mrs Burnett? Warm you up.'

Mrs Burnett sniffed and swallowed heavily. Janice went into the back of the shop to boil the kettle. She could go over for a while anyway, just see what happened. Mr Martin would let her take two weeks off. She would talk to him as soon as Mrs Burnett had gone.

Geordie stood up and walked into the boxroom to get his jacket and trainers. He was going to book Janice's ticket. By this time tomorrow they could be in here together, fucking in bed. He should wash the sheets maybe. Or just open the window for a bit.

Mrs Burnett supped at her tea carefully, like a child, as if it might burn her or spill. Mr Martin had brought Mrs Martin's chair from round behind the prescriptions counter (she was visiting her sister in Newry hospital today) and was now seated opposite Mrs Burnett. He was such a good man, Mr Martin. Janice watched them from across the shop.

'There now, a cup of tea never did anyone harm.'

Mrs Burnett looked up slowly. His head tilted slightly to the side with professional concern, Mr Martin continued.

'So how are you feeling?

'Not great Harry, not great at all. I don't know what it is. I'm not myself . . . I get up and I want to go back to bed . . . I go to bed and I can't sleep . . . I can't do anything.'

'How long has it been now, since Alex . . . ?'

'Three months, nearly three months.'

'Well Jean, these things take time. You don't get over something like that immediately. You're sad now and you should be sad. Nothing wrong with feeling sad.'

'But I can't *do* anything. I can't decide on anything. I can't even decide on a toothbrush.'

She lifted the two toothbrushes that lay in her lap. Mr Martin had picked the dropped one up from under her seat.

'I'll tell you what, why don't you take them both and then tell me which is better? We'll call it market research.' He eased them from her grip and put them in one of her shopping bags. She smiled at him weakly, and nodded, embarrassed at his hands touching hers.

'Okay Harry, thanks. I'm sorry for taking your time.' She bent down and made as if to lift the plastic bags. Mr Martin stayed her arm with his own soft hand. It was hairless and pinkly pale, something new-born.

'Now you stay your ground. We're not exactly busy,' he looked up and down the aisle for effect, 'so sit tight until you're feeling better.'

'I wouldn't be saying that to me, I could be here for months . . . I'll get up in a minute or two.' She leant back in the chair and put both hands around the blue mug, warming them. Her face was almost white. Mr Martin slowly pushed the chair back up the aisle to the counter and went into the back to do his prescriptions.

The glass front door swung open and the electronic singsong went off. Mrs Burnett leant into the wall and looked up to apologize for being partly in the way, but the customer had already moved on, across to the counter where that nice Janice was. He was big and moved very fast. Janice had shrunk back against the cupboard behind her. It was Budgie. He placed his two hands on the glass top and leered across it (Janice thought of the little tented sign on the top shelf she'd scratched out in red biro years ago: *Please don't lean on the counter*). His voice was full of anger.

'Okay Jan? Having a nice day at work are we? And what the *fuck* is all this about you going to London? Are you still talking to Wilson?' He was nodding his head, shouting, becoming more and more enraged. Janice shook hers slowly.

'I don't know what you're talking about. Can we do this later? Mr Martin's going to come out in a minute.' Mr Martin was already coming out. He had walked down the far aisle and was standing beside Mrs Burnett, but looking with evident concern across the shop at the siblings.

'Janice, everything all right?' he asked, his hand on Mrs Burnett's shoulder but with the two of them facing the same way, towards Janice, like in an old style marriage photo.

'It's fine Mr Martin. Greer's just leaving.'

Budgie turned round.

'Why don't *you* mind your own business?'

The chemist bristled and sighed, but Mrs Burnett remained completely calm. She glanced up at Mr Martin, who was now looking away, up at the back of the shop, and then said, quite clearly, 'This *is* his business Greer. Why don't you take your problems outside?'

'Fuck off. I'm talking to my sister and I'll do it where I want to. *All right?*'

Janice came round the counter.

'Come *on* Budgie, outside. *Now.*' She walked to the door and went through it. There was an alley two shops down that cut through to the High Street from one of the car parks. She walked through the shoppers and turned into it, growing angrier with every step. Greer walked after her, bouncing on the balls of his feet. In the alley she turned to face him and screamed:

'LOOK, I DON'T KNOW WHAT YOUR PROBLEM IS. IF I WANT TO GO TO LONDON THEN I'M GOING TO FUCKING GO TO LONDON AND YOU CAN'T STOP ME . . . Sorry, Mrs McClelland.'

Janice stepped aside for Mrs McClelland to pull her tartan shopper between her and Budgie. She scurried through. Budgie made a face at Janice: his tongue pushed over his bottom teeth to create a distended bump below his lower lip, his eyes wide. He had done the same thing, made the same face at her, for maybe twenty years.

'You're just so fucking stupid Jan. You're beyond help. Geordie's a fucking waste of space. A total fucking loser.'

Janice looked at the wall a few inches behind him. He could say what he liked. She didn't care. He could even hit her. Someone must have smashed a bottle off the wall here. There was a little jag of green glass on the edge of one of the bricks. She looked back at her brother's face, its odd bulbous expression and his brown widened eyes. Calm and miles away, she breathed out loudly and said, 'He gave the money back. To some friend of yours in London. Just leave me alone Budgie. Please. Just leave me alone.' Then she turned and walked out of the alley back into the street.

At five twenty-seven that afternoon, Mr Martin walked

197

up the shop to the glass front and stood looking out. He'd been fine about letting Janice have the time off. In fact he'd seemed almost pleased and told her she deserved a holiday. Janice stood watching him now, his hunched back in its white coat framed by the shop window. He sighed with the usual sad and relieved air he liked to adopt at closing time.

'Well, we won't be retiring tomorrow anyway.'

Always the same line, but Janice didn't mind. Being expected, when his statement actually arrived it was also somehow surprising, like the school bell at going-home time.

'And if you want to head on then . . . I have some forms to fill out before I lock up.'

'Okay . . . And I'm sorry again about earlier, about Greer . . . he can be a bit wild.'

'Aye well, these things happen . . . ' He paused by the shampoos, rearranging two bottles that were heading the wrong columns. 'Janice, you know, if these two weeks in London . . . well, if they . . . *work out,* and you want to stay on, Mrs Martin and I . . . Mary and I, we'll get someone in. You shouldn't be thinking we wouldn't cope.'

Janice felt embarrassed. She looked down at the carton of paracetamol she was halfway through pricing,

'Oh I know. I wouldn't think that . . . It's very good of you though . . . thank you.'

Mr Martin had turned his back and was shuffling off. Janice hung her white coat up in the storeroom and left, shouting goodnight up the stairs at the back. Outside, she turned right and started up the High Street towards her estate. Most of the stalls were packing up. At the

corner of Fountain Street Mrs MacNeill was re-wrapping
her ornaments in sheets of the *Newsletter*. Janice managed to get past her without being noticed, and so avoided
the long barmy chat that would consist mostly of pauses
in which she'd try, unsuccessfully, to move off.

Every Saturday, along with the regular stallholders, Mrs
MacNeill would unpack her pick-up truck and set the
contents of her living room, including her fireguard and
black-and-white TV, onto the street. She was the only
person Janice knew who still had a black-and-white telly.
After displaying her goods she then sat in her armchair,
shouting prices at the shoppers walking past. None of
the other traders ever tried to take her space. She was
old and mad and smelt of topsoil but had a reputation
for charms to get rid of warts and other minor ailments.
Janice had gone to her house once – it was the other
half of her Auntie's semi and on the same estate as theirs.
It had been a Sunday and she'd had terrible toothache.
She was only about fourteen. Mrs MacNeill had made
her lie down on the sofa while her slightly retarded son,
Gerry, looked on. She'd then torn a scrap off an old
brown envelope she found in a drawer, poured pepper
on it, and told Janice to open her mouth. Her fingers
were filthy, in keeping with her face and her home. She
then tried to push the paper into Janice's mouth, missed,
and got most of the pepper in her eye. It had watered
for about four days. As she was leaving, and Gerry was
angrily rubbing his crotch against the back of the sofa,
Mrs MacNeill had gripped both her hands very firmly and
growled that Janice needed to bury a tatty in her back
garden. Then as she stepped out the front door and took
deep breaths of clean air, the old woman had thrust a

shopping list at her (*since I can't take any money off you love, wouldn't work then*). When she'd eventually got home her mum had made her take a trowel from under the stairs and bury a white pebbly spud in the flowerbed. It had almost seemed cruel. The potato must have just rotted away in there, stuck back in the dark soil it had managed to get out of. But the toothache was gone by the morning.

At the Fairhill junction Janice had to stand and wait for a wee black Fiat to pull onto the High Street. She took her gloves out of her bag. They were black leather and she had kept them for almost two and a half years. She always set things down somewhere and they'd get lost: her wallet, her keys, her cigarette lighters. But she'd held onto her gloves. The Martins had given them to her as a Christmas present and they were soft, fur-lined, and made her hands look delicate and somehow classy, old-fashioned. There was more of a nip in the air than you'd think from standing inside looking out. Such strange July weather this year. Her denim jacket and pink cardigan weren't enough to stop her from shivering. She crossed over the junction and walked on to Moneyronan Corner. Outside the new restaurant, Palpitations, a car slowed down alongside her. It was Budgie, sitting in the back of a red Astra filled with four other men. It *was* filled, as their arms and heads seemed to bulge from the four open windows, an enormous tortoise coming out of its shell. They were playing techno music but not particularly loudly. She heard the engine's timbre drop a gear as it pulled up beside her, and then she heard Budgie shout, 'Oi, Jan.'

She looked up.

'YOU'RE A FUCKING WHORE.'

They drove off, but Janice could see the driver wasn't laughing. He had looked over apologetically as he pulled off. She knew his face but couldn't think of his name. It almost seemed as if he'd driven away to stop Budgie shouting any more stuff at her. She was sweating suddenly. She looked around but there was no one nearby. She took her bag off her shoulder and pulled out the phone to ring Geordie.

EVENING

Geordie had booked Janice's flight, though he had to ring Danny and borrow his Visa card details. The conversation had been short, curtailed when Geordie revealed that he actually had Danny's Visa card in his hand as he spoke. Danny had left it on his chest of drawers. In such circumstances then, Danny'd agreed. The one-way flight was over two hundred quid.

Danny had been driving when Geordie'd rang. They'd stayed in Lisamore until Margaret and Lillian had put their coats on and sat down at their desks with their hand-bags in front of them like schoolgirls waiting to be told to go home. Danny had finished reviewing the main con-tracts and Ellen had made out a list of any missing agree-ments. It was almost six o'clock when they pulled out of the car park and drove into Belfast, against the rush-hour traffic. The oncoming cars were edging along while they slipped fluently past them. The odd car carried band members or marchers, unbuttoned, relaxed. Danny was explaining how the bidding for Ulster Water worked. He had to write up a report for tomorrow night on the state of the company. Syder's new bid had to be in by Monday at 10 a.m. As it stood now, the board of directors were backing Yakuma's bid and Syder needed to come in much higher. The board of directors would then be obliged to act in the shareholders' interest, which usually meant backing the highest bid. Yakuma's strategy was investment, Syder's to asset-strip and sell off.

'So Margaret and Lillian will be sacked if our bid wins?'

'Made redundant,' Danny automatically corrected, 'I don't know really.' *But I could make an intelligent guess, and that would be yes.* Danny didn't want to think about this. He was feeling hot. He thumbed the electric window button and the pane moved jerkily down, giving an animal squeak.

'They'd probably lose their jobs anyway, with Yakuma. They weren't exactly on top of their game.'

Ellen was silent. Danny interpreted it as a reproach for his unkindness.

'I mean they were nice and everything but a new boss always re-evaluates, puts their own stamp on things, brings in new people.'

'Not new administrative assistants.'

'No.'

It was still too hot in the Focus. The sun was setting in the west, behind them, and all the oncoming drivers had pulled down their visors to protect their eyes. It meant the traffic passing him was faceless, a stream of faceless humans getting carried into the setting sun. He loosened his tie.

'Thing is, Ellen, you can't *be* a lawyer and worry about

that kind of thing. You don't choose your clients. They choose you . . . Everyone's entitled to access the law and . . . it's market forces dictating . . . '

His turn to fall silent. Ellen was looking out of the window at the low flat fields. There must have been a lot of rain recently and little lakes had formed in them. They wore flushed pink transfers of the sky. Danny continued, 'I do feel bad about it.'

He wished she would say something.

'I wish you would say something.' Ellen looked over at him.

'There's nothing to say. Like *you* said, you can't choose what work you get. It's just . . . they seemed nice . . . I'd prefer if it wasn't us.'

'Someone has to do it. You *don't* get a choice.'

Danny was thinking though that *choice* was the only thing you did get. Life is *all* choice. Even life itself is choice. You have to choose to remain in it. The only time he'd not been consulted was birth but from then on he'd pretty much made the calls. Milk or no milk? Sleep? Scream? Life was one big flow chart, a river system you paddle up 'til you're alone and the stream peters out to a lake, in a field, flushed pink by a sun going down. The day was ending.

Ellen was looking at the housing estate they were passing. Some boys were kicking a ball around in a car park. They passed another estate. Another group of boys playing something. They were jerkily moving around one of the kids, blocking him in. Was someone about to be jumped? Then the boy ran into view, casting off, with one arm, an orange blur. They were playing basketball. Basketball?

'You don't often see that. Or you didn't used to anyway.'

The traffic was getting heavier. He pulled up behind

a lorry at some lights. The aggressive smell of petrol. Putting his window up, he held the car on the clutch in second. The lights changed and he pulled away. A new estate on the right had some loyalist murals on the gable ends. Danny couldn't be bothered to point them out, and then have to discuss them. He couldn't even be bothered to see them. He turned the radio on.

Janice was packing. She'd never flown before. The summer after school had finished, when she turned seventeen, the girls in the salon had booked a week in Rhodes and she was meant to go but her granny had her first heart attack two days before they were due to leave, and she had had to drop out. Booking a holiday abroad always seemed like a bad omen then. She would have to find the passport, although maybe you didn't need one to fly to London. Geordie would know about that. She had set all the clothes she owned on her bed and was picking her favourites from each pile. Six of everything basically. She'd found a large black holdall in the roof space, which might have been Budgie's in fact, and it should be big enough, although it had no shoulder strap or wheels. Malandra was across the hall in her bedroom, clicking through her CDs, picking out Janice's. Malandra had seemed pleased she was going, or at least pleased by the idea of a trip over to London to see her, if she stayed on. Both her mum and Malandra had agreed not to tell Budgie that she was leaving in the morning. He could find out on Sunday afternoon. Or Monday. Or whenever he bothered to pitch up, stinking drunk no doubt, and lairy.

*   *   *

'What are you doing?' Ellen asked patiently. They'd pulled into a car park just off Great Victoria Street, between the Opera House and their hotel. Danny was now on his second circuit of it, even though it was half-empty.

'I was thinking that if a joyrider sees our wee Ford Focus between two more expensive cars then he wouldn't choose ours.'

'Okay . . . presumably though, the joyrider could just look around the car park, and pick whatever he likes . . . before he would have to crash through the barrier.'

Nodding, Danny obediently pulled into the next space, between a tiny Micra and a battered Cortina. The view through the windscreen was a concrete wall on which someone had written tidily, in black marker, *Sammy is one stupid cunt*. Danny liked the underlining emphasis on *one*. Presumably there were others. They lugged their bags from the back seat and Danny click-locked the car with the remote on the key ring. They crossed to the pavement. He was feeling expansive.

'The good thing about a city that got bombed a lot is that it always has an excess of car parks . . . All these open spaces created right in the town centre.'

The NCP *had* done pretty well out of the doings of that other three letter acronym, the IRA. Ellen laughed briefly and Danny knew he was trying to be too funny. By the entrance a bald attendant in a navy round-neck with gold epaulettes was perched in his toll booth. He had been unabashedly watching them since they'd driven in, swivelling on his stool as they'd circled. Walking past him now Danny nodded and said hello, giving the attendant the chance to ignore him, which he duly took. He slowed his pace down to Ellen's. She was wheeling her bag beside her and it made the same clip, clip, clip on the pavement that it had at the airport. The weather had cleared up. Though there was a breeze, it didn't seem to have rained here at all. Belfast looked different to how he remembered it. From the livid Cave Hill up on the mountain down to the shop windows exploding only with colour, the town seemed almost flamboyant. Although it was dusk, people weren't hurrying home, angled into the wind, clutching their collars. Instead they appeared to be *sauntering*. He could see a packed café over the street, and another one further up. There were already little single-sex groupings of youths passing, heading out for the evening. The men were dressed the same, in ironed shirts of a singular colour, denim or leather jackets, sensible jeans, whereas the women seemed to be sharing one outfit between two or three, so that each of them revealed a different part of their body. They were approaching their hotel.

'It's been blown up thirty-two times, apparently. The most bombed hotel in Europe.'

'So they've had to build it *thirty-two* times.' Ellen said. She made a slight whistling sound as if to say *wow*. Danny wasn't sure if she was serious. He kept accidentally kicking her wheelie-bag so he paused, let her go ahead of him, and crossed over to her left side.

'I suppose so. Not from the ground. But windows replaced, that kind of thing.'

Danny noticed two short hard-looking boys coming towards them looking at Ellen. As they were passing one of them muttered 'Great baps love.' Danny ignored it, hoping Ellen hadn't heard or understood. He could hear them sniggering. He hoped they hadn't stopped behind them or weren't about to shout something.

Ellen said, 'In fact, if you count the first time it was constructed, it's been built thirty-three times.'

'Yep.'

'So *are* you going to tell me what baps are? Or are you just not going to mention it?'

Danny laughed.

'I was planning not to mention it . . . They're what you think they are.' Ellen made a kind of clicking sound with her mouth, half-tut, half-laugh. Things rolled off her that would have kept Danny awake. A lifetime being stared at must do that to you. A kid on a skateboard went past them. Even *he* was staring at Ellen, so hard in fact that he almost swerved into a lamppost. Danny wished that he'd still been walking on Ellen's right side so he could have just nudged him on into it. *Make it happen*, as they liked to say at Monks & Turner. It was apparent that in Belfast Ellen wasn't just unusually beautiful, she was also unusually black. They stopped in front of the hotel and looked up.

The Europa had been kept from the top spot of The Most Bombed Hotel in the World by some place in Tel Aviv, but it didn't look like any kind of runner-up. Since they'd installed shatter-proof windows the bombings had stopped and it was now shiny, expensive and slick. All steel, glass, and reflected sky. It reminded Danny of some spanking new office block in an Eastern European financial district. It was only medium-sized by London standards. Danny carried Ellen's bag up the stairs and they entered through a revolving door. Danny misjudged the size of it and squeezed in behind Ellen. With both bags.

He apologized and thought for an awful second that they
were about to get stuck but then it moved and Ellen
calmly strode out. As he tried to follow, the momentum
meant the dividing door behind him hit the bags. He
was knocked forward into a stagger and burst with a
grunt into the lobby. The receptionist raised his eyebrows. He was called Mr Andrew Terry, according to his
name tag, and had quite remarkable hair, coated in what
could only have been brylcream and swept to one side
in a very straight parting. He looked like he should be
sitting behind the controls of a Spitfire instead of a reception desk, an impression heightened by an unexpected
posh English accent. Danny hadn't been so frequently
referred to as 'Sir' since he'd played Lord Windermere in
their school play, or been inter-railing and unaccount-
ably held for six hours at a border in Germany. Danny
felt the sarcasm he'd suspected confirmed when Terry
allotted them rooms eight floors apart. *Bastard*. He smiled
very broadly at Danny when he held their keys out.

Danny sat on the edge of his bed in just his suit trousers.
His feet were bare and the rest of his clothes were splayed
over the chair in the corner. He turned on the telly and
caught the end of a feature on the parades. They showed
the main marches in Portadown and Limavady: a collage
of children with ice cream on their faces and old men
twinkling blue eyes at the camera. Mike Nesbitt appeared
behind his desk, reading the UTV news. Actually, because
the reception on the TV wasn't great, two Mike Nesbitts
appeared: the real one and his ghostly doppelgänger, his
guardian angel, hovering just over his left shoulder. They
were both doing a fine job. Danny appreciated their

210

development of a suitable gravitas as in one level voice they recounted the day's events: 'A blaze at a farm in County Fermanagh in which 2,000 bales of hay caught fire, has been brought under control by fire fighters. The alarm was raised just before noon at the farm outside Kesh, close to the border with County Tyrone. Eight fire crews and a water tanker were called to tackle the blaze. The fire service said strong winds made their task more difficult. The oil tank of a nearby house was threatened by the blaze.' A big fire. On a farm. The shot of the studio cut away to a tousled farmer in a woolly hat standing in front of a razed, blackened field. He was nodding slowly. Ropes of smoke still rose behind him, fraying off into nothing. Danny was thinking how he loved the report's last line. *The oil tank of a nearby house was threatened by the blaze.* Something almost happened once, and then it didn't. They should double Mr Nesbitt's salary, whatever it was. He flicked the telly off with the remote and removed his suit trousers. After folding them carefully, so the crease stayed intact, he hung them up in the rattly closet. Briefly, he considered doing some press-ups and sit-ups but decided, instead, to open the mini-bar. He fixed himself an amateur vodka and tonic (no lemon, no ice) and ran the bath.

An hour later Danny was sitting in the lobby, waiting for Ellen, scanning the *Ulster Tatler*. Every page, it seemed, was just photographs of different exhibitions and launches and openings. The socialites always had their arms around each other's shoulders, either for support, which, given the drinks in everyone's hands, was possible, or because they were trying to edge each other out of the frame, which, given their evident joy at being snapped, was also possible. Why would you buy this? Danny thought. Nobody wanted to look at people so much. Ellen swept out of the lift and revised his opinion. He would subscribe to a magazine full of pictures of her. She had tied her hair back and was wearing her dark bootcut jeans and a fitted black open-necked shirt. A long red raincoat was folded over her arms in front of her. She winked at him. 'Ready?'

*   *   *

Janice had packed the holdall and was looking for her passport in her bedside drawers. Malandra was sitting on the other end of the bed. She had started to cry when she brought the CDs in. Janice had told her to keep what she wanted but Malandra said, 'No, it's not that.' A melodramatic sniff. 'I can't believe you're going.'

Janice liked Malandra. She did. People always thought they wouldn't get on. Malandra was pretty, younger and spoiled. But Janice liked her.

'It's probably only going to be for a while ... Och, you wee pet. Your mascara's running. Here.' Janice plucked a tissue from the box on the bedside table and handed it to her. Then she moved down the bed and put her arms round her. Malandra's body was so skinny. Her sharp shoulder blades hurt the inside of Janice's upper arm as she hugged her, awkwardly, from the side.

'I *will* come over, you know.'

'I *know* you will. Maybe you'll even like it and stay.'

'But what about Steve?' She looked up, the big eyes all panda-dark now with smudged make-up.

'Well, only come if you and Steve finish then.' Malandra was in love. Steve sold and fixed lawnmowers. He'd been round for tea about a month ago and Janice's dad had requested that, if the event was ever to be repeated, he receive advance written warning. Steve had spent dinner debating, out loud but with himself, whether an electric or petrol machine would be better for the scorched patch of ten foot by eight at the back of their house.

'But that's *never* going to happen.' Another spell of sobs. 'We'll stay together and then I'll never get to see you.'

'Malandra, honey, calm down.' Janice was whispering. 'Catch yourself on. You *know* what'll happen. Chances are I'll be home in two weeks and be straight back to Martin's, straight back to this bed.' She glanced round her. The room hadn't changed in a long time. The white walls were empty but pockmarked with Blu-tack and scraped in places. The doors of her wardrobe were still lying open and the insides of the doors were plastered with posters that had somehow escaped the periodic cullings. They all seemed to be of pop bands that had long since disbanded: Take That, The Spice Girls, even New Kids on the Block. They'd all gone now even though she was still here, still sitting on this bed, with this same swirly carpet, and the same little sister crying in her arms. This scene could be from any of the last fifteen years. Malandra sat up and her shoulder blades flattened against Janice's arm.

'Do you think then, if you don't come back, that I could have *this* room? It's much bigger than mine.'

Janice was making the tea when Budgie came in. She was grilling gammon steaks and had turned the deep fat fryer on to do chips. She was remembering how as a kid she used to like the sound the basket made when it was sunk into the oil, the hissing and spitting of a cornered cat. You stop noticing those sorts of things. Malandra, face newly made-up, had gone to the shop to get eggs. Her mum was in the living room sewing up a rip in the back of one of her dad's jumpers. No one knew where *he* was – meaning exactly which bookie's or pub – but it was certain that he would turn up on the stroke of seven. He'd sit down at the table and wait on his tea, chatty with the stories from the papers he'd spent all day reading. Budgie had gone straight up to his room. She knew it was him by the way he clumped up the staircase. He always made the house smaller somehow when he entered it, even if he wasn't in the same room. He could fix his own food anyway. She wasn't making him anything. There was a yelp from the landing above, then a bang and a sound like something falling down the stairs but it was only Budgie again, moving faster than usual, descending and bursting into the living room. The door from the kitchen was slightly ajar.

'You know she's only fucking going to London . . . MUM . . . I *said* you know she's only fucking going to London.' Janice could hear the low murmur of her mother's voice in reply but couldn't make out the words. She smoked forty a day and her voice was an effortful growl. She was the only one who could deal with Budgie, and then only sometimes.

'I *can't* fucking believe this.' Janice was sure Budgie was standing with his back to the fireplace. Her mum would be flopped on the sofa, her head down and the sewing up close to her face. She heard the rhythm of her minimal voice again. She would be asking him not to curse.

'Well, you're just as useless. This whole family's fucking useless.'

Janice braced herself for the kitchen door to swing open and Budgie to pound through it. She had horrible thoughts about the deep fat fryer, of him pushing her hand into it, of her throwing it over him. He had better not touch her. If he laid one more finger on her . . . she looked around and saw weapons everywhere: the frying pan on the hob, scissors, a breadknife. But then, instead, the front door opened and made its habitual closing bang, and she heard her mother, voice raised to a half-croak, calling her through to the living room. Janice opened the door. Her mother sat with the sewing held up about six inches from the end of her nose. She made two more stitches, then slid the needle from the dark blue thread and bit off the loose end. With both hands she held the diamond-patterned jumper up in front of her, inspected and then lowered it. She looked at Janice and gave a feeble smile. Her hair could use a wash and condition, Janice thought, and her roots needed doing.

'Darling, I think you're going to have to go *now,* if you're going to go at all.'

'Well I don't see why I should have to. Greer's the one causing hassle.' Janice felt like a child again, petulant and overlooked.

'I don't want you to go but Greer . . . the way he is he might end up hurting you . . . or me. If you're still set on going you should go now. I'll tell him you took a bus and that you're already away on the plane.'

'Where am I supposed to go?' Janice was too tired to argue. She was thinking she could just lock the door of her bedroom but then Greer would hammer on it and her mum or dad would have to get up and calm him down.

'Away across to your Auntie Ronnie's and get her to put you in the back room. Andy's on the roads this week so she won't mind. Tell her to ring me if there's a problem. And tell her that if Greer should come round . . . if he comes round later looking for you, tell her that she's not to answer the door.' Ronnie was Sharon, her mother's sister, who lived three streets over. She was only six years older than Janice. Her husband Fat Andy was a long distance lorry driver. He seemed to spend most of his time parked up in lay-bys in England, on his mobile to Ronnie complaining about rain or the traffic. He was perfectly bald and still fresh-faced, though he must have been almost forty. His appearance, and the fact that when he was at home he just ate and slept and lay on the sofa, meant that people tended, unconsciously, to treat him as some kind of enormous baby.

'Okay. I suppose that's okay. Will she be in now?'

'She should be. She never said this morning she was going anywhere. Have your tea first and then I'll come across with you.'

It was growing dark. As they'd walked over to Ronnie's each held a handle of the holdall. It made Janice think of walking with little Greer, Budgie's son, who lived over in Coagh now with his mother Jackie. Janice and her mum used to walk wee Greer between them like this, letting him swing with his feet off the ground. He'd called them *gliders*: 'Let's do gliders, Auntie Janish.' This was probably the closest they'd get to swinging her own kid: a tattered black holdall crammed with her clothes and make-up and shoes. Greer Junior used to be round all the time but she hadn't seen him for months. There'd been some incident with Budgie and Jackie's dad. They weren't allowed to ask what. Janice had unconsciously started to swing the holdall a little. She stopped. Her mum had been very quiet since they left the house.

'I'll probably be back in a week or so anyway.'

'No you stay there.' She'd said it immediately and it sounded harsh, evidently harsher than she meant since she went on, 'I mean, I want you to make a go of it. You could do with getting away. It's terrible sad but ... ' She broke off.

After a pause Janice said, 'Well, sure we'll see what happens.' They were outside Ronnie's tidy semi. 'Her roses are doing well.' Two rows of yellow rosebushes, their petals luminous in the dusk and sodium glow of the street-lights, flanked the garden path. They set the bag down and her mum opened the gate. The house looked dead apart from a single lit bulb at the back of the hall. It made the rectangular glass pane above the front door a plaque of pure light. The path was too narrow to walk abreast so Janice lugged the bag along behind her mum. There was no response when they rang the doorbell. Janice started to walk round the house to get to the back but the side-gate was locked. Her mum was surprised.

'Where on earth is she? She wasn't going anywhere. We could try her mobile. Have you got yours on you?'

Janice took her phone from her denim jacket and handed it over. Her mum held it for a second, seeming to weigh it, and then handed it back.

'I don't know her number anyway. Only the one for the house.'

Just then the squat bulk of Mrs MacNeill appeared on the doorstep of the adjoining house. She wore a black felt fedora, carried a large cardboard box and was singing a tune without words. She had seen them.

'Mrs Johnson! Hallo Mrs Johnson.' She waddled over to the fence. The box she was carrying was full of old newspapers. 'Hallo Janice.'

'Hello Mrs MacNeill. Your garden's looking very well.'

Oddly, considering that it contained several milk crates and the scattered constituent parts of a bicycle, it *did* look well. She had a few rosebushes and her large rhododendron was in bloom, a little excessively perhaps, beside her wrought iron gate.

'Uh-huh. The flowers look right and nice don't they?'

'They do.'

'Are youse two looking for Sharon? I haven't seen hide nor hair of her all day.' Mrs MacNeill set the box down on her side of the low wall that separated the gardens and, straightening up, noticed the bag by their feet. 'You off on yer holidays?'

'I was going to stay at Ronnie's tonight.'

'Lot of stuff for the one night. If you need somewhere to stay love we've a spare room.'

'No, no, I can always go back and stay at home. I'm sure Ronnie'll be back later.'

Janice felt her mum surreptitiously squeeze her elbow. She wasn't sure what she meant by it.

'Ach sure it's no bother at all. And you know how Gerry loves to see you.'

Janice knew exactly how Gerry loved to see her. He couldn't stop fiddling in his pockets when he walked past her on the street.

'He's got some new photos in his album. You should have a wee look. Some of them are the last word.'

Gerry's album was famous throughout Ballyglass, although neither Janice nor anyone she knew had actually seen it. The story went that Gerry had a CB radio hooked up to speakers around the house. It was apparently set to the police band-length and, as soon as a call went out to the RUC, Gerry would get on his bike and cycle to the crime scene, often getting there before the police themselves. He always brought his camera and took pictures of whatever he saw. Janice was almost considering going into the house to take a peek when Ronnie appeared, moving fast down the pavement, clinking a blue plastic bag which was clinging tightly to its contents: two bottles of red.

'Ladies, how are we all? I ran out.' She lifted the bag towards them, swinging it. 'Just what you *don't* want on a Saturday night. C'mon in, c'mon in. What's in the big bag Jan? Good *night* Mrs MacNeill.' She bustled past them up the path.

LATE EVENING

Mr Terry of the reception desk had been replaced by the smiley Emma Sullivan, who wished Danny and Ellen a sprightly *Good evening* as she accepted their keys. Outside was still dry but it had got colder and a wind had kicked up. As it blew against them he could feel the dampness left in his hair from the bath. They stepped into the road, to cross to the Crown Liquor Saloon, and Danny unconsciously took Ellen's elbow. She jerked it away a little sharply, but then linked her arm through his.

The Crown was the most famous pub in the North and Danny had got drunk there before. From the outside it was a Venetian palace. Two marble pillars guarded its entrance and the whole façade was decorated with Italianate tiles of gilt and rich turquoise. Danny pushed open the doors and it was like being embraced by some love-starved aunt, one who smokes heavily and shouts.

He let Ellen go first. The place was packed and softly lit. The arches at the back of the bar were fitted with mirrors decorated at the edges with painted tendrils of foliage. The booths, illuminated by gas lamps, were accessed through saloon-style swing doors, and the stained glass windows above them were backlit by the streetlamps outside on the pavement. The queue round the bar was four-deep.

'It's Saturday night.' Danny turned to Ellen as they stood, closely together, just inside the pub's door.

'I know.'

'No, I mean that's why it's so busy. Because it's Saturday night.'

'I knew what you meant.'

'Sorry.' Danny looked around. The bar room was lined with oak panelling. Raised highballs or pint jars glinted in the gloom and all the faces were rouged by drink and glossy with laughter. There were no seats anywhere and not much standing room. Danny thought of the hold of an emigrant ship, dark and hot and filled to the rafters with shouty Irish, excepting one quiet black girl who was standing beside him, her skin more polished and dark than the smoke-dark wood of the walls.

'Will we stay here then or go somewhere else?'

'What?' Her nose crinkled.

'Do you want to stay here?'

'Sure. I don't mind.' She shrugged. She could be utterly indifferent, Danny thought.

'What can I get you?'

'White wine. Just a glass of white wine.'

He nodded and left Ellen standing by a pillar. When he came back, ten minutes later, with her wine and his pint of Tennants, she was typing a message into her phone. When he reached her she slipped it back into the pocket of her raincoat.

'Everything okay?'

'Yep.' She gave him a deliberately innocent look.

Danny thought she was trying to provoke him into asking who it was she'd been texting, so he just smiled and said 'Good,' as though to suggest that something had just been decided between them.

They stood at the pillar and talked about work, at first, about which trainers and partners were good to sit with and which to avoid. Ellen had only taken a job at Monks so that they'd sponsor her through two years of law school. She intended to qualify into employment and then leave a year or so later to work at a smaller firm. It turned out she was posh, or posh-ish, having been to a public school somewhere in Hampshire ('You won't know it . . . no, really you won't know it'). Her dad worked as a building contractor and her mum was a child psychologist.

Standing, they had nowhere to set down their glasses, and drank quickly. Ellen went to get the second round and returned almost immediately. The barman had obviously singled her out for service. This both pleased and unsettled Danny: it was another confirmation of Ellen's attraction and yet also a confirmation that being with her must involve continually watching your back. He thought of that bit in *The Golden Bough*, which he'd read parts of at college, where a guy guards the tree with the golden apples. Each guard eventually gets killed and the murderer becomes the new guard and so on. He looked over at her. She was glancing around the pub, and her face, as it sometimes did, seemed so completely closed, so impassable that she was her own guard, her own defence and protection.

Behind her, Danny noticed the snug nearest the front door become free – four short young men tumbled out through its swing doors like circus performers, boisterous with Guinness and the night's full potential. He strode across to it, not even taking the time to tell Ellen in case the delay cost them the table. The commandeering successful, they slid in across from each other. The booth still had a bell-push which was linked to a board in one of the arches behind the bar. When the bell was pressed a disc lit up on the board for whichever snug-dwellers wanted a drink. Danny pressed it firmly, not sure it would work since the pub was so crowded. Like the back of the bar, the booth also contained little mirrors overgrown with painted flowers and foliage, and its entrance was guarded by two carvings: a sneaky-looking gryphon and a lion with his head timidly bowed. Reproachfully bearing their shields and facing each other down across the swing doors that separated and joined them, they had something of the aura of an unhappy marriage. Ellen jumped back up from the table to inspect the inscriptions on the shields.

She read the lion's out to Danny first, 'Amor patriae,' and then the gryphon's, tracing the words with a finger, 'Fortes fortuna iuvat. Any ideas?'

'Let me think . . . I would say *love patriots* and . . . *strength brings luck.*'

'Close. *Love of country* and *Fortune favours the brave.*'

'Seriously?'

Ellen nodded. 'School. Can't speak any French or German but my Latin's still pretty good.'

'Unbelievable . . . What does it mean *Love of country*? That's it?'

She nodded again, her hand still on the gryphon's sly head. Danny went on, 'Not *loving your country is great* or *loving your country is pointless?*'

Ellen turned back to the carved lion. He looked a little shyer, as if he wasn't enjoying the attention and wanted to fade back into the weathered grain.

'Nope. Just *love of country.*'

'I suppose it's suitably ambiguous.' The swing doors were pushed open by a barmaid who grimaced at them. She looked small and overwhelmed, and wore the uniform of the waiting classes: a plain white blouse and a black skirt.

'You looking for service?'

'Please. I'll have another Tennants and . . . ' Danny glanced at Ellen.

'A white wine, please.'

After they'd finished up they crossed back to the Europa. The still-cheerful Emma Sullivan directed them upstairs to the restaurant where they were given a table by the window. The place was busy but with a different crowd from the pub, older and moneyed: the men boxy in blazers and sports jackets, while their fragrant wives, in colour coordinated outfits, looked as if they'd been lowered into huge vats of tea, left to steep and only recently been winched back out. Their colour bordered on puce, although it glinted with jewellery and was shaded with make-up. There was a good view over Belfast from here. The city stretched on and on, down to the docks and the two defunct shipyard cranes, Samson and Goliath, stilled mid-swing, stopped in the motion of giving a blessing.

Danny was feeling quite drunk now and Ellen's eyes had taken on such an emulsive sheen that she must be too, but he ordered a bottle of Pinot Grigio anyway. It was on expenses. He wanted to ask Ellen about men, about relationships, to ensure that if something should happen between them it wouldn't be under the shadow of some recent ex who was still hanging around or that she wasn't in love with her best friend. Danny liked facts. Their food had still not arrived. After spending all day orbiting her he felt he had learned to recognize some of her physical habits: her tuts and her slightly round-shouldered walk, her slow blinks, her hard laugh, the dip of her eyes when she drank. When she spoke about something exciting her hands conducted their way through a symphony complex with feints and grace notes.

'So how come you're single?' He realized immediately, of course, that he hadn't phrased it appropriately. Ellen looked a little startled.

'What does *that* mean? That's just like saying What's *wrong* with you?'

'Of course not. I just wondered why someone who looks like you, and is obviously as nice as you are, isn't with somebody?'

'Not everyone needs to be with people . . . and maybe I'm not that nice . . . I've been single for months. The last guy I was with got a bit too possessive. Even though he'd no right. He didn't give me enough space.'

'Women always say that.'

He watched Ellen twist a battered gold ring on her middle finger. It had a large rectangular garnet, gripped with four prongs, and Danny became conscious she'd been wearing it each time he'd seen her. It was simple

and antiquely beautiful, and all of the gold rings and gar-
nets that before had slipped unnoticed across his vision
were suddenly revealed as chances missed and lost. This
was the wonder of it, the re-apprehension of things.
Although she might only have bought it last week, the
ring seemed entirely a part of her. We fall for people's
things: they earn love by proximity. Danny had once met
a girl at university who'd arrived uncluttered by objects,
an ascetic, whose few items were almost all plain and
gravely functional. In the end, unconsciously desperate
for a place to settle his love, Danny had grown attached
to an Indian buddha her flatmate had bought that sat on
their bath, fatly storing his secret. Danny was a senti-
mentalist, thus random and quaintly democratic with his
love.

Ellen was silent. Danny went on, 'So what happened
with him?'

'Nothing. He's still around.'

'You mean around you or around about? Is he at work?'
Danny heard his own voice come out too quickly, too
high and curious. He coughed a little.

'Let's talk about something else.'

He watched her with a level blue gaze and kept silent.

'I'm not still with him, if that's what *that* look's for.
We don't see each other. Unless by accident.'

'So he is at work.'

'Please. Let's leave this.'

'Okay.' Danny put his hands flat, palms down, on the
white linen tablecloth.

'It was a mistake. It was over six months ago.'

'Over six months ago or *over* six months ago?'

'I don't get it.' She had lifted a bread roll from the

227

basket, and was holding it in mid-air, as if about to lob it at his head.

'Well, I mean, was it over six months ago as in . . . it hasn't really been working for the last six months but we're still sleeping together and having a relationship? Or did it actually finish more than half a year ago?'

She looked stung.

'What it's got to do with you anyway?'

'Nothing, of course.' They sat silently. Ellen broke off a bit of bread roll and mournfully started to chew it. Danny unfolded his napkin and smoothed it onto his lap. He'd cocked all of this up.

'I'm sorry. I just thought it was an ambiguous state-ment. I was trying to redraft it. I'm sorry. I don't *want* to know if you don't want to tell me.'

'There's nothing to tell. He was married and older . . . I was silly and younger. That's it. It was finished, for good, more than six months ago.'

She gave a little shiver and rearranged her cutlery so none of it touched. Danny said, offering it up as an apology, 'Well, I've just broken up with someone. *It* fin-ished, for good, more than six hours ago.'

Ellen moved outside herself again.

'Really?'

'Well, about three days ago. She came round to col-lect her stuff on Thursday.'

'Did you live together then?'

'No, but you know all the things that get left over. Clothes and books and . . . '

'The chattels.'

'Exactly.'

'What happened then?'

'Nothing really. I loved her very much. I was too young and ... '

Ellen interrupted, factually, facetiously, 'Men always say that.'

They drank much too much and bumped against each other getting into the deep-piled lift. Danny pressed the button for 12, his floor, but not 4, which was Ellen's. She noticed and pressed it herself, not meeting his eyes. The lift glided up, smoothly, counterweighted somewhere else, and stopped on the fourth. The doors opened.

'Well then, Mr Williams, thanks for a lovely dinner.'

It hadn't really been lovely, just edgy and drunken and awkward.

'My pleasure Miss Powell. My pleasure. If you fancy a nightcap do feel free to invite me in.'

'I think I've had more than enough.' She stepped out of the lift. Danny pouted a little, and tried for the face of a little boy lost in a supermarket. He was not past begging.

'Well, if you change your mind ... '

'I'll let you know.' The doors were closing.

'Room twelve hundred and one. One, two, zero, one.'

'Okay ... Goodnight then.'

The doors nipped shut. Just me again, Danny thought.

They'd arranged to have breakfast at eight and Danny had just ordered a wake-up call for half-seven when there was a knock at the door, but so lightly that he initially thought it must have been for the room across the hall. Then there it was again, two knocks, small song. He grinned enormously to himself, then settled his face and opened the door. It was Ellen with an opened jar of jelly-beans, the ones that sat on top of the mini-bar and cost about ten pence a bean.

'I thought you might want one, since I'd opened them.'

'Thanks.' Danny stood in the doorway, blocking it, and made his hands into a begging bowl in front of her, so that she could pour some in. She shook out a dozen or so of the sweets, shiny tiny embryos. Danny jiggled them into one hand and then made to close the door with the other. Ellen put her bare foot against it.

'Is that it then?'

'Unless you've any other confectionery.'

'No.' Ellen slumped her shoulders, mock-defeated. 'I'll just be on my way then.'

Danny caught her round the waist with his arm and hauled her into the room. Jellybeans were scattered across the floor. It seemed a bit much, and Danny let her go. They were awkward again. He looked at her feet, half-sunk in the grey carpet.

'Do you want to stay?'

'Have a sleepover?' she asked, wide-eyed, all lashes.

'Yeah. With a movie and jellybeans.'

'Okay. But I get to sleep on *this* side.' She walked over and sat down on the left of the bed.

'Fair enough. Though that's also my favourite side.'

They propped the pillows up against the headboard (Danny found two more in the wardrobe) and flicked through the channels. The fact they were both still fully clothed made Ellen's feet seem even more brazenly naked. He had to make a move. His mouth tasted cigarette-coppery, though he'd only smoked three or four, and he was exhausted. When he lay down on his back at first he thought he was about to lose it – everything swam – but then his focus returned. Ellen was facing forwards, intently watching the television. It was a late-night dating show: some girl who was all teeth was insulting some guy who was all nose. Using the remote on his bedside table, Danny turned the TV off without warning. She looked over at him. He leant forward and half-twisted round towards her, as if waiting for her to adjust the pillows behind him, and she stared blankly into his eyes, not receptive, not aggressive. She smelt of cocoa butter.

'Your eyes are the most beautiful blue.' She said it like she was confirming someone else's opinion.

'Yours aren't so bad either,' Danny said, and she closed hers, granting permission. He leaned a little closer and could feel the breath from her nostrils tickle his own nose. As their lips were about to touch she opened her eyelids again, to check, presumably, that he hadn't disappeared. Her lashes brushed against his cheekbone.

'That's a butterfly kiss.' She'd pulled away.

'What is?'

'*That* was, when my eyelashes touched your face, that's a butterfly kiss.'

She was nervous Danny thought. But she didn't seem nervous.

'It was very nice.'

'Yes.'

'And what's this?' He kissed her on the lips, gently, chastely. She was completely still. He could hear someone running a bath in the room next door.

'That was an orthodox kiss.'

'Really? Greek?'

'I think Russian.' She smirked.

231

'And this?' He leant forward and placed one hand on her cheek, tilting her face up to his, and then moved closer, as if to kiss her again, but at the last moment rubbed his nose against hers.

'I believe that one's the famous Eskimo kiss,' she whispered. Her breath was wine and jellybeans.

'Bang on,' Danny whispered back. Their noses were still touching.

'Well what about this?'

He kissed the side of her throat and she moved her head back slightly, giving the faintest sigh, so he ran his tongue along her neck and, thumbing back the collar of her black shirt, tenderly bit the top of her shoulder. His legs were starting to cramp.

'I think that's nameless at the minute. I think you just made it up.'

'Possibly.' Danny's tone was abstracted. He moved his hand down to the hollow of her waist and held it. It was hard and much smaller than he'd thought. He briefly considered whether he could enclose it in both hands but moved his fingers back up to her neck, brushing them against her left breast. He felt a stirring in his cock, its yawn and its stretch.

'Hold on,' Ellen said, and was up on her feet. She turned the lights off and yanked open the curtains, converting the room to a grey doughy world, moonless, and miles above the hellfire of the street's sulphurous lights.

'That's better.'

Danny lay down on his back and Ellen curled around him. He felt her breasts on his chest and her thigh against his. He turned over so they were facing each other, with their heads on the same pillow, and kissed her, full on the mouth. She smiled an enormous, shameless grin so he winked and kissed her again, edging his tongue in between her lips until it touched hers rising to meet it. Danny felt his cock pressing against his thigh, strapped in by his boxer shorts. He reached down and adjusted it, then undid a button of Ellen's shirt. She was wearing a black lace bra. He licked the dark cleft formed by her breasts and brushed the strap from her shoulder.

'You are incredibly beautiful.'

'Thank you.' Her voice was equally abstracted now, fading quickly into the physical. Danny kissed the small soft button of her nipple until it hardened and then gently took as much of her left breast in his mouth as he could. They were solid, pure creations of flesh, not those filmy breasts that are intangibly soft, that slip from under the touch.

'Shall we take off our clothes and get into bed?'

'Okay.' Ellen's eyes were facing the window and catching the only available light. They looked huge, and vaguely troubled.

'We don't have to, you know. I just thought . . . we have these lovely clean sheets . . . '

'And you thought we should dirty them?'

'No, not that. But clean sheets on the skin. It's a hard one to beat. I need to nip to the loo.'

When Danny came out of the bathroom she was in bed, sitting up, with the covers pulled comically up to her nose. Her clothes were tidily folded on the chair by the window.

'Hello,' Danny said. He was wearing his grey Calvin Klein boxers, and had rearranged his cock again so it was held down against his right thigh. A penny of wetness darkened the crotch and he felt awkward, exposed in the bare light of the bathroom. He turned it off.

'Hello.' Ellen brought the covers down to her shoulders.

'You are *fucking* gorgeous.' The swearword sounded wrong, ungracious and almost angry. He tried again, 'I think you're the most gorgeous girl that I've seen.'

'Hmpf . . . '

'Hmpf?' He had reached his side of the bed but the sheets were tucked in under the mattress. He tugged at them awkwardly.

'You can manage it.'

'I can.'

They were in bed, they were kissing. She kissed the raised bump of his cheek and black eye. He kept touching her face like a man feigning blindness. Then he couldn't stop licking and sucking her breasts. The sensation of holding her waist and kissing them became an imperative, an animal pressure, and the singularity of his ardour seemed to cause her to tense up. She set her fingertips gently on his cheek and pushed his head up to her lips. The sheets came off the bed. Danny felt as if he was grazing on her. She was lying on her back, and he was above her. He moved down the bed, kissing her breasts and mahogany stomach and the hair of her mound. He wet his lips and kissed again, pushing his tongue further down.

'What are you doing?' Ellen asked suddenly, in a calm but loaded voice. Danny looked up the length of her. Her breasts lying lazy and full, her eyes on him.

'I'm going down on you.' Danny kissed her belly button lightly. It was like an eyelid, tightly shut.

234

'Don't do that . . . Why are you doing that?'

'I want to.' She was silent.

'Just for one minute. If you don't like it, I'll stop.'

'I feel a bit naked or something.'

Danny pulled the covers back up off the ground and over them. In his little tent he moved her legs apart and knelt in between them. Stroking her stomach with the tip of one finger, he leant down to kiss between her legs. She was already wet. He began to kiss the tiny part of her, and to work his tongue around it in wider and smaller circles. Eventually he took it all in his mouth and began to suck it. He pushed both his hands down under her smooth round ass. The sheet was coming off them again and he could hear her breathing. He lifted her up, into his mouth, her thighs pressing against his shoulders, and started, gently, to rock back and forwards. She pulled a pillow over her face. He worked his middle finger in until it touched the soft knot of her ass. Immediately she squirmed up off him.

'Oi, don't do that.'

'Sorry, sorry.' He readjusted and went back to kissing between her legs but Ellen gave a different kind of sigh. A pissed-off you've-spoilt-the-moment sigh. 'Sorry,' he said, lamely, again.

'Just come here.'

Danny moved up the bed on all fours. He felt he was prowling suddenly, some big cat. He arched his back and purred. Ellen laughed.

'Come *here*.' She pulled him down to her. 'Your face stinks of me.'

'I know. It's lovely.'

'I'm not kissing you.' She licked the side of his neck

and Danny realized his cock was pressing into her groove. Ellen felt it. Danny pushed very slightly, experimentally.

'Gentle.'

'Sorry.'

'Stop saying sorry.'

'Je suis désolée.'

'Go slowly.'

They were both breathing rawly and she made little whimpers when he pushed too hard. He had to place his hands under her shoulders to stop her sliding up from under him.

'Am I hurting you?'

'A little. Slow down a bit.'

I can't *go* any slower, Danny was thinking, but said, 'Do you want me to stop?'

'Have you got a condom?'

'Yes, somewhere. Shit, hold on.'

'I'm not going anywhere.'

Danny jumped up and walked into the bathroom. He turned on the light over the mirror and pulled out the packet of condoms in his washbag. He grabbed one and returned to the bedroom, ripping open its blue foil cover. Ellen was watching him, grinning.

'Sorry,' she said.

'No, you're right. Stupid of me.'

He kneeled on the bed beside her and put it on. She pulled him back down to her and said, 'Now, where were we?'

'Here. I think we were just here.'

'Are you all in?'

'Nearly.'

Danny tried to hold on. Their eyes kept meeting and

236

making a channel between them, a rushing of something like wonder. Her almond gaze. There was nothing left to protect or defend. Danny tried to hold on. He moved his right hand from under her shoulder to her breast and cupped it, kissing the nipple. He had suddenly misjudged it, whimpered, and came. She dragged a nail up his spine and he shivered, rested on his elbows and grinned at her. She grinned back. Danny couldn't remember smiling as much in bed before.

'You're lovely,' he said, and kissed her nose.

'No, *you're* lovely,' she said, and lifted one hand to smooth down her hair.

Danny was lying behind her, one arm under her waist, his hand cupping her breast, and the other wrapped round her stomach. Her breathing was shallow: she wasn't asleep. He was half dreaming, a voice in his head idiotically repeating *my blackamoor, my paramour* over and over when Ellen suddenly spoke.

'It was Adam Vyse.'

There was a pause before Danny pulled back into himself.

'*Who* was Adam Vyse?'

'The guy I was seeing.'

Silence. Danny dragged his arm out from under her and slid across the bed. She turned over, onto her back.

'You have got to be fucking kidding me.'

There was more silence. It settled on the room like snow. The bed was Antarctica, white and vast and desperately cold. Danny lay motionless. Then the ludicrous sounds of lovemaking, from next door, or above them perhaps, started up. A headboard mockingly banged on a wall.

'Please tell me that's a fucking joke.'

'I wanted to tell you . . . I don't know why I told you.'

Danny lay there, listening to someone else fucking within a few feet of them. He imagined a room identical to theirs but the bed was spotlit, raised like a stage and contained the robust and grotesque coupling of Ellen and Vyse. His trim body and fatuous grin and old hands all over her skin. Danny scrambled up from the bed and tried to turn on the bedside lamp but the bulb had gone.

'I can't believe this.'

He crossed the room and flicked on the main light. Ellen turned back to face the wall, the covers pulled up to her neck.

'Put the light off.' She was irritated and sad. He wheeled the padded seat by the desk round to face the bed accusingly and sat in it. Placing his elbows on his knees, he put his hands over his eyes. He could have been a man who can't bear to watch the penalty shoot-out, were he not completely naked.

'We have to talk. I can't believe what you just told me. He's at least fifty for fuck's sake. You *fucked* Adam Vyse. Jesus Christ, Ellen.'

'He's forty-four. Danny, don't talk to me like that. You don't know me. You don't know anything about it.'

'I know he's got three kids and a wife. I know he's a senior partner. I know you fucked him.' Suddenly, out of the absolute blue, Danny started to sob. Ellen sat up, hugging a pillow. She stared at him, horrified to have caused his tears.

'Danny, it was a mistake. I worked on something for him with Mark.' She'd sat in Corporate with Mark Jefferson, an insolvency lawyer. 'And then after the case ended the whole team went out for dinner. Everybody got drunk. We ended up getting a taxi . . . '

Danny interrupted, 'Jesus, Ellen, spare me the *fucking* details. I want you to go. Can you go? I want you to go now. I want you to get out.'

He was shouting. He knew he was being unfair and overreacting but the thought of her with Vyse just ruined everything. He went into the bathroom and leant against the sink. He could hear Ellen crying now as well, and the sounds of her dressing, the rustle of her jeans being pulled on, their zip, and then the door closing firmly behind her.

The great fallacy is that the game is first and last
about winning. It is nothing of the kind. The
game is about glory, it is about doing things in
style and with a flourish . . .

Danny Blanchflower

SUNDAY, 11 JULY 2004

Ronnie had got her niece drunk. They'd gone through
to the kitchen at the back of the house, keeping all of
the lights at the front off. After unscrolling the blind,
Ronnie turned on the telly and got out three wineglasses,
the corkscrew and a bag of crisps the size of a cushion.
She was always like this, as if she'd been expecting you,
and when you turned up out of the blue, you'd actually
arrived precisely on time. They sat round the table and
her mum explained it: how Jan was to stay for the night,
how they were to pretend not to be in if Budgie called
round, and how sorry they were, how tired they felt,
how awful it was to have a son who behaved like an
animal. Mrs Johnson left after the first bottle of Hungarian
Cab Sauv and after Janice and Ronnie had finished the
second, the two of them moved on to tumblers of vodka
and orange juice before stumbling off to their beds. Ronnie

slept at the front of the house and Janice had the single bed in the small yellow room at the back. Fat Andy and Ronnie had earmarked that room for a nursery just after they married and moved here, ten years ago back before what Ronnie called *their disappointment*. The canary yellow of the walls was now faded out to a dull jaundice. Ronnie was barren. People never used that word any more.

Janice slept but was woken at 2.32 a.m. by her mobile ringing. The time was displayed on its face, flashing above HOME, the code word for her mum's raspy whisper.

'Jan, Budgie's been back and he's gone off to find you. I said you'd left but there was no talking to him and he broke one of the kitchen chairs, the one with the wicker seat. He kicked the leg clean off it.' Her mum started coughing. Jan waited until she swallowed the phlegm.

'Are you two all right? Is 'Landra all right?'

'Your dad's at the end of his tether. Malandra's crying in the bathroom. Make sure you tell Ronnie not to turn the lights on if the doorbell goes.'

Janice, in a purple T-shirt and a pair of navy boxer shorts, knocked gently on Ronnie's bedroom door. No response. She pushed it open and for a second watched the breathing heap of her aunt in the duvet, the lump's tiny bloat and contraction. Janice was thinking how vulnerable everyone was when they slept.

'Ronnie . . . ' She moved across to the bed and pushed at the bulge. A groan whistled from it and then Ronnie sat up, very quickly, and took hold of Janice's forearm.

'Whass wrong? What is it?'

'Nothing, nothing, but Mum rang. Budgie might be on his . . . '

Comedically on cue, there was a banging on the front

door. Ronnie's hand tightened its grip on Janice's arm and she whispered, 'Juss keep quiet.' Ronnie pulled back the duvet and slid across the bed so Janice slipped in beside her and they sat against the headboard, listening and waiting. The banging started again, insistent, malignant. Each bang echoed up through the tinny hall. If he thumped it much harder the door would go in.

'JAN.'

'JAN.'

'JAN.'

Budgie was walking around the front of the garden. They heard him scoop up a handful of gravel, cursing, and throw it at Ronnie's bedroom window. The stones smacked and grazed the windowpane, skittering off. Ronnie whispered again, 'If he puts that window in Andy'll go through him. They're only redone the year before last.'

Janice couldn't imagine Fat Andy, Sweet FA as Chicken called him, going through anyone, particularly Budgie, unless perhaps he sat on him, or suckled him to death.

'JAN.'

'JAN, I KNOW YOU'RE FUCKING IN THERE. COME BACK TO THE HOUSE. I'M SORRY. ALL RIGHT? YOU CAN'T GO TO ENGLAND.'

So he'd reached the stage of apologizing, of trying to make good the damage. This always happened with Budgie. Janice didn't know which was worse: the lunatic anger or the childish attempts to curry favour. Ronnie's bony hand was still squeezing hers, as if to say *Don't worry, we're safe*. Janice didn't feel worried though, not really, just a little tired and abstractedly interested like she was watching all this on TV. She was still a little drunk. Budgie had picked up more gravel and was now pinging single stones at the bedroom window. One tapped on the brickwork, another off the wooden frame, and a third plinked the higher register of the glass pane. The room was dark but ribbed by the streetlight that sliced through the Venetian blinds. Janice watched a fly come loose from a pattern on the wallpaper. It buzzed around restlessly, incredibly loudly, and then re-attached itself to the chest of drawers. Budgie was banging the front door again.

'JAN.'

'JAN.'

The pixel of the fly flicked off the drawers to the deep grey screen of the portable telly. Then they heard Mrs MacNeill's bedroom window open, just to the left of theirs, and her broad, booming voice.

'GOD'S SAKE WOULD YOU EVER SHUT UP?'

'Fuck off.' Budgie's response was slow and half-hearted: he'd taken too much drink.

'You shut yer friggin trap Budgie Johnson. I know who you are. You need to push off. Go *on*. I'll be ringing the police.' Mrs MacNeill's tone was almost kind, as if she was saving him and he just didn't know it.

'FUCK OFF,' Budgie tried again, rousing himself, 'I'LL BREAK YOUR FUCKING WINDAYS.'

'You do that son, you do that, and I'll let Gerry use his Christmas present.' Janice could hear something metal and heavy being banged against a window frame. It had to be an air rifle. Or even a real one.

'I'm looking for my sister. You seen Janice, or Ronnie?'

'Just clear off. You have me scunnered. I mean it now. Get away from the house.'

'I *said* HAVE YOU SEEN *RONNIE?*' They heard Budgie scoop up more stones from the gravel path.

'You throw one more stone at that house and Gerry'll shoot you.' Mrs MacNeill sounded interested by the prospect of this occurring. There followed a confirmatory tap of gun against wood.

'Have you seen my *sister*?' Budgie was almost screaming. In a minute he would either break something or begin crying. They heard his shoes scuffle over the wall: he was in Mrs MacNeill's garden now, under her window, performing an unlikely serenade.

'Just tell me and I'll go. Have you seen Janice? Do you know who I mean?'

'I do, and I saw her today.' Janice moved, to get up and cross to the blinds and peer out, but Ronnie touched her arm to hold her back. Mrs MacNeill was talking again.

'She was walking up the street after finishing work. She works in the chemists, doesn't she?' They could have been standing at a bus stop or in a checkout queue, just chatting to pass the time. Ronnie made a face of disbelief at Janice, as if to say this is much too surreal. Someone was giggling. Gerry. Pointing a shotgun.

'What about Ronnie?' Budgie sounded despondent.

'I haven't seen Ronnie for weeks. I think she went to Tenerife.' She pronounced it Ten-er-ree-fee. 'Now you get gone. The boy needs his sleep.'

There was a long pause, and then the bang of a gate. Mrs MacNeill clanked her window shut.

Elsewhere, in London, in the Lord Gregory Hotel on Kilburn High Road, Ian had closed *his* window after listening, at first with interest, and then with mounting despair, to the outdoor symphony of traffic, and the contralto and bari-

245

tone of a drunken street argument, and then to its crescen-
doed finale: the smashing of several bottles. He was three
floors up but the noise was too much for him to sleep.
He would rather suffer the slow heat that seemed to build
in the room when the window was shut. If only he'd
brought earplugs. They should be part of his basic kit.
Earlier someone had tried the door handle to his room and
it had unnerved him. He'd shouted a deep-voiced *Hello?*
but there'd been no reply, even though a minute or so
later the handle had been turned again. He hadn't crossed
the room to the door to check the spy hole because the
floorboards creaked. You saw people do that in the films
and then get shot through the door. Basic mistake. Nothing
else had happened for more than an hour but he still felt
edgy. He lay naked under the sheet, on his back, and set
his stubby hands over his chest, then tensed and relaxed
his pectoral muscles. He breathed out through his mouth
and in through his nose, slowly. Your standard relaxation
procedure. No good. He was bothered by the idea that he
wasn't fully ready for Monday. He had to cover all the
bases. He thought of his Auntie Florrie in her Elim
Pentecostal home in Larne. How she would feel if . . . well,
it wasn't worth considering. But he should write her a letter
in case something went wrong. He sat up, shifting the
ridged plates of his chest and stomach, and turned on the
bedside light. Its yellow lampshade threw neatly trimmed
shadows on the wall and turned the room a warm sepia.
The exercise book would do for paper and he lifted it off
the chest of drawers beside the bed. There was a Biro
clipped to it. He sat and stared heavily at the pad, before
writing, in tiny stabbing movements, *Dear Florence*. He was
old enough now not to call her Auntie Florrie.

I hope all is well at Five Oaks. I'm sorry not to have been to see you recently. I have been very busy. He would have to explain the situation to her. *It is right . . .* He put a line through that. *It is meet and right . . .* He didn't know what that meant really, but it was what they'd said at church. Still he shouldn't write it if he wasn't sure what it meant. He put a line through it. Mervyn would be able to explain it better than him. Tomorrow he'd write the whole thing out again neat. *I have done a far far better thing than other people. I tried to protect my birthright and homeland. They have asked us to accept government by terrorists who have not handed in their weapons, not ONE, nor halted their illegal activities.* He crossed out *asked* and wrote *expected* above it. *It is too much to swallow. The only thing left is to play a game they under- stand.* He crossed out *play* and wrote *beat them at* above it.

Yours sincerely,
Ian

Or maybe this was all too much. What *were* his rea- sons? He knew all the facts that Mervyn came up with but sometimes it wasn't a question of reasons. It was the third law of Newton's they'd learned in Mr Carson's class. *For every action there is an equal and opposite reaction.* If something was pushed in one direction, an equal force in the opposite direction appeared. And the day his dad was killed in front of him – *mowed down* was the phrase the newspapers used, turning his father to grass – he had become the opposite force. It was the way of things. It wasn't about choice or about reason. The opposite force just appears. He should destroy the letter. He scored lines through it, until he'd forced the point of the Biro through several pages. Florrie was almost senile anyway. His problem was, he told himself, hyper-alertness. He was trying to make sure every eventuality was prepared for, because that was the key to success. What was Sun Tzu's line in *The Art of War*? *Appear at places which your enemy is unable to rescue; move swiftly in a direction where you are least expected.* Well, he wasn't expected by anyone. They'd all be surprised by him. Even Budgie would be fucking surprised. *The enemy must not know where I intend to give battle.* It was a question of adjustment. Ian had realized, had been in fact the only one smart enough to realize, that it made no difference to the English whether the loyalists in Ulster laid down their weapons or not. It made no difference whether they meted out punishment beatings to joyriders or dealers. It didn't even make much of a difference if they kidnapped the odd Catholic (all Catholics *were* odd, Ian reflexively thought), shot them in the back of the head and dumped their corpse. The English didn't give a fuck. There was only one way to make a difference to the English, and that was to cost them money.

Sun Tzu talked about it in terms of water. As its flow was shaped in accordance with the ground so an army would manage its victory in accordance with the situation of the enemy. And as water has no constant form, so warfare has no constant conditions. You had to melt, flow, and eventually immerse the enemy. Ian was staring at the ceiling. At some point in the past a leak upstairs had created a brown tide line that ran the whole way across it. Absolutely everything was tidal. Sun Tzu believed that of the five elements (Ian tapped his fingers on the slab of his chest as he thought of them – water, fire, metal, wood and earth), none is always dominant. And he knew that none of the seasons lasts for ever, that some days are long and some are short, that the moon both waxes and wanes. Well, it was time enough, Ian thought, for the wheel to turn. Their day is over and ours has come. He put the light out.

Danny's telephone rang at 7.30 a.m. He was lying face down on the bed, and wrapped, pupa-style, in the patterned coverlet. He reached out his arm and lifted the mouthpiece, simultaneously croaking *Hello?* The voice was automated, American, and callously cheerful:

'Good morning. This is your wake-up call.'

Never a truer word, Danny thought, as he lay there and remembered last night. Ellen had *slept* with Adam Vyse. He unwrapped himself from the blanket and showered. He would go down to breakfast and if she was there, he would be civil, non-committal, and wholly uninterested in discussing either last night, or Adam Vyse, or any question relating thereto. They'd have to collect Janice in a couple of hours anyway. Funny how he should be thankful now for having to collect Janice. He just had to make it to Heathrow and then he wouldn't have to see Ellen ever again. It would be simple enough: he could avoid the canteen and her corridor, and get someone else to help on the case.

He packed with BBC World on the telly. A global terrorism expert was being interviewed. There was terror everywhere now. Danny felt an unkind thought rise in him like bile: now everyone else would know what it felt like – to live with the backdrop of bombings and guns, with murderers sharing your doctors and schools, your restaurants and surnames. Feeling destructive and sad he decided to walk down the twelve flights to break-fast.

Ellen was in the dining room sitting alone at a table for two. She looked up when he entered (he'd spoken his room number to the waitress too loudly) and he half-raised his hand in an awkward salute. She nodded back, insuperably cool. At the buffet there was a queue of two, a tweeded octogenarian couple who were vocally con-cerned about choice. Should they have pineapple or grapefruit juice? And which was this? Was that yoghurt or cottage cheese? Where was the skimmed milk? Danny jiggled a plate from the heated stack and slipped past them, quickly piling it with cold toast, four rashers of stringy brittle bacon and a congealed but watery lump of scrambled egg. Skipping the cereals, he lifted a pre-poured glass of orange juice slightly bigger than his thumb and headed over to the table.

He seated himself across the table from Ellen. Her two hollowed-out grapefruit halves sat somehow lasciviously in front of her chest. She gave him a brief sad smile and he nodded back, as curtly as he could. He would be untouchable today, stone-like, and he said, brusquely, all-business, from the middle of his mouth, 'Good morning. I hope you slept well.'

It sounded sarcastic.

'Good morning,' Ellen said softly. She looked tired. 'I don't suppose you want to talk about last night.'

'No, I'd prefer not to, to be honest. Let's just leave it.'

'You mean leave us?'

'Yeah. That's what I mean.'

'Right . . . You're pathetic.'

Ellen picked up her coffee cup and drained it. Danny began the fiddly work of opening a tiny plastic carton of butter, a sugar sachet, a miniature pot of strawberry jam. He knew Ellen was looking at him but wouldn't meet her eye. She leant forward, across the table, and he looked up into her face. She was wounded and on the edge of tears.

'Look, maybe I should never have told you . . . but I did tell you, and it's done now, and you should understand that I only told you because I liked you, a whole lot, and I thought that you liked me and I wanted you to know. Your behaviour last night was unforgivable. As if you had a right to . . . Maybe sleeping with Vyse *was* a mistake. Not that it's any of your business. But most people make mistakes. Just not you, obviously.'

'Not that kind of mistake, I don't . . . ' He sat watching her. Her anger neither chastened nor embarrassed him. He just felt again the injustice of it, of her and that smarmy vicious twat, that *ancient* twat, and replied, 'I was just surprised. I mean, are there others in the department you want to tell me about? Have you worked your way alphabetically through the lawyers, all the way down to Vyse and Williams? Who's next?'

'Fuck off.' She said it clearly and calmly, like a serious instruction. Then she pushed her seat back, stood up and left, dropping her napkin several feet from the table. No one was sitting close enough to overhear but a skinny waitress standing in front of the buffet was staring at him. He looked down at his plate and examined the bits of dead cooked animal. He wasn't hungry at all. The waitress was still staring. He'd hurt Ellen very badly. He knocked back the tiny glass of orange juice and then got up to leave. As he was going out of the dining room Danny picked up Ellen's napkin, and thought of those knights' tales where the heroine drops her 'kerchief and the hero journeys and travails and eventually tracks her down to return it to her, on the payment of a kiss. He strode back to their table, still being watched by the waitress, and dropped the napkin back on his plate.

Upstairs he telephoned her room. She answered with a sniff, as if to dispel any notions he might have that he hadn't actually made her cry.

'Ellen, I'm sorry. I had no right to say any of that stuff.'

'Forget it. I don't want to talk about it.'

'Okay. But I'm sorry. I'm a complete arse. Let's meet in the lobby in five minutes, okay? We need to pick Janice up in Ballyglass at ten so we should hit the road soon.'

'Fine.' She hung up awkwardly, clattering the receiver on the phone's base.

The drive was along the M1, one of Northern Ireland's two motorways, and then through Dungannon, a hard hilltop town, before taking the backroads to Ballyglass. As they were leaving Belfast Danny had pointed out local landmarks, the Black Mountain, Cave Hill, but his comments had been left to hang in the air and he'd retreated back into silence. Around Lisburn he turned the radio on. Ellen was sitting with her head turned away. He couldn't tell if her eyes were closed or she was watching the scenery. When they were passing the turn-off for Portadown he asked her if she wanted to listen to a different station. She sat up, evidently awake, but didn't reply so he childishly switched it to a Gaelic channel and then, when that got no reaction, detuned it so the car was filled with hissing and white noise. Ellen leaned forward and turned it off. They sat in silence.

They were on the Ballyglass backroads before anyone spoke again. Ellen suddenly said, 'I'd like you not to mention what I said to anyone.'

'Of course not.'

'Not to Albert, or to your secretary, and mostly not to Adam Vyse.'

'Of course not. I'm sorry for reacting like that last night. I was shocked. I hate him, you see, and I was feeling very happy and suddenly . . . '

She interrupted, 'Well I *only* told you 'cause I was feeling happy.'

Danny slipped the car down into second to take a tight corner. As they rounded it Danny was forced to pull up sharply behind a red Astra trailing a herd of Friesians. A young boy in an oversized anorak and salmon-pink baseball cap was goading them along, shouting and tapping their massive haunches with a blackthorn stick. His cap was the same colour as the cows' lolling tongues.

'Bloody hell . . . We're going to be late.'

Although they were at least ten feet away from the cattle, and inside the safety of the car, it was apparent Ellen was nervous of them. She stared through the windscreen and held onto the door handle.

'I don't think I've ever seen a cow before, up close I mean, like this.'

Danny laughed despite himself. Then her casual revelation made him think how different they were, from what different places, and the residual anger he was holding seemed to evaporate. Who was he to judge? He knew nothing about her at all. He wanted to ask her forgiveness again but said nothing. They sat in voyeuristic silence. The cows dawdled along, grazing at the verge's long acre and blowing steam clouds out through their soft nostrils. Occasionally one would turn its melancholic eyes towards them. Ellen eventually said, in barely more than a whisper, 'They're so *huge*. I didn't realize they were so big.'

'Walking larders, I suppose.'

'Walk-in larders?'

'Walk*ing*. It doesn't matter.' He went on, after watching them intently again for a moment, 'I like the way they jostle together, scared of being left behind, and then one at the back will panic and bolt. A real mob mentality.'

Ellen said nothing. She seemed to be holding her breath. The cattle patiently swung the sacks of themselves along and the cars, a tailback of five or six now, purred after them, meekly reverent as a funeral cortège. A Friesian calf strayed into a field through an open gate, and, chased by the boy, came back out level with their car, at the passenger's side. Ellen shrieked and recoiled, then laughed at her own reaction. She leaned slowly forward, until she was eye to eye with the enormous ponderous face at the window. It looked at her, sniffed the glass and then crushingly turned away, definitively uninterested. The boy in the baseball cap grinned and slapped the calf's rump with his hand, setting it off at a canter towards the rest of the herd.

They drove past his dad's estate agency at the top of the town and Danny pointed it out to Ellen. They could have called at his parents' bungalow for a coffee but they were in Spain for two weeks, golfing with some other couples. Over the brow of the hill was the Esso garage at Moneyronan Roundabout, and, standing beside a litter bin overflowing with takeaway wrappings from the Golden Dragon on the corner, were Janice and some small bird-like woman in a tracksuit. He pulled up by the air pump, got out and walked over to them.

'Danny, I'm Janice.'

'I remember you.' He went to kiss her cheek just as she thrust out her hand for him to shake, so that he walked into it, and then succeeded in grabbing her in a kind of face-hold. He quickly let go after kissing the side of her head.

'And this is my aunt, Ronnie.' Janice had turned away slightly, to try to wipe Danny's saliva from her earlobe.

'Hello.' Ronnie was looking at Danny like he was abducting her niece for his harem. She said, 'You get into a fight on the way here?'

'Oh, this?' Danny pointed towards his eye. 'No, nothing like that.'

She raised her eyebrows.

'I got mugged.' He had to stop lying. It would get him in trouble.

'In London?' Ronnie said, looking at Janice as if to say *I told you so. It's a dangerous place.*

Danny decided to change the subject. He looked at Janice and said, 'Anyway, how's it going? Shall I take this?' He lifted up her battered holdall.

'Please. I'm sorry, there's no shoulder strap,' Janice said, and then felt embarrassed at saying it.

Ronnie stepped forward and tapped Danny on the shoulder.

'Now you listen to me. You take care of this one. She's my only niece.'

'Well, there's Malandra,' Janice said, even more embarrassed now.

'I mean apart from Malandra.'

'And Lizzie, on Andy's side,' Janice added helpfully.

'Well obviously I mean apart from Lizzie.' Ronnie now closed one eye and tilted her head to light a fag but kept on staring at Danny. He was tempted to point to the petrol pumps and suggest that she didn't smoke, but said nothing, nodded reassuringly and carried the bag to the boot of the Focus. Ronnie and Janice walked along behind. One of them was whispering something.

Ellen got out and said 'Hello' across the roof of the car.

'Hi.' Janice made a tiny wave back. 'I'm Janice.'

'Geordie's girlfriend, I've heard all about you.'

Janice looked at Ronnie with open pleasure. *You see,* she wanted to say, *you see?* Instead she gave her aunt a lengthy hug and slipped into the back seat. Ronnie stopped her from closing the door and pushed a brown envelope into her hand.

'No, no, I'm not taking that.' Janice shook her head firmly.

'It's nothing. Put it in your handbag. Do as you're told.'

Janice took it and then squeezed her aunt's wiry hands.

'Thank you. You're too good to me.'

'Nonsense. Now have you your passport?' It was the third time she'd asked this.

'Yes. And tissues, and money, and fags.'

'Good girl. You take care now. And ring me when you get in.'

'I will of course.'

AFTERNOON

In the car Janice texted Geordie to tell him she'd been collected, and then Danny, in the check-in queue at Belfast City Airport, had tried to ring him but neither of them had got a response. Back in the flat Geordie's mobile was balanced on the arm of the sofa but he was still in bed asleep, motionless in the mid-stroke of a front crawl and lightly wheezing. He'd stayed up 'til 4 a.m. watching Danny's DVDs. After an initially unpromising start (he tried *The Seven Samurai* but quickly got bored by the subtitles) he'd watched *Ghostbusters*, then the entire first series of *Fawlty Towers*, before taking a break to make beans on toast. He'd then trailed Danny's duvet through to the living room and watched *Crouching Tiger, Hidden Dragon*, three episodes of *The Office*, and lastly *Lord of the Rings: The Two Towers*. Throughout the viewing Geordie kept up a steady industry of rolling spliffs, smoking spliffs, and drinking tea.

When he awoke on Sunday afternoon then, he couldn't watch any more television. That capacity for inertly receiving information was severely impaired and he had at least three hours to kill before Danny arrived back with Janice. He took a long bath, putting in a concoction of the various crème foams and herbal oils that Olivia had left behind. The result got him mildly high and afterwards, with a blue towel round his waist, he sang as he shaved, with Danny's electric razor, in an attempt to look sharp for Janice. Geordie, though no one had ever told him, could hold a tune, if all of the tune's notes happened to fall within an octave of middle C. However the song he had chosen, 'Danny Boy', didn't work like that at all and the high notes were bear traps into which he quite willingly walked, and accordingly screeched. He used to sing it to Danny when they were kids, out messing on bikes around Drum Manor forest, or getting drunk behind the church hall. It was a love song of sorts. There'd been a fad for singing 'Danny Boy' for a while: the boys' hero, the Clones Cyclone, Monaghan's diminutive Barry McGuigan, used to have his dad croon it in the boxing ring after his successful fights.

Once Geordie had dressed – having borrowed a pair of Danny's boxers, a pair of his socks and one of his T-shirts – he stood in front of the pine bookcase in Danny's bedroom, still humming. He hadn't a penny, not even enough for a Sunday paper, but there was a glass jar full of spare change on a shelf which he took into the living room and emptied onto the sofa. He picked out a couple of pound coins, a fifty pence piece and several twenties. Plenty. He tugged on his trainers and locked the front door behind him. If he headed down the Kingsland Road he could stop for a pint somewhere.

He walked past a group of Turkish men who were crowding round one pink newspaper. They didn't waste time looking at him. This was a new thing, being invisible. He wasn't Geordie Wilson. He was no one. He could be who he wanted. Maybe he could pass for a Turk. This area Danny lived in was trying to pass for something else. The shops gave it away by protesting too much: Class Boutique, Suavé, Top Marks Salon. Geordie walked by the school where the little bastard with the huge dark eyes had given him the finger on Thursday. The playground was flat and apparently featureless but it made Geordie think of how well, even now, he remembered their playground at Ballyglass Primary. He could see each inch of it practically: the painted yellow and white lines they'd run madly along for a game that someone – Danny maybe – had invented, those divots in the tarmac where they ripped out the climbing frame after Ross Hudson fell from it and cracked his skull, the stain on the tarmac from the blood that came out, the back wall where they'd tossed pennies to win them, the grassy bank where they poked at dead things with sticks. He stopped for a moment at the locked school gates. This playground was silent and still, as if sleeping, as if waiting for its dream about footsteps and screaming to recur.

In the course of half a mile Geordie walked past a Favorite Chicken & Ribs, a Dixy Fried Chicken, a Mighty Chicken & Ribs, a Kentucky Fried Chicken, a Kings Chicken, a Tasty Fried Chicken, and a Chick Chick Fried Chicken. A lot of the shops were closed down and locked up. The takeaways that didn't specialize in poultry were Turkish kebab shops. He passed a Chinese Herbal Medicine store and came to the Kilkenny Arms. He entered it reverently, his small head bowed.

Ian had spent the morning exercising in his dismal room: three sets of a circuit of sit-ups, squats, chair-dips, and press-ups with his feet raised on the edge of the bath. Naked, he stood in front of the cracked wardrobe mirror, flexing the ridges and mounds of his body. He was match-fit, he thought, at his fighting weight. He was a knife newly sharpened, perfectly balanced between hilt and blade, and able to cut through anything that might be stupid enough to come up against it. After showering, he went down to the empty dining room and ate a mountainous breakfast (four small boxes of cornflakes, three poached eggs, half a loaf), and decided to find a park to sit in and read the papers. At the newsagents beside the Lord Gregory he stopped to buy the *Sunday Mirror* and an *A to Z*, and the very young and very fat Pakistani boy behind the counter managed both to serve him and conduct an argument with the bearded man carrying boxes through from the back of the shop. He began by energetically screaming an angular diatribe in Urdu or Punjabi at the man, presumably his father, and abruptly switched to a weary silence for dealing with Ian. Then he held his hand huffily out to receive the cash, and screeched something else over Ian's head before indifferently poking the buttons on the cash register, and, with a dismissive sigh, slopping the change down on the counter. His practised lassitude suggested he'd worked here for forty years, and would for forty more. His father was tramping back and forth through the curtain of transparent plastic strips and gradually building a cardboard wall around the chest freezer. He wore a mask of patience that looked to be in danger of slipping. Ian dearly wanted to lean across the counter and clip the kid around the head. The fact that he had no respect for his father was apparent by his screaming, and that he had no respect for his customer, Ian, was obvious from his studied deployment of silence. After picking the coins up Ian stared at him hard but the boy was too preoccupied with puffing his cheeks out and repeatedly crossing his eyes in childish frustration to notice. Ian pushed the *Mini A to Z* into the back pocket of his jeans and started walking down the High Road.

If a road is still the same road so long as it keeps to a straightish line, then Kilburn High Road actually ends miles off, way out past the huge Brent Reservoir and the old American airbase in Hendon. There it's called The Hyde, and then the Edgware Road, and next it tries on the second-hand threadbare coat of Cricklewood Broadway, though before entering Kilburn, which it does with some apprehension (speed bumps, traffic lights), it changes to Shoot Up Hill, a place once famed for its highwaymen. It then becomes Kilburn proper, or as proper as Kilburn becomes, when it's reborn as the High Road, which it holds for the length of those restaurants and cafés and barbers and shops until it lightly coasts down into the stuccoed complacency of Maida Vale.

Ian had stopped and taken the *A to Z* out. He was standing beside the local tribute to Soviet architecture, the new Marriott Hotel, located on the cusp of where Kilburn ends. He decided the closest park, according to the map, was Regent's. He could follow this street straight down, then take a right onto St John's Wood Road, cross the Grand Union canal and he'd be there. His mind snagged on the words *The Grand Union*. The Union hadn't been grand for a long time now but it could be again. It just needed a little push. He'd feel better for walking, for clearing his head, though he couldn't imagine sleeping tonight.

It had rained all morning, a persistent drizzle, but now the sun was breaking through. Crossing a junction at a set of lights, he walked past a grey BMW at the head of the traffic, which had flurries of white blossom stuck wetly all over it. The wipers had cleared two swathes on the windscreen and bunched the petals up at the bottom and sides of the glass. A young Asian couple peered stonily out. It looks like a wedding car, Ian thought, covered in little bits of confetti. He stopped at another newsagents in St Johns Wood and bought a plastic bottle of orange juice. After entering Regent's Park, he wandered for a while along the brown gravel walkways and sat down on an empty bench facing a path. He hadn't expected the park to be so ornate: it was all tree-framed avenues and neat little hedges, trimmed verges and murmurous fountains. Behind him rows of tulips stood in a gangly assembly. There was something adolescent about their too-long stems and their too-big heads. An old man in a three-piece suit was sitting on the next bench along, a walking stick propped by his leg, methodically eating a carton of chips and gazing into the middle distance. He appeared to be watching a wooden signpost for London Zoo that had been planted in the flowerbed on the far side of the path. Ian had never been to a zoo. Cosseted domestic animals bored him but he loved wildlife documentaries, anything involving a tundra or rainforest. Maybe he'd pop in, just for an hour or two. See a big cat in the flesh. A little black pug waddled past on its own, so inbred its breathing seemed dangerously laboured, and then a strolling couple appeared, crackling with laughter and earthed to an excitable spaniel. A thin man, who couldn't have been more than thirty but had completely grey hair, pushed an elaborate three-wheeler buggy by. Ian couldn't see if there was a child in it. The man was followed a few moments later by a chestnut brown Labrador who goofed about the benches, paused to sniff the tulips, and then bounded offstage. The old man had finished his chips and had just stood up, straightening himself in increments, when a reluctant little dachshund appeared on a very long lead. It was ludicrous as a courtier and yapped to herald the arrival of its owner, a pretty mixed-race girl in jeans and a blue headwrap. Watching the dogs made Ian want to see proper animals, wild ones. He posted the newspaper and empty orange juice carton into a litter bin and followed the signs to the zoo.

'*Thirteen* pounds?'

'Yes sir.'

'For one person? Not for a family?'

'Yes sir. One adult ticket costs thirteen pounds.' The young Asian man with bad skin and very white teeth leaned forward and tapped on the piece of paper listing the prices, which was Sellotaped to the glass partition of the booth.

'Okay.' Ian took his wallet out of the top pocket of his denim jacket and extracted a twenty pound note.

'Thank you.' There was a click and whirr and a white slip of card appeared from a slit on the metal counter. 'Your ticket . . . and your change sir.'

All in pound coins. Was he winding him up? He swept them into his palm, made a show of looking at the handful of coins and dropped them into his jeans.

The zoo was cluttered with families out for the day. The saddest were the divorced fathers trying hard to smile and think of things to say to the blank-faced children trailing behind them. When two of these groupings met on the paths, the fathers would raise their eyebrows and nod at each other, as if they'd noticed they were wearing football shirts for the same, recently relegated, team. Ian walked past the birdhouses, not noticing the bloody plumage of the Scarlet Ibis or the Stanley Crane's oriental serenity. He was looking for the big cats, those huge bruisers lounging in their sleekly muscled fur, watching everything with narrowed, passive eyes. The warm day was turning limply grey again. Ian spotted a sign by the camel enclosure as two disdainful dromedaries tried to stare him down.

The tiger cage was outdoors and sizeable but surrounded by a wall that featured several large windows. The two tigers were slumped in front of separate ones. Both had their backs to the onlookers crowding the glass. One little boy with shaggy blond hair and a rucksack shaped like a koala bear tapped at the window and was lifted up by his dad, who started whispering how tigers didn't like to be tapped at. In fact everyone was whispering, even though the glass was two-inch solid Perspex and, in any event, the tiger looked like it could have used a little distraction. But it was nice all the same, Ian thought, that people respected these magnificent beasts enough to lower their voices. It was only the strong that commanded respect. Ian stood at the side of one of the windows and wished he'd a camera. Each tiger had chosen a view that didn't contain either people or walls. Smart cats. The one at Ian's window suddenly sat up and the little crowd groaned. The tiger turned towards the glass. Yellow eyes peered out from a face both intelligent and utterly bored. It yawned and unleashed a pink tongue the size of a chamois over its jagged incisors before turning again, away from the glass, and slumping back onto the decking.

Seeing the cats hadn't been that good, Ian thought, as he set off back to the entrance. They shouldn't be in here. He walked past the penguin pool, where it was feeding time. The little blighters would totter over to the man kneeling down with a bucket, and jostle and nudge until a fish had been placed in their beak, which they'd then immediately toss away. The ground was flecked with these shiny lifeless sardines. It seemed the penguins just wanted attention. A serious one with a scrawny neck and freckles all over his chest set off for a walk around the rim of the pond and was followed by another, and then another, until a whole column of twelve or so penguins were marching purposefully round and arriving back at the group they'd just left. Two pushed a third one off the pond's rim and into the water. He swam around for a bit and then hopped out, baffled but freshly interested in the big man with the bucket.

A young hand-holding couple, cooing over the penguins as if they had reared them, chanced upon another young couple they knew. The girls spoke loudly in estuary accents.

'Oh my god! Susan! How weird!'

'Frannie! How was Glastonbury? Is this Tim?'

'Tom. Yes, *this* is him.' Frannie, a sturdy blonde, simul-taneously pulled one boyfriend forward and, leaning round Susan, said, a little coyly, 'Hello Michael.' The other boyfriend hung back but nodded seriously at Frannie and gave a tiny wave. 'God, Glastonbury was mad. We were up for like forty hours or something and then Liz was sick all over the . . . '

The girls moved away from Ian and the two men stood looking at each other.

'Tom. How are you?' Tom said, and extended his hand.

'Mike. Nice to meet you.'

'Enjoying the zoo?' Tom said cheerily.

'Actually, I was just saying how depressing it is. You just look around and around, and see all these animals that shouldn't be here – and you end up thinking, God, humans are just this rapacious, horrific species that have colonized the world. It's just awful. What about you two? How are you finding it?' Michael thrust his head forward in a little jab of sincerity. He blinked several times as if he'd just put in lenses.

Tom nodded thoughtfully, 'I don't think there's really enough animals, and the ones that are here don't really *do* that much.'

Ian sloped off. People were odd. Always talking and talking about nothing. He walked past two humourless pacing hyenas and then stopped at a bird enclosure to examine its signs: Black-cheeked Lovebirds, Pin-tailed Whydahs, Lilac-breasted Rollers, Red-billed Queleas. The cage was a speaker box of throaty creaks and shrill whis-tles but none of the birds were moving.

266

He stopped at a large exhibit which claimed to hold two Sulawesi Macaques, although he couldn't see any sign of life. He edged around it and found them in a corner, eleemosynary, watching, their black palms stretched out through the chainlink fence. One began pulling leaves off a bush growing in front of the enclosure and folding them into his mouth. They had tiny black nails on their tiny black hands. They were pitiful. As he reached the Ape House Ian glimpsed the dense black mass of a gorilla slumped in a corner beneath a netting of wooden beams and ropes. It was like a huge puzzle, a Gordian knot, which the gorilla sitting below it just couldn't be bothered to solve. The only other visitors at the window were the father and his son with the koala rucksack. The boy had a camera and took a flash photo through the glass. His father squatted down beside him, obviously his paternal pose, and patiently, poshly, began to explain, 'The thing is, Oscar, the window bounces the light back and that means that when we go home – ' Oscar started picking his nose. Without missing a beat, his dad pulled the hooked finger down, 'and Dora sets up the computer so you can see all your animal pictures, there will probably just be a photo of a flash of light instead of a gorilla.'

Oscar was making a face that suggested a photo of a flash of lightning cooking a gorilla would not sustain his interest. He turned away towards the glass, in order to pick his nose again without his dad seeing. The man straightened up, and tousled Oscar's girlish hair, 'Or what *might* even happen would be that you'll think you've taken a photo of a gorilla and it will actually be a photo of you holding your camera up, taking a picture, or even one of me reflected in the glass.' The father laughed, but only for the benefit of Ian, who coolly ignored him and watched the gorilla pick something off the shiny black sole of his foot.

At the airport, when Danny went off to get a trolley, Janice said to Ellen, 'So Geordie was saying that you two are an item?'

'Not even vaguely. We had a huge argument last night.'

Janice sympathetically tutted. 'I thought something like that must have gone on. Everyone was very quiet in the car. Sorry for . . . Just that Geordie mentioned it . . . Anyway it'll be all right. You *look* great together.' Danny was heading back towards them, negotiating with a mutinous trolley. There was a solidarity between the two women, founded, as all solidarities are, on excluding someone else.

After neatly stacking their bags, Danny said, in his best game show voice, 'Ladies, shall we fly?'

Janice felt a flush of nerves. She hadn't really thought about it, about taking off and being held in the air by who knew what. As they made their way out of the hire car park and over to the terminal, she turned to Ellen.

'Have you flown a lot then?' Janice asked, trying to sound blasé.

'Not loads but a few times. I've been to America a couple of . . . Are you nervous about flying?'

Janice nodded, grateful to Ellen for catching her meaning.

'A little bit, yeah. Mum said I need to suck on a boiled sweet when we take off so that my ears pop. She saw it on some travel programme.' Janice laughed a little, to

show that she thought her mum was being overly pro-
tective but wanting Ellen to confirm it.

'You'll be fine. Honestly.'

They joined the check-in queue while Danny returned
the car keys to the Avis desk. Jackie, the fat lady from
yesterday, was missing and only the thin bald man sat
there, looking a little adrift untied from the huge buoy
of his partner.

'Here you go squire. The keys to our Ford Focus. The
guy in the car park checked it and gave me this form.'
Danny was doing his deferent Ulsterman.

'Okay, thanks. Here's your receipt and deposit slip.'
He seemed very low.

'You on your own today then?'

'I am. Jackie, the lady usually on with me, the one who
looked after you yesterday, she's been taken ill.' He was
slightly breathless, and his tone made Danny stop bustling
with his documents wallet and look up. The man's face
was narrow and unshaven, and his light-blue liquid eyes
were kind but also weak and cowardly. The bumpy dome
of his bald head was pallid and shiny under the airport's
striplights. A few hairs wafted, as if underwater, on its crown
as he leaned in across the counter to Danny. He must have
been fifty-something, but looked somehow inexperienced,
like a man who finds himself frequently surprised.

'Nothing serious I hope,' Danny said lightly.

'She'd a heart attack last night. Forty-three years of age
. . . Just goes to show.'

'That's *awful*. Awful.' Danny didn't know what else to
say. 'Will she be all right?'

'We don't know.' The man looked like he wanted Danny
to do something.

269

'Has she a family to look after her?'

'Lives with her sister. They're very close.'

Walking across to the check-in queue Danny was thinking *Goes to show what? What does it show? That she should have lost ten stone? That she should have got her cholesterol checked? That she should have used margarine and not butter on her scones?* He reached the queue. Janice was pointing out a Northern Irish television personality to Ellen. The man with orange skin was standing two lines over with several friends and three trolleys' worth of skiing equipment. *It goes to show, you blethering fool, that your body might just give up at any moment.* The thought took root in his head and stopped him from moving. It was as if he'd looked down and noticed that it wasn't grey linoleum he was walking across but thin ice. He felt suddenly winded and rocked on the balls of his feet. *This is it, my friend, this is all that you get. No next time round, no trial runs or second laps, no sequels or prequels or reprints. You've just one go and it's your turn now.*

On the plane, even though it was just after noon, Danny drank two small bottles of Chenin Blanc. He felt dizzy, damp-palmed and anxious. Should he be working on Ulster Water, trying to get a bid through which would get people sacked? Should it make any difference if those people were Northern Irish? And how the hell was he ever going to work for that slimy fucker Vyse again? Ellen was sitting in front with Janice beside her. The seat to his right was empty. He gazed out at the acres of endless blue nothing.

Janice couldn't help but stare. Ellen was the first black person she had seen up close and on the plane, when they had talked, she'd been silently marvelling at her hair and complexion. It was so clear and soft-looking. She was dying to ask what her skin routine was but thought it might come across as forward or rude. Her skin was so different. But when they arrived into Heathrow's Terminal One, Janice suddenly felt that *she* was the exception. It was like what you'd expect at the UN or something: people-herds of different shapes and colours and outfits rushing around. Four tall black men walked past in full African dress, great patterned sheets wrapped round them, and she saw one woman, at least she assumed it was a woman, who was tented from head to toe in black, with only a rectangular muslin patch to look out through. It was like something from *Star Wars*. Janice saw more shades of skin in those hurried thirty minutes than she ever had before. She'd love to try putting the same eye shadow on all the different colours of women.

They took a separate taxi from Ellen. Danny kissed her goodbye rather formally on the cheek and, smiling, told her that, as she didn't need to come in to the office that evening, she should give him the files. Ellen nodded, unsure if he was being generous or continuing the argument. As soon as they'd sat back in the seats in the taxi, and the driver was pulling away, Janice turned to Danny and said, 'She likes you, you know.'

'Why do you say that?'

'Because she does.'

'Right.'

'Girls can tell. And anyway, she said so.' Janice nodded and winked at him. Danny raised his eyebrows, as if to say *these things happen to me all the time*.

After a pause he said, 'Did she really say so?' It was

271

easier, pretending things worked in the way Janice thought they did. Boys and girls. Mars and Venus. Black and white.

'Maybe not in so many words. But we were talking and she likes you. Though she thinks you're a bit mental.'

Danny said nothing for a minute or two, and then asked, 'So what's been happening in Ballyglass?'

'Same-old, same-old.' Janice smoothed out the lap of her red skirt as if to read something off it. 'What's the news? . . . Do you know Margery Elliot?'

'Not sure. Who's she?'

'Works in the Post Office on the main street. Wee wiry thing with big glasses. Fuzzy black hair.'

'Oh aye.'

'Did you hear what happened?'

'I don't think so.'

'It turns out Jimmy, her husband – drives for Cuddys' Coaches – was leaving her for some woman he took on a bus tour down south, and then Margery and him rowed and she stabbed him with a breadknife. Just last week. Last Monday I think. She went in under the rib cage.' Janice's fingertips pointed at her stomach. 'Upwards. Three children. And the youngest only a toddler.'

'Fucking hell.'

'I know.'

'Dead?'

'Completely.'

Danny watched the back of the driver's head. There was a talk show on the radio and the driver was mumbling and disputing the caller's point. Danny couldn't make out the topic.

'And there's a new shop opened up on the Burn Road. It sells mobiles.'

'Oh yeah?'

'It's called Phones For You but spelt with the number 4 and just the letter U.' Janice described a horseshoe in the air with her index finger and then paused. She was babbling. She should ask him a question.

'So what's London like? Do you like it?'

'Ach well it's all right. I'm not so fond of my job.' Janice nodded, looked concerned. 'And it's dirty and expensive. But there's lots to do. And my friends are all here.'

'And now Geordie too I s'pose.'

Danny was thinking *Query definition of Geordie as friend* but said, 'Right, right.'

They looked dully out their windows. The traffic was light. Danny started reading the notes for the report he would have to draft in the office that evening and Janice closed her eyes. They reached Dalston in just over an hour and a half.

Geordie had returned from his wander and cleaned the flat. It had been a proper operation, involving hot water, the ravenous Hoover and a yellow duster, although he had restricted the action to the living room and kitchen. To demonstrate the enormity of the task, he had left all the drying crockery and glasses arrayed upside down on a tea towel beside the sink. When he heard the key scratch into the lock he lunged towards the door and opened it.

'All right mate,' Danny said, and clapped him quickly on the shoulder before pushing by.

'Big man,' Geordie replied, nodding deferentially and leaning back to let him past.

Janice was on the doorstep, head dipped, smiling at

him. The slight squint of her left eye made it seem like she was looking into sunlight.

'Hey sexy,' Geordie said, and stepped down to her level. They were the same height, pretty much, although Janice's heels usually made her appear an inch taller.

'Hello stranger,' she said and hugged him. He felt so skinny, stringily muscled like a twelve-year-old boy. 'You miss me then? Long four days?'

'I never said *that*. I just got bored.'

Still embracing him, Janice traced the nail of her index finger in a light circle on the back of his neck. He shivered before steering her inside and showing her round the flat. Danny was setting his satchel on the kitchen table when they appeared in the doorway. Geordie had his hands on her hips and his dark little head poked round her shoulder. 'Here, Dan, there'll be things found tonight that were never lost.'

EVENING

After a quick bath Danny'd put on a fresh T-shirt and the same jeans he'd been wearing. He had left Janice and Geordie in the living room, on the sofa, engrossed in the *Antiques Roadshow*. Geordie was arguing that no painting of a horse could ever be worth the ten thousand pounds some berk in a bow tie claimed it was. *And anyway its head's all wrong. Looks more like a greyhound.* Janice had already made Geordie two cups of tea since she'd arrived. They were tactile and easy with each other, and Danny noticed that Geordie fidgeted less when she was around, as though in order to balance her femininity he had to be calmer.

He caught the almost empty 76 bus from the end of Sofia Road. He wasn't cycling home knackered at four in the morning. The bus route ran straight down Kingsland and into the city. At Moorgate he got off by himself and

walked along London Wall to cut through to Cheapside.
The city was as deserted as it ever really got. Passing the
merchant banks and law firms and brokerages, Danny'd
look in to see an occasional figure glancing up from
behind a reception desk or steering a huge motorized
mop across a marble lobby, shiny and sterile as an oper-
ating theatre. On London Wall he heard the ringing asser-
tion of bells, and when he turned onto Wood Street
realized they came from the church tower that sat abandoned on the traffic island in front of him. It was *only*
a tower: whatever church had been attached to it had
long since disappeared. Nor did it seem to have an
entrance though sometimes, late at night, Danny had
noticed lights on in the windows just below the belfry.
He walked carefully round it. The sound was enormous,
peal upon peal to summon an imaginary congregation
to imaginary worship. Danny reached the building site
at the end of the street. A digger sat abandoned in front
of scaffolding badged with billboards and hoardings. He
thought how advertisements were the only things left
singing praises.

On Cheapside the shops and coffee bars were all
closed and the only people around were cleaners or security guards arriving or leaving. Two African women sat
companionably in silence at a bus stop. As he passed
behind them the 25 pulled up, and opened its doors in
a loud exhalation. The African women got on. Dan looked
at the bus's windows – there wasn't one white face. These
were the dark ghosts of the City of London, those invited
to the party but only if they arrived at the back door,
ate nothing, and left before it began.

When Danny worked late, which he usually did, a

cheerful man in the regulation navy polo-shirt, which appropriately signified Monks & Turner's blue-collar staff, would appear in his corridor around eight o'clock. He would be pushing an enormous red wagon, a movable skip, and collecting every office's rubbish, before replacing each bin-liner with one slipped from the wad of white plastic bags he kept tucked in his belt. When he came into the room to empty the bin he wouldn't speak until Danny had said something, though then he was friendly. José was from Nicaragua, specifically from Managua, the capital, and his favourite line was *You work too hard, yes?* Danny's response was to widen his eyes and nod in agreement, but then to suffer the curious guilt of accepting pity from someone paid to empty his bin, and someone who'd fled from hurricanes, earthquakes, poverty and war. The Nicaraguan, though, was continually grinning, and he had a smile that made Danny respond in kind. It was not pretty – José possessed about double the usual number of teeth – but it was unforced and so generous that Danny would find himself sitting up in his seat and beaming happily back.

On the days that he worked through the night a Nigerian cleaner would appear in his office along with the dawn, around six or so in the morning. She would bustle about him and refuse to make eye contact, and by that stage Danny would be too tired to stretch to the effort of speech. Those were the nights when he would stumble out to the street at seven o'clock to transact Starbucks' first sale of the day, a latte and still-warm croissant. It was always the same pretty Italian girl serving, and she was always brusque, though there never anyone waiting behind him. The cleaner, whose name he didn't know, would wipe the keyboard and telephone handset (provided he wasn't using them), and place a wet and folded, lemon-scented tissue (the kind reminiscent of aeroplanes and Chinese restaurants) under the mouthpiece of the phone. Once she'd prodded him awake as he lay slumped over the desk, his forehead being embossed by the lid of a pen, because a small pool of saliva was growing on top of a file. Normally she was kind enough to let him sleep.

His corridor tonight, for 5 p.m. on a Sunday evening, wasn't too busy. Vyse's office was empty. Danny paused in the doorway and looked at the photographs of the happy Vyse clan on the far wall. It occurred to him that he could easily deface them: add beards and glasses, scrawl obscenities. He could unpick a few threads from the seam on the seat of every pair of his trousers, or dribble a neat coffee stain onto the ties. He could tangle his Archimedes' balls. But all of those things would be disrespectful and childish, and besides each corridor had CCTV. He felt entitled to vengeance. It was as if all of the casual agony and hassle Vyse had previously caused him had now been given a specific hook on which to hang his hate. Ellen. The lovely Ellen. Vyse had spoiled everything.

In his own office, Danny had a bundle of e-mails demanding responses. The whole corporate team working on UW appeared to be in, down on the second floor, including Freeman, the nasty abbot, and Tom Howard, the managing director of Syder. They were all at work on the bid. It had to be made by 10 a.m. Danny was supposed to have his report already done. He felt his head itch slightly above both ears. This meant he was getting hot and he was getting hot because he was getting worried. He pushed at the smooth patch of skin between his eyebrows with the middle finger of his left hand while searching the online info-bank for a precedent.

He began drafting. Scott's notes on his part of the diligence were thorough but needed reorganizing and polishing. There were no real reasons for not bidding on the company. There were no poison pills hidden in the articles or main contracts, no change of control clauses, no crystallizing financial liabilities or options that kicked in and altered the capital structure of the company. Ulster Water had become a lost cause. The law that applied to it now was the law of the jungle. Syder would bid, UW would be taken over, and the bloodbath would begin. It would be a natural cull. Business was business. Danny bullet-pointed the issues raised. There were minor quibbles on copyright and outsourcing contracts but nothing of any substance. A pack was only as fast as its slowest member. The lame couldn't be saved. Danny daydreamed for a moment about making up a provision in the company articles that meant the issue of a new class of share capital, to a charity say, in the event of a takeover. It was a stupid idea. They would all have copies of the company's articles. There was nothing for it. Hunt or be hunted.

He searched the intranet's *Who's Who* for Freeman's details and the photo of his sacerdotal face appeared on the screen. Danny dialled the number listed and after one ring it was picked up – snatched was probably more accurate – and Freeman said, impatiently, 'Yes?'

'John, it's Danny Williams here. I just wanted to ring down ... '

'Where's the report? We're waiting for it.' Danny purposefully coughed loudly into the phone and pressed on regardless.

' . . . and let you know that I'll have the final version of the due diligence report ready in a few hours.'

'Anything in it?' Freeman spoke like he had his coat on, and Danny had caught him just nipping out the door. He hadn't of course. Freeman would have his shirtsleeves rolled up and his little bulbous head would be glowing sunset-pink with stress. He was going about his business. Soon, probably, he would die.

'A few minor issues, no deal-breakers, at least not in the contracts I saw.'

'Good. No deal-breakers, glad you think so.'

There was a mordant edge to everything Freeman said. It was the corrosion caused by having too much money and too little time.

'John, I wanted to ask about when . . . '

He'd hung up.

Danny lifted the plastic ribbed bottle of Evian from the shelf above his desk and walked down to the facilities room. There were three other lawyers in the corridor. All of them were, like Danny, contravening the firm's open-door policy. He held the bottle under the water cooler as it noisily filled, pulled two plastic cups from the dispenser and headed back to his office. The Black Bush was nesting in his lockable drawer, among his clean gym clothes, and he poured out a small peat-coloured shot, watered it down to a tawny hue and went back to the document open on his screen.

By midnight Freeman had rang him eight times. Danny still hadn't quite finished the report and was now dangerously close to being drunk. Everyone else in the corridor had gone home. He had printed out a fairly coherent thirty-page draft and was taking it by hand to the Corporate team. To get to the lift Danny had to walk along his own and then another corridor, both bookended by security doors requiring a pass. Danny pressed the release button by the doors at the end of his, forgetting that his security card was sitting on his desk, propped against the base of the Anglepoise light. He walked through the doors and, just as they clicked shut behind him, realized that he couldn't get out.

He was stuck in a vestibule that boasted the facilities of a disabled toilet and views along three empty corridors. No one was around. There is nothing lonelier than an empty corridor. It is not like an empty field or a forest, where humans are neither expected nor wanted. A corridor exists for the traffic of people, and without them is as bereft as a dry riverbed. He sat on a plastic crate that someone had left outside the toilet and set the report on the floor. Then he dragged the crate to the centre of the CCTV's view, sat on it again and waved at the camera. After a while he stood up and rattled each of the doors. It was already past midnight. 12.27. For fuck's sake.

Half an hour later Freeman himself came rolling towards him. He was like a little ballbearing, tiny and hard, and Danny's apologetic grin and open-handed shrug did nothing to temper his scorn.

'Dan Williams?'

Danny nodded. He knew Freeman would abbreviate his name like that.

'You prick. You get yourself locked in here?' His tone was pretend-jovial. Danny nodded again.

'Sorry, I forgot my security card and . . . ' He stopped talking. He had nothing to say. Even though it was a Sunday the partner was still dressed for business. He wore a blue shirt, the sleeves, Danny happily noted, rolled up, and high-waisted navy trousers with yellow braces. The fat Windsor knot of his dusky-pink tie seemed a watery reflection of the nose it sat a few inches under. Freeman looked like he drank too much, and he looked angry.

'Tom wants to see the diligence report before he signs off on the bid. That it?'

The head jerked towards the floor in front of the disabled toilet, where Danny had now spread the report out to spell

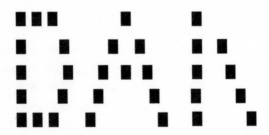

Danny nodded again. There hadn't been enough pages to finish his name and he hadn't bothered to rearrange it so it worked. Freeman barked, 'Pick it up, sort it out, bring it with you please.'

Danny was staring at his exceptional head. It was magnificently bald and ridged above the temples where the tectonic plates of his skull met. The partner had reversed and was holding the door open. Danny scrambled around picking up the pieces of paper, and then Freeman started rolling back up the corridor. Danny felt he was being irresistibly dragged along in his wake.

'And what the fuck happened to your eye?'

'Oh nothing. Tennis injury. Is the bid all done?'

'Yes.' Freeman hardly opened his mouth when he spoke. 'I've sent my team home.'

They were waiting for the lift and standing shoulder to shoulder, figuratively speaking. Literally speaking they were standing shoulder to elbow. It occurred to Danny to ask Freeman whether he was officially a midget. There was a height requirement and he was pretty sure Freeman filled it. It was something like four foot eleven or under. He decided to ask about the offer instead. 'And what's next then?'

'Well, we *print* it. And then we *deliver* it.' Freeman sounded like it was all he could do not to punch Danny in the crotch. Danny wondered if he was married. He looked down, without moving his head, and spotted a gold band embedded on his finger. In that case he hoped he didn't have any kids, particularly slow ones. He was the type of father who would convince his children of their dumbness on a daily basis, and leave them unable to open a window or envelope without feeling anxious and useless. The lift pinged its arrival and the doors slid back. The raging dwarf strode triumphantly in and Danny followed. Freeman jabbed at the button for the second floor, changed to attacking the one saying *Close Doors*, and then returned to jabbing the 2 again.

'Great. All sorted out then.'

'Almost. As my team's gone home, you'll be taking the

bid to the printers. I'm going to sit down with Tom and run through this.' He took the report out of Danny's hands and turned back to the lift door.

'Right . . . What happens if there *is* stuff in the report that impacts on the bid?' Danny was thinking *what a fucking waste of time*.

'Well, it's like you said, there were no deal-breakers in it.' He could detect a smirk in Freeman's voice. 'So can you manage to take the offer document to the printers? You won't get yourself locked in the cab or anything?'

Danny grinned at the side of his head, ready for the partner to look up and smile, but instead Freeman just stood there, facing the door, and staring up at the numbers lighting and fading as the lift descended. Danny smothered an urge to elbow him in the back of the head.

'Sure, I can do that.'

'Good. Adam Vyse rang me earlier to see how we were getting on and he said you should take it down. Good experience for you. Adam's overseeing the bid logistics tomorrow morning.'

Tom Howard was sitting at the oval meeting table in Freeman's office, papers fanned out in front of him. He was a handsome, cleanly-drawn man in his late forties with the slightly dampened demeanour of a person reformed – alcohol, Danny thought, or possibly gambling – but the heat of his smile when Danny approached made it obvious that Howard detested Freeman as much as he did. The partner bobbed like a spring at his elbow, and thrust Danny's report back at him. 'Make two copies of this.'

Ignoring him, Howard reached over the table and offered his hand to Danny.

'Tom Howard.'

'Danny Williams.' Howard had a businessman's practised grip.

'You've been over in *Belfast*, I hear.'

He said it like Belfast was just south of Baghdad.

'That's right, doing the due diligence.'

'That where you got the shiner?'

'Oh no, nothing like that.' Danny raised his hand to
his eye. There was still a slight puffiness.

'Anything to worry about in the contracts?'

'Not really. A few small points you should be aware
of. They seemed a good team over there.' Danny lifted
his report off the desk.

Freeman snorted, 'Tom, couple of issues we actually
do need to resolve this evening . . . I'm concerned . . . '
– he sat down at the table opposite Howard and thrust
out his hands to hold an invisible bowl – ' . . . about
capital.' Howard nodded thoughtfully. Freeman gently
shook his bowl a few times.

'I'll go and make some copies of this,' Danny said,
brandishing his report. As he moved to the door, Howard
glanced over at him a little fearfully. The look reminded
Danny of something. In the corridor he realized it was
the standard look that the abused wife in a soap opera
gives the policeman, unable to speak but aware that his
imminent departure will leave her alone with her husband.

LATE LATE NIGHT

Security rang through to tell Danny the cab had arrived. The bid – all 173 pages of it – was ring-bound with a plastic coil. He put the blue folder containing it into his leather satchel. The bottle of Bush was nearly empty. He shook it and then squeezed it into the bag alongside the folder. It was 2.37 a.m. He wanted a cigarette. The problem with taxis at this time in the morning was the talkative drivers. Normally his cabbies were terse and polite but in the early mornings, when most fares were presumably trying to fight or fuck or puke in the back of their vehicles, the drivers would invariably want to chat to a sober passenger. Sometimes it was pleasant. Often it was not. The driver would frequently describe a detailed legal case involving a relative. And then ask your opinion. Danny climbed into the cab.

'Evening . . . Borough is it? You know the road?'

'Marshal Street. 224 Marshal Street.'

'Yeah I know it. Bermondsey side.'

Danny leant back against the seat. The driver pulled away from the kerb.

'You working late then?'

'Unfortunately.'

'What? Big court case is it?'

'No, not really, a takeover.'

'Oh yes?'

'Yep.'

They were driving down Ludgate Hill. Small grey clouds massed on the horizon below an impassive moon. The streets were shrink-wrapped and glossy so it must have rained. There was a cold breeze coming in through his window so he shut it. The lights went red and the cab pulled to a stop. There was no one about. Danny listened as the timer for the green man frantically tick-tick-ticked.

'You get in a fight?'

'Smashed my head on a chair,' Danny said. He could change the story. It was his choice.

'You drunk?' the driver continued.

'No, just clumsy,' Danny said apologetically.

'You Scottish?' This driver has a nice line in question formation, Danny thought, as he accidentally made eye contact with him in the rearview mirror. Both looked away immediately.

'Northern Irish.' Danny was trying to unscrew the cap from the bottle of Bush without the driver noticing.

'Really? My mum's Northern Irish. Lives in Cardiff now though.'

'Right.'

'She's from Donaghadee.'

Danny kept silent.

'We used to go there all the time when I was a little 'un. She used to have all these rhymes. Not rhymes. I don't know what you'd call them. Sayings. *Augher, Clogher, Fivemiletown*. Funny things to teach kids.'

'It's a funny place.'

'It's a *lovely* place. The Northern Irish are really friendly to tourists.'

'Just not to each other.' The driver wasn't listening.

'She used to say to us *If I weren't so Ballymena with my Ballymoney . . .* '

'I'd build a Ballycastle for my Ballyholm. I know that one.'

The lights had changed and they still weren't moving.

'It's green now,' Danny said, trying to sound relaxed but feeling absolutely crushed. It was almost three in the morning and he was reciting nursery rhymes in a cab. He shouldn't be doing this job. He shouldn't be making so much money for banks and corporations; and for himself. He earned more than a doctor. He should have *been* a doctor.

'You over here long then?'

'About eight years I suppose. In London for five.'

'You like it? Very different I suppose.'

'It's okay. I've too much work.' The standard response. Danny felt bored by himself.

'I picked a girl up last week. Twenty-one she was, and she'd been working three days on the trot. No sleep.'

'From Monks?'

'No, one of the others. The one over by London Wall. What do you call it? Crazy bunch you lot. Can't be good for you. I said to her, *You'll wreck your health love . . .* '

'Yeah.'

'Look at me. What age do you reckon I am?'

The man looked about fifty.

'Forty?'

'Fifty. I'm fifty years of age. No one can believe it. And you know why I look like this? No stress. I work when I want to. Or when I need the money. And then when I don't, I play golf.'

'That's a good life.'

'No, it's not. It's rubbish. I told my son, *You study so you don't have to drive a poxy cab all day. You get good grades and you'll end up in a nice office, have a career.*'

'What does your son do?'

'He's a fireman. Marshal Street, did you say son?'

'Right.'

Danny had lost track of the sense of the conversation. He felt he was being obscurely tricked. They were crossing the Blackfriars Bridge. He wanted to get out and walk. London looked best from the river. Seeing the city sliced into cross sections gave you a sense of distance and scale. They were heading to a place called Lion Printers. Danny was thinking about tomorrow morning. He would have to get up, go to work, and take shit from Vyse. He was delivering a bid that would get people sacked. Margaret and Lillian. Jack Shannon. And another few thousand besides. He was the instrument of their demise. The team and the client would go out for a meal if their bid was successful, and he would have to watch Vyse gloating and grinning in victory. The taxi had reached Borough now. The nervous flicker of a TV played on the window of someone's first floor flat. A white man in a long black coat was walking very fast along the pavement. They stopped at more lights. The driver started singing, in a surprisingly mellow voice.

'*I wish I was in Carrickfergus, only for nights in Ballygrand.*

I would swim over the deepest oceans, the deepest oceans to be by your side.'

His head tilted to allow him to make eye contact with Danny in the rearview mirror.

'She used to sing that as well, my mum. Lovely song that.'

'It is.' Jesus Christ, Danny thought, I'm about to start crying. I am very unhappy. I am an unhappy person. The taxi driver went on talking.

'You know, the last time I drove through Borough at night I saw a fox.'

'There's a lot of them about.' Danny drew the tissue from the pocket of his jeans and quietly blew his nose.

'No there isn't. That's the only time I've ever seen . . . Marshal, Marshal, here we are.'

They turned left into a narrow one-way street.

'It's along here somewhere. There's 18, 22, what's the number again?'

'224. It's called Lion Printers.'

'Must be way up the other end.'

The street was lined with huge buildings, gyms and lofts and art galleries converted from workhouses, tanneries, factories. It was a valley of industrial death. This was what was left of Victorian Britain: this ironwork of gates and fire escapes crawling over the regimented brickwork, an orderly world where Christian salvation could be reached through a solid work ethic. But Danny didn't believe in God. And he had lost his faith in work. He heard himself speak. 'Actually mate, can you take me back towards the office?'

'You forgotten something?'

'Yeah I have.'

He was wasting his life. *Let someone else do it.* The cab took a sharp left into another alley and turned again back towards the river. The buildings thinned and then they were out onto the wide thoroughfare of Blackfriars Road. As they crossed onto the bridge again Danny leaned forward and asked the driver to pull up for a minute.

'Are you going to be sick? No puking in the cab son. Fifty quid to get it valeted.'

'I'm not going be sick. I just need you to stop for a second, okay?'

'Well . . . no puking in the cab. Or boking, that's what my mum calls it. No boking.'

The cab pulled up in the middle of the bridge and Danny got out, carrying his satchel. The driver wound down his window.

'You're not depressed are you son? Not as bad as all that is it?'

'No, I'm fine. Just want a breath of air. I'll be two minutes.'

'Take as long as you fancy. Meter's running.'

Danny lifted the bottle of Bush and the blue folder out of his bag. He unscrewed the whiskey and tipped the few drops that were left over the side, into the Thames. Then he wedged the empty bottle under his arm and opened the ring-bound folder. The first few pages of the bid fluttered and he ripped them off. He dropped the folder on the pavement and rolled the pages up before pushing them into the bottle. Their whiteness darkened where they touched the wet sides. He screwed the lid back on tightly and held it over the side by the neck, swinging it like a pendulum. And then he let it go. One second, two seconds. A remote splash sounded. He watched for the bottle to bob back up before it passed under the bridge but it didn't. It was making him dizzy looking down into the water. There was a breeze lifting off the river that brought the smell of the whiskey on his hands up to his face. He lifted the folder off the pavement, peeled the top sheet from the rest of the bid, and let go. It flickered away and then swung down to the water. He ripped off another. And then he whipped off a flurry of them, five or six, and they turned and wheeled like paper planes. It seemed an age before they reached the water, patching it for a second with wet white squares before they were carried out of sight. He opened the ring binder and emptied the rest of the paper over the side in a clump but before it hit the river the wind caught it, and broke it up into a stream of frantic doves. And then they were gone.

He turned around, still holding the empty blue folder. The bemused cabbie was staring at him out through the open window.

'Should you have done that son?'

'Yeah . . . It had a mistake.'

He climbed back in.

'Could you take me home? Sofia Road? Off Kingsland?'

'You're the boss . . . You going to be all right?'

When Danny stepped out of the cab by his flat, his legs almost gave under him. He was fucked. He had done

293

something irrevocable, something unfixable The bid must be halfway to Deptford by now. Everything flowed. If he'd delivered the offer to the printers, Margaret and Lillian would have lost their jobs. He preferred not to deliver it. It would have been like sacking his aunties. It had suddenly seemed pretty simple. He didn't *have* to deliver it. To pretend there were no other options was the easiest thing in the world. He got a monthly salary, not to mention free gym membership, health insurance, a private pension plan and subsidized canteen food, to compensate him *for* pretending. He got business cards to carry in the jacket pocket over his heart, where soldiers used to keep their Bibles. There was an employment contract of course. But there were other obligations apart from those set down in twelve point font to be countersigned and dated. He could survive pretending his actions were small and complete in themselves but this was untrue. It was misstatement. Lawyers know about consequences. They know about loss and they know about fault. He had made so many mistakes. He could have helped Hughes.

Leaving a man dead or dying on the floor of his home. Which you've just broken into. He should look up *Allen's Criminal Law* to check if the charge was murder or manslaughter. It would turn on intent. He was panicking now, and leaned into his stone gatepost to steady himself. The satchel slipped from his shoulder and he set it onto the wall. There was no going back to fix that or change this. He had left Hughes. And now he had fucked up the bid. He had, intentionally, fucked up the bid. He would be fired. And he would have to sell his flat. He might even be sued, and then maybe jailed. He had to calm down.

He would explain that he'd suddenly felt ill and needed to come home. And that then he'd passed out. Food poisoning. A safe bet. Overly graphic details. He remembered once ringing up his first trainer Jim and describing the colour of his imaginary vomit (pearly yellow) before spending the day in bed with Olivia. He would get all of this sorted. He would write out a list. He would have a large spliff and write out a list. He lifted his bag and walked towards the door. As he slipped his Yale key into the lock he was momentarily cheered by a sudden thought: Adam Vyse's week would get off to a wonderfully shitty start.

He turned the key and pushed but the door snagged short. Geordie, the idiot, had slid the chain across. He turned to see the tail lights of the taxi wink out of the end of the street. He took his mobile from his satchel and tried Geordie's number. As he waited for the call to get through he glanced up and down the road and became sharply aware of a sensation unusual in the city. He was utterly alone. Then he noticed a window was lit several doors down on the far side. Every residential street in London seemed to have its own insomniac, in the way that the best country estates used to boast a hermit secreted in their grounds, someone to live on in our absence. Each road also required a single extinguished streetlight, the puzzle of a broken chair on the pavement, and one locked-out tenant trying to wake his slumberous flatmate. Geordie's mobile was turned off. He would have to shout. Pushing his head into the three-inch gap, he stage-whispered, in short syllabic bursts, 'Geord.'

'Jan.'

295

'Geord.'

There was no response. The silver Ikea clock ticked in his hallway. A television was on somewhere but not in his flat. He tried again, louder this time.

'Geordie.'

'*Wake* up.'

This was ridiculous. First he was locked in and now he was locked out.

'GEORDIE.'

A door scraped open and timidly Geordie asked, 'Hello?'

'Geordie, it's Danny. I'm *here*. You put the fucking chain on.'

'Shit, sorry mate.'

Geordie shut the door and opened it again the whole way. He was only wearing a pair of pants. 'You're back late. You get it all sorted out?'

'Kind of. Are those my pants?'

'Yeah, I ran out of clean clothes.'

Danny walked past him into the kitchen.

'You want a cup of tea?'

'Aye, all right. Everything okay?'

'No, not really.'

Geordie nodded, crept into the boxroom and reappeared in the kitchen in one of Dan's T-shirts and a pair of his tracksuit bottoms. He closed the kitchen door behind him very carefully. Janice was still asleep in the bed they'd made from the sofa's cushions.

'Thanks for getting Jan by the way. It was brilliant, really.'

'Nice to see her then?'

'Oh aye, nice to see *all* of her.'

'She *is* very pretty, great figure,' Danny said judiciously.

'Oh aye.' They both stood in silence for a second, before Geordie, realizing that Danny was still thinking about Janice's body, asked, 'So what's the crack? What happened?'

'I chucked the offer for Ulster Water into the Thames.' Danny sat down at the table. Geordie did the same.

'What do you mean?'

'I *mean* I stood on the Blackfriars Bridge and threw it all into the river.'

'Fuck. Well what does *that* mean?'

'It means I'm in a lot of trouble.'

'Sure you never really liked that job.'

'No.'

Geordie laughed. For a second Danny stared at the wooden surface of the table, in an effort to maintain the gravity of the situation, but then joined in. When the laughter trickled to a stop he shrugged suddenly, a little helplessly, and Geordie stood up, reached above the big blue fridge and opened the cupboard of booze. It looked like a town full of churches in there: vodka steeples, brick towers of whiskey, a Limoncello spire at the back.

'What'll you have?'

'I've been on Bushmills so I'll stick with that.'

'Wise man . . . Here, your eye looks fucking awful.' Geordie grinned, lifted two glasses from the crockery on the draining board and sat down at the table. He poured a couple of shots of whiskey and handed one to Danny.

'So why'd you chuck it off the bridge?'

'Not sure really . . . I went a bit mental. Kept thinking about home. And Ellen's been sleeping with my boss.'

Geordie breathed out a long note-less whistle. 'Gutted,' he said. 'When did you find out?'

'Saturday night, after we shagged.'

The word didn't taste right: they'd had sex, even, at a push, made love.

'You shagged her? Is she going to stop seeing the boss?'

'Oh no it's all stopped already. Been over for six months apparently.'

'Ach, well what are you whining about? Did you think she was a wee virgin?'

'No of course not . . . '

'You should be pleased she's single at all. Girl like that, surprised her boss didn't marry her.'

'He's *my* boss. And he is married already. He's got three kids.'

'Is that what it is? Have *you* ever slept with a married woman?'

'No.'

'Well what about someone who was going out with someone else?'

'Yeah.'

'And have you ever played away? When you've been seeing someone?'

'A couple of times.'

Geordie raised his eyebrows at him and said, 'And was Ellen cheating on someone when she was seeing your boss?'

He was enjoying his theatrical role as inquisitor a bit too much, Danny thought. He wouldn't have made a bad barrister.

'I don't think so. No.'

'So *you've* done worse than her . . . '

Geordie looked at Danny levelly then added, in a softer tone, 'Did you go mad?'

'Ballistic. And then I started to get upset.'

'What – crying?'

'Weirdly, yeah.'

'Wanker.'

'Cheers.'

'To a new job.' Geordie said, raising his whiskey to eyelevel.

'Aye. Maybe even a new profession.' Danny chinked the glass and sipped unhopefully.

'*Mate*, she's fucking lovely you know. Really fit, and sweet and friendly. You fucked up there, I reckon. You should be more concerned about chucking whatever you chucked off the bridge than who she's slept with.'

'Aye . . . ' So that was it over then. He'd expected the story of Ellen and Vyse to last for several hours when he first recounted it. If Albert was here he would have sympathized, analysed, and discussed the various consequences and outcomes. Then he would have recommended a self-help book entitled something like *The Ex-Factor* or a therapist who specialized in Jealousy Management. There should be more to the story than this. He had sat up crying for Christ's sake. Even so, Danny couldn't remember him and Geordie talking like this before: a conversation not constructed entirely from loose insults and brinkmanship. He could mention the other thing now. He *should* mention it now.

'And I tell you what . . . this whole weekend's making me think about Hughes. I feel sick to the stomach. I've let a lot of people down and I keep thinking about Hughes lying in the hallway, his leg all . . . '

Danny faltered. Geordie tapered his eyes into slits and then opened them wide, sighed and said, 'That Hughes thing . . . It was nothing to do with you.'

299

'I *know*, but I should have told someone about it. I could have . . . '

Geordie interrupted him, 'No, I mean it was *nothing* to do with you. You want to know what happened?'

Danny kept silent. Geordie chewed at his thumbnail, then looked at it, and began talking again.

'Me and Budgie were burgling the place. That's what happened. I'd just been in there when I met you. I was coming from his house. Budgie'd just squealed off in his Corsa.'

Danny looked at him blankly.

'What?' He was speaking very softly.

'It's true. I was legging it from the house and then you comes walking up. Budgie had been using me to squeeze in through the back windows. No one else was small enough.'

'What?' Danny said again, even softer this time. He set his glass down on the dark table.

'You *fuck*ing . . . '

'It's years ago.'

'It's fourteen years ago tomorrow. The Glorious Twelfth.'

'Exactly.'

'What happened in the house?'

'Just what I said. They were burgling it and then . . . '

Danny interrupted, '*They* were burgling it?'

Geordie shrugged.

'Okay. So *we* were burgling it. All right? And then I met you . . . '

Danny was staring balefully at him. Geordie paused and then said, slower, 'I'd gone in through the back window, into the bathroom and then . . . let me get my fags.'

He got up and reappeared a moment later with the silver ashtray and his Regals. He lit one – preparing himself – and started again. Danny remained motionless and watched.

'I came down through the window onto the cistern. It was white and my trainers left dirty marks on it from the grass. Then once I was in I wiped them off with some toilet roll and threw it into the bowl. Then I opened the back door for Budgie and Chicken. He was there too.'

'What?'

'Chicken. He was there too.'

'Right.'

Geordie tapped some ash out and looked at something under the nail of his right middle finger. The smoke twisted into loose prehensile loops above the tabletop. Danny took one of the fags.

'Chicken went to the living room to unplug the telly and video and Budgie went up the stairs. I was looking through drawers in the kitchen and there was a thump. Hughes must have been sleeping or something. It was hot – middle of July wasn't it? – and all I heard was a thump, really loud and heavy, like a big sack of spuds dropped from a lorry. I went out into the hall and there was Hughes lying all twisted. No blood or anything though. Chicken was just stood there looking down at him and then up at the landing and then back down to Hughes. I looked up then too and Budgie was peering over the banister and looking half-scared with himself and half-pleased. You'd have thought he'd brought down a tiger or something.'

'Just tell it straight.'

'I'm not joking. This is what I remember . . . We were just frozen. Budgie started to come down the stairs then and that unstuck us. Chicken starts talking. He was going *You stupid fucking cunt, you stupid fucking cunt* and I thought he was talking to Hughes so I said something like *Well, it's hardly his fault* but he was talking to Budgie and he started shouting then: *Of course it's his fucking fault, he shoved him over the banister, he pushed him over the fucking banister.* And then Chicken gets down on his knees and starts listening to Hughes's mouth and I thought Hughes was speaking to him so I said *What's he saying? What's he saying?* but Chicken was trying to hear if he was breathing. Then Budgie was in the hall with us and he pulls Chicken up away from Hughes and says *Let's go.* Just like that. *Let's go.*'

Geordie stopped. His face was lit with an unusual emotion. Danny identified it as excitement.

'And what? And then what?'

'And then we went.'

'I don't understand.'

'I reckon he must have been sleeping and came out of the room suddenly. Just appeared on the landing and freaked Budgie out.'

'But I don't understand why *we* went back there. Why'd you bring *me* into it? It was nothing to do with me.'

Geordie shrugged again. The gesture angered Danny. Geordie would never square up to things. He would never shoulder responsibility.

'I don't know really. I wanted . . . I wanted to see if he was dead. And I couldn't get in without someone to help me up to the window . . . We'd picked a corner house. It weren't overlooked by anyone else's so I knew we'd be safe enough to get back in, and if we were caught . . . well, I think I thought everyone would believe what you said – that we'd done nothing, that you wanted to use the phone, that you were running away from some boys chasing you, all that.'

Danny lifted the bottle of Bushmills and poured another dose into his glass. He hadn't killed anyone. None of this had anything to do with him.

'Jesus Christ . . . You *should* have told me this.'

'Aye. Sorry.'

'I've got to go to bed.' Danny didn't want to look at him any more. He was a moron, an idiot, a dangerous lunatic who pulled people into vehicles that were moving too fast and had no seat belts or brakes. He was trouble wrapped up in a wink and a pint and a cloud of smoke.

'Not yet. Wait up a bit. Sure you've no work to go to.'

Danny stared at the kitchen window. It was dark and shadowy as a photographic negative. He felt like Geordie had broken into *his* flat. This man wearing his clothes and sitting at his table and drinking his whiskey was an intruder, a liar and a thief. He was a stranger.

'I didn't get you to come to the house 'cause I wanted to get you in trouble you know.'

'No?' Danny was too tired to do this any more.

'If I'd met someone else that day I mightn't have gone back at all . . . When we were younger you were always the good one, the kid who did everything right . . . I mind the time you stopped Davy Thom from making me drink that piss in the Top Deck can. Hammy'd already drank it. Do you remember? He said *I knew it was piss because it was warm.*'

Despite himself, Danny smiled.

303

'And maybe I wanted to be good too, or something, when I saw *you* . . . though you'd just smacked some cub in the balls.'

'Slim.'

'Aye, Slim, that's right. *He* was a real fucker.'

'They're everywhere.'

'They are . . . I *am* sorry about it.'

'So am I.'

'Apologies mate . . . Really.'

They sat in silence. Danny stubbed out his fag and said, 'You remember his eye? The way it was watching the wall? How fucking scared it looked?'

'He was all mashed up.'

'Yeah.'

Silence again. He hadn't murdered anyone. Danny solemnly topped up Geordie's drink, lifted his glass and whispered, 'Cheers.'

'Cheers.'

They drank and after a pause Geordie said, 'Would you ever credit that whole thing about Ian? I couldn't believe it.'

'Unbelievable.'

'He *was* immensely strong,' Geordie said respectfully.

'Immensely?'

'Yeah, immensely.' Geordie looked serious and Danny smirked.

'That's a funny word. Immensely . . . How're your immense wounds?'

'You laugh but I swear he gave my head a serious smack with the door. You can feel the bump . . . here.'

He pulled Danny's fingers across the table and held them just above the hairline on his forehead. How odd it was to touch his head, the hair baby-soft and thin. There was a protrusion, curved as an egg, as seemingly delicate.

'Did he break anything in the flat?'

'Nope. Took all the cash though.'

'Thank fuck. You're best out of all that ... Budgie Johnson. I can't believe he killed Hughes.'

'I'm not sure *he* did, to be honest. *Something* happened. I know that ... ' More silence. Then Geordie started again, 'What do you reckon Ian's going to spend all that money on?'

'I dunno. Not on a present for us anyway ... Maybe he's buying a load of something to take back home and sell. Pirated DVDs or smuggled cigarettes.'

'Or drugs. It might be drugs.'

'Could be drugs ... Do you know where he said he was taking the cash?'

'Naw. He mentioned ... now what *did* he mention? He was staying in Kilburn, or at least he said he was, at some place called ... the Gregory, the Lord Gregory. And he said "Anything the IRA can do we can do better" or something. It probably is drugs.'

'We could try and stop it. Try and dob him in to fuck up his and Budgie's plans.'

Geordie nodded. Danny was on a high, winched up by Geordie's revelation and the whiskey. He hadn't made Geordie break into Hughes's house. They hadn't caused Hughes's death, although Budgie Fucking Johnson had. And he'd been wrong about Ellen. What did it matter what she'd done with whom? And besides, now they'd both fucked Vyse. He would love to see him explain this one to Freeman, Tom Howard and the rest of the Litigation partners. Ulster Water wasn't about to be bought and hacked up. He might have saved thousands of jobs. He felt a new looseness in himself, like he was oiled and running properly. He could *change* things. He could *fix* things. He looked at Geordie, who pulled Rizlas and a lump of hash from the cigarette packet and began deftly skinning up, and he was reminded of being in a gang again, a team. He said, 'You know we should try and see where he is maybe. Follow him. Nothing stupid obviously. But see where he is and then make an anonymous call or something.'

'You serious?'

Danny nodded.

'We could I suppose. Get up early and drive to his hotel.'

'And wait for him to come out. Just follow him.'

'You're not going to work then?'

'Nope,' Danny looked at his diving watch, 'and it's already gone four. We might as well stay up and wait.'

They are the Lords and owners of their faces.

William Shakespeare

MONDAY, 12 JULY 2004

'Here ... Check it out.' Geordie was nodding through the windscreen. A voluptuous white girl was walking down the pavement towards them. She wore tight jeans and a pink cropped top that was trying and failing to control her breasts. They'd parked outside the Kingston Shamrock Bed & Breakfast (which, surprisingly perhaps, had NO VACANCIES, according to a handwritten page blu-tacked to its front window). The Lord Gregory was opposite, several times larger, with upper parts that faced onto the High Road. Its blue front door, on this side street, was for now firmly shut.

'Okay but wait ... wait ... wait ... There ... Minging.'

'Yeah, not a great puss on her.'

'Albert would term your problem the eternal optimism of the hopelessly short-sighted.'

On the train to a departmental conference in Brighton,

Danny and Albert had sat facing forward and across the aisle from each other. They'd spent the hour and a half watching women walk down the carriage towards them. Danny hadn't his glasses on and Albert had accordingly diagnosed his misjudgements as the eternal etc. Geordie ignored Danny's comment: he didn't seem to like Albert. After a lengthy pause he said, 'I keep thinking I can see Ian's big baldy head popping out the door. I'm on tentative hooks with this waiting.'

'Tenterhooks,' Danny murmured reflexively.

'Tender hooks.'

'*Tent*erhooks.'

It was 7.13 a.m. and they were sitting in Danny's musty red Polo on Butler Street in Kilburn. He hadn't driven it for over a month and each time he'd spotted the parked car out the living room window he had felt vaguely guilty, like it was an unwalked dog. Despite this neglect the car had started first time and the traffic through London had been pretty light.

Geordie was wearing a red baseball cap that was too big for his head and gave him the look of a child with leukaemia. Danny, his partner on the stakeout, the sensible one, had put on his glasses and a floppy navy sunhat. Geordie said it was like a reconstruction from *Crimewatch*. Danny had wound the window down a few inches to let in some air: Geordie was jubilantly farting. Although their hangovers were not yet biting, they were both knackered, and their initial enthusiasm for the big adventure had quickly dried up. After smoking a couple of spliffs at the kitchen table they had adjourned to the sofa and watched *In the Heat of the Night*. Sitting in the car Danny tried to keep focused. He was Sidney Poitier as Mr Tibbs: maligned and mistreated, but dignified, handsome and coolly determined to bring wrongdoers to justice.

Around six, after Mr Tibbs had overcome the racism, apprehended the killer, and the final credits had rolled, Danny had grilled some bacon while Geordie made two mugs of coffee. There was no blind in the kitchen and the pale dawn gave the white work surfaces the ghostly sheen of milk. They sat at the kitchen table again, in the same seats as before, eating the sandwiches in silence and staring at nothing. Then they'd sloped off to get dressed and organized. When Geordie gently opened the door of the boxroom Danny caught a glimpse of Janice's silver-blonde hair fanned over a pillow. He hadn't seen it down before. She looked like a nineteen-forties movie star.

He rang directory enquiries and wrote down the Lord Gregory's address, then found an *A to Z* on the windowsill in his bedroom. Geordie had washed and was now pottering around the kitchen filling a plastic bag with supplies: a full two-litre carton of milk, the fat yellow claw of a bunch of bananas, and an unopened packet of Jaffa Cakes. They were ready.

At half-seven Geordie stated for the fourth time that he could *murder another bacon bap* and started peeling a second banana. The smell of Geordie's bananas and flatulence was advancing the cause of Danny's nausea. He wound the window down further and opened the biscuits. His stomach was burbling, bewildered at all the abuse it was getting. A street cleaner slowly crossed by the lights at the junction, pushing his cart like a barrow boy heading to market. Danny slid a whole Jaffa Cake into his mouth. This was quite a nice road, although the trees that speckled the pavement with shadow were inconsistently spaced, and so near to the terraced houses that Danny found himself thinking about subsidence insurance. He was trying to worry about what had happened at work, about what he had done *to* work, but found that he couldn't concentrate. They would probably sack him. That was true and it was serious. But he had some savings. Maybe he would go travelling. Or move back home. Or get another job. There must be other jobs. All of the people who lived in *these* houses must make enough money to live on.

By eight o'clock Geordie had fallen asleep and was snoring, but very faintly, as if miles away someone was using a chainsaw. Danny had finished cleaning his nails with a paperclip he'd found in the ashtray. He noticed a fleck of something in the vitreous humour of his right eye and played ping pong with it for a moment, flicking and skiffling it from the treetop to the lamppost and back.

By seventeen minutes past eight Danny had nodded off and Geordie'd woken up. His head had slipped down off the edge of the car seat and knocked into the window. He was restless and opened the glove compartment where there was a road atlas of the United Kingdom and a thick black marker. He started flicking through the atlas. Who knew Birmingham was there? Or that London was so far south? The satellite picture of the British Isles on the cover made it look as if Britain was trying to hug Ireland. Or eat it. He uncapped the marker. Danny shifted around in his seat, still asleep. Geordie leaned over and carefully daubed a Hitler moustache across Danny's philtrum. Danny stirred and Geordie withdrew, rocking about in his seat in excitement.

At 8.32 Danny was woken when a kid on a skateboard went past, clack-clacking over the slabs of the pavement. Geordie was grinning and chuckling softly to himself.

'What's funny?' Danny said, irritated.

'Nothing,' Geordie ventured.

'You wouldn't think so.'

Geordie immediately capitulated: there was no one else to appreciate the joke.

'Stop being such a Nazi,' he said, still grinning. Danny noticed Geordie glancing at his upper lip and leaned over to look in the mirror.

'You stupid cunt.' He tried to wipe it off but just managed to smudge one half of it into a Mexican's droopy moustache. Geordie cackled. Danny grabbed the pen from Geordie's hand and chucked it out the window. Immediately he regretted not keeping it, and not holding Geordie down to scrawl an obscenity with it on the plaque of the little shit's forehead.

At a quarter to nine Danny removed his sunhat and eyed his reflection in the rearview mirror. He had rubbed his upper lip red and the moustache had still not come off. He was less Sidney Poitier now and more a Spanish game show host who had just learned his series was not being renewed. And who had been recently punched in the eye. It was not a good look. Danny pulled his hat back on. He was so tired that when he moved his head it took his eyes a moment to re-focus, and the street seemed to shift a little, airpocket and shudder. Geordie was describing the serious trials his bowels were currently

311

undergoing, and the casual heroism he needed not to complain about them. Danny's response was engaged and direct:

'If you fart again, I will chuck you out of this car.'

'Fair enough.'

'I'm serious.'

'*Okay.*'

'You just farted, didn't you?'

'Fraid so.'

Just before nine the blue door of the Lord Gregory hotel (prop: N. Patel, rating: one star) opened, and Ian appeared, swinging a black sports bag. He was walking fast and away from them. Geordie needlessly exclaimed, 'Fucking hell, there he is,' and Danny started the car. Ian was smaller and broader than Danny remembered. His arms and legs were little pistons on an incredible engine that was gathering momentum. He vanished round the corner onto the High Road.

'We're going to fucking lose him,' Geordie leaned across Danny and tried to chuck the banana skin he'd been absent-mindedly holding out of the window. It hit the glass and fell down the side of Danny's car seat.

'You twat.' Danny pulled out and drove up to the junction. Geordie tugged his cap down even further – his ears were already inside its rim – and slinked an inch or two into his seat. Ian was within thirty metres of them but walking purposefully away. He wore blue jeans and a black shirt tightly tucked in. His back was an isosceles triangle, and so wide that his shaved head seemed tiny upon it, like an egg rolling around on a table.

'He's turning in.' Geordie had leant forward and

was holding onto the dashboard with one hand.

'Mate, can you calm down a bit? He'll see us. Check the *A to Z*.'

'What for?' Ian stepped out of sight again, back off the High Road and into a street called Wallace Row. Danny pulled up to the kerb and stuck his hazards on.

'I don't know. See if it's a cul-de-sac or something.'

'Well there's no dead-end sign.'

'True.'

Danny waited for a bus to go round him and then pulled back out. He indicated and turned into the street Ian had just thundered down.

'I can't see him.'

'Me neither.'

'Let's pull up somewhere.'

Danny reverse-parked in front of someone's stone-cladded home and turned the engine off.

'Well what do we do now?' Geordie sounded truculent.

'I don't know . . . Wait a minute, what shoes does Ian wear?'

'What? Not sure. Brown leather?'

'I can see his fucking foot. That's his fucking foot.'

Across the road and three parked cars away sat a white transit van with its driver's door ajar. Someone appeared to be lying halfway under the front bumper, working at the registration plate. Their foot poked out into the road, displaying a brown leather shoe and a band of white sock.

'What's he doing?' Geordie asked, excited again.

'I don't know.'

A stubby hand moved into view and set a screwdriver

onto the tarmac. It rolled for an inch or two before the hand reappeared and stopped it.

'Can you read the reg? Is he taking the plate off or putting it on?'

'I think it's Northern Irish. I can only see the last three digits. Looks like he's taking it off.'

'What the fuck's he doing that for?'

Ian was up on his feet – 'Watch out,' Geordie whispered and scrunched lower – and then Ian crouched back down again, placing something into a black holdall. Just then Danny's mobile rang. He gingerly took it out of his jeans and looked at the display. Number Withheld. That meant it was Monks. His stomach tightened with expectancy.

'It's work. Fuck. Will I speak to them?'

'Give it here.' Geordie pressed the button to accept the call.

'Hello? . . . No, this is Mr Wilson . . . George Wilson Esquire.' Danny tried to grab the phone back but Geordie pushed him away. 'No, I haven't seen him this morning. No, he's not in his room. Okay, let me write it down . . . ' Geordie looked over at Danny, who was shaking his grimacing head, and winked to say *it's all under control*. He tapped the mouthpiece of the mobile on the dashboard for a second and then said, 'Okay, I've a pen here. Fire away. Carrie, uh-huh, Adam's secretary, uh-huh. And Mr Vyse is out for blood . . . I quite understand. Hold on.' He tapped the phone against the dashboard again and pointed at the white transit: Ian was getting into it. Danny lifted a newspaper from the back seat – a year old *Guardian* – and opened it out in front of his face.

314

'Sorry about that. My pen's not working properly. Right . . . yes . . . jeopardised the bid. Got you, yep . . . Empty his desk? Of everything? Okay. Right. Yes . . . *Lying* Printers? Oh, *Lion* Printers, yep . . . At five in the morning? Right, Adam came in and rushed another copy round . . . So the bid was made . . . Thanks to Brad. Is that short for Bradford? Bradley. Yes, I've got that. Okay, I'll pass the message on . . . Thanks for *your* time, Carrie . . . No, thank *you*.' He turned the phone off completely and pretended to forage for something down by his feet.

'Not good then?' Danny said.

'He's about to drive past . . . He's just driven past. Start the car. Unlucky, mate. You've been sacked for gross misconduct. Effective immediately. You can clear your desk or they can send you your things.'

'Okay,' Danny said simply. He turned the key in the ignition, and felt whatever energy he had left flow out of him and into the little car. It shuddered and then started pulsing impatiently.

Geordie gave a little purr of calculation, then whispered, 'It's not the end of the world, boss.'

'No.' Danny was too shocked to speak. He was unemployed. Like Geordie. He was out of work. After years of staying anchored to a desk, witnessing his gradual submersion by the high tide of a job he didn't like and couldn't do, he'd been cut loose. He was floating on the surface. This was good. This was a good thing, he repeated in his head, not quite able to swim across to the far side of the persuaded.

Suddenly Geordie bellowed in his smoker's thickened voice, 'Come *on*, we have to follow him.'

Ian was at the junction behind them. Danny worked the car into a three-point turn. Ian was pulling out.

'Watch where he goes,' Danny mumbled. The Polo reached the T-junction and the white van was on the other side of the road, waiting at the traffic lights. Danny pulled out into the path of a bus. After braking and giving a long blast of its horn, it sailed up beside them. Danny looked across to see a row of faces watching him impassively, like a jury. They were two cars away from Ian but the colour of the bus reminded Danny that their vehicle was similarly conspicuous, a red too bright and noticeable to tail the van successfully. He should be driving something khaki. But there were so many cars in London: every corner brought a new herd of them shuffling out to join the northerly or southerly migrations along the High Road. The lights changed and Ian drove forward a few hundred metres before pulling into Ritchie Street. Danny turned in after him but the van was gone.

'It's disappeared,' Geordie said.

'Like the white rabbit.'

'Drive on down slowly. He must have gone in under one of those arches.'

A huge solid yellow gate started to slide across an entrance.

'There, he must have pulled in down there. The street's blocked at the far end so we should turn and park facing up to the main road, 'case he comes out.'

In the yard Ian had reversed the van up to a garage. Tomek, Bartosz and Jerzy were standing in front of its open doorway like picketing miners or shipyard workers, arms folded in solidarity. Ian turned the van off and watched them for a second in the wing mirror. He felt a little nervous, but that was natural. It was like the closing minutes of a game. He got out.

'Good morning.' Ian's mouth was too dry and his voice gave a little. He swallowed some saliva.

'Ian, good morning. You have the rest of the purse?' The three of them were still standing there, a defensive wall waiting for the free kick to be taken. It was the one with the abbreviated nose who spoke. Tomek, Ian remembered, thinking of his mnemonic, one of the tricks they'd learned in their LifeSkills class: the name Tomek contains a toe, which is a body-part like a nose. Tomek has a broken nose. He'd had a back-up memory device as well: the name Bartosz contained a bar, and a bar could be used to connect things, like a bridge. Bartosz's nose had a bridge.

'What purse?' Ian said, causing Tomek to look at his brother. Bartosz said nothing and remained eerily motionless. His eyes were a neutral grey in their deep sockets, the kind so sunken that the cheekbones suddenly rush inwards.

'The other money, the balance of the purse.'

'Oh aye, of course.' He went round to the side of the van and opened the front door. When he reappeared, holding the black holdall, Jerzy was pointing a handgun at him. Ian noted that it was a Browning Challenger, not a bad choice.

'What the fuck is this?' Ian asked, quite reasonably.

'Just a little of the caution,' Tomek replied. He was the only one who had spoken so far. Jerzy moved across the other two men and stood about six feet from Ian. Then Bartosz moved over and lifted the holdall out of his hand. He passed it to Tomek and patted Ian down. Nothing. Tomek stepped in under the brim of the garage door and set the holdall down on an oily carpentry bench. He unzipped it and pulled out a white plastic bag, loosely rectangular with stacked bank notes. Ian, self-consciously staying completely still, watched as he endlessly, professionally flicked through the cash once, and again, before finally nodding and murmuring something in Polish to the others. Jerzy lowered the pistol and then casually thrust it into his cheap leather jacket like it was his wallet or phone.

'Okay, thanks for this . . .' Tomek's voice was amplified by the garage and sounded lower than before. 'And now, for *you*.' He moved across the gloom and unexpectedly, with a matador's flourish, whipped back a sheet of tarpaulin.

Danny and Geordie were parked up on the pavement about fifty metres from the gate. The street was quite empty and only a single car, a silver Ford Puma, sat between them and the yard. Geordie's mobile was down to one bar and he wanted to save it in case Janice should text, so he turned Danny's phone back on in order to ring her. He hadn't left her a note to explain where they'd gone. As soon as the mobile had initialized three voicemails and four text messages beeped up on the screen.

'Here, Hitler, you're a popular man,' Geordie said drily. 'Your fan club are looking for you.'

Danny checked the voicemails. Albert: frantic and almost erotically excited about the unfolding drama. Ellen: upset and concerned, explaining that Adam Vyse had

questioned her over the missing bid. Danny felt sick at
the thought of the two of them speaking. Jill, his Welsh
secretary: bemused and repeating the tenor of Carrie's
earlier message but advising that Danny apologize, feign
illness, a breakdown, and kindly referring to Vyse as a
needle-dicked bastard. This was solely for his benefit. He
knew that she had, in fact, quite a soft spot for Danny's
antagonist and he had often heard the hawking drainage
of her laugh when Vyse, sitting on the edge of her desk,
regaled the secretarial pod. The texts were all from Albert
again: expressing mounting levels of curiosity about what
was going on. The last one was simply three rows of
question marks with one final full stop.

When Jerzy was loading the van, Ian found that he
couldn't stop watching the flywhisk of the Pole's pony-
tail whip about. A couple of times it brushed Ian's arm
when they moved round each other. He was a big man,
a solid rod of muscle. Ian was thinking he would make
a good training partner. They should spot each other.
Jerzy could maybe outpress him on the bench but Ian
could definitely clean snatch a bit more. The big man's
legs didn't look so strong in those tight jeans. Ian climbed
into the back of the van and made the final arrangements (it only took a couple of minutes) while the three
Poles stood and smoked in the garage. He backed carefully out and gently closed the van door. The men stood
four-square and shook each other's hands with compet-
itive, monkey-wrench grips, and then Jerzy disappeared
into the back of the shop. Ian climbed into the van's
driver's seat. The two brothers, who were to leave that
night for Warsaw, stood side by side again in front of

the garage. Both had miniature smiles playing at the corners of their mouths. Tomek folded his arms over the white plastic bag filled with money. Through the windscreen they looked to Ian oddly like a family on a doorstep seeing a visitor off, with the mother holding the swaddled baby. He wiped over the surfaces and steering wheel with a chamois from the passenger seat, pulled on his mesh-backed driving gloves, and started the transit.

The yellow gate started to move back behind the stone wall in a jerky eclipse. Geordie sat up a little and said, 'Here we go. Open sesame.' Danny started the car, then unfolded the *Guardian* again to hide his face. The paper was from 4 July 2003. The news in it was more than a year old but could have been yesterday's. Occupations. Terrorism. Posturings. The same but different.

Ian had pulled out of the yard very slowly and was now inching over the speed bumps at the end of the road. It had all gone smoothly. He had to ring Mervyn. He'd be sorry to have missed all the fun. Fucking Budgie. How had he managed to cock it all up? All he had to do was keep the money safe and give it to Mervyn to bring over, and he couldn't even manage that. He was going to be surprised though. Budgie thought Ian was going to arrive back with a vanload of drugs. Only Merv knew what the cash was for. They'd talked and talked it through, sitting at Mervyn's kitchen table drinking endless cups of tea, and occasionally folding up bits of newspaper to set under the one short leg of the wobbly table. It had to be a methodical decision. The money had to make a dam that would turn the flow of the river.

Mervyn knew his stuff. The British government only ever treated the Ulster Unionists as conditionally British. Useful enough when there was a war to be fought or an Olympics to compete in but otherwise fit only for caricature and ridicule – the bigot braying on the telly, marching sternly past the camera in his archaic bowler hat and ludicrous sash, awkward, brash, unfashionably religious.

There was an assumption in the British media that the Union only existed for the security and comfort of the English. The Ulster Protestants were expendable. They had been in Ireland since well before the Mayflower landed at Plymouth Rock, but who was calling for the descendants of those settlers to go home? It was ludicrous. And it was time to say no properly. The Union wasn't something the English could decide to grant or to withhold. The Protestants would not be pushed into a foreign state. Mervyn could list the names and dates of the betrayals: the 1920 and 1949 Government of Ireland Acts, the 1973 Sunningdale Agreement, the Anglo–Irish Agreement of 1985, the Good Friday Agreement of 1998.

We are honourable people, Mervyn would say. We tried to play by the rules, and those rules were broken by the English, so we're entitled to do more than politely dissent. Today was the day. The Glorious Twelfth. Three hundred and fourteen years ago, in 1690, the Protestant William had fought the Catholic James at the Battle of the Boyne and won. Ian was lifting up that mantle. He was ready, he was willing, he was able. It was time to shake the world awake.

Mervyn thought they could learn a thing or two from the Muslims. You had to make the buck stop, you had to break the bank. The only way to hurt the English was to cost them something, to make them pay, to bring to a halt the City's jingling circuit of money. In the enormous silence people would listen. There was another strong currency aside from the sterling or dollar, and he possessed a whole vanload of it. He could spend violence for ever. Let's see them laugh at this.

'There's a lot of stuff in there, whatever it is. He's driving like a granny.' Geordie was in bullish form. The transit pulled out onto the High Road and set off south.

'Where's he heading now? He should be going north, to the boat,' Geordie continued as Danny waved across a stringy white mother in front of the Polo. She was manoeuvring a pushchair in which a chubby black toddler with bark-brown curls was grinning. 'We should just write everything down and ring Crimestoppers. They have Crimestoppers over here don't they?'

'Yeah, they're called the police.'

'Hitler, can you remember all the names of the roads?'

'We can check them on the *A to Z*.'

'Good . . . I'm cracking for a piss.'

It was now just after ten and the traffic was sluggish all the way down through St John's Wood and on to Maida Vale. When they approached the turn for St John's Wood Road Ian got caught behind a car in the wrong lane, and Danny and Geordie found themselves driving past him. Danny angled his head so the top of his sunhat was pressed against the window and then pulled the Polo over onto the pavement a hundred metres or so further on. Geordie arched round in his seat, and stared at the van.

'I think he's on the phone. He's definitely on the phone.'

When they got to the top of the Edgware Road Ian started to sing. He had never been a confident vocalist,

not since Mrs Logan, the choirmaster for Edenmore
Primary School, had asked him just to mime the words
at the Christmas concert, and he only liked to sing when
he was completely alone. He crooned in a low murmur
to himself. It was the words of 'The Sash' but set to the
tune of 'Amazing Grace'.

*'It was old but it was beautiful, and the colours they
were fine . . . '*

'We could just ring the police now,' Geordie said. 'He's
bound to have something illegal in there.'

'Could do.' Danny was tired. The phone which he'd
chucked onto the back seat kept ringing and beeping
with messages. He felt sick with nerves and nausea. He
needed water and a feed and a warm place to sleep.

'Though he might be going to pick up more videos.
From Brixton maybe.'

Danny smirked at Geordie's showy display of his new
London knowledge.

'Really. From Brixton you think?'

'Fuck off.'

*'It was worn in Derry, Aughrim, Enniskillen and the Boyne.
My father wore it as a youth in by-gone days of yore . . . '*

Danny watched the van drifting down with the rest of
the traffic towards the eye of the whirlpool, Marble Arch
roundabout, but then it swerved off, into the inside lane,
to turn left into Seymour Street. As the van slowed to a
stop at the traffic lights, Danny tried to pull into its lane
but cars were already tightly packed behind it.

'Oh shit.'

'Get into the right lane.'

'I can't.' The traffic to the right of them was solid as well. There was only one way to go. They were being forced to pull up alongside Ian. Geordie pulled his cap right down and turned towards Danny, who was staring straight ahead.

'For fuck's sake,' Danny said, without moving his lips. The van was right beside them. He had to slow to a stop. The whiteness of the transit filled the two windows on Geordie's side. Danny kept staring ahead as Geordie squirmed in his seat. He was wedging his palms in under his thighs.

'What the hell are you doing?'

'Sitting on my hands. He might recognize them.'

'*What?* Why would he recognize your hands?'

'*I* don't know. Because they're quite small.'

'Act normal, you berk. The lights'll change in a second.'

'I want to look up at him.'

'Don't fucking dare.'

The lights flicked to green and the van turned left. Danny indicated, and tried to pull across but a large black Mercedes blocked him out. The car behind him began to beep. And then another started. Danny put his hand into the air to acknowledge his stupidity and contrition. A little red Clio let him in. They turned into Seymour Street. The van was three cars ahead. The traffic slowed again. An African – Senegalese, Danny guessed – crossed in front of them. He was carrying a large wooden board wrapped in a cloth. Items bulged under it. Sunglasses, or maybe watches. Danny thought how London itself was a whirlpool's eye, a huge centripetal machine dragging bodies towards it from across the world. Like Scott Atkins, the Australian in his department. Like this Senegalese selling sunglasses. Like Albert, Ellen, Geordie, Janice. Like himself. London had seemed to promise to put him at the centre of his life, but the city kept turning, and the song of one small existence became quickly subsumed in the hum of its engine. He was fuel.

The van pulled across Tottenham Court Road and onto Goodge Street. 'He's heading east,' Danny said absently. They cut down Gower and onto High Holborn. Danny was entirely focused on the path of the white van, as if its movements were those of a roulette ball and he had his savings staked on the outcome. The van was getting further away and for a few minutes they lost it.

'Stop for a bit. He might have turned off somewhere.'

'Then we'd definitely lose him. We have to keep going straight.'

When they rounded Holborn Circus the van reappeared up ahead, stuck in traffic on the old viaduct. They joined the queue of cars and inched along after it. Concrete dragons, sitting back up on their haunches, appeared on either side of the road, marking the entrance to the City of London. At Cheapside, a grey sky slowly turned on the spire of St Paul's dome and Danny pointed out Monks, its huge glass windows reflecting the buildings opposite.

'And it's on the twelfth I love to wear . . . ' Ian drove over the junction at Bank, took a deep breath and pretended to shout *'THE SASH MY FATHER WORE.'* He indicated and slowed before he pulled in, then put the handbrake on and killed the engine.

When Danny drew up to the lights by the tube station, they could see the van across the junction, parked up on the kerb on Threadneedle Street, just outside the grey steel door of the Bank of England.

'He's stopped.'

'I should park up onto the pavement. If I cross the junction we'll have to drive past and we'll lose him.'

Geordie shifted around in his seat.

'There's nothing behind you. Put her into reverse.'

A number 25 bus was coming towards them fast but Danny managed to get back from the lights in time. He swung the Polo onto the kerb as the bus blasted its horn and glided round them.

During Ian's dummy run on Thursday night he had seen the place, but this was the first time he'd stopped. He sat for a second, lifted his phone off the passenger seat and got out. He locked the door of the van, walked across Prince's Street and started back towards Cheapside.

EARLY AFTERNOON

If it was dodgy videos, why had he parked the transit by Bank underground station? And if it was drugs, why was he walking away so friggin' fast? And if the van *was* a shiny roulette ball bouncing through London then zero had just come up, and all the bets were off. Geordie said it first. 'It's a fucking bomb. There's a bomb in the van. A bomb. In the fucking van.'

Danny had realized the same thing at the same moment. They were *so* stupid. So unbelievably stupid. Of course. It was a bomb. They sat for a second in astounded silence before Dan's mobile started its mating call from the back seat, and was answered by a pneumatic drill from the roadworks straddling Lombard Street. There was too much noise. Ian's van was sitting across the junction, outside the Bank of England. And Ian was striding towards them, passing two girls in school uniforms who had just stepped off the number 25. Now he was swerving out of the way of a cycle courier wearing a luminous vest.

'Fucking hell,' Danny breathed, 'there's too much . . . ' He couldn't say what he meant. 'That's the Bank of England. He's going to blow up the Bank of England.'

As they sat and watched, Ian walked right past. His mouth was set into a neat line but his eyes were smirking. He hadn't seen them.

'Cunt.' Geordie breathed the word out. Danny was silent. Turning round in his seat he looked through the car's rear window. The people on the pavement seemed to have slowed way down and the black triangle of Ian's back could easily be seen weaving and slipping among them. Then someone was tapping his window. Ian was getting further away. Geordie had opened his door a fist's width but hadn't moved. A traffic warden was standing outside the car. He tapped on his window again. Danny automatically lifted his hand to acknowledge him but didn't turn round in his seat. With his eyes still following Ian he said, 'What do we do now?'

Geordie answered immediately, 'I'll go after him.'

He had spoken with a tone of such solid authority that Danny looked across to check he wasn't being sarcastic. Geordie didn't smile and he said it again.

'I'm going to go after him.'

'Okay.'

'You should call someone.'

Someone? Who? He thought of how interested his mother would be and then realized Geordie meant the police. He grabbed the phone from the back seat. Another bus passed round him and beeped its horn. He was blocking the traffic. The traffic warden started to bang on the glass with the ball of his palm. Dialling 999 with one hand, Danny wound down the window with the other. The warden was young and white, and had an adam's apple that jiggled alarmingly. He looked vaguely nervous. Well, Danny thought, he was about to get more so.

'Sir, would you mind . . . '

'Listen, I don't have time to explain. I think there's a bomb in that van. The white one. A *bomb*. You have to . . . Hello, police please.' Danny waggled his finger in the windscreen at the white van. The traffic warden looked at him and then across the junction towards the van, one eyebrow raised. He was of the school of cynics.

'Sir, if you *could* just move your vehicle . . . '

'I'm not joking. Hello, hello? My name's Danny Williams and I think there's a bomb in a white van parked outside the Bank of England, by Bank underground station. Me? I'm on Cheapside . . . Cheapside . . . No, Bank underground . . . Of course it's in London . . . There's no plates on it . . . White. A white transit van.' The traffic warden had stepped away from the car and was talking into his radio. Then he strode into the lobby of the nearest building, said something to an enormous security guard and started pointing over at Danny.

About a hundred metres behind the black stack of Ian's shoulders a small man in a baseball cap was pounding along the pavement. What if Ian got on the tube? As he ran, baseball cap jiggling and T-shirt flapping, Geordie patted the pocket of his jeans to see if he'd cash for the tube fare. At the last possible moment he noticed a small black dog attached to a lamppost and managed to leap over its lead. Then the backs of two large women in business suits were in the way. He ploughed between them, shouting *sorry*. Ian had been forced to wait up ahead at a junction. A huge maroon car pulled across the road and stopped in front of him, blocking his path. Geordie was going to catch up with him. He ran on and then, as casually as he could, slowed to a saunter as he came within twenty and then ten metres of Ian. The running had attracted attention and now people were staring at him. The two fat girls he had jostled apart were approaching so he pretended to look at his watch and leant into a doorway. As they passed him the blonde one spat, 'Rude little prick,' and the other one laughed. Geordie felt a pang of injustice. He had always wanted to have sex with a really fat girl. No time for that now. Ian had set off again so Geordie tugged his cap down and followed. What the fuck was Ian doing? Was he taking this seriously, like a dutiful soldier? Or was he smiling madly to himself, chuffed at how things had gone so far? This wasn't funny any more. He didn't want to get thumped by Ian. And he couldn't run much longer. And he didn't want his heart to burst out of his chest like it was trying to. And he didn't want there to be a bomb at the end of the street.

Meanwhile, Danny had got out of his car and into some trouble. Although he'd decided to try to clear the nearby shops and offices of people, the traffic warden had set his heart on detaining him until the police arrived. Every time Danny tried to walk away the warden would hang tightly onto his waist and make the animal grunts of a pro wrestler. Danny was therefore limited to gesticulating to the bemused security guards and shop assistants who had gathered to watch the free street theatre.

Danny eventually pretended to sit contentedly on the Polo's bonnet but then made a lunge towards the greetings card store. One of the shop girls standing in front of it screamed. The warden, assisted by a Nigerian security guard, held Danny in an armlock.

'Sir, I *have* to *ask* you . . . ' the warden gave the arm a little twist with each emphasis, 'to *calm*ly *wait* by your *car* . . . '

'Listen, you have to listen. There's a bomb in the white van over there, I think. The police are on the way.'

The Nigerian security guard said something to the traffic warden. Danny focused on the guard.

'Mate, I'm serious. You have to clear the buildings. I'm a solicitor at Monks & Turner. Check my wallet. It's in the side pocket of the driver's door. The hat's a disguise.' The Nigerian was staring at his upper lip. 'It's felt-tip. It's a felt-tip moustache. Someone drew it on when I was sleeping. *And* I know I have a black eye. A friend hit me in the face. But I'm absolutely serious.'

The guard sighed heavily and delved his huge arm into the car. He pulled out the brown leather wallet.

'Open it. There's a Monks security pass and my business card. I'm not a crank. You have to clear the buildings.'

The guard flicked it open and showed it to the warden who lightened a shade and let go of Dan's arms. The guard said, in a sonorous African lilt, 'How come *you* know about there being a bomb?'

'It's a long story. I've already called the police. They're coming right now.'

And indeed the police *were* coming, albeit on horseback. At that moment Danny turned to see an officer bobbing up the street towards him on a huge blinkered mare. He tugged off his sunhat and threw it into the car before rubbing at his felt-tip moustache again.

Fear is one of the few contagious emotions. Humour is another. The staff outside GAP had been happy laughing at Danny and striking poses in front of their shop, unconsciously imitating the mannequins over their shoulders but then they heard the police sirens and saw the first cop car pull up. Four policemen jumped out and one of them immediately started to wrap plastic yellow tape round a lamppost to cordon off the road. The air began to build with the static of police radios and the chatter of human voices. Three assistants appeared from the card shop trailing handbags and coats. The last one locked the front door behind her, and then they were off, up the street, gesturing and talking to whoever they met. Then suddenly the pavement was awash with faces and limbs. The police had ordered the offices to be cleared and a steady stream of workers, ties aflutter, poured from the marbled lobbies. Even the warden had changed his mind. He was sticking his head into the coffee bars and shouting, 'Everyone out, everyone out.'

Ian was rounding the huge redbrick building at the top end of Cheapside when he heard the police sirens arriving at Bank and turned – to see Geordie walking straight towards him. *What the fuck?* He bolted into the road, dodging around a Range Rover and almost knocking over a girl carrying a cardboard box. Geordie unenthusiastically hurried after him into St Paul's churchyard. This was stupid. He was out of breath and in not a little pain. He was wheezing so badly he thought he might puke.

The churchyard was empty, except for the sprinklers

shaking their heads and spitting at the pigeons strutting among them. Ian ran in between the benches and onto the lawn but the grass was glossily wet from the sprinklers, and he slipped. There is a difference between chasing and catching. Geordie had been quite happy to follow Ian but he wasn't particularly keen on the idea of catching him. Ian was down, sprawled on his side, and Geordie was only a few metres away. Maybe he should just walk right past him. Maybe he wouldn't notice. He stopped. Ian sprang up – mud and grass stains all down one side of his jeans – and turned to see Geordie standing motionless by one of the benches. He smirked at him, nodded contemptuously, and said, 'This is big boy's stuff. You should walk away before you get hurt.'

Geordie just stared at him blankly and Ian started to saunter off down through the churchyard. Geordie let him get about fifty metres away before he started to follow. When Ian crossed the top of Ludgate Hill and headed down the walkway to the river, Geordie slipped his mobile out of his jeans.

Danny headed up Cheapside, towards Monks & Turner, telling everyone he saw to clear out. He rang Monks on his mobile and asked for Ellen Powell. After two beeps she picked up. 'Hello?' There was a ringing sound on the line.

'Ellen, it's Danny. Listen, I think there's a bomb further down Cheapside. You have to get everyone out.'

'They must know already. The alarm bell's going off. Everyone's leaving.'

'Well it's not a drill so hurry up.'

'Where are you? Are you okay? The bid didn't go through you know. Ulster Water won't accept it.'

'Why not? I thought it was in time.'

'It was but Shannon and the board are backing Yakuma, even though it's lower. Vyse has just sent an e-mail to the whole team.'

'You're *joking*. Can they do that?'

'Apparently, if they think it's in the best interests of the shareholders.'

'Vyse must be spitting.'

'Jill said she could hear him shouting from her pod. He has to explain it to Syder. Apparently he'd told them it was a shoo-in.'

'Brilliant.' There was a beep on Danny's line. He pulled the phone away from his ear and looked at the screen. 'Hold on, Geordie's trying to get through.'

'I've got to go out to the churchyard. Come and see me if you have time.'

'I will.' Danny swapped calls.

'Danny?'

'Yeah, where are you? Have you lost him?'

'No, he's heading over the footbridge across the river, on down from the cathedral. And he's not even running now. Get the cops down here.'

'Okay. Nice one mate.'

Danny could see three police cars blocking the cross-roads by St Paul's tube and he ran across to them. A very tall female police officer came towards him, hands raised as if to push him back.

'I rang you earlier. About the bomb. My name's Danny Williams. The bomber's walking down to the Millennium Bridge from St Paul's. He's wearing a black T-shirt and jeans. And he's being followed by a skinny guy in a base-ball cap.' The giantess was looking at his top lip. He put his hand up to it. 'And this was drawn on when I was asleep.' Then he gestured to his eye. 'This is real.'

The woman nodded indulgently. She spoke as if she had enormous experience of pacifying simpletons. 'Okay, sir. Could you repeat that to me slowly please?'

Danny showed her the IDs in his wallet and she began to take him seriously. He then explained him-self again and she relayed everything he'd said into the radio clipped to one of her epaulettes. All the units converging on the City were looking for a muscular suspect in a black T-shirt, being chased by a small man in a red cap.

Geordie pushed the phone into his back pocket. The Millennium Bridge was all ribs and struts and spine. It looked like the skeleton of a new type of dinosaur. A surprising amount of wind buffeted through the wire-strung sides and Geordie thought that his cap might fly off. He looked down through the metal floor into the lazy, unstoppable Thames. Ian was up ahead, walking quickly but not overly concerned. He hadn't looked back for a while. A group of tourists had stopped in the middle of the bridge, and Ian had just pushed through them. They had segregated themselves along gender lines and the men stood apart at the back, uninterested in listening to the toy-squeak of the tour guide. Their nationality was apparent because the petite guide had chosen to carry, instead of the usual umbrella, a long pole flying a minia-ture red, yellow and black German flag. Geordie reached them and slipped through a herd of moustaches and beer guts before reaching the men, who dolefully shuffled apart in time to see Ian up ahead, and opposite him two burly cops.

Where the Millennium Bridge runs onto the South Bank the pathway turns back on itself in a gentle slope down to ground level, presumably to allow wheelchair access. The police officers had just rounded this turn and were walking towards Ian. Geordie shouted, 'That's him. In the black T-shirt,' and confusion broke out. As the cops made what looked like a three-legged dash, Ian vaulted over the handrail down to the lower level. The policemen turned awkwardly back on themselves and Ian was in front of them again, legging it down to the river and heading west for a second before more cops became visible, pounding towards him and screaming into the radios fastened to their shoulders.

Geordie scurried on down the ramp to ground level. The male constituents of the German tour group were now displaying much more interest in the view. They lined the bridge's handrail and clapped and cheered, all while the tiny tour guide carried on recounting, to the nodding frauleins, the story of the princes in the tower.

Ian was trapped in a pincer movement. There were cops behind him and coming towards him. He ran into the open space in front of the colossal brick edifice of the Tate Modern. Two huge crocodile lines of children were entering the building from the left and the right. He found himself funnelled between them and in through the doors. It was suddenly cool and dark. He ran on. He could hear footsteps behind him. The low roof of the entrance gave way to the vast space of the Turbine Hall. An enormous metal spider, maybe fifty feet high, was standing to the right of him. He was on a kind of platform, and looked over the balustrade to see dozens of plinths arranged below in neat rows, each holding a different head. The floor below swept up on an incline to another entrance. That one was extremely wide and the way the light came through it made the whole thing look like the opening of a ship's car-door. He thought of sitting in his van a few days ago, waiting impatiently to start his engine, watching the *Ulster Enterprise* lower its door into Stranraer. He needed to get out again. And here were metal steps leading down. He could hear someone shouting *Stop! Stop that man!* He leapt down the staircase and started pelting up the gentle slope towards the daylight. It felt like running up a drawbridge that's being slowly raised. Two guards appeared in the mouth of the exit, and started towards him, each in a fluorescent yellow Tate Security jerkin. He spun round and ran back past the foot of the steps just as two cops were clattering down them.

He was in the middle of the exhibition and he was trapped. There were heads all around him, arrayed in their various tribes of plaster and metal and granite. There were stone bonces round as boulders lifted out of a river, bronze faces thumbprinted and pinched into careful expressions, and, at the far end, some black televisions sat on the plinths displaying faces that were trying on various emotions. There was also Ian, his shaved and brutal skull jerking around and around for a way to get out. There were policemen and Tate security guards on every side of the exhibition. He stopped running. The police started to approach, their heads moving steadily among the sculpted ones like chessboard pieces setting up a checkmate. They were shouting stuff to him. Ian tried to yank free a bronze head that Giacometti had plucked and gouged to almost a blade, but it wouldn't come loose. He ran towards the TV screens. There was a fire exit at the far end, and if he could just . . . He was brought to a stop by the wall of a sixteen-stone Turkish gallery attendant named Abdullah Yalcin. Ian's running head had bounced off his shoulder and hit the industrial floor.

He awoke a few seconds later with four of her majesty's finest kneeling on various parts of his body, and his head was twisted up so all he could see was two TV screens: one featuring a black guy who looked like a second lieutenant from *Starsky & Hutch*, and the other showing a housewife-y type, white, wearing a frilly collar. They were speaking but Ian couldn't hear what they said. Two sets of headphones lay where their feet would be. The sign attached to their column said '*Good Boy Bad Boy,* Bruce Nauman'. Geordie was a few feet away grinning and watching, leaning with one hand on the tin head of Paolozzi's *Mr Cruikshank*. A stroppy-looking female attendant appeared and brushed his arm from it. Geordie jumped a little, then gestured with open palms to apologize. He sloped over to Ian. He had to walk round him to get into the line of his sight. One of the policemen shouted 'Stay back please sir,' but Geordie ignored him. Fuck it, he thought, I've nothing to lose.

'Hello,' he said and raised his eyebrows amenably at Ian, as if they'd just met in the street. He had intended to try to stick a toe poke into his side but the police looked pretty angry. Ian remained silent – he was a soldier – and Geordie followed his gaze to the video screens. He watched the faces mouth emptily and then picked

up one set of the headphones and put them on, partly
to show that, unlike Ian, he could do what he liked. The
two American voices ran together, overlapping each other.
The man was angry and the woman almost serene.
Geordie listened. It was a weird litany of phrases, like a
grammatical primer.

'I eat . . . you eat . . . we eat . . . this is eating . . .

*I am a good boy . . . you are a good boy . . . we are
good boys . . . '*

Ian was being handcuffed and slowly lifted to his feet.
A police siren could be heard from the far entrance.
Geordie went on listening, and gave Ian a cheeky little
wave.

*'I am a bad boy . . . you are a bad boy . . . we are bad
boys . . .*

I pay . . . you pay . . . we pay . . . this is payment . . . '

A policeman tapped Geordie on the shoulder and
Geordie pulled the headphones off.

'You'll have to come with us, sir. Answer a few questions.'

The bomb didn't go off. When the area was emptied (it
had looked to Danny, from the top end of the street,
like it had been cleared for shooting a movie), the police
had sent in a skeletal robot. After several botched attempts,
it eventually opened the door of the van, and not with
a bang but a rusty whimper. The BBC in White City had
received a telephone warning from a phone box outside
Ballymena (eighty metres, it turned out, from the bungalow of a bachelor farmer called Mervyn Watterson) in
which it was claimed that a bomb would go off outside
the Bank of England in forty minutes. They'd passed the

message on to the police but by the time the robot trun-
dled towards the van fifty-eight minutes had elapsed. As
it happened, the bomb could never have exploded: the
timer was faulty, and anyway Ian had somehow set it
for forty hours instead of forty minutes. In court he unsuccessfully tried to claim that this had been a last minute
decision to avoid endangering lives.

Danny had stood by the police cordon the entire time,
watching, and telling the tall female officer the beginnings of the story. When he heard the police radios confirm that the bomb posed no danger, he turned to walk
up to the churchyard. The officer, Constable Finch,
touched him on the arm and asked him to come with
her. She eventually agreed he could go and speak to his
colleagues but only if she accompanied him. In St Paul's
churchyard certain departments from Monks & Turner
had gathered in the sun, chattering excitedly, not about
the bomb threat, but about being outdoors in the heat.
The sprinklers had stopped and the grass was now dry
enough to sit on. Albert, squeezed onto a bench with
three other lawyers, was bent right over, wiping one of
his shoes with a tissue. He had a large glass bottle of
still spring water sitting on the ground between his feet.
Albert placed a huge importance on staying adequately
hydrated.

'All right mate?' Danny said. Albert stood up, lifting
the bottle by the neck, and patted Danny's shoulder with
two of his fingers.

'Where have you been? Everyone in the department
was going mad this morning . . . Are you in trouble?'
he added, noticing the enormous policewoman behind
him.

'I don't think so. I'm just helping them. I'll give you a ring later. I'm not going to be in work tomorrow.'

Albert nodded to let him know that there was someone approaching behind him. Danny felt a staccato tap on his shoulder. Vyse. Danny turned round slowly. The partner looked older in daylight.

'You decided to make an appearance today, did you Mr Williams? Just in to collect your belongings? I see someone else has tried to get their point across.' Vyse was looking with pleasure at his black eye. Danny glanced at the bottle Albert was carrying and then back at the partner's polished face. He was briefly tempted to bring the two things together in a glorious union but instead he nodded, unsmilingly.

'Yes. Sorry about the bid. I don't know what happened.' *I threw it in a river.*

'Well that little stunt you pulled almost cost us the deal.' *I don't give a fuck. I've beaten you, you little bastard.*

'So it's all gone through has it?' *Really? Have you?*

Adam pushed at his expensive fringe and said nothing while Danny continued, 'Because, *oddly*, I heard that they didn't accept it, and went with Yakuma anyway.' *Oh my friend, my little friend, you're shit and I'm champagne.*

Vyse pushed Danny backwards into the lap of Ryan Smith, a senior Banking litigator who was sitting on the other end of Albert's bench. Danny stood up again, and was murmuring an apology to Ryan when Vyse started to scream, 'You stupid little fucker, you prance around thinking you're too good to be a . . . '

Danny had noticed Ellen walking over from the church-yard gate and he looked back at Vyse, smiled, and then

341

pushed past him. The partner stopped shouting and watched him. The policewoman started to say something to Danny but decided instead to follow him.

'Hello.'

'Hello.'

Ellen put a hand up to his face.

'I like your moustache . . . Everything okay?'

'Yeah. You know I've been sacked?'

'I heard.'

'I just need to get my things from the office.'

'I'll come over with you. They're starting to let people back into the buildings.'

They picked a way through the Monks lawyers and secretaries and canteen staff, the Monks security guards and delivery men and IT specialists and librarians. It seemed the entire staff of the London office were sitting or lying around in easy groups on the warm grass as though they'd just brought in the harvest. When Danny reached the churchyard gate he looked back to see Vyse sitting with his head down on the steps of St Paul's Cross. Andrew Jackson, the senior partner of the department, and Graham Ammons, the managing partner of the whole firm, were standing in front of him talking demonstratively. Danny decided to view it as a victory.

In his office the solicitor Danny Williams gathered up the belongings from his desk and placed them into a single cardboard banker's box. It didn't amount to much: a sleeping bag and a cushion, some gym clothes and a pair of trainers, a couple of ties and a spare suit, a pin-stripe, that he'd kept hanging behind his door, a box of tissues, two unread novels and a desk calendar of the picturesque glories of Ulster. He told Constable Finch he just wanted to get a glass of water before they left and the three of them trooped down to the facility room. The policewoman stood in the doorway and effectively plugged it. Ellen leaned on the copier and watched as Danny filled a plastic cup from the water fountain and then drained it in one.

'So are you going to tell me what happened?' she asked, but Danny didn't reply. He was feeding the roll of paper from the dispenser into the shredder. The police-woman was engaged in a conversation with the radio on her epaulette. He turned the shredder on and took a step back into the middle of the facilities room, to properly admire his handiwork.

The paper was neatly unspooling into the shredder. It was mesmeric and would continue for ever. Or until the paper ran out. He turned round to face Ellen.

'If you fancy dinner later, I could tell you about it.'

'I should come with you now.'

He grinned. 'Well, I could probably do with a lawyer . . . No, just see me off the premises. I'll ring you afterwards and explain.'

The lift was emptying out, with Albert among the silent returners. He stopped and nodded at Danny to ask if he was all right. Danny nodded reassuringly back and walked on into the empty lift. The policewoman and Ellen came in and stood on either side.

'How long do you think this will take, Constable?' Danny said.

'Not that long, shouldn't think, though these things can depend.'

A lawyer's response, Danny thought, as the lift doors closed and Ellen pressed the button for the ground floor.

343

The lift began descending but then slowed and, with a slight sigh of far-off machinery, stopped completely between the fourth and third floors. This had happened periodically over the five years Danny'd worked at Monks & Turner. The policewoman futilely pushed at the buttons. Ellen picked up the emergency phone but it was dead. The constable started describing their whereabouts into her shoulder. Danny felt the unusual sensation of having nothing to do. It was like getting your hair cut or sitting in the back of a black cab. Ellen suddenly, secretly, ran a light fingernail over the back of his hand. She glanced up at him from under her lashes and, as she smiled, revealed that beautifully crooked front tooth. She said, 'So now what do we do?'

Danny shrugged, smiling. 'Wait here until it moves again, I suppose.'

ACKNOWLEDGEMENTS

Many thanks are due to my agent Natasha Fairweather and my editor Clare Reihill for their encouragement, good humour and enthusiasm; to Nik Bower for reading an early draft; and to Zadie for her patience, advice and support.